THE END AND THE DEATH
VOLUME I

Other Novels and Novellas

*Many of these titles are also available as abridged and unabridged audiobooks.
Order the full range of Horus Heresy novels and audiobooks from*
blacklibrary.com

Download the full range of Horus Heresy audio dramas from
blacklibrary.com

—THE HORUS HERESY—
SIEGE OF **TERRA**

THE END AND THE DEATH

VOLUME I

Dan Abnett

BLACK LIBRARY

A BLACK LIBRARY PUBLICATION

First published in 2023.
This edition published in 2024 by
Black Library, Games Workshop Ltd.,
Willow Road, Nottingham, NG7 2WS, UK.

Represented by: Games Workshop Limited – Irish branch,
Unit 3, Lower Liffey Street, Dublin 1,
D01 K199, Ireland.

10 9 8 7 6 5 4 3 2

Produced by Games Workshop in Nottingham.
Cover illustration by Neil Roberts.

A CIP record for this book is available from the British Library.

ISBN 13: 978-1-80407-641-5

See Black Library on the internet at

blacklibrary.com

Find out more about Games Workshop
and the worlds of Warhammer at

games-workshop.com

Printed and bound in the UK.

For Ian Watson.

—The Horus Heresy·—
SIEGE of TERRA

It is a time of legend.

The galaxy is in flames. The Emperor's glorious vision for humanity is in ruins. His favoured son, Horus, has turned from his father's light and embraced Chaos.

His armies, the mighty and redoubtable Space Marines, are locked in a brutal civil war. Once, these ultimate warriors fought side by side as brothers, protecting the galaxy and bringing mankind back into the Emperor's light. Now they are divided.

Some remain loyal to the Emperor, whilst others have sided with the Warmaster. Pre-eminent amongst them, the leaders of their thousands-strong Legions, are the primarchs. Magnificent, superhuman beings, they are the crowning achievement of the Emperor's genetic science. Thrust into battle against one another, victory is uncertain for either side.

Worlds are burning. At Isstvan V, Horus dealt a vicious blow and three loyal Legions were all but destroyed. War was begun, a conflict that will engulf all mankind in fire. Treachery and betrayal have usurped honour and nobility. Assassins lurk in every shadow. Armies are gathering. All must choose a side or die.

Horus musters his armada, Terra itself the object of his wrath. Seated upon the Golden Throne, the Emperor waits for his wayward son to return. But his true enemy is Chaos, a primordial force that seeks to enslave mankind to its capricious whims.

The screams of the innocent, the pleas of the righteous resound to the cruel laughter of Dark Gods. Suffering and damnation await all should the Emperor fail and the war be lost.

The end is here. The skies darken, colossal armies gather. For the fate of the Throneworld, for the fate of mankind itself...
The Siege of Terra has begun.

DRAMATIS PERSONAE

| THE EMPEROR | Master of Mankind, Last and First Lord of the Imperium |
| HORUS LUPERCAL | Primarch of the XVI Legion, Ascendant Vessel of Chaos |

The Defenders of Terra

| MALCADOR THE SIGILLITE | Regent of the Imperium |
| CONSTANTIN VALDOR | Captain-General of the Legio Custodes |

The Loyalist Primarchs

ROGAL DORN	Praetorian of Terra, Primarch of the VII Legion
SANGUINIUS	'The Great Angel', Primarch of the IX Legion
VULKAN	The Last Guardian, Primarch of the XVIII Legion

Legio Custodes

DIOCLETIAN COROS	Tribune
ARCATUS VINDIX CENTURIO	The Emperor's Eagle
IOS RAJA	Hetaeron Companion
HARAHEL	Aedile-Marshal, Warden of the Sodality of the Key
SHUKRA	Companion, Warden of the Sodality of the Key
CAECALTUS DUSK	Hetaeron Proconsul
UZKAREL OPHITE	Hetaeron Proconsul

DOLO LAMORA	Sentinel-Companion
KLIOTAN	Sentinel-Warden
ARZACH	Prefect-Captain
CAZADRIS	Sentinel-Warden
KINTARA	Hetaeron Companion
DAMORSAR	Shield-Captain
KRYSMURTHI	Hykanatoi
AVENDRO	Shield-Captain
TELEMONIS	Host-Marshal
CAERCIL	Companion
TYRASK	Sentinel
SYSTRATUS	Sentinel
ESTRAEL	Companion
GELIDEN	Sentinel
ASTRICOL	Companion
VALIQUE	Sentinel
MENDOLIS	Sentinel
VANTIX	Companion-Captain
HELIAD	Hetaeron Companion
AMALFI	Shield-Captain
ENTAERON	Vestarios
JUSTINIUS	Sentinel
LUDOVICUS	Proconsul Hykanatoi
SYMARCANTIS	Warden
XADOPHUS	Warden-Companion
FRASTUS	Companion
ANDOLEN	Prefect-Companion
KAREDO	Tharanatoi (Hetaeron)
RAVENGAST	Hetaeron Companion
BRAXIUS	Hetaeron Companion

TAURID	Hetaeron Sentinel
NMEMBO	Hetaeron Companion
ZAGRUS	Hykanatoi (Hetaeron)
AMON TAUROMACHIAN	Custodian

Sisters of Silence

KAERIA CASRYN	Oblivion Knight, Steel Foxes Cadre
MOZI DODOMA	Sister Vigilator
VEDIA	Vigil Sister

The Chosen of Malcador

KHALID HASSAN	
ZARANCHEK XANTHUS	
MORIANA MOUHAUSEN	
GALLENT SIDOZIE	
GARVIEL LOKEN	The Lone Wolf
HELIG GALLOR	Knight Errant

Officers and Seniors Militant of the War Court

SANDRINE ICARO	Second Mistress Tacticae Terrestria
ILYA RAVALLION	Strategist
JONAS GASTON	Junior

Lords of the Council of Terra and Lords Principal

ZAGREUS KANE	Fabricator-in-exile
NEMO ZHI-MENG	Choirmaster of the Adeptus Astra Telepathica
EIRECH HALFERPHESS	Astrotelegraphica Exulta of the Higher Tower

The VII Legion 'Imperial Fists'

ARCHAMUS	Master of the Huscarls
VORST	Veteran Captain
FAFNIR RANN	Lord Seneschal, Captain of the First Assault Cadre
FISK HALEN	Captain, 19th Tactical Company
VAL TARCHOS	Sergeant, 19th Tactical Company
MAXIMUS THANE	Captain, 22nd Company Exemplars
LEOD BALDWIN	
BRASTAS	Captain
CALODIN	
LIGNIS	
BEDWYR	
CORTAMUS	
DEVARLIN	
MIZOS	

The V Legion 'White Scars'

SHIBAN	Khan, called 'Tachseer'
GANZORIG	Noyan-Khan
JANGSAI	Khan
CHAKAJA	Stormseer
YIMAN	
ATRAI	
SOJUK	Khan
ZHINTAS	Khan
GAHAKI	Khan of the Burgediin Sarhvu
AINBATAAR	Khan
NAMAHI	Master of the Keshig

The IX Legion 'Blood Angels'

RALDORON	First Captain, First Chapter
AZKAELLON	Herald of the Sanguinary Guard
TAERWELT IKASATI	Sanguinary Guard
ZEPIION	Dominion, 'The Bringer of Sorrow'
NASSIR AMIT	'The Flesh Tearer'
SARODON SACRE	
MAHELDARON	
ZEALIS VARENS	
KRYSTAPH KRYSTAPHEROS	
RINAS DOL	
KYSTOS GAELLON	
KHOTUS MEFFIEL	
SATEL AIMERY	
KHORADAL FURIO	
EMHON LUX	

The Shattered Legions

ATOK ABIDEMI	Draaksward, XVIII Legion 'Salamanders'
ARI'I	Pyre Warden, XVIII Legion 'Salamanders'
MA'ULA	Sigil Master, XVIII Legion 'Salamanders'
HEMA	Sergeant, XVIII Legion 'Salamanders'
BÖDVAR BJARKI	VI Legion 'Space Wolves'
KRATOZ	Spearhead centurion, X Legion 'Iron Hands'
KHRYSAOR	Sergeant-at-arms, X Legion 'Iron Hands'

The I Legion 'Dark Angels'

CORSWAIN	Lord Seneschal, the Hound of Caliban
ADOPHEL	Chapter Master
TRAGAN	Captain of the Ninth Order
VORLOIS	
BRUKTAS	
HARLOCK	
BLAMIRES	
VANITAL	
ERLORIAL	
CARLOI	
ASRADAEL	
TANDERION	
CARTHEUS	
ZAHARIEL	

House Vyronii

ACASTIA	Bondsman-pilot of the Knight Armiger *Elatus*

The Imperial Army (Excertus, Auxilia and others)

ALDANA AGATHE	Marshal, Antioch Miles Vesperi
PHIKES	Her adjutant
MIKHAIL	Captain, 403rd Exigency Stratiotes
JERA TALMADA	Colonel, Corps Logisticae
LANTRY ZHAN	Forward observer, PanCon Fifth
MARTINEAUX	Hort Captain
SKLATER	Sire-Militant
HETIN GULTAN	Sergeant, Royal Zanzibari Hort

KUCHER

DERRY CASSIER — Junior loader

NAHEENA PRAFFET — Corporal, 467th Tanzeer Excertus

N'JIE — Captain, Kovingian Light Ordnancers

AND OTHERS

Prefectus

AHLBORN — Conroi-Captain, Hort Palatine (Command Prefectus Unit)

STIGLICH — Hort Palatine

HELLICK MAUER — Boetharch

The Order of Interrogators

KYRIL SINDERMANN

LEETA TANG

The Citizen Conclave

EUPHRATI KEELER

EILD

PEREVANNA

WEREFT

KATSUHIRO

The Traitor Host

The XVI Legion 'Sons of Horus'

EZEKYLE ABADDON — First Captain

KINOR ARGONIS — Equerry to Warmaster Lupercal

ULNOK — Equerry to the First Captain

Azelas Baraxa	Captain of Second Company
Itha Clathis	Second Company
Kaltos	Second Company
Tarchese Malabreux	Master of the Catulan Reavers
Hellas Sycar	Master of the Justaerin
Taras Balt	Captain of Third Company
Tyro Gamex	Third Company
Vorus Ikari	Captain of Fourth Company
Xhofar Beruddin	Captain of Fifth Company
Ekron Fal	Centurion, Justaerin
Lycas Fyton	Captain of Seventh Company
Kalintus	Captain of Ninth Company
Selgar Dorgaddon	Captain of Tenth Company
Zistrion	Captain of 13th Company

The XIV Legion 'Death Guard'

Typhus	First Captain
Serob Kargul	Lord Contemptor
Vorx	Lord of Silence
Kadex Ilkarion	
Caipha Morarg	
Melphior Craw	
Skulidas Gehrerg	

The XVII Legion 'Word Bearers'

Sor Talgron

Barthusa Narek

The VIII Legion 'Night Lords'

Khagashu

The Dark Mechanicum

CLAIN PENT	Fifth Disciple of Nul
EYET-ONE-TAG	Speaker of the Epta War-Stead linked unity

Others

BASILIO FO	War criminal
ANDROMEDA-17	Selenar

The Long Companions

OLL PERSSON	Perpetual
JOHN GRAMMATICUS	Logokine
KATT	Unsanctioned psyker
HEBET ZYBES	Labourer
DOGENT KRANK	Trooper
GRAFT	Agricultural servitor
ACTAE	Prophetess
ALPHARIUS	
LEETU	Proto-Astartes

'Not for that city of the level sun,
Its golden streets and glittering gates ablaze–
The shadeless, sleepless city of white days,
White nights, or nights and days that are as one–
We weary, when all is said, all thought, all done.
We strain our eyes beyond this dusk to see
What, from the threshold of eternity
We shall step into.'

– Early poet, circa M2

'Sicut hic mundus creatus est.'

– *Liber Hermetis de alchimia*, circa 200.M2

'Behold! I tell you a mystery – we will all be changed.'

– 1 Corinthians, 15:51

'The Emperor Must Die.'

– Banner slogan

I

Look at their pathetic legions, their ruptured hosts,
their walking corpses, living to kill and killing
to kill. There is no longer any point to their
psychopathic exertions or their hysterical sacrifices.
Nothing remains to be won or lost. Not now,
not for them. Nothing survives of their motives,
reasons or agendas. Look! Do they not see it too?
The past is gone, and there is no future. There is
only now, and there is only war, and the war will
burn for as long as there is fuel to feed it.

II

Which won't be long. Look at the rock that they
call the world. It is being dismantled wholesale by
a relentless concentration of absolute fury. They
fight – *look* at them! – they fight for the world, by
dismembering the world. They think the world is
so important. They believe it *matters*. The mindless
killers on each side, their labels of traitor and
loyalist long since erased by flame, they still think
the place matters, the rock that they kill on and for.

III

Think… well that is too strong a word. None of
them are *thinking* any more. But I will say some
impulse, then, some twitch in their lizard brains,
that convinces them, in their inchoate frenzy, that
they are standing their ground, that they are fighting
for what is theirs. Some birthright, some cradle,

some legacy, some place that belongs to them and to which they belong, as though such connections matter. They do not. Only by some tenuous and sentimental thread are they tied together, world and species, some whim, some happenstance, a freak division of biological contamination that gave rise to their ephemeral lineage on that irrelevant rock.

That's all. It could have been anywhere.

It happened to be here, this lump of matter, this scrap of earth, this... What do they call it? Terror? *Ha!* No, Terra. Their minds invest it with significance, their language gives it a name, oh-so-mockable. It is just a rock, of infinite rocks, swirling around infinite suns. It has no meaning, no special property, no singular quality.

IV

Yet how they fight for it! Look at them. They fight, because war is the only thing they have left. They fight to conquer or deny, driven by the notion, which is utterly devoid of meaning, that it matters who wins here. Who claims the rock. Who is left standing at the end.

It does not. It does not. It does *not*. Futile! They are wrong. Pathetic and wrong. Look at them. Fools all, deluded by incoherent compulsion and debased ideals. This place, this Terra, has never been special. It's been a symbol, at best, for a short span of time, and even that symbolic value is now exhausted. They burn themselves up in one last convulsion of psychosis, utterly unaware that the fight is not here.

It is *everywhere*.

V

My name is Samus. Samus is my name. That is
the only name you'll hear. I am the one who walks
behind you. I am the footsteps at your back. I am
the man beside you. Look out! I am all around
you. Samus! I am the end and the death. I tell you
now, I have seen this before, so many times. How
many, I do not care to say. Time is worthless to me,
and I do not bother to remember all the biological
contaminations that spurt up, and I don't have the
patience to memorise the names of rocks. Rocks are
just rocks, and my name is Samus. Samus will gnaw
upon your bones. This – *look* at them kill! – this is
mere repetition. The cycle, the dawn and the nightfall.
It will happen again, and it is happening everywhere.
It is trivial. A dynastic quarrel. A fight between nests
of insects that I might step over, without noticing, on
my long walk to somewhere else.
Unless…

VI

Unless one of them finally notices what *is*
possible. What might be *accomplished* here.
The potential, the beautiful potential, which,
though none of them sees it – *none* of them –
is closer at hand than they realise. I can almost
taste it. It is closer than it has ever been, closer
than it was even in the un-times of the war
that broke heaven.

VII

Who among them has the courage to reach for it?
So few of them, so very few, are even in a position
to see it or comprehend its meaning. I can count
them upon my fingers. Him? The boastful king on
his tiny throne, his feeble light guttering out? Him?
The squealing pretender, hunched in the howling
gullet of hell? Him, perhaps? The maniac prophet
slithering through the open wounds between
unblinking stars? One of them might see, before it
is too late, what could be achieved today. One of
them might recognise, at the very last, that none of
this matters... the annihilating rock, the measureless
slaughter, the pathetic rage... unless they elevate the
war to where it *truly* belongs. Not here. Not Terra.
But outwards and inwards and everywhere, until
that which is Ruin, and that which is Ruin alone, as
it was in the beginning and shall be at the end, is
everywhere and everything.

VIII

That is the only victory that matters. That is
the only end that has any meaning. Alert,
intrigued, alive not to the death of a rock but
to the birth of a reality, I watch. I am Samus.
My name is Samus. I am the man beside you.
Samus is here. I walk into your meaningless
flames and I rejoice. For this time, perhaps *this*
time, there will be a victory.
For this is the end, and the death.
And, finally, the beginning.

PART ONE

CANNIBAL GALAXIES

1:i

Sympathetic magic

When he was very young, no more than two or three hundred years old, he watched a man paint shapes upon a wall.

The painter used his fingers as brushes, and the skull-cups of animals as his pots. He painted antelope and bison, side-on, mid-leap. Startled, deer broke and ran across the wall. The painter drew men too. They had bows, and spears. He had never seen anyone paint a man before. He was very young.

It was not art, or decoration. It wasn't a memorial of the hunt they had conducted the day before. It wasn't a record of something that *had been*. That would have been a waste of valuable pigments. They had their memories for that.

Watching intently, he understood the painter was painting tomorrow. It was a statement of intention, of what *would be*. The painter was making a plan, and executing it. He was imposing his will.

This, the painter was showing them – the antelope, the bison, the men – this *will be*. The animals will break and run, like so. We will be here. These are the bows and spears we will carry. This – as his fingers moved from spear to ante-lope – this will be the path the spear will follow. This is where it will strike, this flank here. This will be our kill.

Watching, he understood that this was sympathetic magic. A ritual rehearsal to vouchsafe that what was once imagined would later come to pass. What was set out here on the wall in pigment would happen in life tomorrow. The antelope would not evade and get away, for here, see? It was already struck and dead.

The man was modelling the future.

To sanctify this, to commit to this specific configuration of tomorrow, the painter dipped his hand into a pot and pressed it, palm flat, against the wall. He left his mark, the mark of himself, on his plan. This is what will happen, and with my hand I signify it. It cannot be undone.

The antelope is already dead.

For this version of tomorrow to fail, the gods would need to turn against mankind and undo the laws of the world, laws which they had promised could not be undone.

By then, even so young, he had already learned to distrust gods. To distrust even the existence of gods. But the natural laws of the world seemed to operate, whether there were gods or not.

He watched the man paint, and he learned to plan. It was, in every sense, a revelation. He learned that a plan might secure the future, and it might be the work of one man, and to be cer-tain of its success, it had proudly to bear the mark of his hand.

His handprints have been on his work ever since. He has been modelling the future for over thirty millennia.

He told me that story himself, years ago. I look at his hands now, hands that have since held the galaxy in their palms. I observe the fingers twitching slightly.

Very few people are permitted to stand this close to him. Few, indeed, are even admitted into his presence, much less allowed to approach so near that they are able to notice such subtle signs of human suffering. But I am his Regent, his advisor, his confidante. I am *supposed* to stay close to him. It is what he requires of me, so I have been as near to him as his shadow for a very long time.

Those hands. Those great and capable hands. They are sheathed in auramite, not because it is golden and regal, but because it is almost quantum-inert, and thus most efficacious for psionic sculpting and the manipulation of immaterial forces. Bare skin would be better, more precise and conductive. I know he has touched the immaterium with bare hands and a bared mind many times, but even *he* has his limits. The saturation of immaterial power now stands at such a level that direct contact would scald his flesh if he but brushed against it. Longer exposure would sear the meat off him, boil his blood, and fuse him to the seat he occupies.

So there he sits, armoured and warded in gold, silent and still, like some graven idol. No, *worse*... I fear he resembles the gaudy chieftain-kings and prophet-monarchs of the past, the petty upstarts and megalomanic bullies who carved dominions out of the carcass of humanity, and built frivolous nations, and caparisoned themselves in jewels and precious metals, and set crowns upon their heads, and declared themselves more than mortal. They were not, and he scorned them all, chastised them for their hubris, and had them cast down, by actions direct or indirect. He has dismantled nations, and ended dynasties, usurped tyrants and dictators, razed palaces, and cauterised bloodlines. He has painted the walls of innumerable throne rooms with blood, and left thrones empty.

He cannot leave this one.

I wait forever in the silence at the foot of the great dais.

There is no one else close enough to heed what I notice, except for Uzkarel Ophite and Caecaltus Dusk, the exquisite ogres who stand watch either side of the steps. But the Legio Custodes proconsuls face outwards, immobile as sculpture, their backs towards him. They do not see what I see. They do not see his fingers tremble.

And subtle signs, be they traces of suffering or otherwise, are my art. Signs, symbols, signifiers, sigils: these are my instruments, the diacritical marks of reality through which I discern the true text of the world. I am his Sigillite, and I have fulfilled that role since this age began.

It is now about to end. Both my long service to him, and this very age itself.

Because his sons are coming to kill him.

1:ii

Fragments

They have crucified Titans along the Ultimate Wall.

Smoke, powder-thick and as dark as rancid meat, flows sideways across the sky. In places, the bodies of the dead are so numerous they look like sacks of grain stacked after harvest. The corpse-mounds have changed the contours of the ground.

On the Canis Causeway, in what would have been the shadow of the Lion's Gate Wall, Maximus Thane yells to be heard above the endless howl of firestorms and shelling, and draws the Astartes of 22nd Exemplars into *Repulse Formation Exactus*. There is no cover. They lock-brace shields that are now grey with ash. Thane's tactical sensorium counts barely seventy men left in his company. He tells himself the device is broken. The display is cracked and wires swing loose. It shows him nine hundred enemy tracks on the causeway alone. He *orders* himself to believe it is broken.

* * *

Inside the Lion's Gate, the upper parts of which are entirely missing, lynched Knight engines of House Vyridion hang like game, trussed in spools of razor wire, and hooked from ramparts. Waste fluid – oil, coolant, blood – drools from their mangled cockpit-faces.

The traitor host boils in like a tidal spate, through broken gates, through breached walls, across the oblique slopes of once-vertical ramparts. They are gleaming scarab-black, horned and howling. A flash-flood surge, they pour through gaps, through fissures and cleft walls, beneath arches, and along once-golden avenues. They are deformed things, remade men, remade again, tusked ogres, semitaur obscenities, warrior-beasts with heads like whale skulls or skinned elk. They spill like a mudslide into the last, untouched sanctum of the Palace.

Abaddon, once the First Captain to whom all others aspired, is among them, both leading them and carried forward by the torrent. He is made destroyer, despoiler of worlds and life, arch-mythoclast. He will tear everything down, all the legends and structures and orders, even his own myth, which he once so proudly forged. He will cast off his hard-won glory and replace it with a new one, more glorious and far more terrible. He yells to his men. His words are no longer human.

They understand him anyway.

1:iii

Record of
an interview conducted
by Remembrancer Oliton

My father? I'll tell you about my father. Of course. Anything you want to know.

My father, Mamzel Mersadie, my father once... Now this is a famous story, but I'll tell it anyway... My father once reached a river, and he knelt down and wept. Famously, *wept*. He–

Wait. If I might suggest, let's move off the bridge. At this hour of the watch, the bridge decks of the *Vengeful Spirit* are a busy place. My First Captain, that's Ezekyle over there, he's about to brief the Mournival and the senior company officers. The Interex are proving to be problematic. It's unfortunate. There was a mistake born of misunderstanding. As you must appreciate, first contact protocols are complex. The meeting of two advanced civilisations inevitably involves issues of trust and comprehension. This is not easy work, as I think you've seen. I certainly regret what's happening at the moment. Deeply. So let's move through here into my apartments.

Yes, after you.

That's better, you see? We can converse and hear ourselves

think. Ezekyle can be so strident and intense. He's briefing on the projected military operations that we are, sadly, now obliged to undertake. As I say, I deeply regret that it's come to it. Yes, that's correct. Military operations. Yes, there will be another war. In truth, my lady, there will *always* be another war.

No, I don't have to be there. First Captain Abaddon is more than capable of handling the watch meeting. Yes, of course I trust him. I trust him with my life. He's my son.

So, take a seat.

Anyway, my father. As I was saying, this was a very long time ago. It's said he was known then as Alysaundr, or Sikander III ho Makedôn, I believe. He told me that, so it must be true. Anyway, he came to the River Hyphasis and crossed it, and wept, for, as he put it, 'there were no new worlds to conquer.'

No, I think–

No, you misunderstand my point. I'm sorry, I didn't make it clearly. I agree 'conquer' is an aggressive, militaristic term. A freighted word. Of course, the word he actually used was κατακτώ, for he was speaking a proto-form of Eleniki there, on the banks of the Hyphasis. So we can allow for some interpretation. It was a long time ago. I was citing the story as an example of aspiration. Our aspirations define us, I believe, more than anything. Beside the Hyphasis, my father wept because, at that time, he felt he had accomplished all he could. His ambitions were achieved. And the revelation shook him. He was not proud or satisfied, he was bereft.

Of course, as it turned out, there were *many* more worlds to conquer. The work had scarcely begun. On the banks of the Hyphasis he had won, not for the first time, nor for the last, the throne of the known world. Not long after that, he found another throne. A *literal* throne. That changed everything. Yes, found it. Well, that's what he told me.

But I digress. The point I was making, however poorly, is

that aspiration is the fire that drives us. We are restless and we strive. 'To strive, to seek, to find, and not to yield,' if I remember the old verse correctly. There is always another world, Mamzel Mersadie, always another goal. We all take after him in that respect.

I'm sorry? And always another war. Yes, *quite so*.

You look at us, remembrancer, and you see beings wrought for war. No, no, don't deny it. I know you do. I see the trans-human dread in your eyes when you regard me, or when you look at First Captain Abaddon, or any of my sons, my Luna Wolves. I don't blame you. I terrify you, and I'm sorry for that. Truly. I look at you here, in this room, dwarfed by the scale of it. Like a child in that chair, a child on a throne, your feet swinging. It was built for my frame, not yours. I feel for you. You put a very brave and confident face on it, but I am sensible to your terror. To be here, to be surrounded by inhuman giants. It must be intimidating. I wish I could say something to reassure you, something to assuage your fear.

I will say this, Mersadie Oliton... I am more like you than I am *not* like you.

1:iv

Fragments

The dead and the living are now quite alike: all will burn on the same pyre.

Barely ten seconds dead, Uris Katjor, battle-brother, Imperial Fist, leans against the round-bitten rampart as though he is resting. His helmet is gone, and so are both of his hearts and the contents of his chest cavity. A sigh is still leaking out of him. He stares at the war through blown pupils.

Beyond, more bodies, hundreds more, left where they fell in the act of running away. Some appear asleep. Most are tossed in disarray, clumsily bent or poorly folded, in postures both uncomfortable and undignified. War has no patience for dignity. Some bodies don't really look like bodies at all: too small, too awkward, too thin, too still. Death has made them mere debris, just fallen scraps of a falling city, tumbled in amid the shingle of cracked stone and fragmented metal. Just bundles of rags with sticks inside.

On the soaring ramparts of the Delphic Battlement, the sealed ring of last defence that surrounds the final fortress of the Sanctum Imperialis, Amit called Flesh Tearer weeps.

The Blood Angels legionary feels the constant concussion of the wall guns around and below him, and he weeps for what he has done, and for what he has left undone. Around him, ten thousand of his kind, other loyal sons, more perhaps, wait and weep too. They wait, armed and armoured, for the traitor flood to break against the last wall, and for the final battle to begin.

Blade braced against his chest, almost in prayer, he looks out from his high vantage across the landscape of the Palatine Zone. He looks out into hell. He sees great bastions burning through shrouds of smoke. Meru, Hasgard, Avalon, Irenic, Razavi, Golgotha, Cydonae... each one a symbol of Imperial power that once commanded a swathe of Palatine territory, each one now a colossal bonfire. The smoke stinks of shame and lost hope.

He weeps. His genesire, the Bright Archangel, has closed the Eternity Gate forever. Such a thing. A feat unparalleled. His Bright Lord saw off the greatest daemons of the world, broke them, and killed them, to hold back the tide long enough for the Gate to be sealed. Amit was one of the very last to make it inside.

Sanguinius, the lord of Amit's life, paid grievously for that deed. Amit saw it with his own eyes: the brutal wounds, the ravaged plate, the immortal white wings – oh, how piteous! – stained and scorched, the feathers plucked, torn out, burned, charred–

He weeps for it. The sight of his lord so wounded will stay with him forever. But that is not what grieves him most. True misery lies in the *meaning* of the deed his lord performed.

The Gate has been closed. Amit cannot imagine the burden

of that decision. To close Eternity is to concede defeat. It admits, to friend and foe alike, that the armies and champions of the Emperor, even Sanguinius of the Blood Angels Legion, can no longer prevent the enemy's merciless advance across the Palatine, just as they could not stop the enemy at the first wall, or at the Outer Palace, or at the gates of Helios, Lion, Eirenicon or Anterior, or at Eternity Port or Colossi or Ultimate, or at any other site where they have been met and opposed. Months of war, the most ferocious Amit has ever witnessed, have done nothing but delay the inevitable. Closing Eternity is an act of desperation. It means the end is here, the death. It means the hour is so bleak that no choice remains: the Sanctum Imperialis must be sealed, for all that lies outside it is truly lost.

Lost, but not yet dead. The full horror of closing the Gate is that it consigned legions of their brothers, whole armies and hosts, to their doom. There was no time or room for retreat, no time to recall them or allow their withdrawal. They had to be left outside. Amit weeps because he knows this decision will haunt his lord longer than any wound he took. The decision feels like desertion. It feels like a second betrayal.

Amit thinks of those who did not make it through the closing gate, those left outside engulfed by frenzied World Eaters, his brothers, his kin, the armies stranded in the field, the brigades and regiments still warring on the Palatine plain, the men and women, the commanders and the common troopers, the battle-brothers, the great champions... abandoned all, to fight and strive and die beyond hope of salvation, selling their lives one by one in a storm of unhinged violence, doing whatever they can to slow the enemy's inexorable progress towards the wall Amit now guards.

He weeps. He waits, he stares out at their hell, and he weeps for them all.

* * *

Flames dance upwards. The dead are just the dead. The living are just the dead who still feel grief and pain.

1:v

His persistent mystery

Respectfully, I call to him.

I don't use my voice. I use my mind. My call is hushed and cautious, more like a murmured invocation and, I'm sorry to say, rather too much like a prayer.

He does not answer. I look for a sign, some intimation of response. There is none. I notice his hands clench again, involuntarily, against the arms of his throne, but that's just another spasm of pain. My concern for him makes my own, weak hands clutch more tightly at the staff that keeps me upright. It wounds me to see him suffer. The pain he feels is intense – though he has known far worse – and it is continuous. He has been subjected to it for several years. It gnaws at him, and he endures. He will not let go, or break concentration. There is too much at stake, and still too much work to be done. He has harnessed the constant discomfort, and uses it as a drishti to focus his intent. This, I suppose, is why he does not hear me. He is too focused. The immaterial presses at him. Though the room is quiet, the warp howls in his ear.

However, I *need* him to break his concentration. That is why I've come to him, with great reluctance. We need to speak. We can no longer avoid the conversation that we have been postponing.

But he seems oblivious. He does not respond to my gentle psychic whispers. He does not even appear to know that I am here. He remains precisely the way he has been for months: still, silent, unseeing, immersed entirely in his vital, invisible labour. So, I must risk his displeasure and be persistent.

+My King-of-Ages…+

I have been his Sigillite long enough to know that he is aware of how he looks. He so detests this unfortunate aspect: a golden king, idle upon a golden throne. He dislikes seeming to be the very thing he has emphatically opposed. I have always known him to be very deliberate in his presentation. Over the millennia, he has worn many masks, each suitable to the task at hand. His mind, his greatest gift, allows him significant flexibility in such things. He has appeared as male or female, or neither, as child or elder, peasant or king, magician or fool. He has been an entire cartomantic arcana, for the Master of Mankind is also a master of disguise. He has performed all of these roles well, with delicacy. He has been humble when humility was needed, gentle when softness was the best device, sly, amiable, reassuring, commanding, caring. He has been terrible when terror was the only recourse, and sometimes meek in order to inherit the Earth. He has been whomever and whatever it has been necessary to be. No one has ever seen his true face, or learned his true name.

Not even me. I have known him by as many names as he has worn masks, and by as many faces. It occurs to me, belatedly, in this last hour of the final act, that perhaps, just like everyone else, I have only ever seen what he has allowed me to see. Perhaps, even if this room was filled with a multitude,

I would still be the only one who would see a golden king upon a golden throne, the only one for whom those fingers would appear to tremble.

The notion is amusing that even now, after all we have shared, he still hides from me. It's said I am a wise man, but I know only two things for certain. The first is that there is always something *more* to learn. His persistent mystery has taught me that.

The second is that, just a short while from now, he will finally grant me the opportunity to see and know *the rest*, all the things I have not yet learned, the full and final truths of creation.

And it will kill me. But I won't refuse the opportunity. Who would? Who *could*?

I wait. I try again.

+Speak to me. Open your eyes, my Lord Imperator, my King-of-Ages, my old friend. Show me a sign. Wake, stir, speak to me. We have to talk.+

He *has* been a king, of course, many times. A regal aspect has frequently been required. During the years of global unification, it was often necessary for him to manifest as a warlord, because humans respond to authority when they are frightened or confused. During the period of galactic reclamation, he was obliged to stride among the stars in the guise of a warrior-king, armoured in gold, for that was the version of him that his young sons best understood. He had to seem like them, yet more glorious, so he could command their loyalty, their respect, and their devotion. It was war, so he became warlike. They would not have followed him otherwise, or obeyed his instruction. They would have doubted. He needed to be able to command them to the very ends of the stars, to secure their obedience across unimaginable distances, and sustain unswerving devotion even after he had left them.

So he played that card: *the Emperor*. It was a version of himself that he found quite odious, but they rejoiced in it. They saw what they wanted to see. His sons committed utterly to the material war, and were so fortified and resolute that he felt he could leave the completion of the work to them.

Because he had to return. Time has never been his ally. He had to leave his children to conclude the material war among the stars and return to this seat underground, for the immaterial war had to be fought simultaneously. One victory was nothing without the other.

After Ullanor, he set that guise aside with relief. He set aside the plate, the helm, the incomparable blade, believing he would not need the aspect of war-king again, for he had left the material war in their capable hands.

In the hands of his chosen successor.

His sons…

I suppose they are my sons too, in a way, for I helped to make and shape them. The current pain of his immaterial toil is nothing compared to the pain of his grief. He is only human, after all. I lament, likewise. We both knew his sons would die, one day, one by one, casualties of the Great Work, for his configuration of tomorrow could not be accomplished without collateral loss. When he marked out his plan upon his wall for me, so that I could grasp the scope of it, he allowed for contingency and redundancy. If a son fell, there would be another to take his place. Even so, we thought they would last for centuries, or even millennia, a great dynasty devoted to the accomplishment of his design for, from the very start, paint on his fingers, he knew that he could not do it alone. Thus, we made sons for him. We believed that when the necessary wars were done, those sons and their father would enjoy the long peace together, and they would walk alongside him towards tomorrow.

Those sons, at least, who could be rehabilitated from the brutal mindset of warfare.

But the gods are against him. The false gods, the False Four. They have been trying to thwart him since he began his work, for they know that his success will signal the end of them. Fearing his version of tomorrow, they have turned against him and undone the laws of the world. We have known disappointments before. Failures. Setbacks. Many times, we have been forced to revise, and fashion a modified path around an obstruction. One does not sustain a plan across thirty millennia without a degree of flexibility.

We have known defeats, but not this.

His plan is damaged. I'm not sure if we can salvage it and set it back in motion. That is his avowed intention, and mine too, but the gods are devious. They have spilled the pigments, and smeared their handprints on the wall, erasing his marks, over-painting, altering, desecrating. Without finesse, with crude and primitive fingermarks, they have daubed their own sympathetic magic, contrary to his. The spear in this man's hand is broken. The antelope has startled and run clear, out of bowshot, lost in thickets that were not there yesterday.

+Speak to me. Show me a sign. Open your eyes, my lord.+

Unable to contest the immaterial war, the gods, to my dismay, have turned the material war against him instead. The world that we carefully built together is being hammered into fragments.

And his sons are dying.

+Wake, stir, speak to me. We have to talk.+

To win now, to reconfigure tomorrow, he will be required to kill more of them.

1:vi

Fragments

A lance, planted in the rubble like a flagpole; from its tip, the bloody rags of a man, flapping like a banner.

Treads gone, the Carnodon tank of Geno Ten Sairus lies upside down in a pool of putrid waste water. All its hatches are submerged. The drive wheels grind intermittently – forward and seize, reverse and seize – a post-mortem twitch of dying systems. A feeble knocking comes from inside the sunken hull, but there is no one around to hear it.

Arcatus Vindix Centurio, the Emperor's Eagle, holds Marshal's Court and the Kepler Gardens. Nothing survives of those places. Only a map overlay on his visor display identifies his location, a digital ghost of the parkland and noble square that existed just the day before. The Custodian captain's golden wargear drips with blood and grease. Loyalists rush in to flank him, either side of the garden's one remaining tree. There is no battle order any more. Those around him are Solar Auxilia,

Excertus Imperialis and Auxilia, militia reservists, Legiones Astartes, a few Oblivion Knights and null-maidens, a handful of Old Hundred veterans, and a few civilians. It has come to this.

What spills towards them isn't human, nor even Astartes transhuman. It is a keening wall of sarcophile horror, the vanguard of nightmare, exoplanar things that the galaxy once decreed could never be born, not here, not anywhere in the mortal plain. But the telaethesic wards are snuffing out like spent candles, and these things *have* been born and they *are* here, fright-winged and coarse-whiskered, coal-eyed and shrieking, skittering on bird-legs and hooved feet, baring their fang-spikes and mattock carnassials.

Centurio has seen their ilk before, but never in realspace, and never in such swarming numbers. He rests his hand, for one startled moment, against the scorched trunk of the one, miraculous tree, a splintered rampike that is the only point of reference in the shredscape of mire and smoke.

The man beside him, an Auxilia sergeant whose name Centurio will never know, dies of fear. He simply dies, and drops. He does not scream or flee, but his mind and heart give out.

Centurio blinks, humbled by a mere mortal. He raises his sentinel blade so that all around him can see it, and his voice so all can hear.

In the ditch below Regnum Way, the roasted shells of tracked war machines have collected like dead beetles in an exterminator's box-trap. They are overturned, jumbled, piled up so that the uppermost appear to be trying to crawl out over the bodies of the rest. But they are not. They are lifeless. The only thing rising from the ditch is a slow fume of smoke and dust.

On the banks beyond the ditch, and all the way up Magistary

Rise, their skulls have been mounted on stakes. The stakes are girders and pylon spars. The skulls are turrets, Shadowswords, Sicarans, Russ-patterns, Slayerblades, Fellblades, Carnodons, Glaives, Stormhammers, some still snouted with weapon mounts, others with barrels snapped off. Such has been the fetishistic desecration of the World Eaters, raising trophies of decapitated tanks like a forest of elephant heads.

Wet bones in a dry gulch. Dead hands fused to cremated weapons in mausoleums formed by neutralised bunkers.

Kratoz, Spearhead Centurion. Khrysaor, sergeant-at-arms. Both are of the Iron Hands, both are of the Shattered Legions that were so cruelly mauled when this insanity first began. That seems to them like centuries ago. They have fought across the disintegrating territories of the Imperium to be here, to be here *now*, seeking only to serve as they were made to serve, and perhaps claim some repudiation and vengeance.

On the majestic Processional of the Eternals, which runs from the temenos of the Inner Sanctum for sixty kilometres to where the Lion's Gate once towered, they line up among the Imperial Fists to make good those claims. They yell the battle cry of their Legion as the World Eaters approach. Their words are lost in the unison roar of the Imperial Fists declaiming their own martial cry around them. Their shout is out of step with the glory-chant of the yellow-clad ranks. But they both hear it. Kratoz and Khrysaor, in the sealed shells of their beaked helmets, hear the utterance of the Iron Tenth, diminished and outnumbered, but not gone. Not quite yet. And they know that, though the words of their cry and the Imperial Fists' are different, the meaning is the same.

They will not retreat. Their flesh will not be weak, and their deeds will endure.

1:vii

Record of
an interview conducted
by Remembrancer Oliton

I am mere flesh, Mersadie. When all else is said and done, and the panoply of war is stripped away, and my physical enhancements set aside for what they are, which is merely the instruments of my duty, I am just human.

You do not have to be afraid of me.

But yes. Yes. I was wrought for war. We *all* were. Because war is one of our duties, and we must be capable of waging it well, better than any before us. However, we are more than warriors. War, my lady, is but one of our functions. The bitterest, yes, but merely one role among many. We were made to do myriad things, and we were wrought to do every one of them supremely well.

Ah, I think of my bold Luna Wolves at Aartuo, and the Keskastine and Androv systems, the superlative implementation of their battle-craft...

My mind strays into memories, forgive me. I was going to say that, one day – and I truly believe this – war will no longer be a necessity. It will no longer *have* to be one of our duties.

I look forward to that. I do not want to die in war. I want to die in the peace that war has built.

We are, fundamentally, builders, you see? That's what I hope you'll understand. We are makers. Yes, sometimes stone must be cut and dressed with a hammer, and worked until it fits, but *only* so it fits and we can build securely upon it. We are constructing civilisation, remembrancer. It is not easy, and it is not quick. Any blood that is spilled is only necessary blood, and I weep, like my father on the banks of that river, when it occurs. I would honestly offer my life in payment if the Great Work could be accomplished bloodlessly. But let's not be naive about it. It *can't*. I am sanguine about that. You should be too. We do this for you. For the whole of humanity. And we do this, I believe, Mersadie, *together*.

I'm sorry? Well, no. He is *not* with us now.

After the Triumph of Ullanor, when my father left my side, I felt genuinely lost for a while. Of course, I was flattered and honoured to be named his proxy–

Surprised? No, I wasn't surprised, I'll confess that. My lady, your questions are astute. Perceptive. You wish to get to the heart of me. Well, I'll tell you, no, I *wasn't* surprised. It had to be me. I was really the only choice. I was flattered and honoured, but *relieved*. I would have been offended if the mantle had passed to one of my brothers, worthy though they *all* are.

But I was bereft too. Just like my father beside that river. For I felt, if he was leaving us, that the work was done, and I was inheriting a hollow crown and an empty title. Aspiration, you see? It is coded into me. I felt lost, for I wondered what there was left to accomplish.

There *were* more worlds to conquer, though. I soon discovered that, just as my father had. And, before you ask, I again use the word 'conquer' in the loose sense we discussed. κατακτώ.

There were worlds to bring to compliance, worlds to liberate, societies to embrace. We have made more *peace* than war. We have made peace with thousands of cultures, all of them the lost and scattered treasures of Old Earth. We have found our kin, and the branches of our family, and we have known them as our own. Every world we come to, Mersadie, I hold out my hand first, before I reach for my sword. *War, Warmaster, Crusade*… these are just words chosen to inspire humanity. They're proud, strong words, intended to impress, and to emphasise the prowess of our deeds. But they are propaganda, much like the histories that you write and transmit home. They speak of strength and courage, of unity in purpose, of determination. Nevertheless, they are *just words*, and they express only a small part of what we do. Soon, I think, we will be able to do away with them entirely. They will be obsolete.

No. How funny. No, remembrancer, I do *not* think I will become obsolete with them. My role has only just begun. Mamzel Mersadie, if you expect me to be humble, you are speaking to the wrong man. I know what I am. I tower over you, Mersadie Oliton. I am four times your size. I tower over all men and women. I am *well aware* of my nature. I am human, remembrancer, but if I was coy, and claimed I was *only* a man, I think then you would have real reason to fear me, for I would either be lying to you, or afflicted by some dangerous denial. I need to *know* what I am. I need to be secure in that fact. I am post-human. I am a primarch. I am Lupercal. I am, in the terms of the ancient Eleniki, a *demigod*. I can't hide it. I shouldn't. Denying that fact is denying myself, and denying myself is denying my purpose. I embrace what I am, and I rejoice.

I was made for great things. That's not arrogance. I know you didn't say so, but I see the look on your face, so… It's *not* arrogance. It is frank acceptance. You do not place this much power and potential in a single frame without making sure it understands what it is. It would be arrogance if I pretended it *wasn't* the case. If I pretended I was... *less*. If I demurred and affected modesty, well... that would be cause for concern.

I know what I am. I am, in the healthiest way, *afraid* of what I am. Otherwise, I would be very dangerous indeed.

1:viii

Fragments

Crater lakes everywhere, lakes of promethium. Some are violently ablaze, lagoons of fire that fog every crease of the air with soot. Other lakes, lakes of coolant, chemicals, or stagnant water from transected cisterns, are filmed with rainbow slicks of fuel, and where that burns, it burns softly and almost invisibly, transparent skins of colourless flame that make an insect flutter. Some pools are lurid pink from copper swill. Some pools are viridian from cyanide.

In the lee of the Sanctus Wall, Sojuk of the White Scars rallies the rearguard. Other White Scars, Praetorian Fists, some Blood Angels, stir to obey him. Sojuk is bone-weary and drained by grief. Mere hours ago, he brought the body of his fallen Khagan to its rest, and thought he would kneel in mourning beside the bier for the remainder of his life. But great walls toppled, and the sanctuary to which he had delivered the Great Khagan's corpse was no longer safe, and war came ever closer. So Sojuk rose, with only a wordless nod to his grieving mistress Ilya Ravallion, and went back out to rejoin the field, which had raced in to find him.

Eternity Gate is now closed. There will be no further opportunity to retreat. He is doomed to stay in the field and do what he can.

Morten Lintz, the fine captain and blood-son of Dorn commanding this portion of the rearguard line, has fallen, skull destroyed by heavy bolter fire. Sojuk is ranked *khan*, the senior man present now Lintz is gone. The line is his now, this thin, diluted line drawn up before the churning hosts of Death Guard units. He shrugs off thoughts of grief like a fur pelt at the start of steppe-summer, and feels in the same instant the sharp focus of *yarak*, the hunting-hawk's yearning to slip and kill. On the plains, they would feed the hawks scraps to keep them strong, but *only* scraps so that their appetite stayed as sharp as their talons.

This is his open plain. He is the hawk. He tenses to fly, and calls so that the others will fly with him.

A stiffened corpse, held upright by mud, grins forever, and points at nothing with a rigor-raised arm.

Crowds flee. Wailing multitudes. They choke the streets, stumbling blind, asphyxiating in the dust, calling out and ringing handbells to be heard or seen by others, for to be alone is to be lost. They flee along once-proud streets, beneath the blood-writ words *The Emperor Must Die* and the obscene symbols of Chaos and heresy.

They flee to nowhere. The bunkers and shelters, prepared by Dorn, are already filled to capacity. The broken city is trying to shield its citizens, but the survivors of Magnificans fled into Anterior, and then fled again alongside the survivors of Anterior into the Palatine Zone when Anterior burned. There is no longer room to shelter the millions who hoped the final fortress would protect them. The bunkers are full and, according to military order and tactical necessity, all access points to the Sanctum's vast subterranean levels are sealed at the surface.

Trapped in the streets, the crowds flee to nowhere. Mortality salience wracks them to the core. They see the words upon the walls – *The Emperor Must Die* – and they know, without doubt, that they must die with him.

Nowhere is safe. No one is safe. Nothing is untouched. Debris rains from murdered buildings, killing those fleeing or sheltering in the streets. Glass falls like blades. There are squalls of blood-rain, of pyrochemical sleet, of ash-snow. Nothing seems breathable any more. A gasp inhales smoke, dust, microparticles of rock and grit that grate the lungs, bacterial vapours, weaponised chemicals, toxic bio-waste. Throats close, gums bleed, tongues rot, tears track cheeks red from burst blood vessels. Eyes are sanded raw and lungs curdle with froth.

On the Via Aquila, someone is calling her name. There's always someone calling her name. Even when there's no one there.

1:ix

On the Via Aquila

On the Via Aquila, vast crowds swirl around her. Euphrati Keeler sets down the old woman she's been carrying, perching her on a low plinth that has lost its statue. The old woman is dumb with trauma, unresponsive. Her feet are in a pitiful state. Wherever she started running from, she did so without shoes. The streets are covered in broken glass.

'Wait with her,' Keeler says to Eild. 'Ask again if anyone's seen her relatives.'

The old man nods.

Keeler turns and looks for the source of the voice calling to her. It could be anyone. There are so many people. Wereft estimates over seventy-five thousand on Aquila alone. Lost, displaced, fleeing their homes, the civilians – and that is *always* who they are, just citizens or workers or families – come looking for something, a place to hide, a place of shelter, a way out. Somehow, they find her instead.

And when they call to her, they want all manner of things, most of which she can't provide. Help. Answers. Reassurance.

Promises. They want to know why any of this is happening. They want to hear what she has to say.

What *can* she say? There are nominated speakers in her makeshift conclave, though what they teach has little to do with any spiritual philosophy. Many call them preachers, but she thinks that's too easy and misleading a word to use. She has trained them to offer secular guidance, instructions on organisation, mobilisation, and simple habits of survival. To stand up and teach, by word and deed. This is no time to debate higher truths.

The state of things is shifting by the hour. The Palatine Zone is breached and overrun, and the Sanctum Imperialis, the ominously named 'final fortress', has been formally sealed. Death approaches from every direction. The handful of Astartes that were escorting her have been obliged to fall back and form a rearguard. Now, for her and the conclave, what began as a stopgap effort to organise a few hundred into acts of resistance is no longer tenable. There are *so many* people, and not enough weapons, not even improvised ones. Short of driving the unarmed masses wholesale at the enemy formations in the hope that sheer numbers will slow their advance, the conclave has become engaged in a frantic endeavour to manage the mass exodus and steer the crowds towards the few districts of the Palatine that remain unviolated.

After that... Well, there *is* no after that. The outer dominions, all of Magnificans and Anterior, are gone. The Inner Palace is shrinking, like a boat slowly sinking, or a log burning up in a grate. Soon there will be nowhere to go at all.

It seems the voice belonged to Perevanna. The old apothecary-general is shoving through the dense crowds towards her.

'Via Sardis is blocked,' he tells her. He is plastered with blood – tunic, apron, hands and face – and none of it is his.

'Fire?' she asks.

'War engines,' he replies.

'We move them north, then,' she says. It's not a question. There *is* only north.

'There are thousands more coming,' Perevanna says. 'Along Chiros and Principus and Navis Heights. Thousands. I've never seen–'

Keeler nods.

'As if they know you're here,' he adds. 'How do they know you're here?'

'They don't.'

'Word spreads…' he says.

'They *don't*, sir.' Keeler turns and points. She points past the monumental spires around them at the sky beyond, at the throbbing glare underlighting the cloud over Lion and Gilded and Europa. 'Firestorms,' she says. 'Slaughter. They come this way because there is no other.'

It's true. But neither of them fully believes it. Word *has* spread. She's tried to keep her message simple, so the nominated speakers can promulgate it effectively. It is an essence; call it faith or belief, not in the Emperor as a god – for He denies that as firmly as she refuses the label saint – but in the idea of the Emperor as a leader with a *plan*, a Great Purpose, a dream of Imperium, that must be supported and preserved.

If the masses come seeking truth, there is too much truth already. That hesitant question of divinity seems so laughable now. She's known that since the Whisperheads, the first epiphany that opened her mind. She has struggled over it, argued over it, been imprisoned for it. Now her heresy seems quite tame. The immaterial Neverborn are everywhere. If you are looking for signs and wonders, here they are, in staggering abundance! And if daemons exist, then surely the divine exists too? Reality could not be so cruel and mindless to create darkness without light.

Still, proof denies faith. The Emperor has denied His divinity at every turn. There must be a reason for that. That reason must be a crucial part of His intention.

Keeler thinks she knows what the reason is. She doesn't know if private contemplation has led her to this, or if it is a revelation that has been granted to her. It is simple: any recognition of power beyond the material admits the *immaterial*. To accept Him as god accepts *simultaneously* the darkness. The Emperor forbade His own worship so that darkness could not be allowed in. Humankind is too delicate a vessel.

That's her truth. Her metaveritas.

Since the Whisperheads, her life has demonstrated in harrowing ways that she has been singled out for something. Early on, she thought it was to light the first flame and speak the word of the Emperor's true glory. To be an apostle. The Emperor, in humility, could not name Himself a god. Perhaps He needed others to name Him so.

She is no longer convinced that is what was intended for her. She now believes her purpose is rather different, part of the Great Purpose she has been allowed to glimpse. Faith is the key after all. Not the assured faith in a proven truth, but the liberation of unconditional faith, the blind trust that needs no proof or verification. To cast free and commit to Him, to believe in Him, not as a god nor yet as a man, but as a process, a path, a configuration of the future.

He has a design. It has been in operation for thousands of years. To truly serve Him, one must commit to it and be part of it. One does not need to understand it.

That is the only possible expression of faith.

That daemons have arisen, that Horus Lupercal, in infamy, has turned and broken every bond of fealty and blood, is not proof of the Emperor's theophany, neither is it evidence of His humanity and fallibility. It is not even a confirmation that His design has failed.

It is simply a testament to the eternal significance of the design itself, for if all this has been done to stop it, if the *warp itself* has risen to prevent it, how sublime must it be?

Perevanna has already moved away to help incoming wounded. Keeler moves back through the crowd, along the Via Aquila, to try to clear the way ahead. She ignores the sound of tumult echoing across the city behind her and the frightened screaming of the crowd.

So many people. Some reach out to touch her as she passes, as though they know her.

'Keep moving,' she says. 'North. Go north.'

1:x

And on other byways

Some in the Palace territory move with greater purpose and certainty. When the Xigaze Wall collapses, toppled completely like a dropping drawbridge, the smoke-filth dammed behind it rushes free in a wave one and a half kilometres high and thirty wide, like an oozing flow of dark resin out of which a new Old Night will be cast and cured. Things move in that rolling smoke, borne by it. Here come the spider-engines, the reptile-tanks, the hunchbacked, rust-caked war machines, the glossy scarab-Titans. Here come the lizard-treads, ox-horned and snorting; here come the daemon-devices of war, trailing chains and cycling powerblades. Here come the corrupted instruments of Martian nightmare, spiked and towering, dwarfed and misshapen, dripping oil from piston limbs, and spewing soot from exhaust vents.

They all know where they are going. There is only one direction, *forwards*. They move towards the heart of all things, clanking and grinding, booming and whirring. Some are guided by auspex or the ping-returns of rangefinder systems.

Some are guided by adepts poring feverishly over charts, calling out direction orders as they trace dirty fingers across map paper. Some are guided by the pre-locked code of hypno-planted orders. Some are guided by moderati perched in crow's-nest masts or steepled turrets, straining amplified eyes into the atmospheric broth, relaying what they see by neural impulse. Some, behemoths that are no longer sentient, are guided by hindbrain, animalistic lusts or appetites. Some are guided by Neverborn whispers that cluck in the ears and dreams of insane princeps.

They all know exactly where they are going. Forwards, inwards, towards the heart, the destination, the end, the death.

There is delight in certainty, and that certainty belongs almost entirely to the enemy.

But some, a very few, elsewhere in the stricken city, have a certainty of their own. And they are guided by secrets.

The Imperial Palace is the most inviolable place in the galaxy, so of course the Alpha Legion has a way in. If a secret exists, they make it their business to know it.

Alpharius leads them, his iridescent blue-green armour slipping through the shadows. The exact colours of its scales are elusive and motile, like a sheen of oil on water, and suit the character of his perfidious Legion.

Or so thinks John Grammaticus, trudging at his heels. He has dealt with the last Legion before. The one thing he knows he can trust about them is that they can't be trusted. This warrior isn't even Alpharius, in that there *is* no Alpharius, and even Alpharius isn't simply Alpharius. They *all* are, or *none* of them are or... or... may they all burn in hell for plaguing his life.

But this one knows him, so the reverse must be true. From where? From Nurth, years ago? That all seems like a dream now, every truth of it un-truthed, denied, redacted and shredded. John is the antithesis of the man he was then, an Omegon to that Alpharius. Where once he laboured to secure the triumph of Horus, he now offers up his perpetual life to prevent it.

What of this Alpharius? Which version of the truth is he? Which slippery aspect of the schizophrenic hydra does he answer to?

Alpharius says little, but when he does speak, John listens carefully. He applies the subtle scrutiny of his logokinetic gift. A mortal man will struggle to tell one Astartes transhuman from another at the best of times: they are all muscled puppets cut from the same pattern. But with the Alphas, forget it. They actively play upon their anonymous interchangeability.

However, words don't lie, no matter how carefully they're spoken. Idiolect can be as unique as a fingerprint. When 'Alpharius' speaks, John mindglosses for microexpressions of tone and affect, nuances of vocabulary, foibles of word repetition, unconscious traces of accent, emphasis traits, pronunciations. He savours each word, and hears within them the inner shape of the mouth, the particular acoustics created by teeth, tongue and palate, the nanoscopic idiosyncrasies of voice, and he compares them to his memories.

To gather clues, he initiates conversation as they walk.

'You have a way into a place that there shouldn't be a way into, but you haven't used it?' he asks.

'Secrets are to be kept, and only used when they have the greatest value, John,' says Alpharius. 'You know that. You know how we operate.'

'And you haven't thought to, I don't know, tell Horus you can stroll him into the Palace past Dorn's walls, should he care to do so?'

'No, John. I haven't.' The stress there, on the first person pronoun. Interesting. What does that betray? An independence of thought, of action? Is this Alpharius somehow rogue, or is he simply alone?

'But if he asks…?'

'He does not ask, we do not offer. It would be inconceivable to any of them, the Lupercal, the Lord of Iron… the Praetorian, come to that… that we would have a way in.'

'They don't know you like I do, then, do they?' says John, with what he hopes is an endearing grin.

'No, John, they don't.'

'I'm just saying, it would have saved them all a lot of bother. A *lot*. I mean, holy bloody hell…'

'You're not wrong, John.'

'So, you're sharing the secret with us now because… because, *what*? This is its moment of greatest value?'

'The world's about to die, John. When it does, a great number of secrets will perish. Then they will have no value at all. So it's use it now, or never.'

'To help us?'

'If you like.'

'You know what I'd like?' says John. 'I'd like to be able to trust you. Just once.'

They pause, and look back along the trail, a thin tear in the rock, which winds down into the secret heart of the Earth. Lumen globes bob behind them: the others of their party slowly catching up in the breathless underground heat. The woman, Actae, Oll and his ragged band, whom John has affectionately dubbed 'the Argonauts', and in the rearguard somewhere, Erda's solemn warrior, Leetu.

'Not here,' says Alpharius. The words – simple words containing a fearful admission – alarm John.

'What do you mean?'

'I mean, not here. Not in earshot. Not in mindshot. Let's

press on, maybe pull ahead of them. Then, perhaps, we can broker some trust.'

'All right. All right, then.'

They clamber on, up a steep flue in the rock, John scrambling to stay upright on the glittering mineral crust where Alpharius strides effortlessly.

'So, uh, you've been this way before?' asks John.

'I know you're just trying to keep me talking, John.'

'No,' John lies.

'And I know a lie when I hear it.'

'Well,' says John, 'I suppose you would.'

1:xi

Ordo ab Chao

So this aspect – a golden king upon a golden throne – is not the one he would choose to inhabit. It is simply required, a sign, a symbol of his current occupation. But its value is fading and it is no longer enough.

+Wake, stir, speak to me. Show me some sign you hear me. We have to talk.+

I have, may he forgive me, become insistent.

We are fighting one war, and we will soon be fighting two, or be forced to choose between them. His loyal sons, of whom there are now so few, trust him still, to such a degree it is genuinely moving. But I read their doubts. The last walls are falling. The sun is red. They fear he is sitting here idle, immobile, impotent, indifferent. They think he's doing nothing, and that he's been doing nothing since this outrage began. They don't understand, as I do all too well, the silent effort he is making just to prevent the eschatonic rupture of reality.

They don't understand. They have *never* understood him. They barely understand me, and I am but his Sigillite. Despite the wonder of them, their accomplishment, the post-human miracle that each one represents, they remain simple tools, built for purpose. They lack insight. Even the very best of them, his terrible Angel, who can sometimes see more of tomorrow than even his father can, does not fully comprehend. They yearn for him to rise, to vacate this seat and join them. They long for revelation. They want their Emperor back, the war-king who led from the front in the Great Crusade. Surely he can turn this fight? Surely he can smite down the treacherous enemy at the gates? Why doesn't he act? Why isn't he with us? Why does he sit this out as though it is nothing?

Surely, if he gets up, sword in hand, and stands with us, this war will be over in hours, and victory wrenched from atrocity? For in him is not *ordo ab chao*? In him is not *lux in tenebris*?

Is he not *humanus pantokrator*? Why is he *letting this happen*?

So little they know. Time has never been our ally. We seemed to have luxurious amounts of it at the start, but now it is openly our enemy. Tomorrow is almost here. The clocks run out. These are plain facts that even my master cannot change. The last scrap of the aegis shield is about to fail. The armoured ramparts are cracking. The Palace will fall in a few hours. It has already lasted longer than anyone, on either side, anticipated. The world will end in a matter of days. It will be shredded to extinction, unable to withstand the onslaught. These are facts. Despite their unimaginable losses, the traitor-foes are about to win the material war.

+Speak to me. Open your eyes. We must talk.+

How do we reconfigure and deny those facts? Time has never been our ally, and the clocks run down. My lord and master cannot leave his seat, or the immaterial war will be lost. Without his focused operation of this device, this Golden Throne, the torrents of the immaterium flooding the antique webway will breach the conduit beneath our feet, and all will be swept away. The warp will rush in, polluted with the Chaotic annihilators that it carries, and the Earth will die from the inside out. It will perish in seconds, long before the Palace falls or the material war obliterates us. The clocks run down.

It is lose or lose. He can and he cannot. He is damned either way. The gods are laughing.

Wracked with pain, he hopes for salvation, for intervention. I cling to that hope too. It is still a possibility. His other sons, his other loyal sons, sons racing to his side from other suns, fleets at their heels, may be bearing down to smash the traitors and resolve the material war.

Even with my mindsight straining to its limits, I cannot discern a trace of them. I know that my master's mindsight, far superior to mine, is obscured too. My view is clouded, a seeing glass made opaque by milky veils. Terra and its system is occluded by the nimbose miasma of the warp as realspace rots around it. The Solar Realm is sinking into the empyrean, like a boat taking on water in a wrecking gale. I cannot see. They may be coming. I am sure they are. The Master of Ultramar, the Lion, the Wolf, the Raven... any and all of them, rushing to our aid. They could be minutes away. Or hours. Or days. Or months. The clocks run out.

Perhaps they are not coming at all. Perhaps intervention is the false hope of an old man.

They may be dead.

If they are, we will never be able to grieve for them.

The clocks run down. This is the moment. This is the critical hour, the perfect storm we have reconfigured again and again to avoid, every stratagem or ingenious revision blocked, or countered, or undermined. My lord, my master, has tried to avert this pass, but he cannot. He cannot wait. He cannot hope. He cannot stay. He cannot leave.

He could fight armies. This I know for a fact. He could fight daemons. He could fight turncoat sons. He could fight devious gods. He could fight material and immaterial alike. But he cannot fight them all at once, and he cannot fight time. The clocks run out.

There are no timepieces here, in what others refer to as the Throne Room. There used to be, but he asked me to have them removed. The stasis generators and stabilisation engines that he retrofitted into what others refer to as the Golden Throne interfere with time. Clocks freeze, or run backwards, or hover at various moments of un-when. He keeps his own time. I know that there is only a scrap of it left.

We must use it wisely, to maximum effect. Thus, we must reconfigure yet again, adjust and compromise, determine a fresh version of tomorrow. We must effect a teleological reset.

+Wake, stir, show me a sign. We must talk.+

He must make a new plan, and signify its intent with the mark of his hand.

I urge him to do so. I keep my place at the foot of the great dais, and I continue my steady, insistent psychic entreaties.

But the pain is so consuming, I am no longer sure he could hear me even if I was screaming.

1:xii

Fragments

The Palace is screaming.

The voice of its anguish is built from countless parts, just as the Palace was built from countless parts. Every component that was drawn together and assembled to fabricate the great edifice is being pulled apart and scattered to manufacture its death cry: the shrieks of buckling, tortured metal deforming, the wail of disintegrating superstructures, the squeals of splintering stone. As though alive now, briefly, in the hour of its own death, the Imperial Palace awakens to agony, and it is screaming.

Some buildings are simply gone. Landmarks, centuries old, have been entirely erased, or reduced to seas of rubble. Some slump or lean. The Manifold Librarium, the Southern Auxilia Barracks, the Mansion of Syracuse, the Charterhall: great cathedrals of Imperial power and lore are canted like bulk liners on the bed of a dry sea. Others have been cropped or scalped or flayed, or cut in two, the inner strata of their floors and chambers exposed like layers of geological sediment, so they now resemble the scale cross-sections and diagrams Dorn originally drafted to construct and fortify them.

The auspex paints an engine advancing through the Clanium Fields, just west of Europa Quarter, so the tank formations grind backwards, scrambling for position while they reload. The squadron, thirty-eight tanks from as many different brigades, has made five engine-kills in the past half hour, but those were three House Atrax Knights and two bastardised Reavers. This paint shows something bigger.

Jera Talmada fears it's a brute Warlord. It's moving slowly, obscured by the towers of Europa Southside, but the returns on her cracked augur screen indicate a huge mass. It is not broadcasting a transponder identity.

Colonel Talmada is commanding a Banestorm, one of four super-heavies in the pack. From her turret seat, she also commands the whole pack. Not a job she ever saw for herself. She's been tank brigade her whole life, but Corps Logisticae, not active. Her role was to mend, service and replenish, not direct front-line tread-war. But the kill-count has been unbearable. When Colonel Sagil was minced by a shell, there were no line officers left in the makeshift battle group, and everyone looked to her because of the pins on her collar. Twenty-nine of her crew leads were ensigns or drivers three days ago.

She orders *scythe* formation, yelling into a headset still crusted with Sagil's blood. She rolls her one Shadowsword out wide to flank her from what's left of the park's embankment. The gunners are loading below her in the oven-heat of the tread. The shell hoppers are running low. When they're out, then what? Withdraw the line for restock, or push on and attempt to support ground troops with the secondary weapon systems? And if she chooses to withdraw, then to where? Latris Bastion, perhaps? Shreave Depot, where they restocked just after dawn, is gone, by all accounts. According to some, the Sanctum is sealed and Eternity barred. There is no sign of support convoys from Logisticae. Talmada can't even get Logisticae on the vox.

Someone gasps. Talmada hears moans of shock from other crews over the vox. The target engine has moved into view.

It is *Emperor* class. Imperator or Warmonger. It's hard to tell through the rivers of smoke flowing across the fields, and formal ident is impossible because the thing is blackened and scorched. In a landscape of superlatives, it is vast. To Talmada's tearing eyes, it looks like a portion of the Palace has uprooted itself and started to walk. A bastion-fortress on legs.

She had dreaded the Warlords of Legio Mortis and Legio Tempestus. She had heard horror stories of the daemon engines that cut through the Ultimate Wall, scuttling giants on arachnid chassis that rendered wall-stone into irradiated glass with their bulk-meltas, and then cut that glass with their shearing mandibles to build vitrified steps that the baying traitor hosts could climb. But *this*…

This.

Someone speaks. She ignores it. They speak again. Talmada finally listens the third time.

It's one of ours.

It is. It *was*. Its banners and standards are burned away. Its shell-plate is seared. It is headless.

The Emperor engine moves erratically, limping, shuffling. It has been maimed and decapitated. It walks blind, mindless, undirected, walking only because of some residual impulse or muscle memory echoing through its peripheral systems. It staggers, spasmodic, lobotomised, like a poultry-fowl still twitching minutes after its head has been lopped off. It sees nothing. It knows nothing, not even that it is dead. It just walks, across rubble, through buildings, towards some final, inevitable halt.

The great Imperial Viaduct, once ninety-five kilometres long, now ends in nothing, truncated, a bridge to nowhere, or to hell, or perhaps to both.

The name Emhon Lux was writ in glory even before the traitors' Heresy began. His deeds in the Great Crusade won him honour, the respect of his Legion, and a reputation that extended beyond the Blood Angels to fellow Legions, who all, in their own ways, acknowledged his prowess as a warrior-champion.

The name Emhon Lux, the very being of Emhon Lux, is inextricably entwined with agony. At the brutal defence of Gorgon Bar, alongside his beloved primarch, and such hero-immortals as mighty Raldoron, proud Aimery, fierce Khoradal Furio, and the noble brethren of the Imperial Fists, Emhon Lux excelled, and then fell, his legs and pelvis crushed by the siegecraft of the Traitor IV's warsmiths.

There has been no time to heal, nor even repair. After such a grievous wounding, a legionary might face months of delicate reconstruction, of augmetic rebuild, of faceless chirurgeons with scalpel hands, and frowning Apothecaries with syringe fingers. Months masked in the bliss-blur of morphic-induced coma and catalepsean fugue. Months of death-sleep filled by the butcher-scents of resected meat and bone-fusion, the alien cold of pseudoflesh grafts and synthetic muscle where nerves had yet to regrow and reconnect. Months of slippery dreams marked out by the beat of bio-monitors and life support. Then months of learning to stand and move again on unfamiliar limbs.

But no months remain. No weeks, no days. Barely hours. Even the great triumph of Gorgon Bar, for which Lux paid so heavily, is a memory. The Bar, hard won, is now lost, along with Marmax, Victrix and Colossi, and all the rest of everything. Emhon Lux screamed from his bed until they let him up, packed his crushed and broken form with gels and dermal wraps and, according to the instructions he gave through clenched teeth, bound him with chains and ceramite splints to a Mechanicus suspensor throne.

As the Inner Palace breaks open, Emhon Lux rejoins the field. Pain travels with him as he drifts across broken rockcrete, despite the palliative auto-units lashed to the base-plate of his throne that drip-pump pure opioids into his body through nasogastric tubes and plugs sutured into his belly. He blanks the pain, but it will not leave him, despite the opiate-fog and the fixed intensity of his mental conditioning. It will always be there. He reminds himself that *always* is now finite.

Ostomy drains thread his lower half, spattering bio-waste in his wake. He clutches a lascannon, half rested on the arm of his seat, braced by the over-grip. His arms still work. His world is a fever-haze, incandescent and hallucinogenic. He knows that's due to the inhuman load of analgesic compounds flooding his body and brain, but the world seems incandescent and hallucinogenic anyway. It's hard for him to know what is his own garish invention and what is the new real, the manifested daymares of an unravelling materiality.

In truth, he does not care. Such is his mental focus to block pain, he has no effort spare to parse figment from truth. Everything is warped and molten. He trusts only the steady ticker of his visor's target reticle. He trusts the heavy weapon in his grip. He trusts the phalanx of combat servitors that trudge at his heels, lugging their rotary cannons, arc rifles and culverins, slaved to his mind through an impulse unit crudely spliced into the base of his skull. Where he aims, they aim.

He glides through the dust-swirled shadow of Manumission

Arch. He glides through pain. His visor boxes multiple contacts on the Via Hyrax ahead. Digitised silhouettes pick out shapes in the smoke, tracking heat and motion. Iron Warriors, the breacher-scum of the Stor-Bezashk, like spelter golems, leading in the smaller shapes of feral Traitor Auxilia. Lux hears the boom of their war-horns, trumpeting victory.

Premature, you piss-weak bastards.

He raises his cannon, fist clamped on the over-grip, and starts to fire lances of hard, bright light. His throne quivers. Around him, the automata swing as one, and unload in support, cones of flame jagging from their barrels, ejected casings spraying into the air like chaff.

His enemies gave him pain and made him dwell inside it.

He gives some back.

On the Via Aquila, in another part of the human river, Katsu-hiro carries his twofold burden, the gun and the child. He tries to steer through the throng, following the general direction of flow, avoiding people rolling handcarts laden with possessions or the makeshift litters of the wounded. The child in his arms, an inherited responsibility, is silent, head against his chest. His gun is silent too, for now.

He was conscripted Kushtun Naganda Old Hundred once. The remains of his last script orders flutter from a staple on his coat. He has moved through this war, at its very heart, a tiny part of the whole. Now he is nominally part of the conclave, the movement that has grown up organically around the woman called Keeler. It is an odd cause to follow, ill-defined. He doesn't know what to make of Keeler, though he admires her charisma and her sincerity. He wonders if the conclave, unofficial in every way, and possibly illegal if there was anybody left to enforce the statutes, is a fantasy, a group delusion confected to give people something to cling to. In a world that is fundamentally broken, the conclave is a conceit that allows people to feel as though they're doing something, that they still have some agency. Its queasy foundation is religious.

In extremis, people turn to faith. Spiritual faith had been forsaken for so long, its sudden outpouring has nothing to fix on except the Emperor. That in itself is forbidden, proscribed by the Emperor Himself. But no one, not even the Master of Mankind, can legislate against fear or hope or want. In the last days, the human need for something more than just a powerful ruler, a need few of them even knew they had, has been brutally revealed. They have clung to whatever is there, as the child clings to him. They have made a saviour-god out of a man, without asking or caring if He minds.

The great avenue is congested, tens of thousands here, tens more flowing in from the Via Artalia and the Chiros Processional, ten times tens more from Lotus Gate and Navis Heights. Slow waves of panic ripple through the teeming mass every time detonations ring too close, and the grain of the crowd billows every time something flies overhead between the towering steeples and blocks of the habs.

It is always hard to see what the flying things are. Aircraft, bombers, drop-ships, ferries... they move too fast, and the smoke is too dense. Sometimes, Katsuhiro thinks they're not machines at all. He glimpses bat-shapes, vulturine wings, and hears the infrasonic purr of lungs, and the creak of muscle instead of engines.

He has found goggles, one lens cracked. He has bound his face like an outlaw, the child's too, to mask out dust and soot. Some in the crowd burn incense or carry lanterns. Most have also plugged or wrapped their ears, but Katsuhiro wants to be able to hear, to stay alert, even if all he hears is pain and screams and constant uproar. The noise alone is exhausting.

He's not certain he's part of the conclave any more, or if it still exists. He hasn't seen another member of the congregation in three hours. The conclave's basic function was to render aid, to mobilise volunteer militia support, and to operate ad hoc munition supply lines to the front. But the number of people has swollen out of control. The supply chains are overrun and disorganised.

Besides, the munition depots are burning.

The crowds flow on as though they know where they are going. People carry other people. Many display wounds and injuries, or signs of disease. All are begrimed. There are two modes of expression: weeping or blank-eyed. Fights break out in the crowd over nothing, men and women lashing out at each other because they can't lash out at anything greater.

'Stop it,' Katsuhiro tells them, child cupped in one arm, gun braced in the other. 'What good does that do? What the hell is the point?'

What the hell do you know? say the looks that shoot back at him. *You're just nobody too,* say the glares that come his way. But they relent. He's not sure if it's because of his gun, or the child he's holding.

And, anyway, they're right.

The Emperor Must Die. The Emperor Must Die. It is written on the tattered walls, and gouged into stricken ramparts. It is written in paint and tar, pitch and ash. It is written in blood. It is written everywhere, daubed up, marked by hand, cut with blades or scorched by burners.

In some places the words have simply appeared, formed by no living hand at all. The words have risen from stone, like blisters, like urticaria, like scarification. *The Emperor Must Die. The Emperor Must Die.*

It is a chant too, bellowed by a million voices. It fills the air, and it covers the walls.

Around that slogan, where it is marked, other words are written: threats, menaces, the iconography of the burgeoning darkness, the malign symbols of etheric power. Four words. The four names from which there are eight. The false gods.

And one other name, too. With increasing repetition.

1:xiii

Record of
an interview conducted
by Remembrancer Oliton

He chose me. My father, after Ullanor. But there *was* no choice.
I was his first-found son. My father, you see, is a man, but in
the same breath, he is surely not. He is more, far more than
me. In his scope and dimension, he is a god, though that is
a word all of us shy away from. He rejects the term. I think
perhaps our language, all human languages, have failed to
come up with a word for what he is. A man, but godlike in
span and aspiration. He has been working for, what? Thirty
thousand years or more, my lady? Thirty *thousand* years. If the
definition 'man' strains to accommodate what I am, it surely
shatters to accommodate him. I am mere centuries old, a fraction by comparison, a mere green shoot sprouting from a seed
he sowed. He made me to help him in his work.

I was his first-found son. That was the greatest period of my
life, those days. Thirty years we had, just him and me, father
and son. He raised me up from the Cthonic darkness where he
found me, and set me at his side. We had that time together.
I had thirty years of his undivided attention and raising. We

formed a bond. Unbreakable. Stronger than any he formed with his other sons, for none of them had that same time with him that I got. Thirty years. Not much, I suppose. Thirty beside thirty thousand, scarcely a heartbeat. But even so, I treasure that time. He taught me everything.

So, of course he chose me. Of course.

His other sons, my brothers, are all great men. My father and I found them, one by one. The joy we both felt at each discovery! The joy of reunion, of blood finding blood. I cannot tell you. I love each one of them. They are mighty, and I am proud to call them kin. All are great, and some are *truly* great. Mind you, Mersadie, in any family, there are always favourites, though that fact is always delicately avoided.

There were strong contenders, of course. For the role of Warmaster, I mean. I have sometimes been eclipsed by the brilliance of my brothers, and I am happy to admit that. The strength of Ferrus. Perturabo's implacable focus. The cunning of Alpharius, last found but never the least.

I have adored them all, and relished their prowess and achievements. But there are always favourites. Rogal, my dear brother, perhaps the finest martial exponent I have ever known. But also, if I'm honest, dour and unimaginative. Narrow in his outlook. My father always had a peculiar fondness for Magnus, for I think in Magnus my father saw a special legacy. But Magnus is a strange one, always stood apart from us; not aloof, but distant, removed into his own thoughts. My father loves him, but there is always a tension there. I think, perhaps, they are too alike. Magnus is too like his father. Such is the way in families, Mersadie.

Roboute, well… I cannot lie. I admire him. The sheer range of his accomplishments. If we resemble aspects of our parents, Lady Oliton, I think Roboute takes after that version of my father who wore the name Alysaundr. There is no doubt he was a true contender too. He would have made a fine Warmaster.

But when it came down to it, there were only two legitimate choices. Two *favourites*, let's not pretend otherwise. Myself, and the only other son who holds a place in my father's affections as significant as my own. My angel brother, Sanguinius. He came late, but was perhaps the most beloved. He looks most like my father too, more than me. The features... the tone of his voice...

He was the only other choice. Can I tell you a secret? He would have been *my* choice. I love all my brothers, but my love for Sanguinius is particular. I envy him. Does that sound strange? Does that sound weak? Well, I *do*. I envy him. Would that I had an ounce of his numinous wonder. He is... How can I put it? He is... impossible to hate. Have you met him? You *must* meet him. He will take your breath away. He is, Mersadie, the only one I would not have resented. Any of us could have been Warmaster. Any of us would have excelled, and we would all have rallied to them without hesitation or question. I had seniority, as first-found, and my achievements spoke for themselves. But had he anointed any of them over me, I would have been secretly insulted.

Except Sanguinius. If my father had chosen him, I would not have questioned it. Not for a second. I would have rejoiced in his promotion and led the celebration.

If my father has a favourite son, Mersadie, it is Sanguinius.

1:xiv

Fragments

It is raining fire from a burned-out sky.

The traitor host bubbles through the low streets and avenues of the Palatine. In their thousands, in their hundreds of thousands, they ascend the staircases of vitrified waste that the spider-engines have woven from the walls, and spill down into the Imperialis, an inky deluge. It is hard to tell in how many places the towering walls have been breached.

The sky is black flame, the low underbelly of hell. The towers and spires of the Precinct Imperialis, those that still stand, are pockmarked and wounded. They are blackened too, caked in billowed soot and the wash of burners.

The traitor mass is black. It is all the atrocious devils of the Inferno at once. Ebon armour. Butcher hooks. Obscene banners. A reek of putrescence. Gorbellied armour distended like pot-stoves, sloshing with inner ferment. Sizzling clouds of blowflies. Black helms, wolf-mawed, hound-skulled, boartusked, horn-snouted, cage-muzzled, bay at the sky, black against black, or hiss crocodilian whispers to the Neverborn things that follow them in the shadows.

This is the Terracide. This is the utter end and the ever-death.

Shapes irrupt from darkness around the charging mass, are made flesh, and stand blinking and mewling, new-never-born, learning the function of their solidifying senses and limbs, adjusting to their unfamiliar corporeal forms. They stand on moa legs, eight metres high, toe-claws the size of husked palm-nuts, or on goat limbs, or on boneless trunks of glistening mollusc-muscle. They shamble, ponderous under chelonian shells of hard-horn and chitin. They caper and gambol, hopping like vultures at a carcass, swan necks swaying, ibis bills clacking. They snuffle the ground and gnaw at the dead. They unfold wings of necrotic skin on finger-bone rods, and catch the air, and rise, cawing. They hatch like blisters, spilling out, frothing with foams of eyes, or oozing sores that palpate with trembling anemone tongues. They gland hatred and bile. They drip acid and pus. They gnar and bark from drooling pit-bull mouths, and from the sounds, form words; and from the words, the text of their new religion; and from the text, the modes and offices of their demented priestcraft. They begin their rites of sparagmos, and their capering danse macabre. They speak their names into the air, for in their xenolalia they know all names, and they scratch those names and marks upon the city's stones with trocar talons. One name above all, one name more and more, over and over, written in fear and read in glee. The name is not Horus Lupercal.

It is the thanatoxic neverness. It is the then and the now and the when, for the clocks are all run out. It is the vatic promise of the warp. It is the name that ushers in doom.

* * *

Bombs burst, interrupting them. Splinters of shrapnel pass them, hissing like wasps. Agathe reaches to her cheek, and finds a hole in it through which she can touch her teeth.

She sits down. A corpsman rushes to her. His hands are quickly soaked in blood as he tries to close her wound. He is sobbing. She isn't sure if it's because of her, or for some other cause. She doesn't ask. She waves aside analgesic and gets him to stitch it and plug it with a patch of pseudoflesh.

The soldiers she was talking to wait, unsure whether to continue or not.

She gestures at them, irritated, and mumbles something incoherent that causes blood to spill out of her mouth.

'You…?' the officer begins, uncertain.

'Just carry on,' Agathe's adjutant tells them. 'Don't waste time. You were saying who you were.'

'Four-Oh-Three,' says the officer. He looks filthy, wretchedly equipped. *But then aren't we all*, thinks Agathe. 'Four Hundred and Third. We were told to report to you.'

He pauses.

'You are Marshal Aldana Agathe?' he asks.

Agathe nods and grunts.

'She is,' says Phikes, the adjutant. 'Marshal Agathe of the Antioch Miles Vesperi.'

Phikes is Vesperi. He says the words proudly, as though they mean something. They don't. The army of some eight thousand she commands is a scratch-built monstrosity made of all the scraps she could get. She was something once. Commander of a hive-host. She stood alongside Valdor, Raldoron and the Great Khan himself at Colossi. They saw off the Pale King's worst, when such a feat was still possible.

But that time's gone. The Great Khan is dead, so she's been told. No one knows where brave Raldoron is. She's just a filthy soul sitting on the pavement in a dying city having her face sewn back together by a weeping boy.

'Four Hundred and Third?' says Phikes, asking the next question she would have asked. 'Four Hundred and Third what? I don't know it.'

'Does it matter any more?' the officer replies.

'I'll tell you what matters!' Phikes snaps.

The soldiers shift uncomfortably.

'We're from Gallowhill Camp,' the officer says. 'Most of us. Ordered to active service two weeks ago. We're glad to serve, I assure you.'

'Gallowhill?' says Phikes, curious. 'The detention camp? You were guards there?'

Unable to speak because the corpsman's fingers are in her mouth, Agathe grunts and waves to get Phikes' attention. He hasn't caught on.

'No,' says the officer.

Phikes frowns. The facts finally align for him. 'You're... convicts? You're a penal unit?'

'Yes,' the man says.

'The Four-Oh-Three is a penal unit, is it?'

'It is,' says the officer, and seems ashamed. 'Four Hundred and Third Exigency Stratiotes.'

Phikes looks at Agathe askance. She glares back, making her opinion very clear.

'Well.' Phikes sniffs, turning back to the men without disguising his scorn. 'Needs must, I suppose. What are your numbers?'

'About a thousand,' says the officer. He is grey-fleshed and grey-tunicked. He and his men have no helmets, just dirty forage caps with an embroidered patch of the palatine aquila on the front. 'We've soaked up a few scratch companies along the way. Stragglers from Anterior and–'

Phikes isn't interested, and doesn't let him finish.

'You are sanctioned?' he asks. 'You have your marks?'

The officer and his men show the tags stapled like script orders to their collars. Marks of purity and fitness. The Corps Logisticae, under the supervision of something called the 'Prefectus', has been screening people for health, for signs of infection, and for the weals and blisters of immaterial contamination.

These men have been passed fit. Murderers, thieves and deserters, probably, the lot of them, but 'pure' by the current yardstick.

'I'll be checking every one of your complement,' says Phikes.

'You may,' says the officer, quite openly.

'I don't need your permission–' Phikes growls.

Agathe tells them to shut up with her mouth closed. It comes out as an angry snort.

'Where do you want us, marshal?' the officer asks.

Agathe holds up a finger to bid them wait, and tries to ignore the sensation of the blunt needle pulling through her cheek.

The corpsman is done. She stands up, takes a canteen, flushes her mouth and spits pink soup onto the flagstones.

'Name?' she asks. It hurts to speak and the word comes out sloppily.

'Mikhail,' he says. 'Captain M–'

'What can you do, Mikhail?' she asks, making a mess of every consonant.

'We have field guns,' he replies.

That's something. She starts to explain her scheme of deployment, but every word is a slurred labour. She waves them over to the wall of the hab behind them, and starts to draw in the thick dust instead. Simple fingermarks, a suggestion of landmarks, a simplified plan. This is how it will be, she draws, forming basic lines so they can understand. The enemy masses here and here. The support armour will block and enfilade. They will break and run, like so. We will be here. These are the field guns you will bring to bear. This – as her fingers move from rough cross to foe-smudge – this will be your arc of fire. This is where it will strike, this flank here. This will be our kill-box.

The convict-officer nods. Her intentions are clear.

She turns back to mark the anticipated lines of retreat if the gambit fails. The wall suddenly feels wrong to her touch. Not brick, not dust. It feels soft and spongy. It feels like the skin of her cheek.

She withdraws her hand, quickly, and stares. The others stare too. The patch of wall is sarcoid, like stretched flesh or raw hide. Bristles sprout from sagging creases that vaguely resemble the original block-joints and mortar.

She can't look away from the wall. Behind her, she hears Phikes dry-heave. It's not the sheet of mottled flesh that fascinates her. It's the marks she made in the dust. Her plan is gone, and the smudges now spell something out.

Three words.

'Did you write that?' the convict-captain asks.

Agathe shakes her head. She doesn't even know who 'the Dark King' is.

Spilled tarot cards, fallen from the torn musette bag of a dead Excertus sergeant near the Razavi line, flutter in the war-wind, billowing like dead leaves across the cracked and blood-soaked pavement.

Some are torn, some creased, some stained. One of them is on fire.

1:xv

Mortal measures

I cannot bear to watch his hands clench involuntarily on the golden armrests any more. I look away. Watching them twitch and spasm tells me too much of his ordeal.

I look away. I seek distraction. The room is vast by any mortal measure. It, in itself, is a sign, a symbol. It was built to suit the regal war-king he once was, a grand chamber to mirror that grand aspect. He did not object, for he understood the psychological value. Down the ages, architecture has always been used to amplify the status and authority of those who rule. Here is where he set his throne, so here is the throne room built around it, quite breathtaking in its dimension and scale. He told me he remembered the great cathedrals of the old eras, the echoing naves of Chartres, Beauvais, Oaxaca Katholikon and Nu Krasnodar Minster, their solemn hush, their sanctity, their symbolic manifestos of reverence. Of course, they were built to laud false gods, which is why he had them overthrown, but there was no denying their cosmetic effect. They inspired belief and obedience. They instilled awe. Those who came to engage with him needed to feel the same effect. They needed to be humbled. They needed to be reminded, beyond any shadow of doubt, that he was worth listening to.

But it's just a room. It is a throne room simply because, to them, it is a room with a throne in it. Even the Throne is not a throne, not as they understand the word. He does not sit here to project an aspect of exalted supremacy. The Throne is a device, the most important and oldest of his key instruments. The room is simply the room where he works, the central chamber of a suite of chambers that others refer to as the Dungeon, but which he thinks of as his workshop.

Dungeon. Words are strange, imprecise and too easily applied. People see what they want to see. A dungeon, a throne room, a golden throne, an emperor. Just words. It is a dungeon because it is deep beneath a palace, so of course the word for that must be dungeon. Not workshop or laboratorium or studio or adytum or temple of science, sunk deep into the living rock simply to insulate it against fluctuations of matter and immateria. Of course it is a throne room, because it is monumental and contains a throne. Of course he is the Emperor, because what else could he be? He is what they need him to be.

Of course it is a throne, for is it not massive and gilded and ornate? And does the Emperor not sit upon it?

The Golden Throne – I have long since abandoned the distraction of finding a better name for it – is a device with many astounding applications, one of which is the moderation and manipulation of etheric power. I have always assumed that he constructed it himself, but I also assume that he incorporated into that construction pieces of relic technology. This has often been his way. He makes ingenious use of the strange treasures he has found in the course of his long life, repurposing and reverse-engineering them. He did the same with the vast and baffling xenoarchaeological monument known as the webway.

We cannot know who originally constructed the webway or why, and we can only speculate that other cultures may have found it and used it for their own purposes before human history began. We do know, however, that the wise-yet-unwise aeldari inherited it, gave it its name, and used it as a subspace network of travel and communication.

It is a labyrinthine subdimension that stretches across the galaxy. It permits transit to those with the will to use it. That transit is direct and, comparatively, swift. Moreover, that transit is entirely free of the vagaries of the warp. From this, we can discern both the genius and the intent of the aeldari. They were building an interstellar culture that would not depend on the warp in any way. They conspired to shun the warp, and remove it from the equation. They built under and around and above it. They limited their interaction with the warp, because they predicted that the warp would always, ultimately, consume any maturing psychically aware species.

They knew this, but it happened to them anyway.

My lord and master's use of the webway echoes their intent. It was the reason he returned prematurely from the Great Crusade. He had recognised that mankind could and *should* not be reliant on the warp, in matters such as travel and communication, and with all haste and urgency, he embarked on a programme to reclaim, repair and rebuild the webway to make it human-compatible. It was a vital part of his Great Work, arguably more urgent than the unifying crusade itself.

But his sons did not understand that.

Should he have told them? Should he have explained? And if he should have done that, why did he not? I confess, that's another story, and not mine to tell.

* * *

My story is this one. His story. It is the story of mankind, of its triumphs and failures, its fortitude and its wrong turns. It began, once upon a time, millennia ago, when we were still painting our hopes and plans on walls with our fingers, and trusting in something *else* to watch over us, and it has been spinning out ever since, like yarn, like a single precious thread, through the adumbral maze of mankind's clumsy, complex, unwieldy and confused history. Now, here he sits, a lonely magician on a makeshift throne, with the other end of that thread in his hand. It has been his story to tell, his thread to pay out so that we did not lose our way, and it ends here, now, or never.

I had hoped it would be never, but now I am not so sure. The clocks run out, and so does the spool of thread. Time has come, abstract but menacing, to demand what it is due.

He has done his best. Many dispute that, but it's true. He has done his best to protect the human race from its own worst propensities, from malice and evil and the predation of others, from a future that was deemed inevitable and, most of all, from itself. I know there are many, far too many, who regard him as a monster, who reject the path he has measured with his thread, who seek to shame his ambition and wrest control from him. Well, my master does not seek approval, and he does not seek acclaim, and he absolutely never asked for permission. He has been guided by rationality, and a profound belief in the potential of our species. He believes, just as I believe, that mankind can achieve what no sentient form has achieved before, in the whole history of this universe. Apotheosis. Not just for him, for the entire species. He believes, and has always believed, that we can configure our own tomorrow, and elude the inevitable doom of the future.

For he saw, once upon a time, what no one else had seen, or wanted to see. He saw that there was nothing *else* watching over us. No gods, no ineffable, divine *other*, nothing guiding us or keeping us safe. We were journeying alone, and the only fate that awaited us, the only far future, was the one we would make for ourselves.

Of course, there *was* something *else*. But not gods, not gods as we would want them, or need them, or imagine them; not providers or guardians. Not gods at all, though, like 'throne', it is the easiest word to use. Anagogic powers, higher things, outer things, formless and uncontrolled, annihilators that have followed in our footsteps every step of the way, symbolic reminders of the preordained doom awaiting us. Predators, watching us from the shadows as we live our lives, waiting for us to drop our guard or turn our backs.

Consider again that wall, long ago, the bison and the running deer, the fleeing antelope, the men with bows and spears. But if you look closely, there, at the edge, where fingers have painted trees and long grasses, there are the predators, lying in wait, hardly visible, but for the tips of their ears and the glint in their eyes, biding their time, waiting for one of the men to fall behind and lose sight of his brothers. They have always been there, even though we don't see them, in the darkness at the back of the cave, in the night beyond the ring of the camp's fire, in the sun-baked cover of the scrub, watching, waiting, hungry.

They are the only *else*, and they must be shunned and kept out. There are four of them. He knows their names. No one else should.

He stole fire from those four annihilator gods, and used it to keep them at bay. He wielded it in his hand, century after century, to drive them back whenever they came too close. It amused him that they flinched from their own fire.

But he knew from the start it would not be enough just to keep them away. We could be vigilant, torch in hand; we could build walls to keep them outside, we could invent cities to hide in, but they would always be there. So there began the long game, his life's work. To keep us safe, and remove the possibility of a future in which they got in and ate us alive, he would have to hunt them down and kill them.

Except, as he quickly learned, they are not things that can die. They persist. They can only be denied and avoided. And even in that, he has failed, or at least is on the brink of failure. That was the plan he made on his wall, but it is not yet complete, and now the clocks run out, and tomorrow is not what he configured and promised, and we have not built our walls high enough or strong enough. They have been trying to stop us since they first became aware of his intention, and now they are at the gates to end him.

I look out, extending my mindsight to its limit. I cannot see hope or salvation, I cannot see relief coming, but I can see them, in the shadows and the long grass, bellies to the ground, prowling ever closer.

So, it's come to this. He cannot fight everything at once. There isn't time. Time is our enemy. He no longer has the luxury of sitting, mastering this pain as he blocks out the warp. He must choose his battles, and win each one in order of priority. He is not a god, but he has been fulfilling that role for a long time, acting in the stead of the allotheistic figments that never existed, no matter how much mankind believed in them. Though we both abhor the word, and forbid its use, he has been a god for all practical purposes for centuries.

Time is burning. The clocks have stopped. The walls collapse. I am his trusted Regent. I must give my advice now. I must urge him. I must *make* him hear me. To redeem his plan and salvage any hope of the tomorrow he intended, he must rise.

He must stop acting as a god, and fight like a man.

1:xvi

Fragments

They have come great distances to destroy the world. They have come from other worlds, obscure systems, from far-off stars and remoter star clusters. They have come from every corner of what was, for one fleeting and glorious moment, the Imperium of Man.

And beyond. They have come from other spaces, other realms, other layers of creation and other flavours of reality. They have come from the roiling psycho-ocean of the warp. They have come from hell.

Baleful eyes blink at the light of a new world. Baleful eyes in pugnacious horror-faces. The black fur around the glittering eyes is still matted with thawing interstellar ice. They have come a long way to be here.

Helig Gallor kills the last of some Traitor Excertus on the walkway behind Sydal House. Once of the Death Guard's Seventh Great Company, now Knight Errant, Gallor's loyalty is uninterrupted. He looks at the bodies littering the flowerbeds around him. The fools thought they could ambush him. They should have brought more than thirty if they'd wanted a fair fight, though nothing has been fair for a very long time. Gallor recognises the insignia on the blood-soaked tunics. Merudin 18th Assault Cadre… or, at least, that's what they had been once. Merud, he thinks. That's a long way out, beyond Cycax. These men had come a long way to be here.

They'd come a long way just to die.

They've come a long way. The last leg has been a slow, exhausting trek up through the compressed grave cities and ancient stratigraphy of past civilisations on which the Palace was built. They've seen sights, marvels, astonishing relics over which, if he'd had a mind to, Oll Persson might have lingered.

But he hasn't. Time's against them, and the crushed layers of compacted cities seem too much like a precis of his life, which has been long, longer than John's, longer even than His.

Longer than anyone's.

Oll doesn't wish to linger and remember. He wants to get there. He's embarked on the longest and most uncanny odyssey that anyone has ever undertaken, and he wants it done with.

Besides, there's something following them. It's been chasing them since they set out from Calth, something in the darkness that's getting closer by the hour. He can feel it in his old bones.

And in the knife that shivers in his hand.

He was a farmer when he set out, but that life of crops and toil and peace was just a brief interval. His *favourite* interval, it had to be said, the best of all the short stories that make up his history. But it was just a tiny island in the vast archipelago of his experience. He's been many things, as many things as there are to be: soldier, scholar, husband, coward, pacifist, parent, navigator, ruler, friend… He was even Warmaster once, the first ever to bear that title. Most of all, more than anything, he's been a voyager. A sailor, a seafarer, a traveller, a wanderer. He's known the infinite wonders of a voyaging life, and understands that the sweetest part of any journey is always the ending. Land in sight at last. Breakers on the beach. The sloping light of evening marking the rooftops of a longed-for home.

The end of this voyage will not be sweet. He only hopes it will be worthwhile.

This voyage – his last, he is sure – has been the strangest and greatest of all. So strange, so perilous, that it would've been rejected by myth-weavers as too fanciful. He's stepped between stars, across galaxies. He's sliced holes in the curtain of the immaterium with his athame, and slipped through them, from place to time, and time to place, against the linear weft of history and the reassuring logic of material reality, a circuitous route, beset by danger, pursued every step of the way, to get here.

Home. Terra. The last and furthest shore. The sloping light of evening on familiar rooftops. His birthplace, and the place where everything began.

The place where, one way or another, everything will end.

Oll's brought others with him, unwillingly, though to leave them behind would've consigned them to death. Even so, one has fallen already. Oll worries how many of them will survive the last stretch. He's offered them chances to stop along the way, to stay behind in safe ports while he goes on alone, but they've refused. They're in this now, confused, committed, utterly loyal to him in ways he can't credit. John, his friend, his nemesis, calls them the Argonauts. To Oll, that's a slight on both the prowess of the original crew to bear that name, and to the bravery of this company. He has, after all, known both.

They walk with him, his long companions, up through the

cavern track. Katt, the latent psyker, close at his side, simmering
with unease; Dogent Krank, the steady and stubborn soldier;
Hebet Zybes, the simple farmhand to whom everything is
miraculous and thus nothing startling; and Graft, the battered
cultivation servitor, which has trundled far outside the remit
of its task-programming.

They've acquired fellow travellers along the way. Leetu – or,
more properly, *LE 2* – Erda's bodyguard, loaned to John for
the duration. In unpainted silver plate as stoic and unyielding
as his demeanour, Leetu is a Space Marine. Oll believes he's
a prototype of the Astartes breed, perhaps even an early test,
his genetic profile unmodified by any primarch's seed. His
beaked helm, armour pattern and bolt weapon speak of a time
when the first batches were made, and the replacement of the
Thunder Warriors began. Oll wishes he'd been there with John,
to speak to Erda and quiz her about Leetu. Has she always
had him? Did she keep him back when the first samples were
cast in the Sigillite's progenoid labs? Is he a stolen treasure, a
memento? Or was he made for her as a gift?

So many puzzles, and they're not even the start. More than
anything, Oll wishes he'd simply been able to meet Erda again,
to talk of things directly, to construct a plan, to recall the histories they once shared and the man they both knew. But the
rendezvous proved impossible. Something – an imprecise cut
with the athame, perhaps, or the sabotaging efforts of those set
against them, or just the ever-increasing warp saturation around
their destination world – threw them off course, like a sudden
storm in the Cyclades, and cast them up on a desolate shore in
the wrong time and the wrong place. They only survived that
misadventure because John, god bless his determination, found
them and, with Leetu at his side, pulled them from danger.

Oll's missed the chance to meet with Erda, and consult a
soul, the *mater omnium*, who's considerably wiser and better

informed than he is. They could've made a plan for, truth of it is, he has none at all. Except to stop this. By any means necessary. That's it, the top and bottom of it. Oll will have to improvise when the time comes, just as he did with Polyphemus, and that awkward time in Ygrayne's chambers.

Worst of all, Oll fears that whatever's following them will have traced a path to Erda and discovered her after her centuries of careful self-exile. If that's true, if she's been harmed…

Then there's the Alpharius. Utterly untrustworthy yet utterly essential. Only he knows the last steps of the way. So Oll must countenance his presence, even though he has a poor history with hydras. The teeth of the dragon have never been sown in his favour.

Oll knows the Alpharius is vital, because Actae has told him so. She's their other new companion, the blind prophetess in tattered red, a creature of immense, perhaps deathless power, who conjures from his memory the witch-queens of the ancient Aegean and Kolkhis at their nightmarish best and beautiful worst. Like John, Actae's life has been threaded through the tapestry of this war, used and spurned by both sides. She stands with them, now, of her own volition, and according to her own agenda. Or so she says.

Actae and Alpharius. Without them, they can go no further nor hope to prevail. But with them… the question becomes 'further into *what*?' What unifies the band is a desire for salvation. Oll's far from convinced that Actae's vision of salvation resembles his in any way at all.

Katt despises her. In part, that's the friction of two active minds in close proximity, jarring and sparking against each other, but Oll knows that Katt can see more, more than she is able to say. As they walk, Katt glances at him from time to time, warning looks that ask, *Why do you let her come with us?* She's too afraid to explain her fears to Oll.

Finally John, of course. John Grammaticus. Pawn of the xenos Cabal, an artificial Perpetual employed to agitate the war and escalate it to a pitch that would end in Horus' victory and the subsequent annihilation of the human race. This, the Cabal dreamed, would be a means to snuff out the ruinous threat of Chaos.

But that genocidal scheme is abandoned, forsaken by the Cabal when they realised that Horus' power was beyond even their ingenious manipulation. Oll knows that John, forever the cat's paw, now wishes to make amends and break the deadlock of the war. He's taken ownership of his last ration of mortality, and intends to use it well.

John's the reason Oll is on this odyssey. John believes Oll's deep history with the thing now known as the Emperor can exert an influence, and change the course of damnation.

Oll's not so sure. Nothing and no one has *ever* changed the Emperor's mind, or persuaded Him to reconsider His plans. But there's a chance, a minuscule one worth all this risk, a chance to stop the Emperor leading mankind to what Oll always warned would be the inescapable consequence of His ambitions.

Not glory. Not the ascension of the human race. Just the dark and hopeless bonfire of the Triumph of Ruin.

The knife shivers in his hand. The lapped-stone thing is old, Neolithic old. It's played its part in history: the instrument of the original murder, splashed with the blood of Abel, the executioner of Gog. It's lain on the painted top of a great round table, and passed from daemon to man and back again. Oll took it from the Word Bearers, who had come to understand the potency of such objects, and had taken to collecting them. A blade like it, similarly cursed by fate, initiated this cataclysm. Perhaps, as a mirroring ritual, the athame can end it.

Perhaps. The athame's just stone, just old stone, but its

past has created a resonance in the immaterium, the stain-ing shadow of murder. It's tired of cutting time and space. It has killed seven times. It's been promised an eighth death.

If that's what it takes. Oll will do it if he has to. Plunging that blade into...

It wouldn't be the first time.

'Your thoughts are fascinating,' says Actae.

'Get out of them, please,' says Oll.

'I can't read them, Ollanius. You mask them well. But I can taste them. They taste intriguing, as though they are... well, unthinkable.'

'He said get out of his head, so get out of it,' says Katt.

Actae pauses, and turns her head to consider Katt, as if she's looking at her, though her blind eyes are wrapped.

'Then should I peer into you instead?' she enquires. 'Your mind is odd, girl. There is so little of you, as if everything has been wrapped up and put away, out of sight. Did you decide to forget who you used to be, or was there nothing to remember in the first place?'

There's a smack, like a hand striking flesh. Actae's head jerks sideways, slightly. When she turns back, she touches the smile her mouth has become.

'Nice shot,' she says. 'Bear in mind that's the only one you'll get.'

'Only one I'll need,' says Katt, 'if it teaches you to keep your mind to yourself.'

'That's enough,' says Oll, stepping between them. He's too tired for this nonsense. Everyone is looking – Zybes, Krank, even Graft.

'We go together, or we go our separate ways,' says Oll.

'Here?' asks Actae, gesturing to the deep cleft around them with her long, expressive fingers and longer nails. 'Part com-pany down *here*, Ollanius?'

The track is steep, uneven and narrow. The rock floor glitters with threads of minerals. Gloom gathers breathlessly. The walls lean in over their heads. It's like an axe-wound split into the rock.

'I've found my way out of other labyrinths,' he tells her. 'Play nice. Don't pry.'

Actae nods, a surprisingly courteous gesture. 'Of course. I am just incurably inquisitive. And I am fascinated by the company I find myself in.'

'That was your choice,' says Oll.

'It was. I apologise, Katt,' says Actae.

Oll looks at Katt. Her fists are balled, her cheeks flushed, her eyes drawn narrow. She glares at Actae. Katt's life has been miserable. Oll knows that. An unregistered psyker, Katt's spent her years hiding, or being shunned, or both. She's leery of everything, especially uninvited questions. Oll's little band is the first and only place she has found a purpose. She came to him as a survivor, a refugee seeking rescue. But she's the only one he really trusts, because there's no side to her, no agenda. Just tough, honest loyalty. He trusts her more than John. He trusts everyone more than Actae. Even the damn Alpha.

Leetu appears behind them. Their lamplight catches on the silvered un-finish of his plate. He seems as fresh as he did when they set out on this long, slow climb hours earlier.

His hand is to the ear-guard of his helm.

'Message,' he says. 'From Alpharius. He requests we stay here. He's securing an area ahead. Him and Grammaticus.'

'Securing?' asks Krank.

'He didn't explain,' replies Leetu. 'If I ask, I won't get a straight answer. This part of the journey is his call.' He looks at Actae. 'Correct?'

'Yes,' says Actae.

'Let's wait here then,' says Oll. 'Rest.' He finds a low rock, settles his weight against it, eases his aching feet.

Zybes unstoppers a flask of water and takes a sip.

Actae folds her great height onto the ground, and sits cross-legged as if she's taking a stance on a meditation mat in some ashram. She places her wrists on her knees, palms up.

'So,' she says. 'What shall we talk about?'

1:xvii

The Bastion

This was the Grand Borealis, the heart of war, the central chamber of the immense Bhab Bastion. This was the seat of loyalist command.

Bhab Bastion, that imperious and impervious block-fortress, with its surrounding drum towers, has been the Praetorian's command core since the siege began. From here have issued all commands, all directives, all orders and notifications. The peerless operation of the defence has been orchestrated from here since the thirteenth of Secundus.

This was the Grand Borealis. A humbling chamber of cyclopean scale. The data of war has flowed across its countless screens and console stations, and on its strategium tables, the hololithic maps of conflict zones have been displayed, and strategies debated, and tactics devised.

It was the nexus of authority, the nucleus of the War Court. It was awake and active, day and night, without pause or interruption, alive with voices, the bustle of a thousand personnel, the chatter and chirrup of tac, noospheric and vox updates,

the whir of servo-skulls darting by on errands, the hustle of
scribes and clerks and messengers, the fierce discussion of the
Tacticae Terrestria, the voices of summoned generals and lords
militant, the briefings of Council delegates, the hum of projection amplifiers, the rattle of cogitators, the squeal of alarms.

This was the seat of Archamus, Master of the Huscarls,
Second Of That Name, Dorn's proxy at the head of the command chain, a station he did not seem to leave for months.

This, nearby, the chair of Vorst, veteran captain of the Imperial Fists, deputy to Archamus, sidelined from the front due
to old injuries, his mind sleeplessly devoted to the decision-
theory of warfare, mentally waging a campaign that would
be enacted in deed.

These were the stations of the mistresses and masters tacticae... Icaro, Brinlaw, Osaka, Gundelfo, Elg, Montesere, a
hundred others, the greatest strategic thinkers of the age.

This is the billow of smoke. This is the heckle of flames. This
is the scree of glass and plastek fragments across the deck, the
spatters of oil and dirt, the spilled and abandoned files and
reports, stirred and ruffled by the wind that gusts through the
spaces where once were windows.

This is the Great Strategium table, at which Praetorian, Khan
and Angel once debated, smashed and overturned. These are
the cracked and fractured plates of the hololith display panels.
These are the loops of torn cables, hanging like entrails from
the casings of calculation desks. These are the punctures and
scorches on the walls, the impact points of mass-reactive shots
and lasweapons.

This is the blood on the floor, the drips and flecks across
the station panels, the spray on the walls that has started
to trickle and run. These are the bodies of the dead, killed
before they were able to evacuate. These are the ones who
died defending the doorways. This is the boom and howl of

war-horns bellowing from the traitor engines stalking past outside, the massed roar of the host sacking the lower levels. This is the giggling of the Neverborn.

This is the Grand Borealis. These are the flames consuming it and the stink of fresh death filling it. This is the charnel house and ruin that it has become in the past four hours.

It has stood since the beginning. It has fallen now, swept away by the apocalypse-tide that has poured into the Inner Palace. Those within remained at their posts to the last possible moment, determined to maintain their vital work. Most left it too late to flee. Few have survived.

These scraps of meat and hair and cloth are Fourth Master Tacticae Terrestria Julius Gundelfo. This burned husk is Rubricator Senioris Hyton Ki. This mangled form is Junior Administrar Patris Sator Omes. These bloody shreds are Colonel Lin-Hu Kway. This smear of gore and tissue is Data-Adjudicator Perez Grist. This head, rammed upon a spike, is Cogitation Overseer Arnolf Van Halmere. This bundle, draped in green robes, is Nytali Hengmuir, Chosen of Malcador.

These splashes and spots of blood are Mistress Tacticae Katarin Elg, who ran the Saturnine defence operation, and whose body was carried off by fleeing survivors in the vain hope they could save her.

This is Vorst, Imperial Fists veteran captain, who has not left his post. His boltgun slides from his grasp and hits the deck with a crash.

This is Tarchese Malabreux, Master of the Catulan Reavers, Sons of Horus. He hauls on his blade and it slides out in a sudden gout of red, unpinning Vorst's corpse from the Grand Borealis wall. The veteran captain sinks slowly to the deck, and falls on his side.

Bhab Bastion is taken.

1:xviii

Record of
an interview conducted
by Remembrancer Oliton

But he chose me.

Such an honour. I deserved it. He chose me because of our special affinity, those thirty perfect years, and my accomplishments speak for themselves. More than that, my lady, I think he chose me because I have... How can I put it? I have a common touch. I am all things to all men. Sanguinius is a far more noble being. But his ethereal quality, the very essence of what he is and why he is so adored... it makes him unapproachable. His perfection was why he was not chosen. My imperfection made me a better candidate.

I was relieved when I was named. I've never told anyone this. Relieved. It was the right thing to do. I cannot believe how immodestly I am speaking to you. There is something about you, Mersadie, that puts me at my ease and prompts me to speak quite openly and without filter.

I was relieved. And, knowing who he might have chosen, I swore I would not fail him. Fathers and their sons, eh? There is always an order to these things, a complex web of blood and relationship that must be navigated. I know this very well, now I have sons of my own.

We all have favourites, you see.

Ezekyle? Oh, I really shouldn't say. You must decide for yourself. I'll tell you this, though, Ezekyle will do things I will *never* do. In his achievements, he will far outstrip me. I am sure of it. But is he my favourite? Mamzel Oliton, it depends how you measure these things, how you navigate that family web. They are all my beloved sons. Ezekyle is the strongest, the most determined, the most like me. But Sejanus has a different quality of strength. If Ezekyle is my Lupercal, my first son, then Sejanus is my Guilliman. Sedirae is my Dorn, Torgaddon my Ferrus.

And then there's Loken, of course. You've met him, I believe? He is quite unlike me in so many ways. He is a favourite son. If anyone asks, I will deny it. I cannot be seen to show favour. But, between you and me, *he* is my Sanguinius.

As a father, I love and trust them all, for they are, as I am, loyal instruments with which the future may be shaped and civilisation fashioned. All of them, even... excuse me, remembrancer... even Maloghurst here, who knocks upon my chamber door even though he knows full well I am occupied talking to you and should not be disturbed.

What do you need, equerry? You can see I'm busy.

Speak up, man.

'You must come, Warmaster.'

Indeed? Why 'must' I, Maloghurst? I am in conversation with the remembrancer here. Whatever it is, I am sure the First Captain can–

'You must come, Warmaster.'

So insistent. That's not like you, Mal. Tell me, why 'must' I do any–

'It's long past time. Please.'

I resent your tone, Maloghurst. You're being presumptuous in front of my guest. Where did she go? She was just here. In that chair.

'You must come, Warmaster.'

Cease your whining, Maloghurst. Where is the woman gone? Have you scared her away with your pleading–

'I implore you, my Warmaster. You must come.'

Must I? *Must* I indeed?

'Forgive me, but you must. We have waited for so long. We need you. The war needs you.'

War? Xenobia is but a simple compliance that the First Captain can handle in his damn sleep, Mal–

'I beg you, my lord.'

The room is warm. There is an odour of meat, of shaved bone. You open your eyes, not aware they had been closed, and see broken light. A face. The echo of a voice. Have you been asleep? Perhaps. You have been tired, so very tired, these last few days. More tired than you have ever been. But you must not show it, not to any of them, any of your sons. You are Lupercal. You are the Warmaster, as you were just telling the young woman.

'I was meditating,' you say. 'A moment of inward contemplation, to gather focus and clarity. How do we stand, Maloghurst?'

The face looks at you. There is humility there, respect, but also a trace of concern.

'It's Argonis, my lord,' the face says. '*Argonis.*'

You sit up. There is a sour taste in your mouth. A sour taste, like the sour smell in the room.

'Of course,' you say. 'Excuse me, my mind was elsewhere.'

'Please, my lord. It is no matter. I'm sorry I had to disturb you when you were resting.'

You wave it aside with a never-mind of your hand. You feel heavy.

'Where is Maloghurst?' you ask. There is phlegm in your throat. Speaking seems unfamiliar. How deeply were you sleeping?

'He is… not here, Warmaster. I… I am Argonis. Your equerry.'

You nod. 'I know that. You said so. And you were saying something about the war?'

The face, the man, Argonis, hesitates. His armour looks black, which seems strange. He is… Kinor Argonis, that's it. A good man. A good warrior. A good son. He's anxious about something.

'Speak, Kinor,' you say. You force a more gentle tone. Sometimes you have to act the patient, paternal role when the junior ranks have to deal with you directly.

'There has been discussion… consultation,' Argonis begins tentatively. 'It was decided that I should approach you. We need you. We have needed you long before now. We cannot wait any longer.'

'Who is "we", equerry?'

Argonis does not answer. He turns his gaze towards the deck as you stand.

'Tell me of the war, then, my son,' you say. You place your hand against the warrior's cheek and turn his head so he is obliged to meet your stare. Is that fear in his eyes? Why fear?

'We are at a juncture,' Argonis replies, with hesitation. 'Certain… elements are in play that must be balanced and judged. As only you can. We crave your instruction. We long for your command.'

'Show me.'

'A full tactical composite is displayed here, the best our instruments can assemble.'

'Interference? Distortion?'

'Well... of *course*, my lord.'

You consider the vast holo-light image. 'This is a full analysis of the Xenobia compliance?'

'Xenobia? No, my lord. Not Xenobia.'

'Then what am I looking at?'

'At Terra, my lord.'

The name hangs for a long moment.

'Of course. Of course it is,' you say. You try to make it sound relaxed. You try to laugh, to make light of it, but you are quite devoid of laughter. You mustn't show weakness or infirmity, especially not to a junior rank like this man. They adore you. What is that taste, at the back of your tongue? Is it blood? What's wrong with your mouth?

'Let us see now,' you say. 'Let us consider our choices. Equerry, tell Sejanus to attend me at once. I would have his counsel on this.'

'I... *My lord.*'

'And find that woman. That remembrancer. Convey my apologies that I am detained, and tell her that I will speak with her again later.'

The walls breathe. The equerry hurries away. You do not bother to watch him go. The display holds your entire attention. This is where you are now. Where you have been this whole time. Where you were always *going* to be.

Terra. Old Earth. The very beginning and the very end.

You must clear your mind. You must focus. This is important. The most important thing of all. You wish you could remember why.

And then you can. Suddenly. Memory flushes through your system, like a sudden rupture of meltwater from a dying glacier. It sluices through your meat and bone, awakening every knot and ache and throb of pain. So much has changed. You have changed. You barely recognise yourself.

The shadows in the breathing corners of the room, in the folds of warm darkness, are whispering. You realise you know the names of all the shadows, and they know yours.

This is Terra. This is the end, and the approaching moment of death. This is the greatest task of your life, except for the one that will follow it when you have taken the reins of power. Only *you* can do that. Only you were made for it. No one else has the vision or the insight. For now, it is just a simple operation of compliance that has, sadly, required full illumination. This world is proving to be problematic. Most unfortunate. There was a mistake born of misunderstanding. There are issues of trust and comprehension. This is not easy work, and you certainly regret what's happening at the moment. Deeply. But you are sanguine, as calm and capable as ever. There is only one way to resolve the path ahead. If you are to do what you have come here to do, you must be sure and swift, the way your father taught you.

Sure and swift. Resolute in the face of a regrettable and disappointing turn of events. You tried to be reasonable. They didn't listen.

You want that on the record. You must make sure the woman writes it down.

She was just here.

1:xix

Fragments

Ice forms on high parapets. Verglas sheens roadways. Blood freezes in potholes. Thundersnow unfurls across the eastern limits of the Sanctum. The air stains yellow. Lightning, electric red, forks from the churning ice-clouds and demolishes spires. It strikes the Widdershin's Tower, removing an upper section in a spray of stones and tiles.

Those who bear witness are reminded of the thirty-third card of the tarot arcana, which symbolises the overturn of fortune, or achievement obtained through sacrifice, or world-changing inspiration.

Or, perhaps, just a tower brought to ruin by fire.

Derry Cassier, junior loader, hauls his munition cart to Old Lord Rogal. Cassier is seventeen years old. Old Lord Rogal is a heavy artillery piece, one of sixty Earthshakers ranged in a battery along Predikant Rise near the Primus Gate. After nine hours of near-continuous firing, the elevated barrels of the sixty guns are glowing like coals. Many pieces have stopped working due to overheat deformation, breech jam or block shear. Cassier's eyes are crimson with burst vessels and the bandages around his ears are soaked in blood despite his rubberised defenders. This will be Old Lord Rogal's final shot. It will be the battery's final shot. The forty-kilo tet-hel intermix high-explosive shell on Cassier's cart was the last one in the supply dump. Cassier takes out a piece of chalk to write his name on the shell as a last goodbye, but his fingers are too numb to write anything.

Flamers roar, and purge atomised human meat out of vanquished bunkers.

The last waves of loyal Stormbirds and Hawkwings lift from the Brahmaputra Fields in a final effort to run interference on the files of the Traitor Legions flowing, in rivers greater than the Ganges or the Karnali, into the heart of empire. None will return. Those that make it through the torrential frenzy of the anti-air batteries will be broken by the air itself. Cyclonic fury will fold their wings, dash them from the sky, scatter them like petals, or cast them away like dead autumn leaves.

Rogue firestorms, uncontained and uncontrollable, consume entire zones, as though some deranged burn therapy or desperate moxibustion is being applied to the terminal world.

Corporal Naheena Praffet comes to, blind, in a crater ninety metres wide. Her entire brigade, the 467th Tanzeer Excertus, has been caught in a rolling barrage as it advanced on Konig Bar. She calls out for a medic. She gropes around for help. She takes someone's hand. But it's just a hand. There's no one else alive. There's no one else intact.

* * *

Alpharius leans back and offers John his hand. John sighs, takes it, and allows himself to be hoisted over the steep lip of the incline.

The cavern he's been brought to is large. It was larger once, but like everything in the depths, it's been compressed, the ceiling crushed low by centuries of weight above. It was something once. John can't tell what. Part of a manufactory, perhaps, or a transit station. Sections of the old walls are tiled, or panelled with rusted metal plates. There's litter on the floor, the broken and commonplace debris of an everyday life that ended, perhaps suddenly, thousands of years before. A tin badge, a paper drinking cup, an infant's plastic pacifier, the stub of a ticket, miraculously preserved, recording a fare and a one-way trip between two places that John's sure don't exist any more.

A one-way trip.

'What are we doing here?' he asks Alpharius. The warrior gestures.

What John first took to be a shelving part of the chamber's wall is actually a row of large objects, massive things stored under drab weather sheets beneath the lee of the ceiling. Alpharius crosses to one, and drags the cover off. It falls aside, heavy, in a puff of gathered dust, revealing the dirty bulk of an Aurox transporter. The Aurox bears the colours and insignia of the VII Legion Astartes.

'The hell?' says John.

Alpharius moves down the line, lifting the shrouds from others. Two more Aurox, one VII Legion, the other Hort Palatine. The Hort machine's clearly rusted beyond repair. A Militia Gorgon. Two Mastodons, in Old Hundred paint. One of the Mechanicus' Triaros conveyors. An Excertus Dracosan. A White Scars Rhino. A Coronus grav-carrier burnished in the brassy gold of the Legio Custodes.

'Help me check them,' says Alpharius.

'What is this?'

'A way station. A depot-cache. Our advance procured these vehicles years ago, and secured them here.'

'Procured?'

'Use whatever word you like, John. We've come a long way, but there's still a long way to go. We need transport, or the humans will never make it.'

John tries not to mark the way Alpharius says 'humans' as though John's not one of them.

'So you stole this stuff, and stowed it away down here, just in case?'

'Yes,' says Alpharius.

'Warriors too?'

'Yes.'

'In case of…?'

'Whatever we were required to do. Please help me check, John. It'll be quicker. These machines have been left untended and un-serviced. It's possible none of them will run any more. Check for power reserves, secondary or primary. See if we can cold-start any of them. If we can't, I'll have to warm up a generator, hook it up, and try a boosted ignition… That'll just take time.'

John crosses to the Mastodon, leans his rifle against the treads, and clambers up the cold hull. He starts working to unclamp the hatch.

'So,' says John. 'Can we talk now? Are we out of mindshot?'

Alpharius has disappeared for a moment. John hears the hatch on a nearby machine being unfastened. He gets into the Mastodon, hauls himself up into the driving position in the dark, and fumbles for the voltaics panel. He throws the master switches, one, two, three. Nothing even flickers.

He climbs back out.

'This one's dead,' he calls out.

Alpharius reappears. He's retrieved something from one of the other vehicles. It's Alpha Legion tech, a metal pod the size of a field stove. He sets it down beside the Mastodon, twists the top, presses, and the side panels unfurl like petals. A soft blue light starts to glow inside the casing.

A psi-damper. John can feel the deadening throb of it at the back of his skull.

'I want your help,' Alpharius says, standing beside the damper and looking up at John.

'I want your trust,' John replies. 'Maybe we can trade?'

Alpharius nods. John sits on the edge of the cold hull, feet swinging, and stares down at him.

'At the start of the Heresy War,' Alpharius says, 'my Legion made preparations. Contingencies. We placed troop reserves under the Palace, in stasis. We secured depots of procured machines. This is one of them. We mapped routes, in and out.'

'In and out?'

'Like this one, John. Even as Dorn was fortifying the Palace above our heads, we were tracing the cracks.'

'Dorn missed this?'

Alpharius shakes his head.

'Not at all. He knows about it. As far as our operatives can tell, Dorn left six hidden routes open. *Well* hidden, of course, even from Perturabo's painstaking surveys. Dorn's a clever man. This is the only one we found.'

'He left six routes open into the Palace?' John asks. 'What kind of siegecraft is that?'

'Not in, John. Out.'

John thinks about that for a moment.

'Gods,' he says. 'To get out?'

'To get Him out, John.'

'Dorn expected to lose?'

'He decided to win,' says Alpharius. 'But he is meticulous. He prepared for every eventuality. We, in turn, secured it for use–'

'What use?'

'Well, there's the thing. For whatever was needed, John. Once the Cabal's plan was ditched, we prepared for every eventuality. Move in, in support of the Throne. Attack, in support of Lupercal. Whichever turned out to be the smartest tactic.'

'Let me get this straight… You waited to see who would win, before deciding which side you were on?'

'A crude summary, John. We waited to see how it would play out, so we could intervene to our own maximum advantage.'

'And this is you doing that?' asks John. 'You, helping us? That's the side you've come down on?'

'Not at all.' Alpharius is silent for a moment, as if deciding whether to say more. 'It's clear Horus has to be stopped. Whatever he is… John, this isn't a civil war any more. It's not a Warmaster turning on his king. It's not politics, it's not even a material war at this point. All the rules have changed. This is about preventing the full and final extinction of human culture.'

'So we are on the same page,' says John.

'John, I was sent here to begin a rapid-response activation of the buried sleeper forces. Awaken them from sus-an so they could begin combat operations.'

'Against Horus?'

'Covertly. We don't have the numbers but, as you may remember, we can be surgically effective. The thing is, John, the Astartes we buried here have no idea what they're waking up to. They went into stasis without knowing which side they'd be on when they came round. To ensure chain of command, and doctrine imperative, they were all preconditioned to respond to code words. We had a list. One word, John, auto-hypnotically implanted at the moment of revival, and the warrior would instantly understand his parameters, and instantly obey them.'

'One word?'

'Yes, each one is a plan condition. "Sagittary" triggered loyalty to Horus. "Xenophon" triggered loyalty to the Emperor. "Paramus" triggered a directive of mutual annihilation, to bring down *both* if it was deemed necessary–'

'Good god!'

'"Thisbe" triggered evacuation and withdrawal. "Orphaeus" triggered a policy to ignore both sides and focus on Chaos itself. To fight it, or seize the means to control it. And so on, and so on. There were many. Every contingency, every possible option, hypno-coded. I was sent to initiate condition Xenophon.'

'Loyalty to the Emperor.'

'Correct.'

'All right,' says John. He shrugs. 'That's a start. Why does telling me this buy my trust?'

'Because I had only just started when she arrived and found me.'

'You mean Actae?'

Alpharius nods.

'And?'

'You can see her power, John,' Alpharius says. 'I am not doing this voluntarily. Quite the opposite. She has me entirely in her control. Everything I'm doing, I'm doing against my will, and I can't resist.'

John points at the psi-damper.

'Well, you can now. That's shut her out.'

'It's merely muted her, John. Very briefly.'

'Whatever, she can't keep up that kind of mental control forever.'

'She doesn't have to,' Alpharius replies. 'When she found me, she read my mind and triggered one of the code words in me. I am aware of it, but I can do very little about it. I am operating on a plan condition, and that' – he gestures to the damper – 'is allowing me, briefly, enough free will to beg you to trust me and assist me.'

'What? For old times' sake?'

'Yes, let's say that.'

John nods, raises his eyebrows. 'So who are you, old friend?'

'I'm pretty certain you know already, John. You have been carefully monitoring my voice patterns.'

'Ingo Pech.'

'Correct.' The Alpha Legionnaire unclamps his helm and takes it off. The face looking up at John is familiar, but then they all are. They all look so alike. If he'd seen the face from the start, it would have taken John a good while to decide which Alpha Legion warrior it was, and even then he wouldn't have been sure.

But he is now, as certain as he can be. The face, the voice, the little microexpressions of affect only a logokine can discern.

'What was it?' John asks.

'What was what?'

'What was the code word, Pech?'

'Orphaeus,' says Pech.

'Shit,' says John. 'Fight Chaos directly… or seize control of it?'

Pech nods.

'Why?'

'Because that's what she wants,' says Pech. 'She wants this war stopped, yes. This *form* of the war. She says Horus is a puppet, a rag doll so steeped in the warp he is utterly enslaved by it. But he's strong. You know how strong Horus Lupercal is, John. The witch believes he can be turned.'

'From Chaos? You mean, saved?'

Pech shakes his head. '*Towards* Chaos, John. She thinks he can be turned to face it. She believes he's strong enough to take hold of the shackles it has placed upon him, shrug off its control, and use those same shackles to enslave it.'

'Chaos?'

'Yes, John.'

'Enslave Chaos?'

'Yes, John.'

'Well, then she's a colossal freaking idiot,' he says.

Pech laughs, but there's no real joy in it. 'The enslavement of Chaos has been a dream of many, for a long time,' he says. 'Everyone thinks they can do it... Lupercal, the Phoenician, Lorgar Aurelian, the Pale King... even that twisted little bastard Erebus, the so-called Hand of Destiny... they all thought they could do it, and they've all ended up slaves to darkness. That's the way it works. No one can do it. Some think they have enslaved the warp, but that's just the warp telling them what they want to hear while it merrily pulls their strings.'

'The Emperor?' says John.

'Perhaps. If anyone could. Once. Not now. This wouldn't be happening if He had succeeded in doing it where everyone else has failed.'

'But the witch thinks she can?'

'She considers herself a hand of destiny too, John. A better one. She thinks she can steer Horus, correct his course, adjust his approach, even this late in the game. She believes she can use him as an instrument and, because he is so very strong, master Chaos.'

'I refer you to my previous statement,' says John.

'And I refer you to mine,' says Pech. 'I am helping her to do it. I am committed to that course of action. That's what Orpheaus means. I'm fighting it, but it won't work. I can't break triggered plan conditioning. All I can do is see what

I'm doing, as if I'm some detached observer, out of my own body and mind. And I can tell you this... you have no idea of the effort this requires, even with that thing switched on. I can tell you this, and beg you to act.'

'Stop her?'

'Yes. Stop her. And, I'm sorry to say, probably me too. Because the conditioning will continue even if she's dead.'

'Shit-sakes, Pech! How do I stop her? Or you? I think you're wildly overestimating my abilities.'

'You were always resourceful, John.'

John jumps down from the hull.

'I can't do it alone,' he says. 'I'll need to bring the others in. Oll. Leetu.'

Pech nods.

'And not yet, either.'

'Why not?' asks Pech.

'Because, you moron, on the off-chance that, by some freaking miracle, we can take you and the witch out, we'd be lost down here. We've got a mission of our own to complete. And we've come a long bloody way to do it. Get us into the Palace. Once we're there, maybe we can try something.'

Pech nods again. 'Yes, that's wise,' he says.

'Shut that damper down and stow it somewhere,' John says, thinking hard. 'I may need it. Hell, I will need it. And weapons. Something heavy.'

'There are weapon caches aboard each of these machines.'

'All right,' says John. 'Let's find out if any of them actually operate.'

'Agreed,' says Pech.

He suddenly places a huge hand on John's shoulder and looks down into his eyes. John flinches.

'Thank you, John,' says Pech. 'I need to say that now, because I probably won't be able to later.'

'Old times' sakes, eh, Ingo?'

Pech turns and reaches for the damper.

'Wait,' says John. 'Wait… Ingo… why is she helping us?'

'What?'

'If I accept all of this, Pech, if I accept it the way you've laid it out, it doesn't explain why she's helping us. Why she came to find us in Hatay-Antakya, why she pulled our arses out of the fire. Why go to all that trouble?'

'Oh, John,' says Pech. 'I thought you'd joined all the dots. You're part of her plan. She needs you. That stuff she said, about you all being archetypes, drawn together. That might be true. That might have some ritual significance. But she definitely needs Ollanius. Ollanius and that knife of his. She needs you to help her contain Horus Lupercal so she can turn him. That little stone knife, in the hands of a Perpetual like Ollanius, is about the only thing that could possibly, and I mean *possibly*, have a hope of hurting him.'

'Yeah,' says John quietly. 'I had a horrible feeling that was why.'

1:xx

Context

On the Via Aquila, there are so many people. Keeler has been walking against the flow for an hour, trying to locate and coordinate other members of the conclave. At every step, people reach out to touch her. They stare. They call her name.

'Are you her?' they ask. 'Are you *her*?'

'Keep moving,' she says. 'Go north.'

They must all keep moving. That's the only way to serve Him. Keep moving in the firm belief that there is a future to move towards. Keep trusting that He knows better, that He can see beyond the range of our mortal vision. Keep moving so the design can be completed.

She hears a rumble and some screams. The basalt columns of the Navis Mercantile have collapsed into the street, onto a portion of the vast crowd. People are dead.

Her breath catches. What part of the design was *that*? Is suffering part of the design? Must we endure to prove something? Does survival prove worth? Does death winnow out the unworthy?

She hates the turn of her mind, the way faith grates against reason. To stop herself from screaming, she has to trust that He has a greater context, that what is insufferable to her is meaningful to Him. Are we made to suffer? Is our purpose not to merely suffer, but through suffering to prevail?

Then she remembers something Loken said to her before he quit her side to organise the rearguard.

'The Emperor is the shield and protector of humanity, Euphrati, but what is *His* shield? Us. *We* are. It is reciprocal. He protects us and, through our faith and perseverance, we protect Him. We are one and the same, mankind and Emperor, Emperor and mankind, souls bound together. We are together as one or we are nothing.'

Perhaps that's the real metaveritas. Not to become so lost in your own pain you forget the greater context. If everything can be shared, nothing is too much. How typical of an Astartes to appreciate that. How untypical of one to articulate it. But then, Garviel Loken had always been unusual, and he had been there, with her, at the very start of things.

She wonders where he is now, and if he still lives, or if like Nathaniel Garro, he has become another tragic victim of this war.

She climbs onto the raised colonnade to escape the worst of the crowd. From here, she can see the great breadth of the avenue. So many people. All are caked in dust. Many are deaf, or glassy with acoustic shock. Others are being carried. Almost everyone has bound their hands and heads with rags, covering wounds, wrapping damaged ears to dull the constant roar, covering mouths to sieve the dust, covering eyes. So many, blindfolded, walking in human chains, hands linked, each following the next.

Blind faith. We do not need to see the future in order to make towards it, as long as we are all moving together.

She realises her hands are cupped in front of her chest, unconsciously miming the way she used to hold her picter, ready to bring it up to capture a moment. For a second, she is a remembrancer again, just a simple remembrancer with a good eye, observing and recording objectively. She hasn't been that in a very long time, though the instinct has survived. This view of the Via Aquila would make a memorable pict, the sort of pict the old Euphrati Keeler, the famous imagist, would have been eager to capture.

Perhaps that objectivity was why she was chosen for this thankless role. The ability to step back and see the fleeting moment and know that, for all its horror, it was a cropped part of a greater, unseeable whole.

That, or she was just in the wrong place at the wrong time.

She jumps off the buttress onto the street, and hurries to the junction with Glacis Street. The crowds thin out on Glacis. She has to find some speakers to go back and direct the multitude on past the fountains and Diodor Circle, to relieve the throttled pressure further south.

Gang-crews are heaving down Glacis Street towards her, hauling wagons of guns and munitions from the burning manufactories at Tavian Arch. The conclave has been doing this work since the start, manually delivering ammunition and reconditioned weapons to the front-line defenders. It is a back-breaking effort. The wagons, stencilled MM226 on their side panels, are heavy. The gangs are all coffled together, yoked to the mismatched wagons. They are all blindfolded so they can't see the nightmares and desert their posts. Each team is guided by an un-blindfolded leader.

The guide closest to her, a young woman, sees Keeler and calls to her.

'We were making for the Gilded Walk,' she says. 'Can we go this way?'

Keeler shakes her head. The girl calls out to her team, and they come to a halt, lowering the yoke and ropes to steal a moment's relief. The other gang-crews halt behind them.

'Aquila is choked,' says Keeler. 'And Chiros too. There's no way through.'

'Then what do we do with this?' the girl asks, gesturing to the wagons.

'Go across to Montagne Way?' Keeler suggests. 'Perhaps get it to the Exultant line? There are Imperial Fists and Blood Angels holding there in urgent need of resupply.' She shrugs. 'Or leave it here?' she adds as an afterthought.

'Leave it?' asks the girl indignantly.

'You've done a lot,' says Keeler. 'If you push on down Montagne and go into that, you… I don't think you'll make it back.'

'But it's needed,' says the girl.

'It is.'

'I'm not going to give up.'

'I'm not telling you to,' says Keeler. 'We're trying to bring the crowds this way. Move everyone north. It's almost impossible. There are so many people. You can press on, or you can come with us.'

'I'm not going to give up,' the girl repeats, but it's barely a whisper. There are tears in her eyes.

'Is there more?' Keeler asks.

The girl sniffs. 'We cleared out what we could,' she replies, 'what we could load. There is more, but most of the plants are shutting down. At Tavian, anyway. MM Three-Four-One is on fire. MM Two-Two-Six is out of intermix.'

'You were one of Kyril's, weren't you?' says Keeler suddenly.

'What?'

Keeler reaches out and points to the torn warrant paper pinned to the front of the girl's dirty smock below the purity tag. The bold 'I' icon is still visible.

'One of Sindermann's? His new remembrancers?'

'Interrogators,' the girl says.

'I remember. I was one for a while too, you know?'

The girl nods.

'I'm Keeler,' says Keeler.

'I know who you are, mam. I know what you are.'

'Do you? Throne, please tell me.'

'You're hope,' the girls says. 'Our hope in the Emperor and the cause of man. Sindermann told us that.'

'Did he?'

'He also told us not to believe everything you said.'

'Kyril's very wise…'

'But I don't see how we can't, not now,' the girl says. 'Not *now*. I think, mam, that's why I was upset when you said we should give up. If hope gives up–'

'I didn't mean that. What's your name?'

'Leeta Tang.'

'Why did you stop being an interrogator, Leeta?'

'I don't think I did, I just… it just seemed more important to do this.' Tang gestures wearily at the wagons. 'Besides,' she says with a shrug. 'Who wants to remember this?'

'Didn't Kyril tell you?' Keeler asks.

'Oh, yes. Some long and inspirational speech. Something Lord Dorn said. The, uh, the act of recording a history affirms that there will be a future in which people will read it. It's a profound act of optimism.'

'There you go,' says Keeler.

Tang sighs.

'I still don't believe anyone will want to remember this,' she says.

'I agree, but things change,' says Keeler. 'I asked why you stopped interrogating and started hauling munitions because… because it shows that we alter according to necessity. Pulling shells to the front line is important. *Was* important. Maybe getting the helpless out of the kill-zones is more important now. That's not giving up hope, that's just pragmatic.'

'Do you still believe in a future?' Tang asks.

'I am trying to,' Keeler replies. She's thought about this often. 'I remember when I was with the expeditionary fleet. With… Horus. Throne, I can barely say his name. That was all about the future. We imagined the future, and it seemed so bright and inspiring. Now I struggle to imagine anything at all. But I want to imagine something. I need to. We all need to. If we imagine a future, the best version we can manage, then perhaps that's how we realise it. I don't think it will be so bright and inspiring now, but I think it can be better than this, this apparent… inevitability.'

'Everyone's just talking about nothing,' says Tang. 'Have you noticed that? Just, I don't know, phatic conversations among the damned and doomed. Just talking about nothing. At the start, it was all memories of the future… you know, "When this is over I'll go see my aunt and visit the Planalto or Antipo Hive again", or "I can't wait to see my brother"… But now it's all just the past. Like we're stuck. People don't even say *I remember*, they just talk about people who are probably dead, or people who *are* dead, as if they are alive. Like they're fossilising the past as something to cling on to…'

She trails off.

'Or am I going mad?'

'No, I *have* noticed that,' says Keeler. 'And I noticed you said *memories* of the future just then.'

'Did I? I'm tired.'

'No, Leeta. I think we are stuck in the now. I fear we literally are. My chron stopped yesterday. Do you know what time it is? What day it is, even?'

Tang shakes her head.

'I think we are invaded by more than just material violence,' says Keeler. 'I think we are invaded on a... metaphysical level. Time and place is warping, slowing down, getting stuck. A constant now, where the past is barely a memory, with no value at all, and the future is withheld. Someone once wrote, "the future has no other reality than as present hope."'

'Was it Master Sindermann?'

Keeler laughs. 'No, but it's something he told me. It's a very old piece of writing. What I'm saying is that hope contains the future, and it's the one thing we have. More potent than a cartload of shells.'

'Is this where you tell me the Emperor has a plan?'

'Dear me, Kyril really *did* talk about me, didn't he?'

'Everyone is talking about you, mam.'

'All right then. I think He *does* have a plan, and it is contingent on us believing in it. Our hope in it, our faith in it, makes it happen. We are the plan and the plan is us. They are not separate things. The Emperor doesn't have a plan that, if we perish, will still come to fruition. *The plan is us.*'

'It's going to be hard to hold on to that idea,' says Tang.

'I know. It's not easy. Listen, some of the conclave have operational vox-units. If I can find one, maybe we can raise the forward positions. Inform them we're holding munitions here. Have your teams rest. Maybe pull the wagons to the side of the street so the crowds can move through.'

Tang nods.

'The plan is really us?' she asks.

'It always has been,' says Keeler.

1:xxi

Fragments

A marching Banelord Titan erupts in flames and falls, killing hundreds on the ground below. There are so many war engines in the advancing line, its loss is barely noticed.

At the blast of a horn, 12th Austra Auxilia rises to the fire step. Twelve hundred loyalist soldiers in bowl helmets surge out of their lines and dugouts, and charge into the unknown. The unknown is probably their doom, but it is preferable to the trenches they are leaving behind, where every shadow whispered and sniggered at them.

Defenders plunge from the huge bulwarks and curtain walls. Some are burning, and streak like comets into the smoke far below. It is impossible to tell if death has caused them to fall, or if they are falling to their deaths.

In the Khat Mandu Precinct, not far from the Jade Bailey, Acastia, bondsman of House Vyronii and pilot of the Knight

Armiger *Elatus*, walks alone. After the engine war hell at Mercury Wall, and the shattering of the great Titanicus formations, she has formed fealty ties with the Legio Solaria. A temporary pledge, she believes, an exigency troth. Princeps Abhani Lus Mohana needs all the engines she can get in her purview. And Acastia cannot walk alone.

But she *is* alone. Effectively. Sections of Legio Solaria are spread thin across the precinct, and all the links are fettered by distortion and twitching interference. The scratching, intermittent wash of the noospherics is driving migraine scissors into her brain, and *Elatus* is skittish and thready, unable to scent others of its kind.

The place is lonely and empty. Somewhere, according to the last reports, mass engine wars are raging in the southern Sanctum. The Great Mother of the Imperial Hunters is driving the bulk of her remaining Legio, along with five maniples, against the massed daemon machines near the funeral pyre of Bhab Bastion. Acastia can imagine the fury.

But here it is silent. The vacant streets and creeping veils of smoke speak to her more of war's desolation than any frenzy of combat. This was the Palace. Not *a* palace. *The* Palace.

Acastia surveys the deceitful patterns of the sensoria, the choppy flood of thermal tracks, electrostatic signals, motion tremblers. She adjusts her tactical abstracts and walks. Squalls of dark rain that could be oil or blood patter off the Armiger's cowling, off the smaragdine lacquerwork and the polished ivory. The pennants of her broken house, red and silver, swing lank from her weapon arms.

A track lights. Acastia pans, and transmits an alert signal that she is sure no one will hear. Ahead, the 86K Ministration Building, its primary doorway open to the elements. She sees something move, something unreeve through the entrance like a mooring rope slipping through a boat's hawsehole. Like a serpent.

She advances, weapons live. Thermal spears and chainblades. Autoguns. The munition hoppers read low, so she aims to make any kills blades-first.

Her target bursts into the open, slamming through the broken doorway. It emerges, and then keeps emerging, a colubrine shape of pulsating meat and muscle with the girth of an Aurox armoured transport. It doesn't seem to stop coming. More and more of it extrudes from the entrance. The front half of it, pale and colloid, undulates across the wet ground towards her, and raises its head, a maggot-mouth, yawning like a lamprey's sphincter-maw, surrounded by lump-teeth. Fronds of tentacle sub-limbs writhe around the mouth, and lash at her. Her target-auspex refuses to lock it. The thing is huge and *right there*, but the noospherics waver, and the guns refuse to hard-lock.

Tentacles whip out. They are tipped with bone harpagons. Acastia feels the heavy thumps as these organic grappling hooks strike the Armiger's hull, and puncture, and grip. She hears and feels the steel-and-ceramite-shod heels of *Elatus* screeching as the engine, against its will, is dragged across the rockcrete towards the gaping mouth.

Blades it is, then.

As the Palace convulses and dies, noise is everywhere and almost absolute. It is layered: the deep and constant booming of the mass weapons, the sledgehammer thump of the orbital batteries at the port of the Lion's Gate, the pounding of artillery, the horn-blast of engines, the thunder of the falling walls, the chatter and cackle of weapons, the screaming of the masses. The sounds combine and blend, becoming a constant, whirling vortex of noise, a steady roar, a breathless chirm. Millions caught inside the Palace-trap collapse from acoustic shock, or go mad and die.

Some places, odd and eerie pockets, are mysteriously quiet.

The Hall of Governance behind the Clanium Library is one of them. It appears to have been ransacked twice; once by the clerks and administrators in their haste to evacuate, and then by some unknown force that blasted through it like a winter gale.

Fafnir Rann, lord seneschal of the Imperial Fists, advances through the stillness. His weapons are raised. With the surviving chiefs of the Huscarls, via patchy vox, he is attempting to engineer a defence of the north-east Sanctum approach.

The hall is oddly silent. Papers scatter the floor. The paint peels, white flaked back to show arsenic-green primer. The varnish of the railings and banisters has buckled in a cracquelure that suggests intense heat.

He leads First Assault Cadre forward. Mizos and Halen have command of support cadres in the other wing of the building.

They have, Rann estimates, ten minutes to secure the location and the plaza outside, and draw up double lines of Astartes and light armour, before the first of the traitors arrive. They're coming through Exultant Quarter, onto the Maxis Processional and the Avenue of Justice. Tracking suggests Death Guard and Iron Warriors, but Rann suspects the World Eaters and the Sons of Horus will lead the way, for, since the walls broke, they have been the most rapacious and the fastest-moving.

In the next chamber, the old, foxed mirrors that once loomed over rows of rubricators at their desks are bleeding. It's probably rust, seeping out of the wall fixings. What else could it be?

He checks his heads-up. Mapping shows one more chamber ahead before they reach the southern side of the building.

There they can set up firing positions along the second-floor windows that will turn the plaza into a killing field. Mizos and Halen should shortly be in position.

One of his men signals for him. Calodin, one of the newborn, accelerated through the progenitive programme into the ranks. He's studying the old mirrors.

'Leave it,' Rann instructs.

'My lord,' says Calodin.

Rann goes to him. He sees the scarlet drips plinking off the edge of the mirror's frame onto the floor. He sees what so fascinates Calodin in the mirror.

Rann is not in the reflection. Neither is Calodin, nor any of the men. Against the mirror's silvered tain, the room is clean. It is full of scriptorum desks, and cowled scribes working, and cogitators chattering out reams of data sheets, and servitors distributing files. The image moves, but it is silent.

Rann raises an axe to smash the glass. As his blade comes up, the scribes in the reflection all turn and look at him. Their eyes are weeping blood. He sees what is behind them, the vague mass of swarming darkness and ash, the baleful eyes, the barracuda jaws, and he knows that what is behind the long-dead scribes in the reflection is actually behind him.

He turns. The Neverborn laughs.

The shooting starts.

1:xxii

Last rite

I am old. I am tired. I sit on the front pew of the wooden supplicant stalls to the right-hand side of the Golden Throne. I ease my limbs. I rest my staff against the stall beside me. The seats are old and tired too, their gold leaf cracked, their carved finials as bleached and smoothed as driftwood from exposure to the Throne's light. The motionless proconsuls, Uzkarel and Caecaltus, pay me no heed, for I am a part of this place to them, as much a feature of the realm they guard as the great dais and the tiles and the pillars. They are not the sort of guards or sentries that a senior of the court can have a passing conversation with. They are fixed in duty at a post-human pitch that is unsettling in its intensity, and allows no distraction.

Such is the perfection of the weapons he has wrought. I had no hand in the Custodians.

I take my seat and I wait. I have done all I can. I have stood at his side. I have called to him, urged him, requested that he answer. There has been no sign of a response. All I can do now is attend to other affairs of state while I wait.

If a response ever comes. *It must. It must!*

So, though I sit and wait in silence, for all sound is crushed this close to the Golden Throne, there is no silence inside me. Since I came to this place that others call the Throne Room hours ago, to stand watch at his side and plead with him to rouse and listen, my mind has also been at work elsewhere. A multitude of elsewheres. It is noisy inside my head: a thousand thousand thoughts, a host of ideas and concepts semantically condensed into sigils and symbols, the synchronised minutiae of an empire in crisis, a hundred concurrent farspoken conversations with seniors of the War Court or my diligent, labouring Chosen in various parts of the shrinking Palace. Simultaneously, I monitor a score of different charts and updating data-projections, I advise and command, I review every scintilla of the data that comes blizzarding at my mind and convert it into compressed packets of differentiated information, sorted by subject and priority, each one summarised by a sigil, sign or signifier in my mental inventory. The workings of the Imperium become a constellation of sigils in my brain. This is my life. This is how his Regent serves him.

I am old. I am tired. I sit on this worn pew. There is still so much to be done, and I now appreciate that, if what I have predicted comes to pass, I will not live long enough to see it all finished. I divert a portion of my mind to the rapid preparation of a legacy; the compilation – hasty and clumsy, I am sorry to say – of the crucial yet soon-to-be-orphaned tasks I will have to delegate to my Chosen when the time comes. It will test them, but they will cope. That's why I chose them.

One other task occupies me as I await his response. I intend to complete it myself. I won't leave it for others to finish after I'm gone. One part of my mind has, for the last few hours, been permanently linked to the cordoned Theatre of the Chirurgeons fifteen kilometres away from where I sit.

I breathe. I close my eyes. I bow my head. My active conscious focus returns to that mental strand. I prepare to make another try. In my mindsight, I resolve the Theatre.

There he lies, the Great Khagan, the Warhawk, broken in death. Just hours past, Jaghatai slew Mortarion in a humbling duel perhaps most remarkable because they were so unevenly matched and, unlike the treacherous Pale King, Jaghatai could not hope to come back from the dead.

I look down at his face, his shuttered eyes, his cyanotic lips, as almoners wash and anoint his body, and a Stormseer administers his funerary rites. I smell the stink of salves and sterilising liquors.

The Warhawk is dead, by any mortal standard. Because he fell so close by, just beyond the walls, his body was carried in at once, and placed on this catafalque in a balming field of catalepsean stasis and life-suspense. If he had died further out, or on another world, there would be no hope at all. But there is. For now and not much longer, an iota of necromimesis remains. The tattered banner of Jaghatai's soul, gusting into the warp, is still attached to his corpse by a single thread. I have determined this, and I have been trying, repeatedly in these last few hours, to draw it back. Every shred of healing science has been exhausted, for it is a matter quite beyond medicae lore. I have been ministering my anagogic craft to keep that thread attached.

It is slow salvation. Each time I try, the attempt ends in failure, and I am forced to ease away. The Khan's soul will not survive a prolonged effort on my part.

It frustrates and saddens me. It should be possible. I don't know why I can't save him. Perhaps even my will and warpcraft are not sufficient. Perhaps it is hubristic of me to presume I can act like a god and claim the power or right to bring a man back from death.

Perhaps… perhaps Jaghatai is tired of the world and yearns to leave it.

But I will try, and I will keep trying. If my lord's attention was not so occupied elsewhere, it's what he would be doing. It's what he'd want me to do. He would not see another son die.

I bend my mind in again and resume the subtle psycho-surgery to keep Jaghatai's soul secure. And this time… *this* time, I am granted one merciful miracle.

Anabiosis. It is demanding, even for me, but I gather the tattered, dancing shreds of Jaghatai's soul, and I draw them back in, folding them tenderly into the casket of his body.

I exhale.

The Warhawk will live. It will be days, weeks, perhaps months before his corporeal body heals and he awakens, but he will live. If any world remains to live upon.

Then, at the very last, as I look down at what I have done, I realise I haven't done it at all. I couldn't. Such a feat was beyond me. It was shameful arrogance to believe I could do any such thing.

I have not done this. Someone else has.

Someone else has reached in past me and performed the deed, like the god he is not, but appears to be.

Because someone else has stirred, and needs me, and does not want me distracted by other matters.

I look up, eyes wide open. Proconsul Caecaltus is looming over me like a golden titan in his Aquilon plate. He is reaching down to nudge my arm and wake me.

'I'm here! I'm awake, my boy!' I splutter, heaving myself upright.

He tries to steady me and help me up.

'I can do it!' I tell him.

A proconsul of the Hetaeron does not leave his place except under the most exceptional circumstances.

'Regent–' he says, with the sort of voice a mountain would have if it could speak.

'I know! I know! I know!' I insist. I clutch my staff with numb fingers, and hobble past him, out of his immense shadow into the light that casts it.

The golden king upon the Golden Throne seems just as still and silent as he was before. But I know he is present, his mind swung open and directed at me.

It is a terrifying feeling.

'Forgive me that I called upon you,' I say. 'I would not disturb you in your work. But it's time. The clocks run out.'

He nods. His voice is suddenly inside my head.

It says, +I cannot fight alone.+

1:xxiii

Mindsight

I cannot fight alone.

In those four words, he tells me everything. I am lost for words of my own. The implication, the intent, is shocking. It was what I hoped and wanted to hear, but what it signifies petrifies me. It means his assessment matches mine. This *is* the end. We stand upon a precipice so sheer, that only actions of true, last resort are possible. A war that forces him to fight is a war that no one should have begun.

His words resound inside my skull. All I can think is that, from this point on, it will be bloody and costly and messy. He will have a plan already, because he always has a plan, and he will take me through it soon enough, and ask for my advice and wisdom. But whatever form it takes, it will be gruelling and difficult, even for him, each step back from the brink as hard as the next.

'Of course you can't,' I say. 'Of course you can't fight alone.'

I turn aside, and begin preparations at once. I must summon those who need to be part of this. Once they are alerted, and on their way to join us, he can lay out his strategy for me.

He needs instruments to brandish torches and keep the darkness at bay as it comes at him from every angle. Who still lives that he can place such trust in? My mindsight spreads wide, across all that remains visible. I look for his sons. I look for our last allies. Let them be revealed.

There! The first, closest to us yet likewise far away. Far beneath the Throne, in the looping neverness of the webway. His name is Vulkan. I would say he is singular, though each of my lord's sons is singular in his own fashion. Upon Vulkan, my master bestowed a special part of himself. Vulkan is the only one of the primarch sons who inherited his father's aeviternal nature. My master is eternal, and so is Vulkan. It is a trait, in fact, they share with me. Thus, Vulkan lives, and Vulkan dies, and Vulkan lives again. To Vulkan, my master entrusted enduring continuity, the courage to keep the flame alive. Vulkan is athanasy embodied.

Vulkan has not failed his father. Not ever. And it has cost him too many lives and deaths already. I see him, deep in the webway, hammer in hand, trudging homeward to take his place at the gate beneath the Throne. Tears spring to my eyes at the mindsight of him. He is but a charred skeleton, a burned ecorche in an anatomist's dissecting lab, crusted ribbons of flesh broiled to his cracked bones, refusing to die, trying to heal. He stumbles–

His newborn heart, misshapen, has foundered and burst. He falls, dead. And then lives, such is the curse gifted to him. He lives, and slowly hauls his bones upright once more, clawing at the haft of his scorched hammer for support. He stands. He sways. He starts to walk again.

Vulkan has just killed Magnus, the second greatest of his father's failures, the greatest of his disappointments. Because of what Magnus is now, that death won't last. The Lord of Prospero can't really die. But Vulkan has vanquished him and banished his deathless corpse into the outer darkness.

I do not know how many times Vulkan died performing that deed, or how many times he has died on the long walk back from it, starting and restarting as he struggles to fully live again.

Vulkan has killed Magnus, but still the warp screams at his heels, and the screech of pursuing daemons echoes down the hollow psychoplastic pathways of the webway behind him.

I reach to him, and whisper gently into his still-renewing mind. I tell him that we need him *here*. I need him to stand, and guard the Throne, and bar the webway door. He must hold it while his father is gone.

He does not answer. He cannot. He has no lips nor tongue, no throat, barely even an embryonic sentience. But I feel his assent. Vulkan will prevail. He will not fail us, for he is eternal, just as we made him to be. He is the quintessence of infinite patience.

I watch him a moment longer, the halting skeleton, dragging itself back from innumerable graves, meat and sinew slowly knitting on its bones, blood welling forth as from some sacred spring to plump the neoblastic veins and capillaries still sprouting like vines across his reassembling frame, the hammer dragging heavy on the ground behind him. He walks, relentlessly, half-dead, out of the furnace, out of the nocturnal veil, to serve the Throne.

He walks back from death, one step at a time, as his father prepares to walk towards what will probably be his.

Who else? I look again. My mind extends across this chamber that others call the Throne Room, upwards to the cloth-of-gold baldachin suspended above the Throne, a vast canopy embroidered with the contradictory yet intertwined principles of *concordia* and *discordia* that frames the electric-blue aura of my great lord's light; outwards from the Throne's massive plinth, carved from the psychoreactive material known on the craftworlds as wraithbone, and inset with psycurium and dark glass panels, tourmaline and aerolithic moldavite; past silent Uzkarel and Caecaltus at their posts, past the gleaming ranks of their Hetaeron companies at attention beyond them; out, like a rushing tide across the lustrous floor of sectile marble and ouslite; across the susurrating banks of stasis generators, archeotech regulators, and psykanic amplifiers that surround and feed the Throne, prophylactic mechanisms brought here in haste and urgently set to work when the folly of Magnus cracked the harmonised serenity of this adytum; past the diligent conclaves of the Adnector Concillium in their cowls and chasubles, standing amid the fat snakes and intestinal loops of power cables, ministering to the operation of these murmuring devices; then further out, along the frightful height and breadth of the cyclopean nave itself, a canyon turned upside down; between the soaring auramite columns rising like the trunks of mature *Sequoiadendron giganteum*, the Solomonic pillars of twisted bronze, the acanthus-headed colonettes, the gargantuan scissor arches; beneath the shining, ornate electro-flambeaux strung like stalactite pendants from the dizzying ceiling, and between the lumen orbs that float like infant suns; on, past echelons of burnished automata maintaining talismatic psycho-systems; past empty, scarlet-cushioned stalls where once the High Lords of the Council gathered, and the void-manic worthies of the Navis Nobilite awaited audience; past the golden pulpits of the cataleptic astropaths, adrift in algolagnic fugues; around the clattering dream-dynamos and stegosaurian oniero-looms; past the hypnostatic augury kilns breathing steam and dripping myrrh, and the affirmatrix prognometers leaking synthetic plasma, and exhaling the smell of industrially recovered nightmares; past the scriptorums of the noctuaries; past brass reliquaries and vitrodur grails; past mother-of-pearl loggia where bewitched diviners and incanting prognostipractors sift and read the ribbon-tapes of transcribed glossolalia spilled from the chattering indifference engines, searching for morsels of meaning; past prophesires swinging thuribles, and technoseers wheeling scrimshandered feretories; past mendicants in penance at their kneeling desks and anchorites bearing electro-generative monstrances; on, through the sound of melismatic antiphon and canticle welling from the mouthless choirs in chantry niches, screened by lace-pattern iconostases so they cannot catch sight of him and forget the words; past regiments of catachumen observants, seeking expiation and brimming with eucharistic ardour; along the walls of porphery and mica mosaic, frescoes of death's-head putti and cackling ephebes that conceal hidden figures of alchemy; past engraved genealogies, and past the blazoned armorial hatchments of the twenty Legions, all but eight now shrouded in amaranthine drapes of mourning; past the iron tabernacles of the chimerical brethrendae composing, as rapidly and ceaselessly as they can, via feverish automatic writing, new variations of the material truth in a frantic effort to mediate and divert the impending bow wave of fate; past flocks of scurrying serfs and deferential abhumans, all blindfolded so they can remain present and sane at the same time, all rushing to deliver reports that no longer matter; past Zagreus Kane, the Fabricator-in-exile, with his coterie of adepts, weeping for the decimation of his battle engines, and plotting the deployment of the few that remain; past acres of empty marble floor where one day we will have to place tombs; past the great banners of liberty and victory that hang like waterfalls from the high walls every step of the nave's six-kilometre length; beneath the vaulted gloom of the ceiling, wrought of Peruvian gold and tromp l'oeil and crystal mined on Enceladus, a ceiling a kilometre high; past the silent, waiting companies of the refulgent Custodes Pylorus who make their motionless vigil at the door, whispering their ever-mantra of *by His will alone*, to the ceramite and adamantine door itself, the Silver Door, the innermost gate of eternity.

And out. It's just a room. I go beyond.

Beyond, my urgent mindsight stretches.

Through the eternal door, beyond the secular, humanist cathedral of his throne room, into the alabaster halls outside, to the acheronic avenues of approach, the measureless rockcrete tunnels that thread the Inner Sanctum, the radiant bridges spanning infinite cavern gulfs, in the aphotic depths of which crushed grave-cities lay untouched. I do not linger. My mind floods out through the buried halls of the final fortress, through each of the Great Seals, along fusion-bored mass-passageways where armies once marched to crave benediction, and Titan engines strode ten abreast to approach him like supplicants and kneel like men at his feet–

There. Two more. Two more coming through the lambent, sodium glare. Rogal Dorn, the stalwart Praetorian, and beloved Sanguinius. I have no need to summon either of them, for they are already hurrying to us, side by side, flanked by the greatest of their lieutenants, Imperial Fists and Blood Angels, a delegation of Astartes. They are coming to him as a deputation, I think. They have done all they can, beyond all that could have been asked, but the clocks run out. They are coming to tell him it is time.

They are coming to tell him, *demand* of him, that he rise up with them at this second before midnight. And if he won't, they are coming to remove him and escort him to safety.

He has refused this option since the siege began. It is not pride, it is not a refusal to acknowledge the threat. It is simply that there *is* no safety. There is nowhere to go in the entire span of the galaxy where he would be safe from what is approaching.

Rogal, perhaps his truest son, the exemplar of unwavering loyalty. I see his emptiness. He is undone, his body aching and exhausted, his armour battered by combat during the frenetic retreat from Bhab Bastion, his mind spent. That exhaustion is a terrible thing to feel. Rogal, one of the finest strategists in history, oversaw this defence. He orchestrated the fortification of our stronghold, and his tactics, brilliant, ambitious, mercurial, ran the game, the greatest game of regicide ever played. I want to embrace him, and praise him for his labour. He has excelled, and sustained his play, beat by beat, by means of engineered planning, shrewd anticipation and reflexive improvisation, through every harrowing turn of fortune. But his mind is empty. There *is* no more game. There are no more moves to make. I sense the vacuum in him, his weary mind surprised to find itself spinning free and wild, with nothing left to process or decide. The feeling is alien to him, and toxic. He has never *not* known what to do. He has never not known what is coming next.

He hopes his father does. He is coming to beg his father to tell him.

And Sanguinius. His physical wounds are greater, though he hides them from others behind the aura of his being. He cannot hide them from me. Beneath his projected radiance, I can see the damage to his armour and his body, the open wounds, the tattered and scorched feathers of his wings. Now he is back inside the Sanctum, the aegis of his father's protective spirit is healing him, faster than any mortal could ever heal. But it is not enough. He may never be whole again. He will bear some of these crippling injuries for the remainder of his life.

He tries to walk tall. He hopes his sons will not see the spots of blood he leaves behind him on the hallway floors. He has just conquered both Angron, the strongest and most hate-filled of our foes, and Ka'Bandha, the daemon-bane of the IX, but that incomparable pair of deeds has cost him woefully and, unlike Vulkan, Sanguinius has but one life to risk. I see his suffering, the wounds in his flesh and the hurt in his limbs, but more than that, the pain in his heart. Like Rogal, he has given everything and it has not been enough. He has destroyed Angron, broken Ka'Bandha, closed the Eternity Gate, and locked the final fortress. And yet, the walls fall. The sun is red. The clocks run out. He does not understand why we are made to suffer.

None of them do, in truth. Not even the primarch sons have the context to understand the scope of their father's plan, the depth of his allotheistic learning, or the true extent of what is at stake. But Sanguinius, Bright Angel, he feels it most of all. I taste his anguish. There will be no recrimination. He simply wants to ask his father *why*.

In different ways, they both seek revelation.

They are coming to us, I do not need to summon them. They are coming to ask for help, and this time, perhaps to their surprise, my master will be ready to answer them.

Who else? My mind unfurls, spreads wider, out into the body of the Sanctum precinct, where towers burn and walls that should have held forever subside in torrents like a child's toy blocks. The Palatine is entirely invaded, with homicidal urgency and fetishistic glee. The air reeks of ozone and smoke-filth. Trumpets and sirens blast alarums that are too late, or blare orders that cannot be followed. This was mankind's central arcology, the heart of empire, and it is overrun by acronical slaughter and waves of Neverborn carnage. Only the final fortress, sealed by Sanguinius' monumental deed, remains sacrosanct. Those of our forces that got inside, before the great gate closed, now man the last walls, and those that did not – so very, very many – will now never get in, and are doomed to fight to the death in the insanity of the Palatine Zone.

Even the final fortress has been contaminated. Before the Archangel locked the Gate, the first invaders broke through. Now the Gate is shut, and the Sentinels of the Legio Custodes labour to exterminate any traces of the enemy that slipped inside. The daemons are here–

There. Valdor. First of the Ten Thousand. Defender of the inner circle. He is hunting in the Preceptory of the Heironymite, eradicating the squealing horrors that stole in before Eternity closed. Constantin's mind is bright with focus. The master of the Legio Custodes is a dreadful thing, perhaps the most ruthless of all the demigods my lord commands. To Constantin was granted very little latitude. His role is the simplest of all. He has fulfilled it without hesitation. He stands apart from the others, not a son, but both less and more, an ever-vigilant proxy, impartial and unwavering, not biased by issues of blood, lineage or fraternity. He was made to stand apart so there would be one among them who could keep the unprejudiced objectivity of distance.

But in the course of this war, my lord has come to pity him, and has allowed Constantin to learn more, and share more of his noesis. In part, he did this because it would help Valdor perform his duties even better, but he also judged it only fair to let him learn. He gave Valdor a weapon, the Apollonian Spear, and through it, revelation. With each kill it makes, it teaches him. Each thrust through daemonic flesh and bone imparts instruction, feeding Constantin knowledge from the things he kills.

I only hope he has not learned too much.

I fear he might have seen enough to interrogate his creator's design. I know Constantin is acting on his own recognisance now, building contingencies of his own in case my lord's plan fails. He thinks he is keeping this secret from me, but he is not. I know he has permitted the construction of a weapon to be used in extremis. It will end my lord's sons, and their sons too, all of them, without discrimination. Constantin has always questioned the wisdom of the demigods his master made. I have allowed him the consolation of this weapon, accepting even the employment of the genius monster he recruited to make it. It will not be needed.

Or if it is, then it exists, and our master will not be alive to witness its use.

I call to him.

'My king,' he says, hearing my voice as his lord's. He comes at once, without demur, leaving his men to finish the work, leaving Neverborn things writhing and lacerated in his wake, his damascened armour splashed with their blood. He is still, without doubt, loyal. He will hold his secret weapon in reserve, and stand at his master's side as the clocks run out.

Only after that, if his master is gone, will he enact his sanction, draw the curtain down on this bloody revenger's tragedy, and wipe it all away.

Valdor is on his way. Rogal and Sanguinius. Vulkan. My mind drifts for a moment, through the fused ceramite ruins of the Inner Palace, vainly searching through streets filmed with bacterial clouds, and caustic gas, and the wind-blown ashes of a million victims. There should be others to find. Once there were so many who could be called upon in an hour of need.

But there are no more. These four are the last of them. The rest are all dead, or have become the reason that our world is dying.

1:xxiv

Fragments

The gunners are all dead, but the autocannon battery keeps firing. Death has clenched the lead crewman's hand around the fire control paddle. The battery pours tracer fire out into the murk, wide of any target except the sky, and it will keep doing so until the bulk munition drums run dry, or until the end of time, whichever comes first.

The Bayer Ordnance Komag VI is a light assault weapon manufactured in the Yndonesic Bloc towards the end of the Unification Wars. It is one of a hundred antique patterns still in service, cheaply made, easy to maintain, and basic in function, issued to the lower orders of the Army Auxilia.

Sandrine Icaro tries to remember how to work it. It does not represent the instruments of war she is used to employing. The Second Mistress Tacticae Terrestria has not had to touch a gun in years. But she did two tours with the hive territorials in her youth, to fulfil the service requirements that got her into Tacticae War School. The damn thing is basic. It has three controls, and one of those is the trigger. She fumbles. Her hands are covered in blood.

People are milling around her.

'Get into the transports!' she yells. 'Get into the damn transports!'

Clerks and junior staffers, rubricators and assistant desk officers look at her, eyes wide. She can see how utterly mind-less they are, mindless with terror and confusion. She feels it herself.

The street, one side of which has been levelled by mortar fire, is packed with survivors. Smoke is coming in on a weird, angled plane. Icaro's not sure how any of them got out. She can still just see the bastion, three kilometres south, visible through the buildings and towers around her. Bhab Bastion is on fire, burning like some awful torch.

'Get in the damn transports!' she yells again. 'We have to leave this zone!'

People push past her. She tries to shove and steer them. She got the Komag off the corpse of a militiaman a few hun-dred metres back. The Komag, and two spare magazines. She thinks the damned thing's jammed. She focuses her attention on trying to clear its action. It's better than thinking about what has just happened. When the end came, it was so sudden. They stayed as long as they could. Too long. Icaro doesn't think they're going to reach the safety of the Sanctum Impe-rialis now.

Figures stumble past. Between them, they're carrying Katarin. Icaro's not sure why. Katarin Elg is clearly dead. Her body is caked in white dust, but the chalky coating is clotted crimson around the head and chest.

She wants to tell them to put poor Katarin down so they can move more quickly. She can't bear the thought of leaving Katarin here.

'Where is Captain Vorst? Has anyone seen Captain Vorst?' she yells. No one answers. 'Halmere? What about Osaka?'

She tries to herd them towards the last of the transports. The first shots start chasing them down the street. Auto-fire. Someone falls down, as though they've simply had enough.

'Where is Lord Archamus?' she yells. 'Has anyone seen my Lord Archamus? Did he make it out?'

No one knows.

More shots. Traitor forces begin to appear, two hundred metres away. Infantry units, corrupted devils that were once Imperial Army Excertus.

'Where is Lord Archamus?' Icaro yells. A man to her left is smacked off his feet by high-velocity hard rounds.

Sandrine Icaro remembers her basic training. She clears the jammed round, reslots the magazine, raises the Komag VI, and starts to return fire.

Keeler follows Glacis Street, past lines of the shell-shocked, aimless and displaced. The conclave has set up an aid station in the ground floor of a once-celebrated dining house. Wereft is there. She asks about a functioning vox, and he says he'll find one. She stands under the portico for a moment. Survivors shamble past. So many are blindfolded, and some of those stumble onwards, ringing plaintive handbells. Many heave along on stilts or shoes that have been platformed with timber or bricks to avoid contact with broken glass, toxic ground-water or bacterial spills. Most are masked or veiled, or swing foetid censers to ward off the foul air and the caustic smoke.

Officers of the Command Prefectus Unit have set up a check-point nearby. The Command Prefectus is a new agency of the emergency powers that Keeler still doesn't quite understand, despite encounters with Boetharch Mauer and her officers. Founded by the Huscarls Praetoriat, it seems to be more concerned with discipline and superficial concepts of morale than protection. Even Mauer seemed adrift in her duties. Keeler suspects the Prefectus are an idea conceived at the very highest level, to contain and ward off Chaos, without any firm understanding of what Chaos is.

Here, as elsewhere, the officers are checking people for signs of disease and infection, and examining them for the weals and marks of corruption. They focus mainly on the able-bodied, on people of fighting age, or military who have become detached from their units. If any pass inspection, the Prefectus tags them with a mark of purity, using the hand staplers the Corps Logisticae used to pin scripts and deployment tags to service personnel. A purity tag means you are fit to serve. It will allow you access to aid stations and soup kitchens. It also shows you can be trusted. Emblems and insignia, even uniform colours, are meaningless. All the sides have changed. The enemy could be anyone. And anyway, even if emblems meant anything, everyone is too layered in grime for them to be identifiable. The seal of purity has become the only meaningful emblem of the loyalist cause, more than the aquila or any Imperial crest. It signifies loyalty. Those who get them, keep them clean and visible with spit and rubbing fingers.

Those who don't move away, bewildered.

In the long lines waiting for inspection, Keeler sees people flagellating themselves to remove any mark or graze that might be mistaken for impurity. They chastise themselves brutally, hoping that the sight of flayed skin, and their willingness to inflict such damage on themselves, indicates their resolve, no matter what marks or sores blemish them. Other self-harm, cutting off warts and buboes, debriding infected or plague-festered flesh.

'Do they have to do this?' she asks one of the Prefectus.

'I didn't tell them to,' he replies. He is a boetharch. He wears the black storm coat with twin lines of red enamel buttons, crimson gloves, and the silver emblem of his unit.

'Make them stop.'

'I can't make them do anything,' he says. 'Where's your tag?'

'She doesn't need one,' Wereft calls out from the steps. The boetharch shrugs. He's got too much to do to engage in an argument. He's prepared to take the word of a veteran enforcer of the Provost-Marshal's office.

She walks back to Wereft, and is about to speak when something colossal bursts the sky behind her and throws her on her belly. The shock-pulse knocks most people in the street down, and topples the Prefectus station. What windows remain are all blown in.

When Wereft helps her to her feet, she turns and sees a huge, rippling bolus of fire rising into the sky to the east. Single strands of wiry flame, traceries of debris, spill from its underside like the fine ribbons of a jellyfish.

'What–' she says, swallowing hard. Overpressure has muffled her hearing.

'Munition plant,' says Wereft. 'Over Tavian Arch way. MM Three-Forty-One is my guess.'

'She said it was on fire.'

'Who did?'

'The girl–'

'Well, it's just torched off and taken its dumps with it.'

No more munition hauls, then. Not from this area. If the vox still works after the electro-mag pulse of that blast, she'll reach a frontline unit and inform them of the wagons' location.

They have to move on. They have to urge the masses north. There's already panic and jostling nearby. A stampede brewing. They'll have to work hard to keep them calm.

'We'll need help,' she says to the boetharch.

'With what?' he asks.

'Order,' she replies. 'Discipline.'

The line breaks. Close to thirty thousand infantry, Excertus and Auxilia Imperialis, from twelve different regiments including the PanNord 110th, have recovered some momentum in the open plain near the blazing ruins of Principaria Gard, driving into a considerably larger mass of Traitor Auxilia advancing from the Annapurna Gate. After sixteen brutal minutes of choked battle, the traitor force has been levered sideways, partly wedged against the huge earthworks running east to west. It is ugly work. The terrain is iced and frozen, victim of freak etheric weather patterns, and the battle has come down to bayonets and pole weapons. The main combat is a thick, churning melée covering ten square kilometres, thousands of soldiers caught in the savage push and pull of a giant, brawling skirmish. Lit by the flicker of low lightning, the two armies grind at each other face to face, crowds mobbing crowds, the closest of close quarters. The traitor formation is about to disintegrate. Then World Eaters, drawn by the scent of blood, sweep in from the south, and the brittle, determined discipline that has got the loyalist commanders this far shatters almost instantly.

Order collapses. Fortune inverts. The line breaks. Slaughter results.

Thinking they have time to set and range the artillery, Captain N'jie and his platoons of Kovingian Light Ordnancers line up along Quaternary Ridge. But time has been crushed into powder, and the Traitor Mechanicum's skitarii engulf them before they have even unlimbered or planted the recoil spades. The Kovingians fight and die around their unfired cannon, reduced to pistols, knives and shovels.

* * *

Keeler waits in line. She waits in line, accepts inspection, and takes a purity tag. She thinks others will too if they see her doing it. *Teach by word, teach by deed. They see you stand up, they'll do the same.* She also believes it's the only icon that means anything now, an article of faith. A talisman of hope to counteract the symbols of atrocity that are appearing on every wall. She doesn't like the Prefectus' callous process, or the exclusion, but she reminds herself there's a greater purpose at work.

Eild rallies the conclave, and sends out the speakers to start drawing the crowds north. By his estimate there are nearly a million people welling up from the southern Palatine.

'North,' she says to him. 'That's the plan. Tell them "north".'

1:xxv

A Warmaster confesses his crime

'So what *is* your plan, Ollanius?' Actae asks.

'In my experience, plans work best the less people share them,' says Oll. 'It reduces the odds of someone screwing them up.'

His answer echoes in the narrow, sloping chamber they've made their rest-stop. Actae smiles.

'I'll take that as a no, then,' she says.

'No, what?' asks Katt, perched beside Oll, a weight of scorn in her voice.

'No, he doesn't have a plan, Katt,' says Actae. 'I thought as much. That's why I came to find you. To help you. To… I suppose, engineer a plan that might actually work. You have the potential, clearly. Your very long association with the Emperor.'

Everyone looks at Oll, even Leetu. They've set their lamps on the ground, and they blaze like little campfires, throwing their shadows long and lean up the sloping walls until they become part of the pitch darkness overhead.

'Association is a strong word,' says Oll. 'I knew Him, a very long time ago. We stopped being friends. I don't suppose we ever were friends, but… anyway… I ran from Calth, when Calth burned. I was running away, but somewhere along the line, I started running towards something. I believe there are higher powers at work in the universe, powers, forces, whatever you want to call them. I think I have been set on my path for a reason, so I'm following it. And if I can do anything when I arrive at the end of it… if I have any influence left, as one Perpetual to another, both cursed by that state of being, I intend to use it.'

'You believe in god, Trooper Persson,' says Graft. 'This I have recorded about you. You are pious. You cherish a private faith in the old, prohibited religions.'

Oll nods. 'Yes. An old habit. Very old. Too old to be shaken off. But what I believe in doesn't matter. Only what I can do.'

'End it,' says Zybes.

'Yes, Hebet,' says Oll. 'End it. End this incredible, monstrous, unnecessary bloodshed. That's the bottom line.'

'Stab him,' says Krank. 'Stab him with a blade that cuts through space.'

Katt snorts a laugh.

'Stab who?' asks Leetu.

'Yes, Ollanius? Who?' asks the sorceress with a sly smile.

'Horus,' says Zybes.

Oll shrugs.

'Oh,' says Katt, in surprise. An expression of shock and realisation spreads across her face. 'He means either one,' she says. 'Either one of them. Or both. Whatever it takes.'

'Whatever it takes…' Actae echoes.

'But you intend to talk to Him first,' says Leetu. It's almost a question.

'Who?' asks Krank.

'His old friend,' says Actae.

'I do,' says Oll. 'I mean, if there's a chance. I doubt there will be. And I doubt He'll listen. He's never listened to anybody. But I think that's the intention. Otherwise, why me? It could be anyone carrying this knife if it's just a case of stabbing.'

'Because he might drop his guard if he encounters an old friend?' Actae suggests. 'No one else could get close.'

'Maybe,' says Oll. 'But that's not really me. That's more of an Alpharius move. Besides, He'll be wary of me. He wouldn't lower His guard. I've stabbed Him before.'

There is a long silence.

'Are you joking?' asked Katt.

'Expand on that, Ollanius,' says Actae.

'Nothing much to add,' says Oll. 'We had a falling out. This was thirty thousand years ago, give or take, so... a lot of blood under the bridge since then.'

'No, no,' says Krank, wide-eyed. 'You have to say more than *that*!'

Oll looks at them. After the loyalty they've shown to him, he owes them something. This deep under the earth, entombed in rock, it feels like the most secure crypt, where an old secret might be safely unwrapped.

'There was a great tower,' he says. 'It was called, by some, Etemenanki, and stood at a place called Babilin, or Babel. I'm sure that means nothing to any of you, because scripture's no longer taught.'

'It means something to me,' says Actae. 'Was it real?'

'It was,' says Oll. 'The culture that built it had power. They were a dangerous obstruction to His plans. A danger to everything, actually. They had weaponised language. Enuncia, they called it. I was His Warmaster, His friend. We campaigned and brought them down. I thought we'd burn everything. But, to my great disappointment, it turned out He wanted Enuncia for His own purposes.'

It was a long time ago, but it feels oddly fresh to Oll, because he so recently relived the whole affair in the dreams woven by Hatay-Antakya Hive.

'So you stabbed Him?' asked Zybes, wide-eyed.

'I did. To stop Him. That ended what the lady here described as our association.'

He looks at Actae.

'Now you,' he says. 'Tell us something. You're a Perpetual too.'

'Not born so,' she replies. 'Not like you at all. But granted, after death, a second birth and a new lifetime. I was born on Colchis. I was used by the Aurelian's people as a confessor, and as a priestess of their craft. And for that association, Ollanius, I was killed by the Emperor's golden warriors.'

She pauses.

'And in dying, saw the truth of the warp. All of it. Then I was reborn in this form. What you would call sorcery remade me, Ollanius, not some happenstance of biology or evolution, but now I serve the truth. No one and nothing else.'

'The Cabal tried to use you,' says Oll. 'John told me.'

'They did. They sent Damon Prytanis after me. Another Perpetual.'

'He's dead,' says Oll.

'He is. Finally and fully. But I serve no one and nothing now, except the greater cause of finishing this conflict before it finishes us all. The same as you.'

'A loose definition of the words "the same", I think,' says Oll.

'For now, Ollanius, we only have each other.'

'Cyrene Valantion,' says Katt quietly.

Actae turns her veiled face towards her sharply. 'Oh, you're clever, girl,' she says. 'That mind of yours is more cunning and light-fingered than I realised. You hooked that from my thoughts.'

'It was just there, on the surface,' says Katt. She looks a little pleased with herself.

'Yes, I was Cyrene Valantion, the Blessed Lady. My flesh-sight was taken when Monarchia burned. I died in the prelude to Isstvan. After years of tormented enlightenment, or perhaps enlightened torment, I was reborn. I was no longer Cyrene. I had escaped death, and I had been given a different kind of sight. Think what you will of me, Ollanius, but I am a significant asset.'

Oll gets to his feet.

'They're taking a long time,' he says to Leetu. 'Any signal from Alpharius?'

Leetu shakes his head.

'All right,' says Oll. 'A few more minutes, then.'

He wanders a few steps down the passage, the direction they came from, and peers into the darkness.

'Something the matter?' asks Leetu.

Oll looks at him, and drops his voice to a whisper.

'On the way up here, you had the tail end.'

'Yes.'

'Did you hear anything behind us?' Oll asks.

'No,' Leetu replies. 'Like what?'

'Doesn't matter,' says Oll.

1:xxvi

Sharper than thorns

On the Via Aquila, in front of the Scholaster Hall, the human tide parts suddenly. People pull back in stumbling dismay, a hole in the crowd. A man has fallen.

Conroi-Captain Ahlborn of the Command Prefectus pushes his way through the packed crowd, and reaches the gap. Stiglich, one of his best from the Hort Palatine, follows him.

'Keep back,' Ahlborn calls to the people. 'Keep back!'

The man is writhing on the ground. A factorum worker, perhaps, or a labourer from the mills. From his convulsions, it looks as though he has been poisoned. Ahlborn realises that the sight shocks him: not the man in agony, for he has seen far too many humans in agony in the last few hours. What shocks is the empty circle of street around him. The Via Aquila is so congested, there has barely been space to move or breathe. But this man, this writhing man, commands a circle of open, littered ground a full six metres in diameter.

The crowd looks on, wide-eyed and silent. Some pull up their purity tags for Ahlborn to see, but he isn't looking.

'Is there a medic?' he calls out, crouching over the man. 'A medic? A doctor?'

No one answers. They are all as afraid of the crimson-gloved Prefectus officer as they are of a man afflicted with madness or disease.

Ahlborn looks at Stiglich. She shakes her head.

'We have to get him somewhere,' he tells her. 'Carry him off the street.'

He reaches down gingerly. The man is matted with filth, and he has soiled himself. He mumbles something, something Ahlborn can't quite catch, and stares up with blood-blown eyes.

'I don't understand,' Ahlborn tells him. 'Kin? King? King who? Is there someone here called King?'

The man vomits suddenly. Strings of waxy glair spatter the roadway. Ahlborn flinches back. He doesn't want to touch the man. He can see dark spots on his skin, the maculae of disease, the rotting plague that the enemy carried in with them. He wants to put a shot through the man's head, but he can't do that in front of the crowd. And they can't leave him here.

He clenches his teeth and reaches out again.

The man gets up. He rises quickly, swaying. He grins at Ahlborn and Stiglich. Vomit drips from his chin. He says something again, the name, and then shivers. Spines, the size and colour of rose-thorns, sprout from his skin. They erupt from his cheeks and brow, his jaw, his forearms, and the backs of his hands.

Ahlborn cries out in alarm, and draws his sidearm. The crowd starts screaming. The man, thorn-stippled, turns and staggers away. Ahlborn can't take a shot with people all around. Stumbling, the man reaches the steps of the Scholaster Hall. The crowd parts like a curtain to let him pass, recoiling in fear and revulsion.

Ahlborn and Stiglich run up the steps after him. He's gone inside, through the great doors, into the unlit, empty chambers of the hall. Ahlborn leads the way. It's cold, quiet and dim inside. Every step sets off a dozen echoes. The ceilings are high, supported by pillars. A firelight glow throbs through the tall, dirty windows.

Stiglich, carbine raised, nudges Ahlborn and nods. On the ground, a splatter of stomach contents. They edge down the hall, covering each other, their footsteps making hundreds more even though they try to tread softly.

The man is waiting at the far end, under the huge oeil-de-boeuf window that presents the stations of the Scholasticae in glassaic. He is no longer a man. Some Neverborn thing has hatched, thorns first, inside him, and burst him from within. It crouches against the wall, raw-boned and glistening, trying to peel and scratch the husk of the man's skin off itself like rind.

It's not just the Palace that is invaded, Ahlborn thinks. *We are invaded, and conquered from within.* He wonders what awful sin, what crime, what accidental dream the man committed to become so ghastly a conduit.

They both raise their weapons and fire, raking the thing backwards against the stone wall in a storm of dust, stone chips and ichor. Its neverlife undimmed by ballistic trauma, it rushes them. Ahlborn, still firing, manages to get out of its path. Stiglich is lifted off the floor, entwined by thorned fingers, and pulled in half.

Ahlborn will not forget the wet crack of her living spine separating.

Dropping the halves of her, it turns on him. It giggles, chunters and cackles through pin-cushion lips. His weapon is out. He backs up, frantically trying to reload.

It speaks. A name. The words that the man it hatched out of was trying to say.

The Dark King.

When it says it, it shudders, as though just speaking the syllables fills it with terror.

A shadow crosses in front of Ahlborn. There's someone else here, someone huge, moving fast and without a sound. A grey knight. An Astartes legionary in almost colourless plate, like a phantom. He has a sword in each hand, a black combat gladius and a longer battlesword.

The Neverborn rears up at the warrior, hissing, clutching. The Astartes slices back, one blade and then the other. Fluid squirts from massive wounds. As it comes at him again, he buries the long sword into one armpit, and the gladius into ribs.

The Neverborn lurches backwards, the swords wedged through it, wrenching both from the warrior's grip. The Astartes reaches behind his head and draws his third sword, a chainblade clamped to his back. It revs and wails as he brings it down, sawing the Neverborn in half vertically.

Now it dies.

The warrior kills his chainsword, and returns it to his back clamp. He crouches, and recovers his other blades.

Ahlborn knows him. The Lone Wolf. The last loyal son of Horus.

'Loken?' he whispers. 'Loken? Sir?'

Garviel Loken turns and looks at him. Rubio's blade is in his right hand, *Mourn-It-All* in his left. 'It said "The Dark King",' he says.

'I heard it, sir.'

'Mean anything?'

Ahlborn shakes his head.

'You're Ahlborn, correct?'

Ahlborn nods. 'Yes, sir. What… may I ask… to find you here, I…'

'I was with Keeler,' says Loken, 'escorting her. But the war front swept in too close, so I sent her onwards, and dropped back to establish a defence line.'

'When was this?' asks Ahlborn.

'I don't know. An hour ago? Two?' He pauses. 'I'm on my way to the Processional of the Eternals,' Loken says. 'The main fight is there. I heard the gunfire...'

He looks around at the gloomy hall. He seems confused for a moment.

'Sir,' says Ahlborn, 'the processional... it is leagues from here.'

'Where is this?' Loken asks.

'The Scholaster Hall, sir. On the Via Aquila.'

'The Via Aquila?'

'Yes, sir.'

'That's... that's nowhere near where I was. Nowhere near where I was going...'

Ahlborn hesitates. *How does an Astartes get lost? How does an Astartes lose his way? Is the Lone Wolf injured? Is he... Throne save us... is he invaded by the creeping inner madness too?*

'The Via Aquila?' Loken asks again.

'Yes, sir. Right outside.'

'Something is wrong, Ahlborn.'

'That is... an understatement, sir.'

'No, conroi-captain,' Loken snaps. 'I was at Praestor Gate. I was on the avenue there, approaching the processional. I heard gunfire, just a hundred metres away, so I followed the sound. Just a hundred metres... and I was here.'

'But, no,' Ahlborn stammers. 'With respect, no, sir. Praestor is fourteen kilometres from here, at least. Probably nineteen. That's...'

'Not possible,' says Loken.

'Exactly, sir.'

'But true,' says Loken. 'I think the empyric is in us so deep, it is warping everything. Time. Spaces. The materia of the world and the Palace. My being here is not possible, and yet here I am. The impossible, Ahlborn, no longer exists.'

1:xxvii

Hydra

John turns a machined gold dial built for hands larger than human, and hears a slow hum of power rising. Console lights come on around the cabin, pale blue bars of neon blinking in auramite frames as start-up and reboot systems begin to cycle. He eases himself out of the red leather driving throne, and clambers back down the cabin to the Coronus' hatch. None of the other vehicles have shown a spark of power, but the Custodes vehicle has retained some reserve. No surprise. The grav-carrier is a breed apart from the other transports, built using technologies both older and more advanced than the mainstay Imperial standard.

He looks out into the gloom. 'Pech?' he calls. 'Pech? This one's working.'

There's no answer. The Alpha Legionnaire has left the checking to him, and gone to scout ahead, to make sure the next portion of the route is still clear enough for vehicles.

'Pech?'

He climbs back in. He can feel the vibration of the under-deck generator as it begins to sequence, and hear the whine of the grav-system slowly boosting to operational power. He opens some of the built-in storage lockers. Four bolters, too big for anyone except Pech or Leetu. One is a master-crafted piece of great beauty, with silver and emerald inlay, fitted with double-drum magazines. John can't even lift it. The next two lockers contain racks of Solar Auxilia lasguns and autorifles, high quality and manufactory-fresh, still in their plastek wraps. The Alpha Legion were anticipating human agent support.

Prepared for every eventuality. No shit.

The next locker holds handguns, both Astartes and human pattern, including two handsome voltvolvers that look like Mechanicum archeotech. There are metal canisters packed in the bottom of the locker. He opens one, and smiles at the contents.

Pech is taking too long. They should have rejoined the others and been moving again by now. John climbs out of the Coronus to find the psi-damper and make sure it's packed aboard. As he jumps onto the ground, the grav-carrier's restart cycle reaches operational power, and the exterior lamps come on automatically, drenching the area in front of the vehicle with bright ovals of light.

The Alpha Legionnaire is standing there. His return was typically silent, but the lights have surprised him. He stands for a moment, motionless, his armour iridescent, motes of dust drifting around him in the hard glare.

'You found one that works, then?' he asks.

'Yes,' says John.

'Power reserves optimal? No drop off?'

'Enough to start the generation system,' says John. 'Now it's building its own charge. Should be good to go. Is the way ahead clear?'

'The way ahead? Yes.'

'No collapses or cave-ins, then? A transport's going to make the rest of this trek a lot easier.'

'No collapses,' says the legionnaire.

John nods. 'I left something inside,' he said. 'Just a sec.'

He turns to climb back in.

'That can wait.'

John pauses, and glances back at the Astartes. 'That can wait *what*?' he asks. His pulse is racing. He's not sure what to do, because he's pretty sure he's about to die, and his ruse to get back in to grab a voltvolver or something with serious kill-power has just been thwarted.

'I don't understand what you mean,' says the Alpha Legionnaire, and takes a step forward.

John smiles his best forced smile. He's only got himself now. Wits, brains, smarts. The only way he's going to live another minute, another second, is to use what he has. The unexpected. The oblique.

'That can wait *what*?' John repeats, still smiling, maintaining relaxed body language. 'All the way here, you've called me by name, every other sentence, emphasising the fact you know me. Psychological reinforcement. Pretty standard. But now you've stopped.'

The Alpha Legionnaire hesitates for a fraction of a second.

'I don't understand what your problem is,' he says, his tone expressing genial bemusement.

'Well, you wouldn't,' says John with a cheerful shrug. 'You're not Pech.'

'Of course I am,' says the Alpha Legionnaire.

'You can't be,' says John. 'He knows my name. And he's standing right behind you.'

Fooled just for a second, the Astartes turns to look behind him.

John dives for the hatch.

He isn't even slightly inside when the huge hands grab him from behind.

1:xxviii

Xenophon

John's face and forearms slam into the hull as his legs are snatched backwards. When he hits the ground beside the grav-carrier, he's already dazed from that jarring impact, his nose full of a salty stink, his mouth full of blood.

The Alpha Legionnaire rolls him onto his back, pulls the autopistol out of John's belt, and tosses it away. *If I'd thought that was going to do any good against Astartes plate, I'd have tried it already,* John thinks. He tries to clear his head. His nose feels crushed, and there's blood running into his throat. The bastard basically bounced his face off the Coronus.

But he didn't kill him. Not outright. And an Astartes kills when he decides to, so John being alive is a conscious decision.

'Get up,' the legionnaire says.

John can't. He's too foggy. He rolls on his side and cough-spits blood. He's split his lip and bitten his tongue.

'How many of you are there?' the Alpha Legionnaire asks.

John spits again and tries to sit up. His face is numb, but the pain in his tongue is acute.

'Don't play for time, Grammaticus.'

John flinches.

'Yes, I know who you are. You caught me out. But you will be aware of the techniques I can employ. How many of you are there?'

John sits up, clutching his oozing mouth, and shrugs.

The Astartes picks him up and slams him against the grav-carrier. John's sure he feels a rib pop, but the air is crushed out of him so completely, he greys out. The legionnaire holds him there.

'How many?'

Blinking, head swaying, John looks at the burnished visor inches from his face. It's just a frozen snarl of metal. He can see the intricate green and silver scales, the droplets of his own aspirated blood gleaming on its grille. He can't see the eyes behind the lenses in the deep, recessed sockets, but he's so close he can see the orange flicker of the display projecting on the inside of the tinted plex.

'How many?'

John says something, but his split tongue is so swollen, it comes out as a gurgle of blood and spittle.

'Repeat.'

'Xenophon…' John grunts. His words are slurred and impeded by his swollen tongue. 'You're running Xenophon? We're on the same bloody side…'

The Astartes keeps him pinned against the carrier with his left hand, and lowers his right. Power-armoured fingers, as gentle as a lover's, find the rib lesion and track the rib around the curve of John's torso. John winces. A fingertip stops, adjacent to a pressure point. It digs in.

John screams. The pain rips up his spine and into the base of his skull. His legs go numb.

'This flow of information is one-way,' says the Astartes. 'How many of you are there?'

'There's no incentive for me to answer,' John replies, each word distorted by his tongue. 'You're not going to let me live.'

'I might.'

'You're Alpha Legion.'

'And?'

'Everything about you is a lie. Let me live? Lie.'

John has one card left. A word, one of the many words of power he glimpsed in Oll's vision of the word-filled tower back in Hatay-Antakya Hive. It's the only one he could recall after the vision faded, and he's memorised it. It's a word of the proto-language Enuncia, and he isn't sure what it does, but he knows that once he's said it, he'll forget it. He was saving it, saving it as a last resort, for when they finally close with their quarry. But that moment will never come if he doesn't survive this–

The huge right hand moves up and rests a thumb against his brachial plexus.

'Stopping the pain is an incentive,' the Alpha Legionnaire says. 'Preventing pain is an incentive. Live or die is hardly the point. Pain is the significant factor. Pain, and how much of it there is before death.'

'Pain's just distraction,' John gurgles. He starts to form the word.

The Alpha Legionnaire presses with his thumb to prove it isn't. John screams again. His hand goes slack in paralysis. His mind spins, no longer able to compose the syllables he needs. Shock and nausea wash through him. There's raw terror simply in the gentle restraint with which the Astartes is administering pressure.

'How many?'

The hand moves to John's paratoid lymph node, a finger resting on the mastoid process.

'Make me scream again,' gasps John.

The hand stops.

'Making me scream is a great way to find out how many people are with me.'

'Last chance,' says the Alpha Legionnaire.

Metal hits metal. The impact is so clear it's almost as if a bell's been struck. Suddenly released, John hits the ground.

Two huge figures grapple beside him. Both are in green and silver plate. One has a bolt pistol drawn, but the other has clamped the wrist of the hand holding it.

John blinks, and tries to crawl away from the brutal contest. It's not like two men brawling, rolling in the dirt, punching and cursing and grabbing at each other's clothes. It's two giants in power armour. It's fast, transhumanly fast, *nightmarishly* fast, almost faster than John can track: blows, blocks and grips exchanged in rapid, surgical series. It's like lying close to two counter-rotating propellers that are spinning and chewing up the ground towards him, out of control.

Pech is the one with the pistol. He didn't take a shot. Now he's locked. The other Alpha Legionnaire shifts and slams Pech against the carrier. Pech pivots and mashes the other Astartes against the Gorgon parked beside it. Flakes of rust puff into the air. The Alpha Legionnaire spins Pech again, trying to break his grip, and caroms him off the carrier's hull a second time. John scrambles, and then rolls frantically. The two Astartes crash down into the space where he had been sprawled. He'd have been crushed under them, and churned up by their wrestling plasteel bulks.

John tries to get up. His legs are nerve-limp, and his rib is shrieking pain through his midsection. His left hand is paralysed. He slips, falls, gets up again. He staggers clear as the two Alpha Legionnaires thrash over again in a tangle that would have pulped him.

The other Astartes breaks Pech's grip on the bolt pistol by

cracking his hand against the carrier's port grav nacelle. They roll again. Fists connect in a flurry, drawing sparks and grazing armour. Now John can't tell the bastards apart.

John drags himself aside, staring in horror. One Alpha Legionnaire lands a solid blow, and the other rocks back against the nacelle. There's an Astartes combat knife the size of John's forearm already in the fist of the first one. He tries to punch it home, but the other slides away, and the blade gashes the nacelle's plating.

The Alpha Legionnaires lock again, one holding the other's blade back. They plough past John, out of the space between the carrier and the Gorgon, into the pools of light cast by the carrier's lamps, spinning and rotating each other.

Dragging his deadened leg, John blunders back to the carrier and tries to haul himself up the hull. His left hand just won't work. He gets a toehold, and boosts himself up onto the nacelle, falling on his face again. He hacks up blood, hardly able to breathe. Behind him, a green blur moves in the bright wash of floodlights, ceramite clanging and grinding against ceramite.

The glinting combat blade finally bites. It punches through the reinforced undersuit exposed between groin guard and tasset, in and out, as fast as a snake striking. Blood gouts down the cuisses and greaves. Alpharius staggers backwards, trying to reset a defensive stance. The other Alpharius stamps in, blade levelled for the kill-jab over the gorget.

A lance of boiling light vaporises the ground between them with a savage bang. Leaning against the Coronus' hatch frame to stay upright, John aims the voltvolver at both of them, bracing his right wrist with his left forearm to steady the weight of the hefty, antique weapon. Post-discharge voltaics writhe and crackle around the muzzle.

'One question,' John says, his enlarged tongue making him sound stupid. 'How many of us are there?'

'Nine,' says Ingo Pech.

John's shot melts a hole in the chestplate of the other Alpha Legionnaire. He falls on his back with vapour pouring out of the hole. He's still twitching.

Pech limps to him, breaks the combat knife out of his spasming grip, and rams the blade under the lip of the helmet and up into the skull inside.

'One of yours?' John asks, lowering the gun and sagging slightly.

'We're all Alpharius, John. You know that.'

Pech unlocks the dead Alpha Legionnaire's helmet and removes it. He stares down at the face.

'Mathias Herzog,' he says.

'Him? Really?'

'Yes, John.'

'Working to Xenophon?' asks John.

'Yes. Sent here to activate the sleepers, like I was.'

'You should have shot him, Pech,' says John. 'You had the drop on him.'

'There was a high-percentage risk that you'd have been hit,' says Pech. 'I had to separate you and take him down.'

'Appreciated.'

The Alpha Legionnaire turns to look at John.

'We may not all be on the same side, John,' he says, 'but I am on your side.'

'That's the most Alpha Legion thing anyone's ever said,' says John, and slides down onto his haunches with a long, slow moan.

1:xxix

In Lupercal's Court

You stand and wait, patiently, arms outstretched, as the fitters machine your war plate into place. You use the time to think, to run multiple tactical schemas in your head. Perturabo of Olympia had a reputation for such mental feats, but in your opinion, the reputation was largely undeserved. His plans were so complex, so precise, so cumbersome. They lacked panache. Panache is the mark of true war-genius. You only let him orchestrate the whole thing, truth be told, as a favour, brother to brother. Something for him to do. Something to keep him busy. And, of course, to placate his constant, needy yearning to prove himself against Rogal.

Well, he's gone now. Gone to sulk, most likely, because at every turn, Rogal has proven superior. Rogal, stolid and humourless as he seems, has some panache after all. It is such a damn shame Rogal decided to throw in with the other side. Such a damn, stupid shame. It would have been a pleasure to have him at your right hand. He would have cracked that place open inside two weeks, maximum. Faster, if you'd goaded him.

Yes, a shame. But then Rogal, for all his panache, has always been a dull conformist. Rogal didn't choose his side because he thought it was right. He chose it because it was safe.

Oh, Rogal Dorn. You will be almost sorry to kill him, but you will console yourself that it is his own lack of imagination that has brought about his death.

The fitters are taking forever. You have a headache. Some cloud of migraine that is either setting in or in retreat. Did you have a migraine before? You can't remember. You were busy. They are taking forever, fussing with the power connectors of your Talon, as if this is the first time they've done it. And they are whispering. They haven't done that before. Whispering to each other. What is it they are saying?

'Stop your whispers,' you tell them. Softly, of course.

They look at you, and you read alarm in their faces. No, more than alarm. Terror. Terror, and puzzlement. One seems to cower, as though he fears you will strike at him. What's got into them?

'You were whispering,' you explain. 'Whisper, whisper. It's annoying. Stop it.'

'Yes, Warmaster,' says one.

'Begging your forgiveness, Warmaster,' says another.

There's a tone there you don't like, a hint they feel falsely accused. You let it slide. It's trivial, and you have more important things to do.

They continue with the final fitting work. And they keep whispering, though more quietly. You decide to ignore it. You'll have a private word with Mal later, and instruct him to dole out punishments accordingly. Have them all demoted from the personal retinue and sent back to the arming decks. Another team can take their places and their honour.

They step back. The Court, your personal place of grace, falls silent. Even the walls hold their breath. The wargear, the

Serpent's Scales, so miraculously fashioned by Kelbor-Hal and his artificers, clings upon you like the burden of responsibility and decision, the weight of war, the substance of authority.

The fitters bring the wolf pelt, and hang it as a mantle around your shoulders. It takes four of them to lift it. A great beast indeed, taken on the moon of Davin, a lunar wolf for a true Luna Wolf.

You look for approval. Your attendants in the Court smile and nod from their alcoves and ledges. Some bow. Some shiver and tuck themselves behind the drapes that line the chamber, unable to bear your magnificence. Some avert their gaze behind splayed fingers and cower, giggling, in the orifices of the walls.

You walk from your private chamber. Your plate feels light, as though they haven't adjusted it properly. Or perhaps you're just stronger. You've been feeling stronger these last few days. With the end in sight, that's a boost to your vengeful spirits. The prospect of victory at the end of a difficult compliance always feels uplifting. It takes away fatigue and makes you feel like a–

Like yourself again. Unstoppable. Vital. Justified.

You walk to the bridge. It's possible that they have relocated the bridge, because the walk seems to take longer than usual. Perhaps a structural reconfiguration as a result of the additional skins of armour you have ordered to sheathe the hull and fortify the primary compartments. The hallway is now too long, despite the lightness you feel. Corridors intersect and subdivide, leading to parts of the ship whose purposes you seem to have briefly forgotten. That's understandable. You've had a lot on your mind in the past weeks, an inhuman burden of data to process, and decisions to make. You have deliberately spent hours in meditative focus in the Court, clearing your head of all extraneous thoughts, the usual mental garbage of work-a-day duty, to achieve a clarity with which to consider what really matters. A state of oneness, attuned to the core issues of the compliance. You can't be expected to remember where this sub-corridor leads, or what that side chamber is used for. That's the shipmaster's job.

The walls breathe. It is very bright in the hallway, like being outdoors in the sunlight on the wide plains of Chogoris, or the bleached ever-deserts of Colchis. Light, almost sickly bright, strobes slightly, flickering through leaves swayed by the wind. Or something like leaves. You don't care. You don't look. You can hear the whispering again, like dead leaves skittering in the breeze or shushing under foot. Like the dry wing cases of beetles. Like whirring moths–

What is it they are whispering? It's very annoying. You can almost make out the words.

The name.

One name, uttered and repeated.

1:xxx

World's end

It's time.

As we wait for his champions to arrive, he shows me his plan. Effortlessly, he takes my mindsight into his, and melds them together so I see things as he sees them.

I tremble. I am old. I am tired. My frail bones shake, and I cling to my staff to stay standing. *Such power.* My mind feels as though it is about to burst. I gaze, sharing his will and view, out to the limit of his mindsight. I see…

I see what is revealed. The Imperial Palace, all of its dominions, maimed and disfigured, its towers lightning-clapped and tumbled down, its golden avenues scorched to molten streams of clotted alloy, its polished walls baked in soot and befouled. It is numb with terror, rendered vacant by shock. It clings to its last shreds of life. It is as close to death as Jaghatai was, gone past the fatal brink and owning only a fragment of its vitality.

Firestorms seethe. Caliginous hosts of plated men and towering war machines, like swarms of gleaming insects, pour in through sundered walls. Energy beams sear, noctilucent, through the choking swathes of smoke. Pestilential rains, of blood and toxins and biomatter, hammer the broken bastions and churn the dystrophied plains to mire. Cataracts of blood splash from fractured ramparts and splintered battlements.

Wider still, spears of light flash from our last defensive battery, the ransacked port of Lion's Gate, which the White Scars have retaken and somehow cling on to. The orbital lasers stab at the obscured heavens, and are answered a hundredfold by the traitor fleet above. I see a giant void-ship shearing and burning as it falls through the clouds. I see the vast impacts of orbital bombardment, porcupining slow explosions around the collapsing skirts of Lion's Gate. Its defiance is humbling. Its end is near.

Wider still, the outstretched surface of the world, mottled and bruised, shuddering in tectonic agony and seismic convulsion, gashed and lacerated, fall-out plumes rising from the shiver-flash of glowing, irradiated lesions the size of nations. The world is wreathed in smoke and flame, the atmosphere peeling away like flayed skin.

And nothing is whole any more. The warp is spilling loose, coruscating into realspace, suppurating the flesh of the planet, corrupting and transmuting all matter it touches. This is end-stage war, the pyrophoric caress of Chaos metastasising the human home world, eating it away, making its own realm where once we ruled.

Wider still, the buckled sphere of Terra, rotting in its own skin, bathed in un-light, the black specks of the numberless traitor fleet settling like blowflies on its polluted rind. The orb of once-proud Terra is encircled by a noxious nephelospheric halo, a livid puncture in reality, a raw corona, as my master's son, his beautiful, first-found son, our enemy, immanentises his insane transaction with the four false gods of annihilation, and consigns the world into the distended maw of the warp.

The natural laws of the world are undone. This is his configuration of tomorrow, sanctified by the bloody print of his hand.

What is my lord trying to show me? I see nothing that I don't already know, or can't imagine. His first-found's domination is utter and absolute. I expect to discover some tiny flaw, some chink or fissure in his attack, something or anything we can use to leverage a counter-strike. But there is none, and I knew before my lord showed me this that none would exist, for Horus Lupercal has proven that while Rogal and Perturabo might be proclaimed the greatest strategists of the age, none can compare to the Warmaster.

There is nothing. My lord, my master, my King-of-Ages, my friend… you must *accept* this. There is nothing. You must accept that our fight back, which we perhaps have left too late, must be done the *hardest* way, one blow, one step, one metre, one strike at a time, a gruelling uphill struggle against a far superior–

Wait.

Wait.

1:xxxi

Revelation

Can it be? Surely, it cannot. A mistake on my part, a misapprehension of my mindsight. I am old, after all. The sheer weight and wealth of the data that my lord is showing me, the scope of it, the etheric fury… it has confused me for a moment, overwhelmed me, and made me see what I want to see, rather than what actually *is*.

I look again, my mind pushing at its capacity, amplified by his will, mindsight narrowed like a needle.

There. *There?* Surely that can't be true? I refuse to allow myself to hope–

+It is true, Sigillite.+

There it is. A detail so small, so lost in the background storm of system-wide conflagration, that I missed it the first time. I look again to be sure. I check and re-check the veracity of my insight.

+What I show you is true.+

And I see that it is undeniable.

The *Vengeful Spirit*, his first-found's death ship, has lowered its shields.

My mind reels. I blink. I stare up at my lord, incredulous. His hands shiver on the arms of the Throne.

'What does this mean?' I ask.

What *does* it signify? Damage? Error? A malfunction? A boastful challenge? A hubristic gambit? A vulgar trap? It doesn't matter. The shields are down.

The shields are *down*.

There is our variable. It does not matter what it represents, though every instinct in me names it a trap. It is what I have been searching for without thought I would ever find it, the one brief hope that could reconfigure all of this. Whatever it is, we will make it what we need it to be.

The shields are down.

I test it again, to make certain I am not fooling myself. There is no deception. The treasonous heart of the first-found is wide open.

I breathe deeply and slowly. I take one last look, wider still, across the universal madness and cosmic apocalypse, out to the very failing edge of mindsight, and glimpse the reddened whirlpool ruin of the Solar Realm, an open wound in the flank of the Milky Way–

I close my eyes.

I have seen so many of the wars that history has witnessed. I have never seen a war like this.

We will end it now, by his will alone, or we will die.

1:xxxii

The fortunate ones

She's sitting on the steps near the Prefectus station, resting for a moment before setting out. She's peering at the oddly clean tag stapled to her coat. Leeta Tang approaches her, followed by the other gang-guides and their blindfolded, coffled teams.

'Can I stay with you?' she asks. 'Can we all stay?'

'Of course,' says Keeler.

'I want to help you guide the refugees.'

Keeler rises to her feet. She nods. They start to walk, joining the river of refugees shuffling along the Via Aquila. Someone calls her name, but it isn't anybody in the crowd.

'Mam?' Tang asks. 'If we keep faith. If we hold on and actually get there. To some kind of future, I mean. If we manage to get there, how will we remember all of this?'

'As the place where the future started,' says Keeler. 'As the fire in which a decent future was cast. We will remember ourselves as the fortunate ones.'

'And what will we say about it?'

'We'll say, *I was there.*'

PART TWO

HOW LIKE AN ANGEL IN APPREHENSION, HOW LIKE A GOD!

2:i

King of the Hollow Mountain

They have finally found Vassago the Librarian, after days of searching. When Corswain is told the news, he goes at once.

'How?' he asks.

At his side, Adophel the Chapter Master seems to shrug. 'Our perimeter patrols located him by chance on a rock shelf outside the Tertiary Portal, your grace,' he says.

'Not how was he found. How was he killed?'

'Skull crushed to pulp. Massive trauma. No defensive wounds. He was either surprised–'

'Who surprises a Librarian, Chapter Master?'

Adophel opens his huge hands, palms up, to acknowledge the faulty logic of his suggestion. Or perhaps to crave forgiveness for his lack of answers.

'Or he knew his killers, your grace,' he says.

Corswain, seneschal of the First Legion, the Hound of Caliban, halts and looks at him. A chill, world-top wind saws down the ancient metal tunnel.

'Knew his killers?' Corswain asks, weighting each word with lead.

'This beacon hill had become a nest of daemons, your grace,' Adophel replies. 'We have purged it and cleaned it out, and we hold it now. But the taint lingers. Things still lurk in recesses and shadows. Daemonkind beguiles, my lord. We are taught this. They wear masks and change faces, according to the particular deceits they seek to weave. Librarian Vassago was committed to our cause. Our best hope, perhaps, of guiding our smiths and restoring function to the mountain. I venture the malign spirits lingering here recognised that, and conspired to stop him. And wore faces he trusted to lure him to his demise.'

'Whose faces?' asks Corswain.

'Mine?' says Adophel. 'Yours? The face of any friend. Does it matter?'

It doesn't. The loss matters. Vassago was the centrepiece of Corswain's strategy. This place, this hollowed mountain, this 'beacon hill' as Adophel so typically calls it, making everything, even mountains and worlds, less imposing than his own renown, must be brought back to life.

They come out through the Tertiary Portal into the open air. A waiting phalanx of cowled Dark Angels bow their heads. On the fortified buttresses of rock rising sheer above them, defensive stations have been rebuilt and re-manned to watch over the vale below.

Corswain pauses for a moment. The view is memorable. The Astronomican, 'this beacon hill', is the last, glowering mountain of the world. Where once a continental range stood, the mightiest on Terra's face, only this peak remains, solitary and symbolic. The other mountains were ground down and levelled, through feats of engineering that Corswain can scarcely imagine, to form the vast plateau for the Palace

Imperialis, but this was hollowed out and laced with mechanisms of the Emperor's devising. It was fashioned into a psychic beacon, a beacon hill, yes, but one whose light could be seen from distant stars. The beacon light of Terra, the signal of Old Earth, reaching across the trackless territories of the Imperium as a reminder of Imperial order, and a guide-star for any of mankind seeking a homeward path.

It has been dark for too long.

Facing its greatest hour of treachery and murder, the Imperium is blind.

The Astronomican was Corswain's primary objective when he undertook his suicidal counter-strike to Terra. Even with his ten thousand warriors, the backbone of his fighting force for the last five years reinforced with much-welcome Calibanite strengths from Zaramund, he could not hope to engage the traitor fleet head-on, or drop directly into the main warzones of the Palace. Enemy numbers are staggering. His contingent would have been shredded in minutes, overwhelmed. To make the best of his resources, Corswain chose instead to run the gauntlet, a sheer act of bravado or madness, and retake the mountain instead, securing a loyalist foothold on the home world outside the Palace.

He prevailed, though the odds were long and the daemon-war in the mountain abhorrent. Once the beacon hill was secure, many of the First, Adophel among them, petitioned him to push on, with a stronghold at their backs, and drive into the flanks of the besieging traitors in a breaking effort to relieve the Palace.

It was tempting. The enemy host is vast, and the Lord of Iron's investment of the Palace a superb display of poliorcetic warcraft. He has built a constricting circumvallation around the entire Zone Imperialis, but, arrogantly expecting no counter-action from a field army, he has prepared no contravallation whatsoever to guard his heels. A firm strike, ten thousand Astartes, could perhaps drive a wedge through the traitors' careless spines…

Corswain is no coward, but he rejected the idea. He could see the futility. Ten thousand was not enough to break the siege, even from a secured surface footing. It would take more. Far more.

That was his decision, as lord commander. It was upheld and endorsed by the Archangel Sanguinius, in a fleeting, jumbled vox-link. Sanguinius told Corswain to hold: hold the mountain, hold the line, light the beacon. So what Corswain does, he does in Sanguinius' name. In his memory, he fears.

From the rock platform outside the Tertiary Portal, in the bitter wind, he stares out across the vale and the plains beyond. Even from a distance, the scene is piteous. The golden city that once filled the land before him, a crown on top of the world, a palace that was a city that possessed the dimensions of a nation, is lost in a cloud of fire. The sky is scoured to blackness. Smoke encases the heavens. Dull clots of flamelight, red and infernal, throb within a blanket of cinders and dust a thousand kilometres wide. It is no longer possible to glimpse, even from here, the shining spires of the Emperor's city. They may all, indeed, have tumbled. The vale and the slopes of the mountain are caked white, but it is not snow. It is the fresh fall of ash blown back from the Palace, falling softly, forming drifts and samite swathes across the black rock.

Corswain is not the saviour of Terra.

He remembers the joy-turned-to-despair of Admiral Su-Kassen and the valiant Halbract when they realised that his force was not the vanguard of the long-awaited relief, the racing front edge of the deliverers, an eager herald of Guilliman and the Lion. He was all he was. The hope was false. He could not tell them that Guilliman or the Lion were en route, or even if they were still alive.

But they must be. He tells himself they must be. It is an imperative that he cannot bring himself to doubt. His liege-father and noble Guilliman are still alive. They are racing here, closing with every passing second, leading the full and terrible might of the remaining loyal Legions.

They *must* be.

For only they can break this. Only they can turn this tide and crush the infamy of bastard Lupercal and his brother-usurpers. They are mankind's last hope.

To doubt that is to accept defeat.

His duty is to prepare the way for them. For there to be even a shred of hope, Corswain has to hold Terra's beacon hill, and make it shine again. He has to pierce the enfolding shroud of darkness that obscures the very location of the Throneworld, and guide salvation in.

I will light the fire so that my father can see and come to me.

No wonder the daemons conspire to stop him. Vassago's murder won't be their last attempt.

2:ii

Master of Mankind

The Word Bearers have assembled for you, thousands of them, lining the approachways to the main bridge levels. They sing your name, yell it, a raw, bawling chorus of homage. You walk through their midst, nodding, accepting the praise, indulging them, almost shaken by the volume of their massed voices.

None of them dares to look directly at you. None can bear to. You are too glorious for even their post-mortal eyes. As you move through them, as your immense shadow passes over them, they look away determinedly, tears in their eyes, trying not to glimpse you as they chant your name. There is fury in that chant. It's almost manic desperation. It feels as though they are afraid of stopping, or taking breath, or pausing, as though screaming your name is the only thing that's keeping them alive.

Maybe it is. You raise your hand in a modest gesture to acknowledge their adoration, and enter the main bridge.

Inside, they are waiting for you, which is only right. The seniors, the commanders, your inner circle. You smile a generous smile as you enter the grand expanse of the bridge, the smile a father bestows upon his extended family, and they bow, just as they should.

'Rise,' you say.

They rise. They gaze up at you in awe, at the regal, smoke-dark mountain of your towering figure. You loom over them, the stature of a new-forged god, the solemn authority of a dark king.

'You were waiting for me?' you ask, with a wry smile.

'We were, Great Lupercal,' says your equerry.

'Very good, Maloghurst.'

What was that? Did he just correct you, under his breath? Did he murmur 'Argonis'? Did he just shoot a nervous look at the senior officers standing nearby?

He's a fool, but you'll excuse him. Everyone is overexcited. You can feel the tension in the room, like the leaden air before a thunderstorm breaks. The eagerness. The anticipation. This is what they all live for. Victory. Triumph. Conquest. Compliance. This is what the Luna Wolves were bred for. Your sons, not a loser among them. As victory approaches they gather, like wolves indeed, scenting the kill to come, the looming end and the imminent death.

'Let us review, then,' you declare. You move to the great strategium, the projection table upon which you have planned and executed every one of your victories. Such has been the scale of your career, on this warship, with these men, in victory after victory, the table has a patina of use. The auramite edges and control surfaces are almost burnished from the repeated touch of hands, the hololithic plate scuffed and worn from tapping fingertips and demonstrative gestures. It should be replaced, really, or at least fully serviced by the adepts, but you can't bring yourself to instruct it. It is a fine device. It has been your instrument of command down the decades, moulded to your touch, fatigued by your hands, a hard-working tool of warfare and an artefact of your military legacy. It will be in a museum one day. There will be a placard: *Upon this tactical device, Horus Lupercal, Master of Mankind, planned out his conquests and built the Imperium.*

It is fitted to you, like a good sword or a favourite bolter. It is a weapon, a weapon wielded by your mind as your hand wields a blade. You would rather cast out an heirloom gladius.

Sentimental? Perhaps. You may be excused sentiment at this hour. You are human after all.

Someone has left tarot cards scattered on the strategium's surface. That's very sloppy. How unlike the command cadre. *The Harlequin* of discordia, *The Eye, The Great Hoste, The Shatter'd World, The Labyrinthine Path, The Throne* reversed, *The Hulk, The Moon, The Martyr, The Monster* and *The Lightning Tower,* all major arcanoi. *The Dark King* is askew across *The Emperor* card. You sweep them onto the floor. You light the table. The Palace appears, a three-dimensional light-form, expressed in micro-detail at Millisept Sigma resolution, a standard broad appraisal that includes climate patterns and rendered atmospherics.

The smoke bank is so wide and thick, there is virtually nothing to see. Just a blur, a greyness, as though dusty cloaks have been heaped across the plate.

'My sons,' you say. 'Such a pity to behold. Our target site has seen better days.'

You laugh. Someone else laughs, though it's more of a whisper.

Swift haptic gestures peel the atmopsherics back, erasing layers of cloud. When you finally reveal the Palace beneath, it takes you by surprise.

An awful thing to see. A dolorous thing. It is heartbreaking. For a moment you suspect that someone, perhaps Ezekyle or

Tarik, has loaded a simulation of the surface of some blasted moon or volcanic planetesimal as a joke. Just the sort of prank they'd pull to ease the tension.

But it's not a moon. It's not a joke. The punctured, cratered, punished relief is the Zone Imperialis Terra. A ruined wasteland the size of a major nation state. The Palace is almost entirely gone.

The fool, you think. The stupid, blind, unreasonable, arrogant fool. He did this. He made this happen. He brought this hell down upon himself. His pride earned this wrath. So damn him, for he has brought this hell down on millions besides. On billions. They have suffered this because of him. Those innocent multitudes.

It is almost unbearably sad. But the state of the city is inevitable. You can't be stalled by tragedy. You clear your throat.

'Call up dispositional overview,' you tell your equerry.

'My lord,' says one of the command cadre. 'There are issues we should address–'

'An overview first, I think,' you say.

'My lord Lupercal, the issues are critical. We–'

'Are they, Sejanus? *Critical?*' you snap. You pause. Emotion has got the better of you for a moment. You find a smile. 'Forgive my abruptness, Hastur,' you say. 'I meant no rebuke. I would like an overview before we scrutinise details.'

'Of course, my lord. But we–'

'Are you going to press this, Captain Sejanus? What, I wonder, do the Mournival think of you questioning a direct instruction?'

'The Mournival, sir? They–'

'Can they not speak for themselves, captain?'

'They are not here, my lord,' says your equerry. He sounds timid. He doesn't want to point out your slip.

Of course, they're not here. Of course. They're on the surface, even now, leading the compliance. Of course. What a stupid mistake to make. Sejanus is only here to–

Sejanus is only here to report, and the others–

What a very stupid mistake to make in front of them. Correct it. Move on. Show confidence. They're all looking at you, the officers, the tacticians, even the young woman, Oliton. She's there at the back, stylus in hand. Right there between Nero Vipus and Luc Sedirae and the tall things, the tall things that stand by the door and whisper.

'Overview,' you say. 'Now, please.'

Your equerry steps in. He adjusts the display. The tabula topographica shifts to project a tactical breakdown, your armies laid out upon the table.

'Baraxa has Second Company, here,' he tells you, pointing, 'alongside Abaddon and First. They have cut in deep, and approach the limit of the Gilded Walk. Balt and Third Company hold here. Vorus Ikari has advanced Fourth Company rapidly, almost to the Confessional–'

'With typical haste,' you remark. 'Ikari is rash. Too hungry for–'

'Some might say, my lord, but Fifth, under Beruddin, and a unit of the Justaerin led by Ekron Fal have flanked his reckless overstretch here and here, and have actually cut off the Praetorian's southern line.'

They have. It's rather elegant, a daring but precise extension, the sort of spear-tip tactic you might have devised and drilled them in so that it could be sublimely executed. Perhaps you did. Perhaps Ikari was simply obeying your instruction with that bold run of his. Yes, of course. That's it. Beautiful. Your plan exactly. That couldn't have been accomplished without expert oversight, and who else but you is overseeing this?

'Sycar sweeps the remainder of the Justaerin along this line, in support of Abaddon,' Maloghurst goes on, rotating the image. It's funny, you hadn't noticed before quite how much he resembles that battle-brother from First Company's Storm Eagle cadre. What is his name? The one with the unmarked face? Kinor... Argonis, yes. Argonis. The likeness is uncanny. 'Malabreux, Master of the Catulan Reavers, has broken through here, with Seventeenth Legion support, and is on the brink of taking Predikant Bastion and the Hall of Ushers.'

Then it is all as you ordained. As you laid it out. You hope the Lady Oliton is paying close attention. You hope she is getting this all down, word for word, for this is the very essence of your genius, your potency as a martial savant. You have brought your finest game to the table at this, the most crucial moment of your career.

'And of these here?' you ask. 'In the vanguard between Ezekyle and dear Sycar? Which units are these again?'

Your equerry coughs awkwardly.

'Mal? Which units? Who commands them?'

'I... I do not know their names, my lord,' he says to you.

'How can you not know their names?' you ask. It's preposterous. Thousands of men, tearing into the Sanctum, and their units are unidentified?

'We don't know the names yet,' says Layak.

'Not all of them, lord,' says Sejanus. 'Not yet.'

'Are these not the warriors you summoned to support us, Layak?' you ask. 'Are these not the very ones you let in yourself?'

Zardu Layak nods. He smiles. There is blood on his teeth.

'We thought you might tell us their names, lord,' says Sejanus.

Yes, of course. They want you to grandstand a little. Show off your mastery with the remembrancer watching. How clever of them to engineer an opportunity for you to magnify your own legend. You bend down and peer at the display, and you increase the resolution.

You say, 'As I thought,' as though you were testing them. 'We have Kweethul, and there, his steeds, and here the juggernauts, and here, those that are the letters-out-of-blood, and here the pestigorae and the tzaangorae, and here Scarabus, and here the Drach'nyen host, and here proud Be'lakor, and here the ones that are of the Doombreed, and here Rhug'guari'ihululan, and here N'Kari, and here the Bahk'ghuranhi'aghkami upon their palanquins, and besides them the Tsunoi, and the Heartslayer, and Khar-Har, and carnate Illaitanen, and old father Ku'gath, and Skarbrand and Epidemius, and those of the Masque, and Karanak and wily Suvfaeras, and ancient Tallomin, and that which is Uhlevorix, and iron-willed Ax'senaea, and Abraxes and Ulkair, and weeping Jubiates, and Ushpetkhar, and the storming ruin of Madail, and Ghargatuloth, and J'ian-Lo, and Mephidast, and M'Kar and Collosuth, and here, the one who walks behind us, whose name is Samus, and all of them. All that is and was and ever will be.'

You hear them echo it, *is and was and ever will be*. You hear Oliton's stylus scratching at her slate, recording every word.

The air has turned cold. You can tell how impressed they are. How excited. But also, how scared. This is no common undertaking, and there is no reason to pretend that it is. It is time to change your tone.

'We never wanted this,' you say. 'We never asked for it. Sons and brothers, I know how you feel, for I feel it too. This is the last thing we wanted to happen, and it seems unthinkable that we are doing it. I want you to understand that I know that. If I had thought, during the crusade... in the thirty sweet years of... If I had thought, when my father saved my life on Reillis, if I had thought for one moment...'

You take a deep breath.

'He is false,' you say, quite plainly. There is a murmur from them, a whisper and a murmur. 'He is false. He is a false god. And he has played us false. He has used us to further his petty dreams. His... his preposterous vision of the future. We are of his blood, but we are not his children. I am not his son. He made us merely to use us, and to use us up. How much of our blood has he spilled? How many of our lives have we given? He has constructed a plan, shared it with no one, and expected us to blindly enact it for him. Well, my sons, my beautiful sons, we are strong and we are loyal, but we are also clever. We have done enough and seen enough to understand the true abomination of his scheme. It will annihilate everything we love and everything we believe in. So it must be stopped. This I told him. This, we all told him. But he did not listen and he did not cease, so he must be *made* to cease. Though my heart is broken, my loyalty is not. I am loyal to the Throne. I am loyal, unto death, to the Imperium of Mankind. But not to him.'

You look away, as if to contemplate the grandeur of the bridge, and the helm-serfs and steersman at work below, but in truth it is to conceal the tear in your eye.

'He withheld,' you say. 'Shamelessly. He used us as toys, as playthings, and spent us as though our blood was nothing. But more than that. When we beheld, by accident, by happenstance, the truth of all that is, he denied it to us. He denied us the power and the magnitude, the shining glory of Aeternity, claiming it was not for us, and that we were too small and weak to own it or use it. And worse, as it turns out, he had kept it from us all along. Forever. He has kept the truth of what we might be from us, in case, I think, we came to eclipse his status. He wanted it for himself, all of it. Well, I am not weak. We are not weak. And he is not the father I once loved.'

You look to the officers, to Hastur and Luc and Zardu.

'Assist me with this,' you say. You hold out the Power Talon. 'Detach it.'

They come forward, and, between them, unclamp the seals

and disconnect the power and munition feeds. Hastur slides it off your right hand. You take it from him and drop it onto the strategium table. The image of the burning Palace shivers, disrupted, and the glass projection plate cracks. The Talon almost covers the entire tabletop. With your freed right hand, you unclasp the gauntlet of your left hand. You drop that on the table too.

You show them the worn gold ring you wear on the smallest finger of your left hand.

'He gave me this,' you say. 'Do you see it? The motif? It was wrought the year before he was born. It was his gift to me, as Warmaster. He said that I had become his centaur, half-man, half-army, that where I rode, the Legions would ride with me. Well, I ride here now, and he will meet his dreadful Sagittary at last. You are my sons. Unlike him, I will not waste you. I will not squander you and send you to death without a passing thought just to serve my whim. My love for you, and my pledge to you, is *this* – that we will go into this together, and stand together, and triumph together, and free the Throne and the Imperium of Man from this tyrant, together. And after, we will share the truth and wonder of immateria infinitum, for it is in us already, and fills our hearts, and raises our spirits, and whispers blessings in our ears, and it is the strength we need to face him, and compel him, and topple his deceit.'

You look at them.

'And when we are done, after this hour, you will live in glory, and you will be able to say, "I was there, the day Horus slew the Emperor." That is my pledge.'

2:iii

The pride of Caliban

The Librarian's body, wrapped in a groundsheet, is being carried in off the false snows by gun-serfs. The killers left his body where they hoped it might not be discovered, broken on the crags outside the fastness, in among the piles of choir-dead Corswain's men have raked from the stalls of the Astronomican. Corswain sees the warriors escorting it up the winding track. Brothers Tanderion, Cartheus, Asradael and Zahariel. Like Vassago, Calibanite veterans all.

'I sent for them,' Adophel tells him. 'I thought they should know.'

Corswain nods. The Calibanite reinforcements provided by Lord Luther at Zaramund, with the promise of twenty thousand more to follow, bother Corswain still. He needed the men, dearly, but his liege-father's strict orders have stood for a long time: a sword does not unsheathe itself. Luther had been commanded to remain on Caliban to raise and train new recruits, not to deploy in the field on missions of his own devising. His presence on Zaramund had been in defiance of the Lion's command, and to accept men from him was to countenance that defiance.

But the Lion is not here. He has been gone for years, lost in whatever crusading quest he has seen fit to undertake. Corswain is his seneschal, in all respects the acting master of over *half* the First Legion, an avenging son, and his father's proxy. It was his decision to make, and the galaxy has changed since he last saw his father. The strength of the enemy, once unimaginable, has now been miserably revealed. Corswain needed warriors, and the Calibanites were warriors, ready and fresh.

He hopes his liege-father will one day censure him for his decision to waive Luther's disobedience, because, for that to happen, his father will need to be alive. Corswain longs to hear his voice again, even if it has to be fierce with rebuke.

Vassago had been proof positive of Corswain's wisdom in accepting Luther's men. A gifted warp-seer, Librarian Vassago had been an essential part of their conquest at the Hollow Mountain. Without him, they could not have bested the Never-born thing they had found within. Vassago had become a true and trusted friend, and he had thrown himself into the arcane labour of restoring the Astronomican's function. It was a deed quite beyond the martial skill set of a son like Corswain.

He descends the track to meet them.

'The loss will be mourned,' he says. 'Later, when there is time.'

'You still believe in a later, then, your grace?' asks Cartheus.

'I have to,' Corswain says. 'And my brother Vassago did.'

The Calibanites seem to bridle at the word.

'We are together in this,' says Corswain.

'Of course,' says Tanderion.

'Vassago's work had barely begun,' says Corswain. 'But you were close to him, all of you. I look to you to help complete what he cannot.'

'You look to us for counsel?' Cartheus asks.

'I do. And for technique.'

'He was the Librarian,' says Asradael, glancing back at the winding sheet.

'In an official sense,' says Corswain. They look surprised. Corswain looks at Zahariel El'Zurias. 'Brother, I know you too were once of the Librarius, trained in its ways.'

'Before the Emperor's Edict,' replies Zahariel.

'An edict now overturned,' says Corswain. 'The Lion himself ruled on this. I ask you, brother, to assume the role.'

'You ask a great deal, your grace,' says Zahariel. 'I have not used those gifts in a long time. I fear they are weak from neglect...' He pauses. 'But perhaps, as a concerted effort...' Zahariel looks at the other three. 'All four of us were once of the Librarius, returned to the common ranks after Nikaea. With your permission, my lord...'

'I grant it so,' says Corswain. 'For all of you. I need your lore and craft.'

They are startled. The Edict has stood for a long time. Vassago had been a rare example of its sanctioned and tentative revocation within the First. For Corswain, the Lion's seneschal, to reinstate them all, and bid them draw upon their once-forbidden talents is an act of heartbreaking fraternity.

That he does it, without hesitation or formality, there on the cold mountainside, shows them the extremity of the threat they face.

'You trust, your grace, perhaps too much in our potential,' Tanderion says. 'A blade grows rusty and dull without use, and it has been a long time since we even dared–'

'I know,' says Corswain. 'But you, brothers, know more of this art and artifice than I.'

'We know barely–' Cartheus begins.

'But we will do whatever we can,' says Zahariel. 'Whatever

we know, whatever old ways we remember from observation of beloved Vassago, we will employ as you command. We serve you, your grace. And I am honoured to see that you value us, no matter how o'erconfident that faith is.'

Corswain nods. He smiles. Adophel is calling to him.

'Carry him up,' he tells them.

2:iv

The Emperor Must Die

You let your words hang in the air. You pause for effect. You can see that your declaration has made a startling impact on them. Their eyes are bright. Their hearts are strong. Some wipe away tears with hands that are almost trembling. Even the whispering has stopped. Your rallying speeches to your men have always been the keenest weapons on your belt. You needed to set them straight, and you have done so. There will be no hesitation now.

'Let us finish what we have begun,' you say. You turn. 'Now, someone had an issue to raise. A question, when I came in. Does it still stand?'

They glance at each other.

'The shields, my lord...' says your equerry.

'Are down,' you say.

'My lord?'

'On my command, the voids have been lowered,' you say.

'When did you give that command?' one of them asks.

'When I chose to give it,' you snap. 'It was my decision as Warmaster, and I don't believe you get to question that.'

'My lord,' your equerry says, exhibiting some agitation, 'elements of the Fifth have retaken the port of Lion's Gate from your brother Mortarion. Indeed, we fear–'

'The White Scars should be commended for their tenacity,' you remark with a nod that says you are still man enough to acknowledge the courage of your foe. 'What of it?'

'The port's guns are operational,' says Falkus Kibre. 'They are firing upon our fleet elements. Without shields, we are vulnerable–'

'I'll tell you what makes us vulnerable,' you bark, hard enough to make the Widowmaker flinch. 'I have seen the intelligence reports. The intercepts.'

'My lord, Great Lupercal,' says your equerry, 'what reports are you speaking of?'

You pick up the data-slate from a nearby console, open the files, and hold it up.

'Transmissions,' you say. 'Intercepted transmissions. From Roboute and the Lion.'

They look at you in horror. They had no idea. You are forced, once again, to remind yourself how much more capable than them you are. Your perceptions, your insights, your understanding. You have always excelled, and now your powers are magnified by the gifts invested in you. The data on the slate is near gibberish. None of them could make sense of it, or discern the danger it represents. Only you could read the truth.

'Our enemy's reinforcement is rushing down on us, headlong,' you say, projecting the slate's data onto the repeater screens around the bridge so they can all view it. 'They are, perhaps, three days away. I'll stake my life it's not more than five. Roboute and the Lion, with their Legions. With their vengeance fleets. With their indignation and their pathetic notions of loyalty. That's what makes us vulnerable, my sons.'

You set the tablet down and look at them.

'We will destroy them when they arrive,' you state. 'We will break them as we broke the Legions of the Praetorian and the Khagan and the Brightest One. But their intervention will make our task more difficult. An unnecessary impediment. Only a fool fights on two fronts unless he has to. Isn't that right, Lev?'

Beside the table, something nods.

'Indeed so. Then it is my judgment that the Throne must be empty when they arrive. We finish this, and then we turn to face them. One battle followed by another, not two at once. This is elementary combat doctrine, my sons. Why are you struggling with it? We bring Terra to compliance before they arrive. Indeed, that will break them. How could it not? Can you imagine their faces, Guilliman and the Lion, when they realise they have come too late? That the lies they were racing to preserve are all undone? There will *be* no fight. They are not that stupid. They will surrender, and kneel before us, and beg us to forgive them. Or they will flee in despair. Either way, one victory resolves the other.'

'But how does lowering our shields bring about a victory?' Maloghurst asks.

That does it, really. You can't be blamed, in truth. Has the momentous nature of the hour rendered them stupid? Are they deliberately testing your patience? Well, test no more.

You slap him, a backhand across the face. The force of the blow hurls your insolent equerry across the bridge and into the guard rails, which bend under the impact. He collapses to the deck, as twisted as ever. There is blood. Serves him right.

'The Emperor must die,' you tell them all. 'He is the only thing that matters. He has hidden this whole time behind his walls and his gates, behind his armies and his engines. He has cowered from me. He has sent his sons, our brothers, to fight for him, to throw away their lives in a futile effort to stop us. And every one of those lives I have mourned, and

regretted having to take, because it should have been his. He
hopes, prays, that he can remain hidden until his wayward
sons arrive. So we must tempt him out. We must entice him.
We must make him think he has some fleeting chance to win
this and retain some dignity in the eyes of his sons. He wants
me. *Me*. I won't go to him and play the game his way. I will
lure him out. Let him have his try, for I am more than ready.'

'So… it is a ploy? A trap?' asks Sejanus.

'It will seem a mistake, or a malfunction,' you say. You smile.
You show them reassurance. 'It is the flaw he has been looking for and waiting for and praying for. He will not be able
to resist. He will think it a tactical masterstroke that will take
me unawares. Our enemies gather for a final push, but the
Emperor must die *first*.'

There is silence.

'No more questions?' you ask. 'Good. Go. Prepare. Prepare
to greet a boarding action. Tell the First Captain to finish his
work, and sack the Palace. Burn it all. Kill for the living and
kill for the dead. Leave nothing but a heap of ash and stone,
and a throne for me to sit on.'

You see them resolved. Good. Some seem eager. This is
grim work, but it will soon be over. They are relieved you
are taking on the main burden yourself. The rest is just operational necessity.

You wonder if they should refinish their plate in black for
this final stage, to signify respect for the enemy fallen. You
think it would be an appropriate mark of honour if they
dressed their gear in mourning.

But they already have.

2:v

A broken sword

As Vassago's pall-bearers wind up the track towards the Portal, Corswain joins Adophel on an outcrop of rock. The drop beneath is sheer, a natural pass that was left unaltered by geo-engineering because it was well suited for defence. Ash snow billows around them, and settles on the dead below, the jumbled corpses of the astrotelepathic choir that once sang in the mountain. Their bodies have been prised from the mangled chantry-tiers of the Grand Chamber, and cast aside without ceremony. They are tumbled across the slopes, like the scree and wreckage of some human avalanche.

Corswain sees the look on Adophel's face.

'You heard?' he asks.

'It is my duty to hear and know,' says Adophel.

'And advise?'

'Why else would I need to hear and know?'

'So advise me, Chapter Master. Am I slipping the leashes too much on the warp-seers?'

'Far too much,' says Adophel. 'Their employment is governed by the most strict–'

'I know, old friend, but–'

Adophel raises a hand gently to halt Corswain's reply. 'I had not yet reached my advice, your grace,' he says. 'That was your request, was it not?'

Corswain nods.

'You place too much trust in them,' says the Chapter Master softly, 'or perhaps, more correctly, too much hope. Part of me wishes, against decency, that they have more of the seer-craft in them than is seemly, and will startle us by performing the deed you desire. The other part... well, it longs to be confounded. It hopes they will fail, and prove our suspicions of all immaterial dabblers false and defamatory. But what matters now is... well, *all things*, a greater contest... perhaps the greatest of all. There is a beast to hunt and slay, the most infamous of all, and to stand a chance, we must be pragmatic. At the door of death, we must fight by any means, or there will be no First to have integrity. In Aldurukh, in ancient days, there was a proverb. "A broken sword is better than none at all." Those four Caliban-born sons may be our broken sword. Not the most sporting or gallant weapon, but all that we have to hand. So, there is my advice.'

'And it accords with my instinct,' Corswain replies. 'But... you will watch them?'

'Hell's blood, of course. Like a hawk. Which is why I hear and know. And one hint of baneful idolatry, I will snap their spines myself.'

'And mine for permitting it?'

Adophel turns his craggy face. He sees Corswain's rueful smile. 'In a heartbeat,' he says.

'Good,' says Corswain. 'If all is lost, then the honour of our Legion will pass from this world unblemished.'

'I think we will all be cleansed by valour 'fore then,' says Adophel. He unclamps the sensorium from his left vambrace and hands it to the seneschal. Corswain studies the display. The data it presents is incomplete, and scabbed with interference. But enough is comprehensible.

'An army?'

Adophel nods. 'An army, of considerable magnitude. It is, if we can trust the read, three days out at least. But it is advancing rapidly, and without doubt moving towards us. We are the only possible target.'

'A traitor army?'

'Yes. They issue no code signal or cipher, but what else could it be? A formation drawn off from the siege force to prosecute us. There is chatter too, on the vox. I have teased it out and isolated it. Heathen bile, incomprehensible. But a voice we know.'

'It's him?'

'I'd wager my life it's him.'

'Then I command you make us ready for combat, Chapter Master,' says Corswain.

2:vi

The last gathering

The first of the champions are about to arrive.

I sit upon the throne, facing the Silver Door, and wait for them.

Not *the* throne, of course. *My* throne. It is but a poor, high-backed wooden chair, lacquered red, and marked with certain sigils of my devising. It is kept in a side chamber off the main nave, and brought out for my use when I am required to enact the formal duties of Regent. I have it placed with its back to my silent lord and the great dais, so that it appears that the sun is rising behind me.

The intimidating proconsuls, Uzkarel and Caecaltus, have brought it hence for me today, and set it carefully in its spot. Either one of them could carry it on the crook of a single finger, but they insist on bearing it between them, in all solemnity, as though it was an artefact of veneration.

It is not. It is simply somewhere for me to sit, for I am old and almost always tired. *Chairs, thrones, dungeons, rooms, men, gods*. Words are strange and imprecise, and unintended significances too easily applied. I have always found symbols far more fluent and explicit when it comes to expressing sophisticated meaning.

I am old. But I am not tired now. I am fizzing with expectation. I stare at the Silver Door, so far away from me, as though staring at it will make it open faster. I tap my staff – *tick! tick! tick!* – against the tiled floor.

Come now! Come now! The clocks run out! Let us get this matter underway!

An invisible hand rests gently on top of mine to dissuade me from fidgeting with the stick.

I stop. I smile to myself ruefully.

'Yes,' I murmur, 'I *am* impatient, my lord. Forgive me.'

He does.

'Nervous, perhaps,' I reply. 'Preparing myself.'

He whispers.

'No,' I assure him. 'No second thoughts. I have not changed my mind.'

He wonders.

'No, old friend,' I say, 'I fully understand what you are going to ask of me.'

Crowds are starting to gather in this place they call the Throne Room, and in the pavilions and chambers adjoining it. I have beckoned to us all those we will need to support this undertaking: senior lords, war courtiers, high functionaries, intelligencers, artificers. A mere three or four thousand people, the necessary logistical backbone, technical and bureaucratic. I sent my thought-summons, little sigils of compressed meaning and instruction, flashing out like shooting stars through the hierarchy of the Sanctum, hand-picking the appropriate personnel. They enter, in small groups, wide-eyed and hushed, through the side doors and ante-ports around the edges of the nave, and congregate in huddles. I can smell their anxiety, their awe, their dread. There is palpable anticipation, an excitement that I share with them, and have not felt since–

That I have not felt, *ever*. This surpasses the Declaration of Unification, the Call to Crusade, even the Great Triumph. I have, I suppose, grown too used to the monuments and punctuations of history. But this, I cannot deny it, has a suspension, as if everyone, and everything, and everywhere, has turned to look.

At what we do now. What *he* does now.

They gather, meek and quiet, around the Silver Door at the south end of the nave, along the lustrous floor of outer aisles, and they crowd the triforium galleries above. The choirs are singing only the low plainsong needed to maintain psycho-mantic equilibrium. No one dares approach, nor should they. From where they stand, cowed by the scope of this impossible room, all they see is a remote figure on a faraway golden seat, as still and silent as it has ever been. Beneath that outward stillness, my lord does a thousand things every second, a thousand things that only one or two of them at most could even begin to comprehend.

He stokes the wards that guard the last of the Palace. He radiates controlled burns of telaethesic energy that weaken and shrivel the Neverborn instantiating closest to our fastness. He watches and moderates the flow of the endwar, at both micro and macro levels. He moves through the minds of individual warriors as they crunch and gasp and stab, observing the flow of combat at a granular level; and simultaneously, he watches from above, like one of poor Jaghatai's finest hawks, hovering on an updraught, beholding, below him, entire regiments and armies as they twist and pivot and brawl. He shaves and shapes the etheric turmoil of the webway, guiding and conducting immaterial force via the Throne's ancient machineries, so that the doomsday pressure can be held at bay. And he tries, as best he can, to soothe the minds of a billion terrified human souls as they flee and panic and scramble for some vestige of safety.

I fear I will be able to manage but a *fraction* of those things.

The expectant tension increases and becomes razor-sharp as the Silver Door opens and the Custodes Pylorus admit the train of armourers. In they troop, in their imbricated iron-and-brass garb, ceremonial versions of the work armour they wear in the smithies. Every man and woman of them is deaf, the occupational hazard of work in the constant din of the hammering rooms. They haul and push the burnished carts on which my lord's wargear lies, brought from the sealed chambers of the House of Weapons.

A tight, hard hush falls. He has not spoken, but his intent is plain.

I rise from my seat. The first two champions are here.

2:vii

Admission

'Brother,' Sanguinius whispers, an aside. 'Look.'

Rogal Dorn and Sanguinius step through the Silver Door together, blades drawn and centred to their brows in respect and fealty. They enter the eerie, infinite glare of the Throne Room. Dorn is flanked by senior Huscarls, and the Angel by solemn Sanguinary Guards. The golden Sentinels at either side of the great door respectfully drop their chins as one. The growing crowd of worthies parts in deference at the sight of the primarchs to make a path.

Dorn sees what has drawn his beloved brother's attention.

The high company of the Imperial Armoury has entered ahead of them, and their procession is beginning its slow, dignified advance along the six kilometres of the nave.

'Then it is upon us,' says Rogal Dorn, his voice barely audible. Neither he nor Sanguinius have ever become used to this chamber, no matter the number of times they have come here. It triggers vertigo, acrophobia, agoraphobia and kenophobia. Despite the numinous and pervasive light, it inspires a fear of darkness too. It is the only place in creation where such feelings manifest for them. The endless space seems to whisper to them of their mortality, as though every stone and tile and column is intent on reminding them of their insignificance.

But that's not what Dorn feels today. His voice, and heart, are stilled by the sight of his father's weapons, brought through in honour.

The gathering crowd around them stirs, both fearful and elated. Dorn glances at Sanguinius. There is joy and sadness in both of them. Joy, sadness, and infinite fatigue. This is what they had hoped for and also what they have dreaded. Is the drawing-in of the great armours a sign they have failed in their duties, requiring their father to finish what they could not? Or is it a sign of their success, that they have held the line, beyond all expectation, long enough for this moment to become possible?

Simply that it is happening is enough.

They look to the Sentinels. 'You are admitted, lords,' says one.

The brothers sheathe their blades.

'Are we instructed to approach?' asks Dorn.

'At once.'

Dorn turns, but Sanguinius catches his arm and stops him. For a second, they stand shoulder to shoulder, eye to eye.

'You've performed the most extraordinary feat,' Sanguinius says unexpectedly. 'Please remember that.'

Dorn is taken aback by the frankness of the comment, and the innocent sincerity with which it is expressed. His startled half-smile wavers with imprisoned emotion, a flash of light at the high slit-window of an otherwise impregnable keep.

'A mere... fraction of your deeds, brother,' he replies awkwardly. 'You closed the Gate. You locked–'

Sanguinius shakes his head. 'I was a warrior, Rogal. Just a warrior. You were the one who mattered.'

He embraces the Praetorian, the spontaneous impulse of a child. As with his guileless comment, the embrace is unexpected and unselfconscious, a rare display of emotion, especially in such a gathering. For a moment, Dorn freezes, then he completes the embrace. When they step back, a single teardrop glints on the Brightest One's pauldron where the Praetorian rested his head, and a single drop of blood gleams on the Praetorian's backplate where Sanguinius pressed his hand.

'Not yet.'

They both look aside. The crowd has parted again. Constantin Valdor has entered, his spear across his shoulder. The Custodes Pylorus do not drop their chins: they kneel, for they are his.

'Not yet,' he repeats, a growl. 'Your plaudits and self-congratulation.'

'You are owed much yourself, Constantin,' says Sanguinius.

Valdor shrugs. His armour is pitted and filthy. He eyes them both.

'If any is owed and any necessary,' says Valdor, 'then it can wait until the outcome is settled.'

'No,' says Sanguinius. 'Let's imagine it can't. None of us may live to see that outcome, so I'll make damn sure I say it, while I still can, and you can both listen. You've both excelled, and you're both owed, and I am proud to call you brothers.'

'Brothers, now?' sneers Valdor. 'Brothers, is it?'

'In every way that matters, Constantin,' says Sanguinius. He sighs. 'I meant no slight by it, captain-general. But now I see that–'

'Stop,' says Valdor. He sniffs, and his brows furrow. 'I recognise the spirit of your words, Ninth son,' he says grudgingly.

'And… and if this *is* our only moment, as you suggest, then… then I tell you I have nothing but honour in my heart for you both.'

His eyes narrow as he looks at Sanguinius.

'But no embrace is necessary,' he adds. The remark is intended lightly, and the tension slackens. But Dorn can see how wracked with unspoken, perhaps unspeakable pain Valdor has become since they were last face to face, as though the captain-general has seen and done too much. It hurts to behold that in a being of such legendary fortitude. Dorn looks away, at the receding procession.

'Shall we fall in behind?' he suggests.

'Yes,' says Valdor. 'You two should. His will is known to me already. I will follow as soon as I have issued my last instructions.'

He turns aside. Attending him are two giants of the Custodian order whose plate is so coated with soot it seems almost black. The grim Wardens of the Dark Cells are a rare sight even in the Throne Room. With them, Dorn sees, is Kaeria Casryn and seven others of the Silent Sisterhood. They may have been there all along, and their null states only just registered by his senses.

Valdor begins to instruct them, his voice low. Sanguinius and Dorn turn and follow the armourers in, side by side.

'He's going to fight,' murmurs Sanguinius as they advance.

'I think he is,' Dorn replies.

'Should we weep or rejoice?' asks Sanguinius.

'I think it is just cause for both,' his brother says.

2:viii

―――――――

The Order in the dark

In the mountain, the wind sings through odd angles. It has always been a sacred space. In the oldest of all times, when men were mere figures with spears in the great landscape, tracking ibex and deer through the foothills, the mountain whispered, and some men put down their spears and left their game trails, and ascended, against all common sense, to penetrate the darkness of its worming caves and crystal-threaded tunnels. They were the shamans, and to them the mountain granted the first insights of otherness. Their rituals were ancient before the Emperor was born, and the mountain is why the Palace was raised in this high, remote place.

As with all the rest of Terra, the Emperor refashioned the mountain to suit his needs. Tunnels of steel and ceramite replaced the ancient cave systems, and heat-bored shafts replaced connate flues and chimneys. Cavities of intricate and exact geometric design were cut inside the rock surrounding the Great Chamber, in whose gleaming, spherical space was raised the silver and auramite chancel tiers of the astropaths.

Great machineries of secret design were set deep in the rock range, their inlaid conduits aligned to enhance and amplify the natural wonder of the resonating quartz and chyrosite. The mountain's natural sonority was harnessed by rational science, and industrialised by etheric technology, and its eternal whispers were weaponised into a blinding scream.

Yoked to the service of the youthful Imperium, the mountain forgot all of its old names, some already half-lost or cancelled into myth, and became the Astronomican. It became the Light of All Worlds, the inescapable radiance of mankind's supremacy, and the visible expression of the Emperor's guidance.

It mutters to itself, still.

Even now the light is out, the choirs butchered, and the precious apparatus broken and defaced, it mutters still.

The brethren-leaders of the Caliban formation leave Vassago's body in an undercroft, in the care of bedesman serfs, and withdraw to an amplifier sub-vault deep beneath the Great Chamber where they can be alone. The vault, heat-finished and squared off, is nevertheless a remnant of the original caverns. It smells of cold, and its walls glimmer with the mineral traces of quartz and lustrous anthospar. There is no echo, none at all, despite the emptiness. As they speak, sparks of light, cinnabar and violet, dart across the crystal veins, as though triggered by certain words.

'I do not understand you,' says Cartheus. 'We silenced Vassago because he pledged to Corswain's side, yet now you do the same?'

'I do,' says Zahariel. 'And so must you, without demur.'

'If we are to go along with him,' snaps Cartheus, 'why kill Vassago? His death becomes meaningless.'

'His death had meaning for him,' Zahariel replies. 'It showed him he had gone too far. He had spoken too openly. It showed him we Mystai will not tolerate those who break our confidences. I said what I said to Corswain to protect the rest of us.'

'Protect how?' asks Tanderion.

Zahariel, a noted warrior long before he came to Corswain's side, stares at the three of them. He can feel their stubborn disapproval. 'We can't hide forever,' he says. 'Vassago knew that. He had become too enamoured of Corswain. Considered him a brother. I am certain he was close to unburdening himself and telling Corswain of the Order. Of what the Order represents. For that alone, he died. The Mystai tradition must guard itself completely. And I think the sight of what we found here, the daemon that had made this place its nest, troubled him greatly. I believe it made him doubt that immaterial powers can ever be subdued to our will. Such was his trust in Corswain, Vassago was close to speaking out.'

He turns and stares at the dim rock wall, where once men limned dye-marks with their hands to design the future.

'Corswain is a fine leader,' he mutters, almost to himself. 'That cannot be denied. I admire him. I see why Vassago softened in his bearing towards him. If any can lead us out of this, it is Corswain, for we are in this now, my brothers, to the hilt. We have come to Terra, into the mouth of hell, and our side has been chosen for us. If we are to live, and the Order to continue, we must commit.'

'*Has* our side been chosen?' Asradael asks.

Zahariel seizes him by the throat and squeezes. Asradael sinks slowly to his knees. The other two look on, aghast.

'You *saw* what was here, brother,' Zahariel hisses. 'You *saw* what Vassago saw. Have you no wits? It was a thing of Chaos, raw and terrible. I have no doubt its ilk has made slaves of all the so-called traitors, aye, even the dread Lupercal. Did you somehow *mistake* it for the Spirit of Caliban to which we vow fealty?'

'No–' Asradael gasps.

'No, indeed. The spirit that guides us is a pure thing of the immaterial realm, the circle-serpent from which flows the wisdom of the Mystai. We are sons of Caliban, sons of Luther. We will know no master, not any who command from the gilded Throne of Terra. Not Lupercal. Not the Emperor. That is our *side* in this.'

'Let him be,' says Tanderion.

'Yes, fine words, brother,' says Cartheus. 'But in practice, as worthless as dung. This is wartime, and a side must be chosen.'

Zahariel releases his grip, and Asradael rocks forward, gasping.

'Of course it must,' says Zahariel, staring at Cartheus. 'Do you believe you have a choice? Would you side with the others against Corswain? Would you side with the Emperor's Children and the World Eaters and the insane Sons of Horus? Our side is chosen for us, and it was chosen from the moment we set forth under Corswain's banner. We fight for ourselves, not for traitor or loyalist cause, but for Caliban. And that means casting our lot in with the side that will serve us best. Brothers, the loyal alignment must win this war, or all is lost, so we *must* help them. Vassago was on the brink of saying too much, so we took his words away. But we must complete Vassago's work. Make this beacon shine. Win this war. Then our destiny will be ours to shape again.'

'And when all is done?' asks Cartheus.

'Consider the gains we could make,' Zahariel says to Cartheus. 'If Corswain emerges victorious from this bloodshed, and his victory is achieved with our aid, we will have him in certitude. He will value us, and honour us.'

'And we can turn him to our advantage?' asks Tanderion. He grins at the notion, a wolf scenting prey.

'I think so,' says Zahariel. Spark-lights flicker in the rock wall, mimicking his cadence. 'Turn him, or use him. If the Lion is dead, Corswain will be lord of the First when this is over, and we will have his ear. If the Lion lives, then we will have influence over his successor. The brute Lion's been gone too long. The First looks to Corswain, for he has been steadfast and present. The Lion would find he has few friends here, and none on Caliban. So we will serve Lord Seneschal Corswain. To the death, if necessary. We will become invaluable allies that he can never renounce. Brothers, has he not already remade us Librarians, so we may practise openly?'

They nod.

'Then we will build on that and cement that trust. Suitably vizarded to protect its identity, the Order will stand forward and prove its worth to him.'

He pauses, and removes something from the satchel under his robe.

'You'd… go *that* far?' asks Cartheus, amazed.

'Yes, brother. Corswain must understand the honour he is receiving. We must impress him, by our deeds *and* by our appearance. Though not of the Order, he is of Caliban after all. He must be made to feel the weight of tradition and the old line upon him, and marvel that he can be worthy of such prestige. When the time comes, I will wear the face I wore when we came to Vassago. For him, that face was a punishment. For Corswain, it will be an accolade.'

'You would dare?' Asradael growls, rising back to his feet.

'I dare indeed,' says Zahariel, 'with the blessing and permission of Lord Luther. A face is a face, and a mask is a mask, and the meanings and significances are ours to employ. Lord Seneschal Corswain will be served by four loyal Librarians. And by something else.'

He can tell they all have their doubts, but then, they appreciate so much less than him. Though Mystai, they have not yet ascended to his level of enlightenment. He reads their misgivings, and gently steers them with a deft psionic touch. His power is low and silent, but inexorably erosive, like a glacier or a mature river. It firmly alters the course of the other minds it touches. He intends to work on Corswain in the same way. Bring those who are reluctant round to the right way of thinking, without them ever realising they have been subject to persuasion.

One by one, they nod in agreement, even Asradael. Zahariel offers them his hand.

'There has never been a war like this, brothers,' says Zahariel. 'So there has never been a moment like this. The Order can turn this disaster to its great advantage.'

'The gramyries of Ouroboros will instruct us in the repair of these devices,' says Cartheus, almost eager suddenly. 'The lore of the Triumvirate Engines can be applied, if we are careful and circumspect.'

'That was Vassago's plan,' says Zahariel. 'You have that lore by rote?'

'Since boyhood,' Cartheus replies, for they had all been tutored by the Mystai teachers, and each had committed certain texts to memory.

'The Bestiaries of the Great Hunt will serve us too,' says Tanderion, 'and I hold those by recollection. Each verse, each engram. Through them we can channel etheric force.'

Zahariel nods. 'Then we are agreed. Are we not, brother?'

Asradael glares, then joins his hands with the others. Sparks flash around the rock seams of the walls like angry fireflies.

'We are,' Asradael says. 'In my nonage, I was charged to learn the Chanson of Mamenezy. I can recite it without flaw. Its charms and bindings will reinforce the engrams of the Bestiaries.'

'Then we must to work,' says Zahariel. 'But we must work swiftly, for Chaos is coming to claim this mountain back.'

'How do you know?' asks Cartheus.

'Look at the walls, my brothers,' says Zahariel. 'Look at the signs, the marks that flash and resonate, and read them well. The future is writ before our eyes. Chaos is coming hence to harrow us, and its name is Typhus.'

2:ix

What the Angel has seen

And now they approach. The war plate my master has not worn, the sword he has not drawn, since the Great Crusade, are nested on the armourers' velvet biers. Rogal and Sanguinius follow the procession, solemn and pensive.

I heave upon my planted staff, and drag myself up from my little wooden throne. I can taste Rogal's impatience, perhaps even a little eagerness. He has held the reins of command since this began. Now he wants to *be commanded*. Now he wants to fight, and carry his fury to our enemy in person, not through the remote instrument of some army or division.

He will get his wish. We are not about to flee this field of war. There will be fighting enough for all of us.

In Sanguinius, I taste only pain and fear. He is wounded more grievously than he wants to admit or show. He is afraid he has fought too much, and too recklessly, to be fit for the final battle.

I fear he's right.

But he's hiding more than wounds. He's been hiding

something else for much longer. He thinks I don't know, but
my mind is busy, busy, everywhere. I know of the escalating
visions that have been haunting him.

Sanguinius has inherited, like damned Magnus, his father's
more esoteric aspect. A state of higher grace, and in that grace,
a visionary foresight. But I believe that, in some specific area,
that foresight has begun to exceed his father's. The Angel's
visions have been coming with increasing frequency. He tries
to cover them, but they are sharp thorns snagged in the silk
of his thoughts. When his attention has been on other things,
I have slipped into his mind, examined the visions to discern
their value and origin. They have all been glimpses of futures,
some through his brothers' eyes.

But there is one in particular that he keeps close and will
not, through force of will, reveal, even to my mindsight. I
have gently tried to prise it from him, but the way to it is
utterly blocked by a great fortress wall he has built from a
single burning question.

Why must we suffer?

I share my concerns with the one I serve as I watch their
slow approach.

He knows already.

'Of course you do,' I murmur. 'And what of the boy's
question?'

+I will answer him. I will answer every question they ask.
I owe them that.+

'Good,' I whisper. 'Good. But I wonder… why *that* question? What calamity has he foreseen that makes that question
so impenetrable and absolute?'

+Can you not guess, Malcador? He has seen me fall.+

I breathe deeply to steady my nerves.

'And what might you tell him, with regard to that?' I ask.

+I will tell him that I will not. I will face down the Four

and deny them, and I will cut the strings of their deluded puppet, my own first-found, and I will return to the throne triumphant, and take my place for ten thousand years, and ten times ten thousand more.+

I nod.

'Make sure of it, old friend,' I murmur, 'for I will not be here to hold you to the promise.'

2:x

Vectors

There is only the mountain.

We see only the mountain. We turn our backs on the false, golden city and march towards the mountain instead. The Emperor must die, but someone else can kill him.

Our Pale King is gone, but his commandments remain. Death must guard itself, and scythe down the vulgar fraudulence of mortality. Like a fever, we will consume.

Parts of us doubt. Parts of us think the port of the Lion's Gate, stolen from us by the savages of the V, should be reconquered. Other parts buzz with desire to be at the final fortress when it cracks open, so that our name can be recorded as the cause of death.

We will allow some latitude. The corpus of Terra is in its terminal stage, and its palsied, myalgic organs offer no resistance to our infection, so we will spread like wildfire, unchecked, decaying and diseasing that which remains. Under Serob Kargul, alive with meat-flies within his metal frame, we will advance upon the Sanctum and there, with Vorx and Kadex

Ilkarion at our side, we will sow end-stage corruption. Thus will the haemorrhagic truth of the Rot be conjugated.

The stolen port we will assail, but on it waste no great strength. The White Scars are few, and they have, in some great fit, like the false-dawn flare of vitality that spikes just before death, resolved to open active fire on the Lupercalian fleet. Unwise, little hawks. You have drawn wrath and damnation down upon yourselves, for the fleet will answer and annihilate you.

The Pale King's words to us were clear. The mountain, the hollow hope. *That* must be our true target. Hope must be crushed and extinguished, resected and cauterised before it can metastasise and spread. We will not fail in that. And it is our wish too, the death rattle of our father be damned. His death will not hold us back.

So that is where we spread, advancing across the pedregal wastes towards the mountain, to infect and rot away all hope. We will send our dreams before us to plague the foe and eat away all resolve.

We walk with Caipha Morarg, who cannot disguise his scepticism at our decision, but dares not repudiate the order of his beloved king. We walk with Crosius, who understands our aim, and understands our particular ache for this objective. We walk with Melphior Craw and Skulidas Gehrerg and all the other warriors that the fever of the warp has swollen into monstrous, behemoth champions.

We will crush hope, yes, for that is our pathology. We will be destroyers, for the Hive, like a twitching ball of maggots, writhes within us all. But we will also annihilate Corswain, for the Pale King has promised us that Corswain is there. Our long duel, for good or ill, has run its course, and illness will prevail. Corswain of the First will choke on the congealed flux of his own lungs, and rot in our arms.

We will be aggressive. We will be virulent. We will be incurable.

The Hound of Caliban thinks he is immune. He commands a mountain, and believes we cannot permeate his cordons. But we can seep in through the smallest gap, or enter as spores in the slightest breath, and multiply. We will open fistulas in his bulwarks and transfuse our septicaemic influence into his dark angelic blood. We will swarm as prions through pores, ooze as helminths into orifices, and our drones, pouring like sizzling smoke from the bone funnels and flutes of our back, will be numberless, a legion of legions, and bloat the sky with lymphatic darkness.

The mountain, hollow like a cyst, filled with loyalist pus to be evacuated and drained, is distant, a good material measure from our position. For a conventional army, it is three days' march away, four or five perhaps, allowing for considerations of armour advance and terrain. But the lytic malaise of the warp permeates this world, reducing dimensions to jelly, slicing distance and suturing it back together in new proportions. We are closer, far closer, than Corswain imagines. He will feel our bacteriophagic caress long before he is ready.

And our diseased god, grandfather-lord of decay, has shown us another truth, through febrile dream and delirium. Our god has shown us Corswain's comorbidity. The cancer is already within him, eating away at his heart, asymptomatic but congenital. It is morbid, inoperable, invasive and degenerating. When it finally erupts, it will be fulminant and refactory.

For we have seen the sparks of Chaos in his meat and in his bones, a parasitic wastage deep within the body of the First Legion. We sense the flicker of activity, the chancre of Chaos within his own ranks, psyker-whelps sired on Caliban, already picking and scratching at the scabs of the immateria. We will barely have to fight him, for we will already be fighting him from within.

For we are the termination. We are the Death Guard. We are the Destroyer.

We are Typhus.

2:xi

Fear made flesh

Dark, feral figures swarm Logis Gateway and Clanium Square. Fafnir Rann's elements have been driven out into the quadrangles and scholar-courts beside the library, and there is no room to recompose. The entire length of the Hall of Governance is ablaze, wrecked by the daemon-fight they have just endured, and the assault position Rann hoped to establish and hold is lost. As the Sons of Horus – and he knew it would be them – begin to pour through the gateway from the Maxis Processional, his formations are not locked in and waiting to greet them, they are in disarray.

Plans die as fast as men, and the pavements around the burning hall are littered with bodies in yellow plate. Beliefs die too – long-cherished, long-trusted beliefs in method and technique.

Some things don't die. Rann doesn't know what it was they found in the Hall of Governance other than it was nigh-on impossible to kill. He buried his axe-blades in its bolt-shot mass, but he still isn't sure if it is actually dead. He isn't certain it was alive to begin with. Rann thinks it was probably waiting for them, that *it* found *them*, which means that all the normal principles of combat are null and void. Everything he has learned, every battlefield tactic the Praetorian schooled into him, is meaningless. This notion distresses him more than any aspect of the physical danger surrounding him. The art of war as practised by the Imperial Fists is no longer trustworthy.

He feels a sort of numbing loss. The rubrics of the world have come undone. This was supposed to be a bounding counter-attack – hasty, yes, and born out of dire necessity, but calculated and precise. He had identified the threat, the numbers of the foe, the direction of movement, and he had formulated a robust response to meet, block and decapitate the enemy advance. Textbook methodology. Except, suddenly, the enemy was behind them. It was where it couldn't and shouldn't be. It was already among them. What good is rational methodology when the foe can just appear? When it can come out of nowhere? When it can come out of mirrors?

He and his surviving men are pinned. There is nowhere to fall back to. Rann would only consider that option if it allowed them a chance to reinforce a line, but lines are meaningless. Plans are meaningless. The direction of enemy advance is meaningless. The thing in the hall, that shrieking thing that claimed the lives of so many of his men and left raking fingernail punctures in Rann's armour, was the greatest nightmare of the Imperial Fists made manifest.

Rann tries to shake the thought off, but it won't leave him alone. The supreme fear of the Imperial Fists, if they could admit to a fear at all, is to be outplayed by unpredictable variables. *Not to know.* The war-craft of the VII has always depended on knowing: knowing the location, the angles of advance, terrain variables. Such specifics become their weapons, even in a fight this precarious and desperate.

Not any more.

And it is as though the thing in the Hall of Governance knew that. It hadn't come to simply tear their bodies, it had come to shred their minds. It was a psychological coup, severing their faith in method as fast as it severed limbs. It was as if their darkest phobia had come to life. Worse, it was as though their most secret and deepest doubts had *created* it.

Rann tries to gather himself, but there is nothing to cling to. Plans are pointless, and the rules are vanished. The enemy, now in part or totally imbued by some Neverborn magic, can be anywhere and everywhere. Intel and preparation are worthless. The trusted mindset of the Imperial Fists cannot be trusted.

Rann thinks that this is what human fear must taste like. He is conditioned to process fear so it doesn't affect him, but that conditioning seems to have failed or malfunctioned. Rann is heedless of the bolt shells shrieking past him, the explosions that crater the courts, heedless even of the figures in filthy plate that mob through the outer quadrangles. They are just foes and dangers. He knows how to face foes and dangers. He doesn't know how to face unprocessed fear, and now that settles upon him.

He hears men calling for instruction, fear staining their voices too. He forces his mind to focus. He studies the data-flow of his retinal display. His auto-senses are screening out the harsh stimuli of explosions and flash-fire. What his visor's sensoria render is a patchwork of heat-as-colour, laced by the geometric graphics of structures and architectural solids. On that float icons, the tag-markers broadcast by each legionary's helmet system to afford instant overview and identification even during the sensory overload of extreme combat. Each marker is a small fist icon and a name. To his left, Calodin, Lignis and Bedwyr. Then Devarlin and the assault squad teams. To his right, the icon-cluster of Leod Baldwin's fire-team. Across the quad, the jumbled light-dots of Tarchos' squads, holding semi-cover around the buttresses of the Scholars' House.

Between them, icons that have gone still and dropped to a pale half-tone: the markers of the fallen, their systems still transmitting at low power so that bodies can be found and recovered.

So many. Too many.

The Sons of Horus spill into the quads. To one side, armour supports them, tread weapons and sooty war machines that erupt through walls and sub-gates, scattering masonry and crushing barricades. They clatter up new hills of broken stone, and fire their turret weapons, loosing concussive hell into Rann's positions. The side wall of the Archivum collapses like a released curtain and buries three squads in an avalanche of bricks. Rann expected the traitors to have long since turned off their tag-markers, but they have not, and his system still reads them. Wolf's head icons, the old mark of the XVI. But the names appending those icons have become illegible. They are incomprehensible non-names, as though the generating algorithm has corrupted, or is simply unable to form letters and characters graphically.

Wolf's head icons and broken hell-names.

So many. Too many.

Rann yells into his squad-to-squad, and concentrates fire on the largest of the breach points. His fire-teams open up, and so do those of Sergeant Tarchos and, to the left across the range of quadrangles, Fisk Halen. Mass-reactive shells from Astartes boltguns and heavier support weapons bracket the breach point. Visibility drops instantly as the area torches with thousands of explosive detonations and vomiting clouds of dust. Half-seen traitors quake, twist and topple. Some icons go to pale half-tone, but, it seems, so few.

Something is leading the Sons of Horus in. It is a cloven-footed horror the size of a Knight engine. Its wings are vast, but still don't seem big enough to lift its mass off the broken ground. The flex and flap of them, which Rann can hear, like the sound of sawing rope, seems more intended to fan the flames and drive the wall of smoke towards them. The thing is hunched and horned. Its eyes are orange gashes of neon. Rann does not want to look at those eyes. He doesn't want to acknowledge that the thing, somehow, is still wearing the distorted pauldrons of XVI Legion Cataphractii plate.

It has a tag-marker. The icon is a mere blister of contaminated pixels to his auto-senses.

Rann reloads. He orders a sustained concentration of fire. He ignores the thump and thwack of impacts as men drop all around him.

A hail of fire – a stupendous hail of fire – crosses the area from his right. For a few seconds, it becomes a torrential deluge. Rann sees dark, misshapen figures writhe and fall.

A counter-strike comes in, crossing the head of the Maxis Processional like a steady flow of magma, burning everything in its path. Figures in yellow, shields locked, driving in across Rann's flank. Rann sees the raised standard a second before the data of his retinal display updates with marker codes. Archamus. Master of the Huscarls. Second Of That Name. *Archamus…*

For the last months, Archamus has served in the Grand Borealis, Dorn's proxy in the command bastion. But Bhab has fallen, and Archamus, perhaps impatient after so many hours at a strategium, fighting the war with his mind rather than his fists, has not fallen back into the locked Sanctum to continue his duty. He has taken to the field instead.

Perhaps he couldn't retreat. Perhaps the great gate was already shut. Perhaps joining the fight was his only option. Perhaps the sight of him here is a true signifier of defeat and desperation: there is nothing left to control or command, no orders left worth giving, and no strategy to oversee. Perhaps fighting is the only option remaining.

But the sight of him. The sight of him, *here*. A wonder. Six hundred Imperial Fists, many of them Huscarl veterans, advancing in perfect *Antecessum Purgatus* and driving unbelievable fury into the enemy's ribs.

The traitors came in like a flash flood, a dirty torrent. Archamus' formation is much slower, the crawl of molten rock. But water splashes and dissipates. Lava is thick, steady and inexorable, and water turns to steam where it touches.

'He is with us!' Rann roars. 'He stands with us!'

His men roar in response and find some new stocks of courage. Halen's battle squads actually manage to edge forward six or seven metres, and engage close, swinging chainblades or firing point-blank. A portion of the enemy tide, stung by Halen's jab and blocked by the Hall of Governance, turns too wildly and meets the rolling shield wall of Archamus' advance.

A second axe-blow falls across the throat of the traitor column. From the east, bisecting the Avenue of Justice, comes a line of Blood Angels Kratos tanks and Falchion super-heavies, with Sicarans and Basilisk tractors in flank formation. The hammer of their rolling bombardment turns the top of Maxis into a forest of flame-trees. Enemy machines, turning to train on Archamus, are gutted by penetrator shells and bulk-beam weapons. Rann sees a traitor Arquitor hurled into the air, spinning, track-links whipping like a broken belt.

The Blood Angels advance through the rows of their armour, moving with fluid, surgical speed that counterpoints Archamus' steady, relentless roll. Icon markers light up. There, the squad groups of Satel Aimery, of Zealis Varens, of Zephon Sorrow-Bringer. Aimery's assault teams burn forward on their jump packs, led into the air by the rare wonder of Azkaellon, commander of the glorious Sanguinary Guard, whose augmetic wings cast him in the image of his glorious primarch. Airborne Astartes, angels of death, moving like missiles at low level, spear fire and bolter shells into the enemy breaking beneath them.

'One push to snap their neck,' Archamus roars over the vox. The Master of Huscarls' observation is true: despite their vast numbers, the head of the enemy mass is boxed in and blocked on three sides.

At once, both Halen and Aimery demand the honour. Both are well placed, their units in striking distance. But Rann is reading the field. Either strike will be anticipated, and either one could end in an overreach.

In the space of three minutes, Fafnir Rann has subconsciously rewritten the tactical rulebook in his head. Preparation and tested moves are all redundant, the honoured codes of formation warfare hopelessly inadequate. The enemy thrives on the unexpected. The Imperial Fists must learn the knack of it.

'Mine,' Rann voxes.

'My lord seneschal?' he hears the Master of Huscarls respond, trying to isolate Rann's voice from the inter-signal mayhem.

'Hold them hard,' says Rann. 'I have it.'

'Yours indeed, Fafnir.'

Rann orders meltas and flamers to the fore. He gives the command even as his men are assembling. Of all the battle groups in this crossroads of armies, his is the smallest, the weakest, and the most poorly positioned, the least likely to move or attempt a surge. That's precisely why Rann calls it, and precisely why Archamus, after months of studying the evolving madness of battle on his strategium, approves it, without hesitation. Rann, technically, outranks him, but field authority always falls to the commander with the superior position. A fundamental code of Imperial Fists warfare.

Archamus defers. He tightens his line, and communicates

holding restraint to Halen and Aimery. Rann and his men are already moving, charging across the rubble from the dead end that should have been their unmarked graves. They come at the header formations of the Sons of Horus from the least expected direction.

And they burn them.

Howling flamers and squealing meltas cut their path for them. Roasting armoured figures topple before them, incandescent, shrieking and thrashing. Impact follows a few seconds later, the winding, hammer-blow contact of Astartes clashing with Astartes in close combat, swinging mauls and chainswords, driving with broken storm-shields.

Rann's axes, *Headsman* and *Hunter*, bite deep. He guts one traitor son, and keeps running as the brute spins away, then sweeps the axe in his left hand through a spine with crunching force. Slivers of plasteel fly. He keeps moving, splitting a blackened visor in two. To his right and left, the newbloods of his squads keep pace, crashing from one foe to the next, wheeling chainswords and hammers.

Blow by blow, they break the yard open all the way to the Logis Gateway, then clear the line across Clanium Square. The enemy, its numbers vastly superior, is caught in a bottleneck, and by surprise. The mass of them flinches back, stung, and then shatters across its right-hand edge as the Blood Angels armour lights off and rains shells into their confused and tight-packed mass.

The tide falls back. Lupercal's bastard-sons retreat. The cloven-hooved thing leading them is already vanishing into the smoke. It's a brief respite. Rann knows that. The enemy will gather and resurge in minutes. But they've held the line at Logis against a foe that, until now, has not been even slightly checked.

Rann halts the charge at the edge of Clanium Square.

Pushing further, though his blood wants him to, will simply force the kind of overreach he feared for Halen and the Blood Angels. Aimery's guards fly in to land around him, finishing the half-dead enemy with execution shots from bolt pistols or the clinical down-strikes of blades. Archamus, resuming area control, orders rapid repositioning to defend the retaken ground before the assault resumes. There will be no time to rest. Battle will blur into battle.

'My hand, brother,' says Azkaellon, coming to Rann across the rubble and the burning dead, his augmetic wings retracting and folding high like a white banner against his back. They clasp. Azkaellon, Herald of the Sanguinary Guard. He seems like a winged god in gold. Rann feels mortal before him.

'Ingenious,' the huge First Sanguinary says.

'Improvised,' says Rann.

'Indeed, my lord?' says Azkaellon.

'The spirit moved me,' says Rann.

'But of course. You've heard, then?'

'Heard what?' asks Rann.

Azkaellon looks at him. 'That He rises?' he says. 'That He stands with us?'

Rann is silent for a second.

'Is… is this true?'

'Word is spreading. He rises, brother. He rises from the Throne to stand with us. *This* is the hour.'

2:xii

The end of time

I take a moment to steady myself. Curse my mortal shell, but I am old and I am tired. I consider resuming my seat for a moment, just a moment, to ease my old bones, but that would be a symbol of weakness. He mustn't think me weak. He will not be able to trust me if he thinks me weak.

Yet the rising, world-drowning tide of the immaterium hammers and burns at my soul. I feel my lord fight to adjust and correct, re-crafting the invisible, constructing and reinforcing talismatic dykes and dams of psykanic force, opening psycho-mantic outfalls and conduits to relieve the rising pressure.

It is growing ever more disturbed by the moment. In the great chamber of the Golden Throne, astropaths moan and spasm, bedevilled by unbidden dreams, and the oniero-looms spew friction-smoke as they spin too fast. Prophesires weep, lamenting, and prognostipractors bleed from the mouth and ears. Indifference engines judder on their platforms, and archeotech valves spit green and yellow sparks. What new surge wracks the currents of the webway? Keeping it chained is a constant, precise struggle. I wonder... will I be remotely prepared for it when my turn comes? Will–

Another surge. I feel the Throne sigh as it shudders and rides the empyric current, its amplifiers and stasis-nodes straining. What is causing this fresh perturbation?

My mindsight turns upwards. Peerless Terra falls ever further into the void-wound Horus has cut. A caustic halo surrounds it utterly, so that it resembles a great, inflamed, infected eye. The nephelosphere around it burns black, like the petals of a monstrous, poisoned flower, arcs of morbid lightning millions of kilometres long lashing across the Solar Realm. The forces of two universes, cosmic opposites, mingle and intermix, contrary to the absolute laws of cosmological regulation. The warp and realspace are beginning to devour each other, cannibal galaxies starting to feed, to consume, to mutually obliterate. The empyrean will win, of course, for it is malevolently hungry in a way our cold and starry void is not.

And there, hanging over us still, is his utterly vengeful spirit. Unlike every other vessel in the vast murder-fleet circling the skies of Terra like carrion birds, it remains unguarded. Its shields are still down. It is wantonly, brazenly exposed.

A threat, an invitation, a seductive promise. He thinks he's luring us into a fatal mistake. Except this is not his work at all. It is a scheme devised by the four *behind* him, the four anagogic annihilators who govern him. His role is merely their impatient host. The four are allowing him to believe that this is a tactical masterstroke, a summons my lord and master cannot refuse.

Horus Lupercal accepts this. He seeks gratification and triumph. My lord's first-found was always so very eager. Flagrantly, he shows us the trap he thinks he has set and beckons to us. Well, you once-wonderful son, you peevish traitor-child, it is a trap indeed, but not for your father. In your pride and confidence, intoxicated by the power you have so unwisely drunk, you have built your own demise.

So, is it *that*? Is it that indecently bared flagship, shamelessly revealed, that suddenly perturbs the warp so, and makes the Neverborn shriek and gyrate with expectation? That makes the noctivagant horrors in the burning streets of the Dominions gibber with glee? That makes the webway roar? I think perhaps it is. Daemonkind quivers, salivating, at the prospect of the coming moment and–

No. No, it is *not*. It is something else. I feel the pattern of it, the particular gust and eddy of the immaterial gale beneath my lord's adytum. Impossible. Too soon, surely? And yet…

In my mind, he warns me to brace myself.

I feel him take control at once, applying full and conscious mastery of the turbulent ever-seas. Warding bells and klaxons sound automatically. The Armoury procession halts, bewildered. The Custodians stand ready, spears raised. The Sisters unsheathe their blades and their anti-souls. The conclaves of the Adnector Concillium scurry to and fro, adjusting flow regulation and dynamic connection. The lights of the vast electro-flambeaux hung along the arched and echoing nave flutter and dim. A hundred centuries of noetic learning and practice guides his hand.

My lord and master opens the webway door.

Withering light floods out, scorching the flagstones and crusting the auramite fittings of the chamber with fulgurite soot. By his will alone, my lord holds the ether back long enough for the figure to emerge. Then, as his will ebbs and frays, he closes the door again, clamps the telaethesic locks, throws bolts forged from the heavy metals of white dwarf stars, re-engages the dampers, and rekindles the wards.

The light fades. The chamber floor before the Golden Throne is spattered with ectoplasmic fluid and fuming pools of ooze and waste-wash. Spavined and translucent things from nowhere, by-blow organisms from the deep trenches of the warp, splash and twitch, and flop and gasp, unable to survive in a world they were not made for. They die, decay and liquify in the light and air of the Throne Room, leaving nothing but puddles of putrid jelly and a lingering odour of decomposition.

And there he stands, amid the spatter of bio-organic emulsion, whole and home, the acrid vapours of the webway rising like smoke from his shoulders.

Vulkan. The Promethean son.

I share the astonishment of all those gathered here. Vulkan turns and kneels to his father, head bowed. I see Rogal and Sanguinius start, and hurry forward, pushing past the halted line of the armourers.

Vulkan has returned. Joy fills me at the sight of him but, just as quickly, dread. He was hours away when my mind last visited him, clawing his half-dead, half-living way back along the psychoplastic halls. I doubted he would return before it was time for his father to leave.

'Lord father,' he says, the low voice of a flexing fault line, 'I feared I was coming too late. Whole ages it has taken me to reach your side.'

And then I understand. It is an alarming thing to realise that even I can be mistaken in my reading of signs. Vulkan's sense of time, just like his father's, just like mine, is born of the perpetual, and runs outside the mortal flow of hours. But our perceptions here are contradictory. Instants have become centuries, and years moments, for him and for us, in different ways.

I understand now the full degree of the damage wrought upon Terra. The last walls are falling, the sun is red, and the clocks… the clocks do more than just run down and disagree.

The ruin of the warp so afflicts the materia of Terra that dimensions have collapsed. Space and distance, time and duration, those constant and trustworthy arbiters of realspace, have seized and fallen.

Time, a local foible of our reality, no longer counts. It is no longer our ally, or our rival. The Palace, and all of Terra, and all of us, have become pinned in the infinite now of the empyrean, and we will remain there until the grip of Chaos is broken. This is neverness, the abdication of metaphysical continuity. This is the unmoving Uigebealach of the webway's singularity-node. This is un-time. There will be no tomorrow, for there is no longer a today or a yesterday.

There will be no tomorrow unless we wrench Terra from the sucking wound of the warp and allow space and time to reformulate according to Euclidean and Minskowskian principles.

The four, the False Four, know this. To them, this is a step closer to triumph, depriving us of orthodox reality. To them, this is the final state of madness that will carry us off.

I think on this in despair, and then... and *then* I start to chuckle to myself.

They have – because they do not *understand* it – forgotten *logic*. The foul False Four have forgotten that we still think in human terms, and plan human plans, according to human conceptions. They have denied us tomorrow. But if tomorrow is the fall of Terra, then we have been strenuously denying *that* for months! By melting time away, and condemning us to neverness, they have given us a moment of eternity, an endless now in which to forge the tomorrow of our choosing.

'In the webway, my father,' Vulkan says, 'as I walked, I heard a name. It came from the walls and the air, again and again.'

'The Dark King?' I ask.

Vulkan glances around at the sound of my voice and the soft tap of my approaching staff.

'Lord Regent,' he says, and rises to his feet. I shuffle forward, leaning heavily on my staff, until I am alongside him. I reach up, and pat him on the shoulder, an avuncular greeting. Then I eye the splatter on the flagstones around us, dubiously probing one rotting lump of dead flesh with the tip of my staff. I wrinkle my nose.

'Was it the Dark King?' I ask again. 'Vulkan, the name, my boy? Was it the Dark King?'

'It was, Lord Sigillite,' Vulkan replies.

'Yes, I have heard it too,' I tell him.

'And what does it mean?' asks Sanguinius, as he and Rogal join us at the foot of the great dais.

'It is a title sometimes claimed by Curze,' says Dorn. 'And, I understand, an element of the tarot.'

He glances at me warily. He knows full well my fluency in the language of symbols. Though it seems like years past, it is only months ago that I gave Dorn a private reading in which, following the reveal of *The Moon, The Martyr, The Monster*, and *The Lightning Tower, The Dark King* turned to lie askew across *The Emperor*. I place great credence in the working of the cards, and consider my old deck an especially prized possession, but dear Dorn has no stomach for such superstitious frippery, and he is annoyed that this bothers him.

'Yes,' I reply, 'it signifies Konrad, and also the name of an ill-favoured card in the tarot arcanoi. But, in this case, my dear Praetorian, both definitions are mere echoes of the real truth.'

I look up at the Golden Throne, raising a hand to shield my eyes from the glare.

+Will you tell them?+ I ask.

He tells me that I speak for him in all things.

'Very well,' I say. I turn to the three great primarch sons.

'It means,' I say, 'the end and the death.'

2:xiii

A cornered wolf

Loken can suddenly hear a boltgun firing. It's close.

'Stay back, Ahlborn,' he instructs. Ahlborn's been with him for twenty minutes, vainly trying to guide him to the last place Keeler was seen. No one in the crowd seems to know. Everyone's seen her, no one's seen her. It's not even clear which way the crowd is moving. The Via Aquila is choked with people, but there doesn't seem to be an agreed direction. Which way does the great avenue run? North?

He hears the gunfire again. Ragged bursts.

'Ahlborn!' he cries. But he can't see Ahlborn any more. Where's the man gone?

Where have the crowds gone?

He's entered a side yard that's littered with broken glass and a few discarded possessions. There's a groundcar parked, abandoned. Ahead of him are the doors of a large building, perhaps a grand archive or a depository. Is that the Clanium Library?

Sudden squalls of rain hammer down. The raindrops are fat and dark, like oil or beads of dark glass. Through the downpour and the veiling smoke, Loken can make out a great city gate looming above the large building. Is that Praestor Gate? Is it Lotus? How could it be either? They've only been moving for twenty minutes. How has he lost his bearings again?

The rain gets heavier. Where the hell is Ahlborn? Where did the crowds go? How do so many people vanish so completely? All he did was step from the street into the yard.

The great city gate is burning. It must be two kilometres away, but Loken can hear the munching crackle of the flames and the hiss of fire meeting rain. Veneered between those two sounds, something else... another sound, just for a second.

It sounded like someone calling him by name.

'Ahlborn?'

There's absolutely no trace of the conroi-captain. The rain is raising a fine spray from the broken flagstones, and streaming down the walls. The walls are marked with signs and names that Loken decides to ignore.

The gunfire rattles again, closer. He draws his bolter and checks the load. He's getting low on shells. He'll favour blades in a fight if he can. But against a shooting foe...

When the World Eater appears, striding into the yard with an axe in one fist and a boltgun in the other, Loken drops him with a single shot.

The brute is huge. His goat-spike horns look like unwound ammonites. The mass-reactive blows open his chest. He falls hard, cracking the flagstones with his impact. The blood leaking out of him starts to ripple in the rain.

Loken takes a step forward. Instinct tells him to duck, and a swinging maul misses his head by inches. There is absolutely no explanation for how the Word Bearer got behind him.

Loken tries to turn. The maul catches him on the back-swing, smashing the bolter out of his hand and throwing him into the wall. Bricks shatter. He rolls, trying to rise. The Word Bearer ploughs in at him, laughing. The traitor's eyes are insane. He's trying to say something, perhaps tell Loken something, but there are too many fat, wet tongues in his mouth to leave room for coherence.

The maul sings down. Loken blocks it with his chainsword. The grinding teeth chew the maul away at an angle, and wrong-foot the gibbering Word Bearer. That gives Loken enough time to get upright and recompose. He starts driving the Word Bearer back. The traitor is forced to use his heavy maul to make defensive blocks and fend off the stabbing, slicing strikes of the chainsword.

A warrior of the Death Guard lumbers out of the rain. He's wider than he is tall, his rusted, sweating armour bloated and distorted. His helm, or his head, or perhaps both, have become some ceratopsian fight-mask with tusks over the eyes and a snout horn. The back of it flares into an iron frill and the entire left cheek and jaw are swollen like a metal balloon. The Death Guard, plodding at first, starts to jog as soon as he sees Loken. He lumbers across the yard from Loken's left, hoisting his warhammer.

Loken blocks the Word Bearer's maul with his chainblade, and then kicks out, putting his right heel into the Word Bearer's abdomen and hurling him away. The Word Bearer sprawls on his back. Loken snaps left out of the path of the Death Guard's clumsy assault. The down-swinging warhammer hits the wall, and the wall tears open like mummified flesh.

Loken rotates and catches the Death Guard across the pauldron with his biting sword. The pauldron cracks in two, and dirty blood gushes down the traitor's right arm. He issues a gurgling roar, and sweeps the warhammer in a wide, horizontal arc. Loken evades. He hears the whistle of it passing him.

The Word Bearer is back on his feet, yelling something

unintelligible at his fellow traitor as he closes from the left. And somehow, the World Eater is upright again too. There is an appalling hole in his chest plating, a crater of impacted ceramite, metal and meat. His hands, blood drenched, grasp his bearded axe.

Loken fends off the Death Guard, sidesteps, and draws *Mourn-It-All* in his left hand. As Death Guard and Word Bearer come at him simultaneously, he smashes the traitor-son of Mortarion to his knees with a ripping down-slash of the chain-sword, reverses, and runs the entire length of *Mourn-It-All* through the Word Bearer's head.

He wrenches the blade out of the sagging body just in time to block the World Eater's axe. Despite his size, and the size and weight of his axe, the World Eater is hacking frantically, as lithe as a boy with a stick. The axe comes at Loken again and again, without wind-up or balance compensation. The World Eater seems oblivious to the gaping wound in his torso. Loken fends off the raking axe, first with one blade, then the other, drawing sparks. The Death Guard, chips of torn cera-mite flaking from the oozing chain-wound in his shoulder, charges from the right, head down, helm-horns angled like an angry bull. Loken clips aside the World Eater's axe, and barely dodges the lunge. As the Death Guard blunders past, Loken hacks *Mourn-It-All* across his lower back, and severs his spine.

The Death Guard drops on his face, writhing and sputtering, froth and noxious slime weeping from the long gash across his back. He tries to crawl, then succumbs to a fit of wet cough-ing and choking, and falls limp, his head propped up at an odd angle by his snout horn.

The Nucerian axe catches Loken and knocks him over. Pain flares across his ribs. The World Eater shrieks a war cry, bringing the axe down with both hands. In desperation, Loken rolls. The axehead embeds in the flagstones, biting stone. Still prone, Loken sweeps the World Eater's legs and drops him on his back with a crash.

Then it's simply a matter of who gets up first. The World Eater is fast, but the Luna Wolf is faster. The chainsword takes the World Eater's head off as he rises to vertical, and his body collapses again with a scrap-metal clatter. The head bounces, rolls, and comes to rest like a caltrop on its horns.

Loken pauses, a sword in each hand, alert, breathing deeply. The rain hammers down, mingling the blood of three foes in the broken gutters of the yard's pavement.

Nothing stirs. No one else appears. The black rain is so heavy, Loken can no longer see the burning city gate.

2:xiv

Anabasis

At my lord's instruction, I explain to the four of them the corruption and suspension of time and how this, inadvertently, might actually favour us. Then I tell them his scheme of attack. Its code name, quite utilitarian, is *Anabasis*.

Our defenders hold the sealed walls of the final fortress, while outside the last of our warrior-armies fight a hopeless rearguard to delay and thwart the enemy advance. Neither will last long, but while they do, we must strike. A boarding action by teleport assault, so only the most formidably armoured will be capable of withstanding the transition. It will be a spear-tip thrust against the primary, just the way my lord taught his first-found. Taught him so well, indeed, that he owns the tactic as his signature.

'He will expect it,' says Dorn, unable to stop being a strategist.

'Well, we can *let* him, Rogal,' I reply. 'Let him expect exactly what is coming. Expecting something, and stopping it, are different things entirely.'

'But to walk into a trap–' he insists.

'Oh, let us hope it *is* a trap!' I tell him. 'For though time has run out, we have no time left to spare. If it is an error, a mistake, or a malfunction, those things could be remedied at any moment. If the shields are re-lit, this chance is lost. The urgency with which we must act is self-evident.'

Then I tell them that our lord will lead the assault himself. That is why he rises. The four of them will stay here, and hold the Palace through the final hours.

They all immediately turn to look at the Golden Throne. Just as I expected. Each one of them wants to protest. My lord dims the radiance of his aspect a little so they can read the solemn sincerity on his face and not burn out their eyes.

His glance alone has quietened kings and stilled the objections of caesars. It permits no defiance, and they are loyal, all of them. All of his children were made to be loyal, but the grotesque heat of this war has fully proofed these four. The fidelity of Valdor and these last three sons is irreproachable.

I am startled, therefore, when Sanguinius says, simply, 'No.'

Sanguinius! Of *all* of them!

Even Valdor looks at him askance, and the captain-general was the only one I truly thought might utter an objection.

I ask the Great Angel what he means by his protestation. He does not look at me. His gaze remains fixed on the Throne. There is a shining quality in his eyes. It's not defiance. It's… some kind of certainty.

Before he can answer, Rogal speaks too.

'We will not let you go alone, liege-father. Not into this.'

Oh, now *Rogal*! I study him too. The Praetorian dares not speak another word of opposition, but the white heat of his thoughts is clear enough. *This siege,* they sear, *and all the work I have done to hold it, has never been about the Palace. I have defended the Palace because you are in it. If you go to the* Vengeful Spirit, *then my siege defence moves with you. It is as simple as that.*

'My king,' says Constantin. 'What you have commanded is out of the question. The Legio Custodes are your lifewards. They are the only ones fit for this undertaking. They must go with you, and where they go, I go.'

Vulkan does not speak, but he does not have to. His frown expresses his reservations quite plainly.

Well, well. I am dismayed. *All* of them! I know full well my lord will be infuriated by their reaction to a simple order, yet also touched by their determination to defend him. Except, is this response born of high virtue and love, or of something darker? Sanguinius is the paragon of integrity, yet he was the first to refuse. Of them all, Valdor was ever the most unswerving. Now *he* disobeys? Has, as I feared, his deepening exposure to the secrets of Chaos gnawed a discontent in his heart?

Is this a sign that the rot of disloyalty has reached even the heart of fidelity? This war has split brother from brother and father from son, against the rule of nature. At this final hour, do these last sons turn against their master's will?

I look to the Throne. I ignore the painful dazzle of the light in my eyes. I remain calm, for no counsel was ever valued that came from fervent lips.

+Think,+ I say, to him and him alone. +They've given everything for you, as I'll give everything, so you must, in turn, give back. Share now, be it in victory or defeat. You always told me, always, that we were together in this. The whole of mankind, as one thing, striving as one. So... think, my King-of-Ages. There must be understanding here. For too long, as is your habit, you've seemed silent and remote, hiding your schemes from all. I know, I know. You have been most wretchedly preoccupied. Well, my old friend, they've learned to think and decide for themselves. They've had to. And isn't that how you made them, the trait you fostered in them? Don't be the stern

patriarch now and rebuke them for the very virtue you raised
them to uphold.+

He knows I'm right, of course.

I am correct because, in so many ways, I have been his con-
science down the years. He *has* made mistakes. That's only
human. There are things he regrets, for he has told me so. The
greatest of those is that he has kept others out. He was too long
alone, I fear. Too many centuries, working in solitude. There
were sometimes friends and allies, but one by one they left
him, or reached the ends of their natural lifespans. He made
Constantin and the primarchs as sons and first companions,
but their arrival still seems recent to him. He has not grown
accustomed to trusting them the way that he should, or sharing
with them the scope of his intentions.

Well. No more mistakes, old friend. Do not act the tyrant
and bark orders. You must compromise, and show them a sign
that the trust they have in you is reciprocated.

All four, it cannot be denied, are needed on the ground. The
conflict has reached its fiercest pitch, and to remove all four
champions from the field is to remove all the figureheads and
symbols that cleave our forces together. But neither Rogal nor
Constantin will permit my lord to venture alone without their
forces as close protection. Indeed, both thought the hour of
our lord's enforced evacuation was approaching. Vulkan has
fought in solitary for too long, and yearns to wage war alongside his brothers, and Sanguinius has the honour of his Legion
to uphold. Debate now would be fruitless.

I sense my master quell his anger. Good. We are together in
this, and we will end it together, not just through the united
strength of our company, but because you need them to *see
it done*. They need to witness the culmination of this war, and
the end of this horror, and share in the achievement, just as,
afterwards, they must share in the plan. For them to fully

invest their hearts in the future, they must be stakeholders in the present. Understand your oversights. You have withheld too much, for too long, veiling your Great Work from all eyes. They are your sons, and their part in this must be respected.

And, further, this is *owed* them. They have needs of their own to fulfil: honour, justice, catharsis, retribution. They have borne all of this, and show the wounds of it, and those wounds must be assuaged. Each one, in his own way, is also a vengeful spirit.

But there must be accommodation. Just as my master cannot be everywhere, and do all things, neither can they. His mind turns to me, and makes his resolution known. Once again, I become his voice.

'Constantin, Rogal,' I say, my tone as thin as paper, 'you will select your best warriors, a company each. I warn you not to denude our embattled forces on the walls. Our last fastness must hold while you are absent. Rogal, I know you have already made your pick, anticipating this moment days ago. Constantin, choose which Sentinels you require.'

I turn to Vulkan. I lean heavily on my staff, for standing has become a Herculean task.

'Vulkan,' I say gently, 'you deserve to go, but you will not, for I need you. I'm sorry. Your father is about to ask me to ward the Golden Throne in his place. It's not a task I welcome, but I'll do it without demur. I need you here at my side. You know, sadly too well, the reason why.'

He pauses. In the long moment that follows, I see Vulkan's jaw clench. I know he feels robbed of honour in this. But the reasoning is irrefutable. Vulkan has no gift whatsoever for the operation of the Throne, no ethereal magic, which is why Vulkan, and *only* Vulkan, must stay to take my place if I fail.

For if I fail, then all is truly lost, and Vulkan must take the Throne and prevent Horus from obtaining all the riches, secrets, treasures and mysteries of the Palace.

Forever.

Vulkan knows this to be true. Finally, and simply, he nods.

'Sanguinius,' I say. 'You will select a company of Blood Angels to join Anabasis. But we stand in the final fortress at the final hour, my boy. The last of our forces are fighting and dying as we speak, to preserve this last piece of earth. They need a commander. More, they need a figurehead, a warrior they can rally to, and who will keep their courage alive to the very last. You're the Brightest One. You are, and always have been, the embodiment of glory, the shining symbol of all that we cherish. A Blood Angels company will have the honour of joining the *Vengeful Spirit* assault. I suggest Raldoron best suited to command it. But you must stay here and be our figurehead. In this, you will be named the Emperor's *true* War-master, and drive back the hosts of the one who so villainously defames that title.'

I nod towards my lord. His word is stated.

I ask them if they understand what I have told them.

Rogal, Constantin and Vulkan reply that they do.

Sanguinius… Sanguinius says nothing.

2:xv

At the Hegemon

The warriors stationed at the Hegemon inspect her credentials and admit her. Ilya Ravallion, tactician to the *ordu*, counsellor to the primarch Khan, devisor of stratagems for the V Legion White Scars. She is led through the emptied halls, through lines of Custodians, units of Imperial Fists, and makeshift choke-point cordons manned by Imperialis Auxilia. The Hegemon, topped by its massive tower, is one of the oldest and largest structures in the compound of the Sanctum Palatine Imperialis, and it has been repurposed. For the longest time, it has been the seat of planetary government, the domestic counterpart of the Great Chamber legislature, where the High Lords convened to debate Terra-centric concerns as opposed to the grand and outward Imperial policies of the Senatorum Imperialis and the Great Chamber. The armoured bastion tower rising from it is the central fastness of the Legio Custodes.

It has become, in the last hours, the heart of command.

Ilya is weary, and sick, but she walks with determination, her White Scars escorts Gahaki, khan of the Burgediin Sarhvu,

and Ainbataar Khan at her side. In the face of destruction,
there is a spark of hope. She has been told, assured in fact,
that the Great Khagan, fallen in battle, has been salvaged from
death, as though by some miracle. Sigillite magic. Ilya does
not understand it at all, for she saw the Khan dead and carried
in, but she does not question it, and the joy of it has raised
her from her knees, out of her pain, out of her lamentation.
If Jaghatai lives, then she will resume her duties and spend
the remainder of her life fighting for a future he can live in.

She wonders if Sojuk has heard the news. Sojuk was her
bodyguard for the longest time, and she allowed him to leave
her side to join the front line. Fearsome Gahaki and stern
Ainbataar have insisted on filling Sojuk's place and warding
her, for nowhere is now safe, not even in the Sanctum. Does
Sojuk know the Khan lives? Has the news fired his resolve too?

Is he still alive out there?

At the huge entry hatch of the echoing Rotunda, she presents her credentials yet again, and Gahaki and Ainbataar scowl
at the Auxilia colonel examining them.

'You are admitted, mam,' the colonel says to the apparently
frail old woman in the shabby general's coat. Ilya nods. Gahaki
snatches her papers from the colonel's hands, and they enter.

The Rotunda is a circular chamber with a high domed
ceiling. In more peaceful times, it was a political debating
chamber. It has already become a bustling command centre.
Though gangs of servitors and Mechanicus adepts are still
wheeling in and setting up station desks and hololith displays,
and the room is alive with the wail of machine tools, this
didn't happen overnight. It would have taken days to strip
out the tiered seating and galleries, and link up the huge strategium arrays. She detects the Praetorian's handiwork, Dorn's
uncanny knack for being three steps ahead. He knew Bhab
Bastion would fall, or at least made provision in the event of

its possible loss. This is Loyalist Command now, a scene of frantic activity, confusion and effort, three-quarters built and already in use. It is hauling on the reins of control dropped, through brutal necessity, at Bhab. Transition of control, if not smooth, has at least been improvised urgently.

Ilya stands for a moment. She sees the officers of the War Court and the robed seniors of the Tacticae Terrestria hard at work, blind to the industry and disturbance around them, already lost in considerations of vital strategy. She wonders what she can do, and where she might possibly start. She observes the data scrolling on the active displays, the blink of real-time revising maps. Already, her experienced mind can discern structures, connections, possibilities and chances.

She doesn't feel her age any more. She doesn't feel like she's dying. A keen occupation of the mind can keep all things at bay.

She turns to her bodyguards.

'Return to the walls,' she says.

'Szu-Ilya, we are sworn to–' Gahaki begins.

Ilya shakes her head. 'I am home, Sarhvu-khan,' she says. 'This is my place now. My battlefield. You are needed elsewhere, and urgently.'

'But, szu-Ilya–'

'If death can reach me here, ringed in the Hegemon by Custodians and Imperial Fists, then it can reach me anywhere, with the greatest respect, whether you are with me or not. Go, please. I will supply the ordu with the wisest counsel I can from here, as best I can.'

They hesitate, nod and depart. No word of farewell. It's a thing she's always loved about the White Scars. Every leave-taking is done without sentimentality, for every leave is taken in the expectation of reunion. It is a liberatingly optimistic attitude for warriors who live such short lives.

Alone, she turns, reviews the flow of activity around her, and finally lights on a face she recognises.

'Mistress!' she calls out. 'Mistress, I am here to work.'

2:xvi

The sacrifice

I have neither the time, nor patience, frankly, to interrogate Sanguinius' curious silence. I turn to my impassive lord.

'Now?' I ask.

He tells me yes.

'Already? Ah.'

I sigh. It's foolish. I've been preparing for this moment since the day we realised that Magnus was no longer a viable candidate. My lord has been unwavering in his reassurance to me. He believes me capable, and I trust that, for our minds have been strangely entwined for a long time, long before he took up the title Emperor and I became a Sigillite.

It's not that I wanted longer. I've had enough years, more than my fair share. But there is still so very much to do. However, in truth, I wish this had happened when I was younger and stronger, and invulnerable with the recklessness of youth, rather than now, when I am so old and so tired.

Not that it would really have made any difference.

Still…

I am lost in my thoughts as I begin to limp my way towards
the great dais, ordering my mind, settling my estate, frantically
sending out last-moment thought-notes and idea-symbols,
reminders and instructions, so that others can finish what I
will leave unfinished. These sigilised messages swirl around
me like a colony of bees evicted from their hive, flying off
piecemeal in every direction to find new homes. It is sloppy,
haphazard work. I have no time left to be methodical, precise or polite. Everything just *goes*, dumped like ballast from
my head.

I am so lost in my thoughts, I do not really pay attention
to what's going on around me. I stop short when I hear a
gasp. It would stop *anyone* to hear primarchs gasp in surprise and dread, and hear them fall to their knees in abject
obeisance.

At the foot of the gleaming dais, I look up. I look up the
exquisite steps that I will climb and never come down again.

The sun is in my eyes.

My lord. My King-of-Ages. My friend. My Master of Mankind.

He stands. He has risen from the Golden Throne. He stands
above me like the god he isn't.

He *stands*.

That in itself is a minor miracle, for he has not stood in a
long time, and I was beginning to fear he could not. Cloth of
golden light hangs from his frame and his arms, streaked with
trace threads of crimson sunset and scarlet dawn. Microcli-
mate lightning sheets and shivers around him, and corposant
sloughs like blue ice from the arms of the Throne at his back.
There is a halo of white radiance behind his noble head, bright
as a full hunter's moon or a steadfast star, his face cast in
shadow, an eclipse before that disc but for the splendour of
his eyes.

Powers that be! I had *forgotten* this! I had forgotten his majesty! I had forgotten how *tall* he was, how astronomic, how wonderful, how terrible, how–

How did I ever *think* I could take his place? What kind of old and tired fool *am* I?

I ought to bow! *I need to bow down!* I need to abase myself and bury my face in the stones of the floor, for he is too bright to behold! I fuss and fumble, clumsily, my old limbs too stiff to obey me. I stumble–

Hands catch me, and arrest my fall before I crack my face against the lower steps of the dais. The Sentinels, Uzkarel and Caecaltus, have swept from their posts at the moment of my mis-step, but they have not reached me in time. The hands supporting me belong to Rogal and Sanguinius. Vulkan is with them, his hand extended to help me upright. Constantin looms behind them, concern in his eyes.

'Let me help you,' says Sanguinius.

'Oh, forgive an old man!' I mutter.

'Steady yourself,' says Rogal.

'I am as steady as ever, my boy,' I chuckle. They set me on my feet. Vulkan hands me my staff. I look at them. They surround me, their worry for me showing in their faces.

I shoo them away.

'I'm fine,' I assure them. 'These old legs. When you get to my age, eh?'

Sanguinius looks at me. His jaw tightens.

'I'm *fine*,' I insist.

Valdor nods curtly. The two proconsuls step past the primarchs, and stand either side of me to guide me up the steps. They reach to take my arms to support me.

'Oh, no!' I tell them. 'I'll climb these damn steps myself.'

'Give us the honour, lord, of escorting you, at least,' says Uzkarel quietly.

I huff and allow it. I begin my climb up the steps of the

plinth, squinting into the glare, pulling myself up each step with my staff as a prop clutched in both hands. It is a struggle for me, but nothing like the struggle that will follow.

Above me, my King-of-Ages waits. He remains standing, motionless, silent, ignoring the awe that fills the Throne Room, all eyes upon him, eyes that never thought to see him stir or stand again. They have longed for him to rise, and now they are terrified of what his rising signifies.

He looks only at me. Right into my heart.

Halfway up the steps I pause. I glance at the dutiful Sentinels either side of me. 'That's far enough now,' I say. 'I'll go the rest of the way alone.'

Their golden masks express no response.

'You are both Hetaeron Companions, yes?' I ask them quietly. 'Likely, then, that one or both of you will go with him to ward his side in the final fight. I ask you this, then. Do not fail him.'

'We are not conditioned to fail, my Regent,' says Caecaltus.

'Oh, I know all *that*, my boy! I know all *that*! I know how *peerless* you are! I'm not talking about devotion or duty or ability! Those things are wired into you! I'm talking about… about… when it's all done, I mean, bring him back to this seat, you hear me? Bring him back alive. You do all you do for him, but do this for *me*. Here, here…'

I lick the tip of my left index finger, and with it, I draw my sigil on the breast of Caecaltus' plate. The mark is gone as soon as it is made. Then, with another lick, I do the same to Uzkarel.

'I leave my mark, the mark of myself, upon my plan,' I whisper as I draw the shape. 'This is what will happen, and with my hand I signify it. It cannot be undone. Do this for me.'

They make no reply. Staff braced, I resume my climb. The proconsuls stay where they are, respecting my request.

I near the top, the light around me. My lord and master

moves. He steps down to me, and offers me his hand in support. That hand. That great and capable hand that has held the galaxy in its palm. I feel him close. To my surprise, he permits me to share the private working of his mind.

The signs I read there are clear.

'Don't be sad,' I say.

This is more painful than he expected it to be. He is afraid he will never speak to me again, that there will be no more hours spent exchanging thoughts and words, configuring mankind's best fate. His memories are Antarctic-bright: the day he first showed me the Throne, and told me what it did, the shining look of disbelief in my eyes; the evening when we both realised that I could moderate its functions too, that my mind, like his, had the capacity to engage with it and not instantly perish; the night when we concluded, through plain, logical deduction, that there might come a day when I would have to take his place; that, in almost every configuration of the future we could model, someone would have to do it.

I was not afraid. Not then, not now. I knew what that would mean. I brushed it off as a 'thing that would have to happen if it came to it'. He hoped it never would, because he knew what it would mean too. And, for the longest time, it seemed unlikely. He had built a contingency to avoid it ever becoming compulsory. The contingency's name was Magnus.

Now the time is here, I do not hesitate. I take the hand he offers to steady me, and I ascend the final steps to the Throne. I give him a nod and a little smile, and whisper to him, 'Do not mourn,' in a voice no one else can hear.

And then I prepare to take my seat.

There is nothing else to say. After centuries of conversation, in which we have dissected and shared everything, there is nothing *left* to say. Just a look from one friend to another, an unspoken understanding of everything that has passed between us, and the debts we owe each other. This act is my final, everlasting gift to mankind, to the future, to the plan painted on the wall.

But in his eyes, I can tell he knows that I am only really doing it for him. The greatest, most universal acts are always born from the personal.

I am old. I am tired.

I sit upon the Golden Throne.

2:xvii

Unfinished business

Tension breaks into a state of high alert. Orders are already circulating through the Throne Room and beyond, conveyed by vox signal, astropathic command, and by psycho-meme, orskode and thoughtmark. Runners and messengers are despatched, and servo-skulls hurtle along avenues of approach, broadcasting binharic chatter, their tiny, straining lift-systems leaving high-pitched echoes in their wakes.

The shield-companies of the Custodes are already shifting, commanded with almost glance-like ease by Valdor from the foot of the Throne. The commands are complex and detailed, communicated with just a nod of battlemark. Sentinel details realign and change. Selected Custodians move from their vigil places to the arming chambers and deployment areas, their eternal stations instantly filled by replacements. Dorn's Huscarls burst from the Throne Room to ratify and initiate the Praetorian's pre-prepared orders of battle. The members of the High Council and their mobs of officials scatter to set for readiness, to authorise the necessary diversions of main generator power, and to inform the emergency command station at the Tower of the Hegemon of the evolving situation.

In the Throne Room, the company of armourers resumes its slow, ceremonial advance.

Outside the Silver Door, in the aching halls of the Sanctum Approaches, Khalid Hassan, Chosen of Malcador, hurries to his post, his mind sore from a sudden psyk-burst of symbolic instructions that the Sigillite has just planted there. He steps aside, a green-robed ghost, as Imperial Fists Huscarls hammer past, wipes tears from his tired eyes, and continues on.

At the door itself, another delay. Supervised by Sisters of Silence, labour gangs of Adnector Concillium automata are hauling huge hexagrammatic generators into the Throne Room on lifter carts. There are eight of them, drawn from the Dark Cells, each one the size of a main assault drop pod. Behind them come more wagons and carriers, laden with additional and emergency talismatic apparatus, void-screen broadcasters, and portable telaethesics.

Hassan stops and watches them roll past, scrupulously checking the accuracy and completeness of the consignment. There are more to come. Other resources are being carefully withdrawn from storage as he stands there, to be brought up from the bowels of the Palace by freight conveyors. Hassan taps the cowling of one hexagrammatic turbine with his middle finger as it is rolled past. He hears the harmonic of the impact ringing. Yes, it is correctly tuned.

This is Sigil Protocol, one of eight hundred and fifteen contingency measures held in readiness. Some were prepared long before the siege began, others are recent – somewhat desperate, in Hassan's opinion – additions. Sigil is one of the oldest, and was written into contingency shortly after the devastation of Magnus' folly. It is a sequel, an appendage, to the necessary horror of the Unspoken Sanction.

Hassan had hoped Sigil, *this* dreadful sigil, would never need to be enacted. His breath is short in his chest, a flutter of panic. It's come to this. Whatever the end turns out to be, this is it. According to the psycho-meme instructions the Sigil-lite remote-printed into his mind not ten minutes earlier, a crushing load of symbology he is only just beginning to parse, Sigil is now active. What's more, the Unspoken Sanction must also be made ready.

Throne of Terra… Throne of Terra…

Others of the Chosen, others of his kind with the same mark on their cheeks, are already abroad in the Palace, beginning the preparatory tithe and selecting the required psycho-able, not by lot or on a volunteer basis, as was once considered, but by ruthless exaction. They need the best, the most compatible, whether the best and most compatible wish to submit themselves or not.

Hassan turns, using autonomic techniques to calm his galloping heartbeat, and finds Kaeria Casryn behind him. She bows.

'Sigil is enacted… You have full protocol instructions?' he asks.

She nods again.

'It must be entirely precise,' Hassan says.

The Oblivion Knight seems to sigh, as if frustrated by his fastidious manner, a relic of the military discipline drilled into him in his former life.

It is precise, she replies in thoughtmark. *Every detail, according to both the written edict and the verbal instructions. I have checked and rechecked.*

'And the instructions came from–'

Yours, from the Great Sigillite, I imagine, signs the sister of Steel Foxes Cadre. *Mine, directly from the captain-general.*

'We should compare–'

We do not need to.

'If there is even a minor discrepancy, Casryn–'

Are you disputing the accuracy with which the captain-general compiles his instructions?

'No,' says Hassan. 'No, of course not. Forgive me.'

We have rehearsed this, and rehearsed this, until we have it by rote, she signs.

'I know. But even so, are we ready? Are *you* ready?'

Casryn stares at him. He can detect something in her eyes, framed above the grille of her half-helm, that wavers between misery and terror. She, like him, played a key role in the oversight of the Unspoken Sanction the last time it was enacted. The only time. She has had to live with that horror too. She knows what is about to happen, and what may happen as a consequence.

Yes, Casryn replies.

He nods.

The Eighteenth is here, she signs. *That's something, at least.*

'It is,' he replies. He knows this. The Sigillite flash-filled his mind with a bewildering quantity of order-signs and information markers. The presence of Vulkan was one of those facts. Vulkan's unique gifts will be a distinct asset in this endeavour. But he also represents a fail-safe that Hassan would rather not contemplate.

'Carry on,' he says. 'I will join you shortly.'

Casryn bows and turns away. She has vanished before she has even moved into his peripheral vision.

Hassan struggles to sort through all the information memes his master has bequeathed him. There's just so much of it, in no clear order, the usual precision of signifiers sloppy, as though Malcador was running out of time and simply trying to say everything and anything he could think of before he forgot. He has clearly been detained by the Emperor's business.

Every last thing the Regent needed to impart, every idea, every meaning-dense sigil, every passing thought, every last minute, while-I-remember notion has been delegated to his Chosen to free his mind.

One sigil carried particular emphasis. Malcador has marked the thought-file it condenses with the meme-tag *Terminus*. Hassan sees figures emerging from the Throne Room, coming his way. They are giants, wraiths of black smoke and jet shadow that flicker along the fusion-bored walls of the mass-passageway towards him like an approaching nightmare.

He stands in their path anyway, and they halt.

'Aedile-Marshal Harahel,' Hassan says.

The two Wardens of the Sodality of the Key glare down at him. They are Legio Custodes giants, but the terrible glory of their golden plate is dulled with soot to a menacing black. The Dark Cells and archives in the catacombs deep beneath hold all the forbidden technologies and secrets of Old Night, curated and secured by a specialist Excertus taskforce. The Sodality of the Key is the Custodes coterie that supervises the handling and transfer of such devices when they are called for.

'Stand aside,' says one.

'You know my rank and my authority, Warden,' says Hassan. 'I have business with you.'

'Our directives have been issued,' the dirt-tarnished Custodian answers. Hassan wants to shrink and flee from them. He stands his ground.

'I should hope so,' he says, 'and I am here to confirm them. And to see that they are carried out with complete diligence.'

'They were issued by our master,' says the Warden, making no effort to keep the warning growl out of his voice.

'And mine were given by mine,' says Hassan. 'With respect to the captain-general, the Sigillite's wish in this is absolute.'

'Stand aside.'

Hassan draws breath. Without hesitation or error, he begins to recite the entire name-sequence of Aedile-Marshal Harahel. It is four hundred and nine name-units long, inscribed on the inside of Harahel's blackened armour, and known to only a very few. To know it is to command authority at Throne Room level.

Harahel raises a giant hand and stops Hassan forty-six names into the recitation.

'You've made your point,' he says. 'Speak, then.'

'You are charged with the handling of the individual known as Fo, and also of the device he has constructed.'

Harahel does not immediately reply.

'Come, marshal, let us speak as men,' says Hassan. 'The employment of Fo, and the existence and purpose of the device he has crafted is known to the Sigillite. Did the captain-general really think such a thing could be concealed?'

'Then what?'

'It is the Emperor's will, and thus the will of the Sigillite also, that the device be preserved and held in reserve. For use in last resort only. It is signified Tier XX, and deemed a terminus sanction. It must be made safe, and its architect too.'

'Then our directives match,' replies Harahel. 'The captain-general was precise. We are to manage the individual, Fo. We are to withdraw the device to the Dark Cells for safekeeping. You have no further need to detain us.'

'Pending transfer,' says Hassan. 'You left that part out. The Sigillite is aware that Captain-General Valdor intends the device to be secured in the Dark Cells. This is appropriate, for the Custodians of your sodality are by far the best suited for this responsibility. But your custody of it is *pending transfer*. When... *if*... the time comes, and transfer becomes viable, it will be supervised by me at the behest of the Sigillite. Are we clear?'

'This was not as it was communicated to us,' replies Harahel. 'Nothing was said about transfer.'

'Then I have communicated your directives more fully, so that mistakes cannot arise. Be thankful I was here to intervene.'

'This was not as it was communicated to us,' Harahel repeats. 'You will need to present confirmation.'

'Very well, I will obtain it.'

'I do not think there is time left for that,' the Warden replies.

Hassan goes cold. He looks past them, then pushes past them, and starts to run, leaving the sable giants standing there.

He rushes to the Silver Door. It is open, the convoy of wagons still rolling through. Hassan ducks around one conveyer and runs through the doorway. Golden Sentinels turn, spear-blades down, to stop him, then step back into place when they recognise him.

He starts to sprint now, along the colossal nave, hoisting up his robes to prevent himself from tripping. He sees other figures in green robes, others of the Chosen like him, running forwards too, breaking from the gathered throngs at the back of the Throne Room, rushing along aisles parallel with him.

None of them are going to get there in time.

Hassan sees the Throne, far away. He sees the small group of figures around it. The view is blurred, because of the frantic motion of his headlong sprint, and because there are tears in his eyes. All the while, he's still frantically unpacking and sorting all the data his master dropped into his head to be actioned.

He sees the figures. A great form in gold has risen from the high throne. It stands, bathed in a flare of white light. There is another figure on the steps below it, tiny, crooked and hunched. The shining figure reaches out a hand to help the other the last few steps of the way. A moment passes between them, as though they are exchanging words.

Then the great shining form gestures towards the high throne. It seems to be burning, as though the entire dais is on fire. The tiny, crooked figure seems to nod. He shuffles forward.

He sits upon the Throne. The flames, it seems, reach higher and engulf him.

Hassan stops running. He pulls up, bent double, hands on his thighs, panting. Tears stream from his eyes and splash on the sectile patternwork of the nave floor. He has found and unpacked the last note-meme planted in his mind. A scrap, just words, barely forming an integrated sigil. Almost an afterthought.

It says, *Khalid. Do not fail me. Goodbye.*

2:xviii

Only as a hero

The Sigillite sits upon the Throne. He does not and will not speak. His eyes are open but sightless, or rather they see nothing of the chamber that others call the Throne Room. They see only the immeasurable deeps of the empyrean. He sits still, upright, his hands resting, just as his lord's did, on the arms of the Throne. His staff lies at his feet. A dazzling swathe of radiance, like ball lightning, encases him and the Throne, boiling and flickering. The glare of it drives all shadows backwards from the great dais, stretching them out, long and narrow, across the chamber, the shadow of a father and those of the sons at his side, long, radiating lines of darkness in the blinding light, like the shadows of humans on a ridge, watching the sunrise at solstice.

Vulkan, standing beside his towering father, his two brothers, and the captain-general, finds it hard to watch. Malcador is making no voluntary movement, but he is trembling, every part of him, every bone, every atom. Vulkan gazes at him in the heart of the fire and sees the jitter, like a pict-feed stuck and jumping, wobbling, vibrating, the REM-twitch of the Regent's open eyes, the shiver of his jaw, the flutter of his robes, the minute and cycling quiver of his hands on the armrests. But the Promethean lord can also sense the masterful and assured operation of Malcador's guidance at work, the strong mind, the purpose, and the absolute concentration. Vulkan can hear the mechanisms of the Throne responding to the Sigillite's every subtle adjustment. He can feel the immaterial flood obeying his directives and commands.

'I can feel his focus. And his pain,' Vulkan murmurs. *I can feel his cells dying, one by one,* he thinks.

'And his sadness,' says Dorn quietly.

'It's not his sadness, brother,' says Sanguinius. He glances at their father, silent at their side. 'It's yours, isn't it?'

The Master of Mankind makes no reply. Is he overwhelmed with love for his old friend, with speechless admiration at the scale of the Regent's sacrifice? He is only human, after all, and the sensation is coming from somewhere.

Valdor turns away, grim. Another last survival of the Long Yesterday has passed from the world, leaving precious few remaining. 'We must begin,' he says.

Vulkan shakes his head wearily. His resolve is granite-hard, for he understands more than any of them what this signifies.

'The Sigillite–' he begins.

+The Hero,+ a voice corrects him gently. Vulkan looks at his father, eyes narrowing at the radiance of his aspect. He nods.

Down the scope of the nave, a few others have dared approach, pushing past the halted armoury train. They have come to stop a few hundred metres away, men and women in green robes, perhaps a dozen of them. They stare at the Throne. Vulkan sees their grief and shock. A couple of them have sunk to their knees.

They are known to him. The Chosen of Malcador, the

individuals of special ability and particular aptitude that the Sigillite hand-picked down the years to serve as his aides and proxies. Through them, the Regent has conducted his inscrutable business. Only these twelve or so have made it here in time, and even they are too late. Others are still on their way, pulled by the psychic bond they shared with the Sigillite. There has been no opportunity for a farewell in person, no last fond words or whispered wisdoms. Required by circumstance to put his affairs in order without ceremony, Malcador has brusquely decanted his thoughts into all of them, distributed piecemeal and without finesse. Their minds ache with the burdens they have been handed so suddenly, and which they have barely begun to process, making this loss even harder to bear.

There is a change in the air suddenly, a winnowing aura of calm that moves like a summer breeze from the Master of Mankind down the great length of the nave towards the Chosen. Everyone in the room feels its soothing aspect. He is alleviating the worst of their immediate suffering, for they will all need to be sharp and capable from this moment on. They must complete the tasks the Regent has left to them. They are the executors of his legacy. They contain the Sigillite's last testament.

+The greatest sacrifice of our age,+ the voice tells them softly. +Our Sigillite is no more. Regard him now, as you fulfil his bequests, only as a hero. Your duties are not finished, and neither is his. What we do now, all of us, we do because he has made it possible. Remember him. Remember that. Use that memory to prevent even a moment's falter.+

They nod. Some weep. They all bow.

Hiding his own grief, the King-of-Ages Risen turns to his sons and the captain-general.

'Now we begin in earnest,' He says.

2:xix

At the Hegemon

Sandrine Icaro looks up from her station. Her robes are dirty and stiff with dried blood, and her mind is on a thousand other things. It takes her a moment to identify the thin, dishevelled woman who has appeared at her elbow.

'Ilya Ravallion,' says Ilya.

'Of course,' says Icaro. 'You'll forgive me–'

'If I may, I'm here to assist. Tell me where you need me.'

Icaro blinks. Ilya can see the Mistress Tacticae's hands are shaking, and there is a neural tick twitching under her left eye. There is, incongruously, a light assault weapon – a Komag VI, if Ilya is not mistaken – resting across the edge of Icaro's workstation, as though she wants it in sight and in reach at all times. Ilya has heard that Icaro, and a very few other seniors from Bhab, were among the last to reach the final fortress before the Archangel sealed the Gate. Icaro looks as though she doesn't quite believe she made it.

'If you're fit,' says Icaro.

'No one's fit for anything, mistress, not any more,' replies Ilya, 'but I am capable.'

'We lost a lot,' Icaro murmurs. 'The War Court was decimated coming out of Bhab. We–'

She pauses, listening to data feeds coming in through her plugs and earpiece. She realigns unit graphics on her lithic display, and punches in an augur cross-feed.

'Two Seven advance to Gilded six-six-eighty, radial and bracket. Confirm,' she says, and waits for a response Ilya can't hear. Satisfied, she glances back at Ilya. 'Yes please, then,' she says. 'Station six.' She points. 'Access authorisation is "Icaro".'

Ilya raises an eyebrow.

'I know. We haven't had time to be sophisticated about it. Light the desk, please. We have data-stacking from the eastern line. I need someone to start processing it. Main items to me, everything else…'

'My judgement?'

'It'll have to be, yes.'

Ilya nods, and crosses to the vacant station. Icaro's attention is already submerged in data again. At every station nearby, War Courtiers are locked in concentration so intense it seems like they will burst, their hands moving like hummingbirds on the console haptics.

Ilya sits, punches in the laughably make-do code, and wakes the desk. The desk is new, dragged in from somewhere else and connected to power and noosfeed barely half an hour earlier. It floods with data-blocks the moment it's initialised. She starts to sort and process, triaging information. Her brow knits. She understands at once the intense concentration of the others. Some data is broken, some incomplete. Some seems like it's been transcribed into xenos code. And there is so much of it.

'Ravallion!'

She looks up. Icaro is standing, looking in her direction

through the throng, glancing at an order wafer she's just been brought by a man in a green robe. One of Malcador's Chosen.

'Mistress?' Ilya calls back.

'Dump what you're doing. We need a priority link to Fifth Legion units at Lion's Gate port. Standard connectives are out, or they're refusing to respond. I presume you have Legion-specific combat codes or vox-authentics they might trust?'

'I do,' says Ilya.

'Fast as you can, please.'

Ilya turns back to her screen, and conjures vox and hardline links. She initiates a signal, coding in the encrypted battle-cant of Chogoris. The Chosen is suddenly standing at her side. He's not one of those she met when she brought the Warhawk home. He's a middle-aged man, augmetic traceries gleaming bright against his black skin, the sigil on his cheek.

'Ravallion,' she says.

'Sage mistress,' he replies. 'I am Gallent Sidozie, of the Chosen.' There is a huskiness to his voice, as though he has recently been crying. In this hour, Ilya thinks, our emotions take us by surprise.

'Content of this message?' she asks, fingers hovering, waiting.

'Instruct Lion's Gate to cease firing at Target Principal.'

'Cease firing?'

'Yes.'

'Target Principal?'

'I believe you heard me.'

'You mean the traitor flagship?'

'I do, sage mistress,' he says.

She looks at him. 'May I ask why? If the White Scars can strike at Lupercal while they are still able–'

'It is not your place to ask for clarification,' he says.

She holds his gaze for a moment, then nods.

'As you like,' she says, and turns back to the console to enter the message. 'I'll despatch by data-burst and then try voice.'

She hears him sigh gently. In a low voice, he says, 'I have just delivered an operational directive from the Throne Room. Mistress Icaro will announce it shortly. To understand its importance, I will advise you in strict confidence that we will shortly have spearhead deployment on the *Vengeful Spirit*.'

Ilya swallows hard. She does not react. She does not turn and look at him. She keeps her eyes on the display.

'Teleport assault?' she asks, barely audibly.

'Primary strength. Its void shields are down. He has risen to lead it Himself. Operational reference is *Anabasis*.'

2:xx

Shiban, Fifth, Lion's Gate

At Lion's Gate space port, a broken relic of its former magnificence cradled in the firestorms of hell, the main batteries speak again. Lances of power, kilometres in length and as pearly-fluorescent as deep-ocean eels, retch and spit from the massive orbital gun platforms into the dust-caul of the sky. Ship-killing beams shriek upwards at the traitor fleet.

The port, its skirts and out-flanks reduced to scrap and wreckage, is like an island in the midst of the inferno, its main superstructure bent and almost listing, such is the catastrophic damage done to the bedrock it sits on. It is hundreds of kilometres from the Sanctum, hundreds of kilometres from the nearest loyalist force, entirely cut off and surrounded. An atoll of defiance, the only Throne-held position in the entire Palace Dominions outside the final fortress, it is slowly drowning in the maelstrom of warp-corrupted ground, furnace-storms, super-orbital bombardment, and encircling enemy assault. It is raging, furious, as it dies.

Battles boil through the port's hems and lower levels: loyalist forces, principally White Scars and Imperialis Auxilia, waging a futile, fall-back fight against the vastly outnumbering echelons of the Death Guard and the swirling horrors of instantiating Neverborn. Devastating fire from the traitor fleet ruptures the territory around it, and explodes entire spires and freighting platforms off its shoulders and spine. Its remaining void shields soak up some strikes in crackling ripples. It feels as though the voids are doing little more than simply holding the disintegrating port together.

In the smoke-clogged, half-lit ruin of the primary fire control, deep in its upper structure, Shiban Khan, called Tachseer, has just been crowned *ahn-ezen*, Master of the Hunt. It is not a title he will hold for long, but the khans of the ordu have insisted. When the V dies, it will not die leaderless.

Shiban accepts the honour with brief solemnity. He turns from the others, from Ganzorig the noyan-khan, Jangsai Khan, Chakaja Stormseer, and Yiman.

'Finish the work,' he tells them. 'Kill what may still be killed while we yet live.'

They bow, and hurry to their places. Shiban can hear shooting from below. It sounds close. He calls for target solutions.

Atrai, the White Scars legionary manning the augurs and sensoria, tries to locate clean paints on the warfleet above them. Nothing is returning true, as though malfunction or distortion is corrupting even the port's immensely powerful detection and ranging systems. Power is also ebbing. It is taking far longer each time for the main batteries to cycle back to full charge.

But Shiban can see from the fluttering hololiths that the one key truth remains. The *Vengeful Spirit*, unguarded, voids down.

One direct strike…

'Acquisition?' he calls.

Atrai and the others shake their heads.

'Damage observed from previous cycle?'

Atrai looks at him, as though wishing he could say something other than a helpless negative.

'Again!' Shiban yells. 'Kill that thing!'

The deck vibrates as the bulk generatives whine back to capacity.

'My lord?'

Shiban turns. A young White Scars warrior, wounded, is handing him a data-slate.

'Direct from the Sanctum, lord,' he says. 'Authentication is confirmed.'

It reads correctly. They've been ignoring all contacts, assuming that every transmission is a pack of traitor lies. But this, this is genuine.

The message, however, makes no sense.

'Do we have operational vox?' he asks.

The wounded legionary replies with a nod that suggests he will die trying to provide it. The message had an encrypted channel appended to it.

'Channel as indicated,' Shiban orders. He links his armour's vox-system to the main comms grid. An icon tells him when the connection is established. It wavers, threading in and out.

'Shiban, Fifth, Lion's Gate,' he says.

'Hegemon Control, authenticated,' a voice crackles back. He knows it at once. *Ilya.* There's no time to acknowledge that, or ask after her. There's no time for anything.

'Confirm instruction, Hegemon Control,' he says.

'Instruction – deselect firing solutions, Target Principal.'

'Repeat and confirm. Target Principal is shields down, repeat shields down. Do you understand?'

'We understand. Instruction confirmed, and sanctioned by the War Court. Deselect firing solutions, Target Principal, effective immediate.'

'Yes,' he says.

'*Shiban, we don't want you to hit it,*' the voice crackles, fading in and out.

'I copy,' he says. 'I will comply. But, Hegemon Control, you don't understand. We have been targeting it for the last sixteen minutes. Its shields are deactivated. Our battery strength is at prime. Our target-plotting systems are damaged but functional. It should be dead already.'

'*Explain.*'

'I cannot, Hegemon Control. It's not a matter of us *not* firing at it. We *cannot* hit it.'

Ilya Ravallion pulls out her earpiece and rises to her feet.

'Mistress Icaro!' she calls out. 'Lion's Gate confirms receipt of instruction.'

Through the bustle, Icaro hears her and nods to her. She is about to make her announcement.

'Mistress Icaro!' Ilya yells. 'I need you to stop, listen and comprehend. Right now. It is not what it seems. There is something wrong.'

2:xxi

Marked as ready

Proconsul Caecaltus Dusk has been selected. Proconsul Uzkarel Ophite has not. Or rather, they both have, but not for the same duty. Uzkarel will remain at his post, and will assume direct command of the Hetaeron Sentinels in the Throne Room during the absence of the captain-general and Tribune Diocletian. Caecaltus will assume direct command of the Hetaeron Sentinels assigned to their king's company for the assault.

Neither of them regards the captain-general's choices as favour or disfavour. Uzkarel does not feel passed over, nor does he resent his brother-Sentinel's selection. Caecaltus does not register pride, or feel singled out for special preference. They are Legio Custodes. They are nothing like the other warriors fielded in humanity's cause. They are precision instruments of absolute focus, refined and conditioned way past such trivial distractions as pride or envy or disappointment or ambition. All that they are, their minds, their souls, their wills, is forged into one quality; all that they are, and it is so very much, is concentrated into unqualified faithfulness.

Not for them the tawdry rivalries and passions that seem to flash so very often among the Astartes, always feuding and boasting and seeking to outdo each other. Uzkarel and Caecaltus both deem Astartesian behaviour bafflingly counterproductive, though they seldom spare it any thought at all.

Uzkarel and Caecaltus do not even exchange glances when Caecaltus leaves his eternal post in the Throne Room. No farewell, no wishing of good fortune. At the silent signal, Caecaltus just removes his helm and starts walking away, pausing only to meet his replacement, Sentinel-Companion Dolo Lamora. They pause, touch their bowed foreheads together, then continue on their separate ways. The forehead touch is not a greeting, or a gesture of respect, it is merely a rapid neuro-synergetic transfer that instantly acquaints Dolo Lamora with the circumstantial detail of Caecaltus' vacated post, as though he had been standing there himself all this while.

Uzkarel Ophite does not look up to watch Caecaltus go, nor does he look up to see Dolo Lamora arrive. He is simply aware of the situational change. His concentration and alert remain pure.

In the arming chambers below, two full war companies of Legio Custodes are priming for war: Valdor's assault company, and the Companion company that will flank the King-of-Ages. In truth, there is little to do, for every guardian has been fully and permanently war-ready for months. Weapons, cells, plate seals and armour systematics are simply checked and approved by white-clad adepts. Only a handful, like Diocletian, and the captain-general himself, who have been in recent combat, are obliged to submit to more thorough attention. Weapons are reloaded, cells recharged, blades re-edged. Damaged plate components are cleaned, re-finished, re-polished, or entirely replaced. Minor wounds are treated. Dirt, grease and blood are washed away. Perfection of wargear ensures perfection of performance.

It is almost silent in the Custodes arming vault. No one talks. Caecaltus Dusk submits to inspection. Serfs take his paragon spear and his praesidium shield aside for examination. Diagnostics check his sensoria, his refractor system, and his arae-shrike device. Scanners play inquisitive light across every segment and component of his ornate Aquilon-pattern plate.

The check seems to take longer than usual.

'Done?' Caecaltus asks.

The adept-supervisor nods, but asks that the proconsul's breastplate be removed for cleaning.

'Why?' Caecaltus asks.

To wash away minute traces of an unknown organic residue, he is told.

Caecaltus looks down at his golden chest plating. The old man. The spittle on his finger. The mark's not visible any more. It barely ever was.

'No,' says Caecaltus.

Passed ready, Caecaltus walks through to the inner chamber. He passes the Companions assembling in the holding area. Marked as ready, they draw up in perfect, silent rows, steady as statues in the amber light. From the arming chamber across the wide hallway outside, Caecaltus hears the chosen company of Imperial Fists Astartes taking their oath of moment. The voice of a Huscarl leads them. An instant timbre/tone match with Caecaltus' mental archive identifies the voice as Diamantis. An adequately proficient warrior, for a Space Marine. Human voices, human customs. The Legio Custodes need no such rituals, no bold evocation to summon up courage.

The voices fade behind him. The proconsul reaches the inner chamber. Few are let in here. The armourers are finishing their work. From the threshold, Caecaltus finally sees something that causes him to register a flicker of emotion. His heart rate shifts imperceptibly for two or three seconds.

Then he hears a step behind him and turns at once. His paragon spear sweeps instantly to 'guard' position.

'You cannot be here,' he states simply.

'But I am,' says Sanguinius, 'and you will let me pass.'

2:xxii

Fate denied

Sanguinius stands fully armed and plated for war. He has never looked more regal or magnificent.

'He will send for you when He is ready,' says the Custodes proconsul facing him.

'I will see my father now, Companion,' Sanguinius replies.

'You are defying His will.'

Sanguinius hesitates.

'I am, Proconsul Caecaltus,' he admits.

The Sentinel does not move. His paragon spear is held more firmly and steadily than Sanguinius has ever seen a weapon proffered. The micro-muscular control of the Legio Custodes is extraordinary.

'Proconsul,' says Sanguinius gently, 'I wish to explain myself to him, and I need to do that before–'

He pauses. He is aware of the others now. Four other senior Sentinels, summoned no doubt by the proconsul's neurosynergetics, have arrived behind him in complete silence. They have all come from the holding area. They are all members

of the Anabasis protection company. They are all gloriously
armed for war. They take their positions behind him, in a perfect half-moon suppression formation. Sanguinius hears the
slow whine of charging Adrathics.

Sanguinius raises his hands, open, and shows them to the
proconsul facing him. No threat, no weapon.

'I will see my father now, Caecaltus,' he says very calmly
and very clearly.

'You are defying His will,' Caecaltus repeats.

'Which is why I must see him now,' says Sanguinius.

'He will send for you when–'

Something ripples in the air. The proconsul tilts his head
for a moment, then nods, and steps aside.

The Bright Angel steps past him into the inner chamber.

The light inside is emerald, crossed by the white beams of
focus-lights deployed by hovering servitors. The air holds the
perfume of industrial incense.

Oh, my father…

A telepathic signal has just dismissed the armourers, and they
step back from their final refinements and adjustments. His
father's wargear, as it flexes in test and evaluation, moves with
the fluid perfection Sanguinius remembers from the fields of
Ullanor. Years of expert crafting have refined and enhanced its
systems and its subtle calibrations, and years more of finishing
and fining have made it gleam and glow like molten gold. His
father turns, and his scarlet mantle billows behind him, casting
an impossible shadow across the floor of the arming chamber,
like the rolling terminator of nightfall across the face of a world.

He has put on his new aspect. He is no longer Master of
Mankind, or King-of-Ages. He has put away the symbolic
masks of 'Lord of Terra' and 'father'. He has cast aside the
graven idol, and the aspect of the idle king upon a golden
throne, which he was obliged to wear for too long.

He is as Sanguinius first knew, as all the sons knew him, first-found onwards, in the glorious days of the beginning. He is again what they want him to be.

The warrior-monarch.

The Emperor.

Sanguinius' eyes widen, and he smiles. Then, as he becomes aware that the mighty proconsul and the other four Sentinels have sunk to their knees behind him, he bows his head in shame and humility.

He hears his father approach. He stands his ground, awaiting his rebuke. His polished, mended auramite plate conceals his lingering wounds.

No rebuke. Just a gentle question. Sanguinius looks up again.

'No, I will not be Warmaster,' Sanguinius says. 'Not here, not now. I will not take the name. It is a tarnished symbol.'

+Someone must stay. Someone must be seen to lead.+

'Fafnir Rann,' Sanguinius replies.

+Rann is a great hero.+

'Or Aimery,' says Sanguinius. 'Or Azkaellon. Or Thane. Or Huscarl Archamus, Second Of That Name. Any one of them would command the hearts of all loyal men. Any one of them. And there are others besides. Amit, in his great fury. Diamantis. Any of the golden Warden-chiefs of the Custodes. Diocletian Coros would–'

A small gesture cuts him short.

+You are refusing to stay?+

'I am insisting on going,' says Sanguinius.

+Is that not the same thing?+

A small, almost boyish smile crosses Sanguinius' face, partially masking the pain he is suffering.

'No, father,' he replies. 'After everything we have endured, the day is here. I absolutely refuse to let you go alone. It is my right, just as it is the right and honour of Rogal and Constantin.'

Behind the Angel primarch, on their knees, heads bowed, the five Sentinels Hetaeron listen, monitor, ready to react. Once more, the emotional turbulence of the late-born sons complicates the issue. They know their king's will profoundly well, for it is through that will alone that they function. It is never to be disobeyed.

+Proconsul? Companions?+

'My king?' says Caecaltus.

+Stand.+

Caecaltus rises. The other four rise with him.

+Companions, elucidate my son. He does not listen to me.+

Caecaltus and the others fan out. They form a wide circle around the Angel, their guardian spears upright at their sides. Sanguinius eyes them warily.

'My lord king could deny you, even now,' says Caecaltus, almost without inflection, as though the words are not his own and he is merely reporting them. 'He could cite the wounds that you think you have successfully concealed. You have not. You are too weak, too hurt.'

'My king is even afraid that the injuries done to you by Angron are mortal,' says Companion Andolen, 'and that death has already got its grip on you.'

'I will not listen to this,' says Sanguinius, glaring at the Sentinels. 'Not from them! Father, why do they speak for you?'

'My king wanted you to stay to protect you,' Caecaltus continues, without hesitation. 'As a rallying figurehead for the Palace, you can excel despite your wounds.'

'You do not need to fight, or find new reserves of strength and fortitude,' says Companion Nmembo. 'You can simply be present and visible, a presence signifying inspiration.'

'But to tell you that is to humiliate you,' says Companion Kliotan.

'To remark upon your weakness, and your lack of fitness,

to suggest your lord father is sparing you the effort of the onslaught to keep you out of harm's way,' says Companion Systratus, 'that would be hurtful.'

'That would be the greatest shame you could know,' says Caecaltus.

+But to face me, unflinching and defiant, shows your courage is not weak.+

'If you know all this, father, then you know that it is more than honour or reputation that drives me to defy you,' says Sanguinius.

+Tell me what you saw.+

Sanguinius hesitates.

+Your vision. Your foresight. The true reason you are so determined to join the assault.+

'If you know my visions, father, then you know already.'

+I do not see them as you do.+

'My king was alerted to your visions by the Sigillite,' says Caecaltus.

'My king scarcely knows their detail or specific content,' says Companion Andolen.

'My king only knows them as things that move upon you from time to time, like fever-fits,' says Companion Kliotan.

+Tell me what you saw.+

'You already know,' Sanguinius replies.

+This?+

Sanguinius grimaces as a fevered, nightmare image passes through his mind.

'No, father,' he says. 'I did not see you die. I did not see you fall. I do not demand to come so I can change that vision of heresy.'

The Angel blinks. A tiny tell, but enough. It wasn't that at all.

'I foresaw a different death at the hands of Horus,' the Angel says, a whisper. 'I have been seeing it for a long time. I have worked to outplay the prediction at every turn, at every step of the way, each permutation, each possible version, as it has come upon me, I have evaded it and refused its truth. I have denied the prophesy several times. But the possible permutations diminish. It wasn't Signus. It wasn't Ultramar. It wasn't Gorgon Bar. It wasn't Eternity Gate. The possibilities are finite, and there is one remaining. It must be now. It must be the endgame and the *Vengeful Spirit*.'

+Your death?+

Sanguinius pauses. He nods.

+You intend to go to see this fulfilled?+

'No, father. I intend to go to see it denied one last time.'

'It is far too great a risk,' says Caecaltus.

'No, proconsul! No!' Sanguinius declares. 'The alternative is a greater risk altogether!'

He stares at his Emperor-sire fiercely.

'If it is ordained that I am to die at Lupercal's hand,' says Sanguinius, 'then I cannot let you go alone. Because that means that Horus will survive so he can come for me again, afterwards. Don't you see? If I stay, Horus lives. And if Horus lives, then you will have failed.'

+Sanguinius–+

'I must face the last permutation. I must force it. I cannot allow for the possibility of another, for the cost to us will be too much.'

'So you would go willingly to your doom?' asks Nmembo. 'Sacrifice yourself for–'

'No.' Sanguinius has never sounded more sure. He has never sounded so much like his father. 'I intend to reject it. To defy it. To change it as I have changed it every time so far. Father, I will kill him myself if that's what it takes. But I cannot allow the permutations, now reduced to one, to breed and multiply again. I cannot allow a future with Horus in it.'

Silence. The moment of quiet is so utter, it is uncanny.

'My king, your father, has always called them configurations, not "permutations",' says Andolen softly. 'The models of the future He has set, refined and revised across the lifespan of mankind. They are always subject to variance.'

'We make our future, and that future is only grim darkness if we fail to be wise and cunning, and refuse to reconfigure our designs to match the fluctuations of fate and the vicissitudes of history,' says Kliotan.

'This has been my king's process since He first watched a man's fingers smudge paint on a wall,' says Systratus.

'As if by some beautiful symmetry, and because you are His son and His blood, you have intuitively learned to do the same,' says Caecaltus. He pauses, and then adds, 'My king is proud.'

+But still, you gamble everything.+

'Yes,' says Sanguinius.

+You would walk knowingly towards death.+

'Yes,' says Sanguinius again. And he smiles.

'My vision says that the day I face Horus is the day I die,' he says. 'So if I face him today, that day is here. But Malcador told us, father, as we stood in the Throne Room, he told us that time has *ceased*. Today is not today, or any day. We are caught in the un-now. Horus, father, will not kill me today, for there *is* no today. By the time a tomorrow comes, a tomorrow of any kind, Horus will be done, defeated by your wrath, and my vision will be voided. This is how I know fate can be denied. The permutation… the configuration… can be defied if we act together.'

A nod. Permission.

'Prepare to join your company, lord primarch,' says Caecaltus.

2:xxiii

The last testament of the enemy

They are preparing to kill him.

'Inevitably,' says Basilio Fo. He has been expecting it. There are only so many reprieves a man like him can expect to get (especially given what I've done). He has found loopholes before, proved his usefulness to postpone the hour of execution, but there may not be any left to find.

He waits, then, for the inevitable. He hears heavy footsteps approaching outside his chamber. The captain-general (a particularly vicious piece of work, in my unsolicited opinion) has granted him quarters in the depths of the Sanctum Imperialis. The last days of Fo's long life have been spent close to the very heart of things, barely eight kilometres from the Throne Room (barely eight kilometres from Him!). Fo wonders if He knows Fo is here. The Custodians are a strange breed. At times, they seem like automata, mere vulgar extensions of His arrogant will. But, at others, they seem oddly independent and secretive, as though they are working to an agenda of their own. (Am I kept a secret even from Him? Am I a highly confidential resource, a secret weapon project, like the device I made for them?)

He doubts it. The Emperor (and it is excruciating to use the inflated, grandiose title, though ultimately preferable to the even more objectionable pronoun, as if 'He' is the only 'Him' that anyone could ever, possibly be referring to) is omniscient, isn't He? Possessed of a 'mindsight' that perceives all? That's the myth He likes to sell, anyway. If there's any truth in it, surely He would be aware of Fo's proximity? And aware of what the captain-general's had him doing.

But if He does, it's surprising that He hasn't simply descended from on high in a pillar of flame, and reduced Fo to ashes. They never got on. Too many ideological differences. Too much (what is the phrase?) blood over the weir.

The quarters provided for him are very spare, so spare they barely earn the name 'quarters'. Fo has a cot, a chair, a basin, and he has been allowed a few books. There are no windows, and the door is kept locked. It's a cell, really, though of a better quality than that rancid hole in the Blackstone. Nearby, a short walk away under guard, is the small laboratorium where they let him work. No one has come to fetch him today (undoubtedly because they consider my work to be finished. The device is, after all, essentially complete, as a prototype form at least. In hindsight, I should probably have ignored the captain-general's demands for quick results, and spun the work out to keep myself indispensable). His quarters, the laboratorium, that's all he gets to see. Fo was free, briefly, thanks to the gene-witch, but now this is his entire world. Two rooms. He is in the greatest palace in the galaxy, the greatest treasure-store of learning, and he gets to see two small rooms of it.

It is, perhaps, the greatest and cruellest punishment of all, to be so very close to so much knowledge (He always did like His books) and yet not be able to touch it, or see it. Fo never expected to return to Terra. Never. He expected to die somewhere out in the stars, his name forgotten, his latest host-body finally expiring of old age or some systemic failure he lacked the technology to repair. When, once in a while, every couple of lifetimes during his long exile on Velich Tarn, he thought about Terra, Fo dreamed sad dreams of the world that he would have made from it, the future he would have shaped. Fo's Imperium would have been superior, a post-human extrapolation of the species devised along pure biomechanical lines, not this dystopian, hyper-militarised hierarchy. Fo would have eschewed any dependence on legacy genetics, psionics, and most especially the warp. He would not have called it an Imperium, and he most surely would not have declared himself Emperor.

But he'd lost that fight, lost it long ago, during the ferocious centuries of the Age of Strife. The Emperor had prevailed, and Fo had fled to the stars. And because, as the old adage says, history is written by the victors, the Emperor is now the saviour of mankind, and Fo is a war criminal, a monster, the personification of all the wrongs that the Emperor has come to make right.

Except, Fo wasn't wrong. The world is literally falling apart. Doom has come to Terra. Fo takes little satisfaction from that, but there is some vindication there. The Emperor's overweening scheme has brought about this calamity. His militarised hierarchy, His legacy genetics, His careless employment of psionics, His foolhardy dalliance with immaterial power; these things, the foundational principles of His Imperium, are precisely the elements that have brought about its fall. They have combined (with, deliciously, an elegant garnish of hubris) in a perfect hellstorm. This end, this death, is His doing. It is exactly the catastrophe Fo predicted and fought against.

Vindication is a small consolation, something to cling to and smile about as he waits for the end. Fo won't die alongside the rest of mankind, even though that annihilation can be no more than hours away. He will already be dead, because they are coming to kill him.

Does he have regrets? Some: that no one ever listened to him; that he didn't prevail in the Age of Strife and divert this benighted future; that he never got the chance to look Him in the eye and say, 'I told you so.' Nothing worth stewing over. What's done is done. If Fo has any real regret at all, it's that he did, against all expectation, return to Terra but, once there, he never got a chance to examine the wealth of knowledge and advancement that had accumulated in his absence. That would have been the only reason ever to return: a few days, left to his own devices, in His libraries.

The footsteps stop outside his door. Fo hears a voice, and the activation of a key. The inner hatch opens with a sigh, sleeving into the wall.

His executioner enters.

2:xxiv

Beyond reason

The air throbs. The lights are dimming to half power. In the great basalt vaults nearby, the mass teleport platforms are being drawn to power.

They walk into the holding area, father and son. They are flanked by the proconsul and his four impassive Sentinels Hetaeron.

The light smokes in the dim, heavy air as they halt in the centre of the chamber. Around them, the four companies of Anabasis stand assembled: the burnished Cataphractii, the assault squads, the Terminators, the majestic Sanguinary Guard, Dorn and the Huscarl Praetorians, Valdor and his towering Custodes, Raldoron and the Blood Angels, Diamantis and the Imperial Fists, all geared and plated for war, all in panoply as beautiful as it is terrifying. All bow their heads in reverence.

The Emperor has returned and stands among them.

'One last question,' Sanguinius says.

+Why do we suffer?+

Sanguinius laughs in surprise that he is not really surprised at all.

'You know my question before I ask it?' he says.

+Of course.+

'It is in the forefront of your thoughts,' says Caecaltus.

'It is the bedrock of your mind,' says Systratus.

+Ask it.+

'Very well,' says Sanguinius. 'Why do we suffer? Knowing the trials and pain we would face, why did you make us to suffer?'

+Because whatever we are and whatever we do, we are, and must always be, human.+

'That simple?' Sanguinius asks.

'Nothing is simple,' says Proconsul Caecaltus. 'But my king vowed to the Sigillite that He would answer your questions as they came. So, understand. Suffering, pain, grief, they are all extremities of the human condition.'

'It would have been too easy to shed those things,' says Andolen, 'to excise them, to remove the messy and illogical mechanisms of emotional response, those non-verbal animal reactions of our early hominid forms.'

'My king could have made his sons, and their warrior-sons too, without emotion,' says Nmembo, 'freed from feeling, concern or care, unburdened by hurt and loss and sadness, coldly proofed against the galaxy with a biological armour stronger than any ceramite plate.'

'But that would have made them less,' says Systratus.

'That would have made them mere flesh-machines,' says Kliotan, 'bloodlessly cold, and driven only by instruction and intellect.'

'Even we, His Companions, woven by a different craft, were not forged to lack that spark,' says Caecaltus.

'But, what? You just hide it better?' asks Sanguinius wryly.

Caecaltus makes a grudging shrug.

'But isn't rationality the very essence of your working?' Sanguinius asks his father.

+Most certainly.+

'And the feeling heart and the hurting soul can be an impediment at times,' says Systratus.

'It was for the aeldari, as we understand it,' says Kliotan.

'Reason, and rationalist stability, and the empirical operation of high science, these must be our unshakable touchstones,' says Andolen.

'Then what? You strove for a balance when you made us?' Sanguinius asks, frowning.

+It was more than that.+

'I realise it is a hard question to answer,' says Sanguinius. 'Even for you. Even with a mouthpiece as articulate as the proconsul. Forgive me, I–'

He stops short.

The world has altered, without warning. The holding area has gone, the proud companies of war vanished. Sanguinius realises he is being granted his answer after all. He is being *shown* it, a symbolic answer blending signs and devices, his gift of foresight commandeered by his father's will to display a last personal, privileged vision, exclusively shaped for his eyes alone. The powerful telempathic rapport enfolds him for a second, sharing memories that run back deep into time. It is immersive, more than any vision he has previously experienced in his life, and bewildering at first. The shift of scale, of intellect and perception, is giddying. Stars of all magnitude, each one singing its eternal electromagnetic song, circle him slowly in void without end or edge. He is not sure what he is supposed to be seeing, or how to decipher it.

'Father?'

Then, slowly, he begins to see. Meaning, structure, the long, tenuous thread of a plan.

He sees a world below him. It is perfect and bright, its vivid blues and greens mantled with lace of white cloud as dazzling as ice.

Terra. No, no. He begins to understand better. Terra, before it was Terra. Old Earth.

Young Earth. A species upon it. A species in its youth, young, virile, headstrong and rash, but brimming with potential, far from perfect, but with the capacity to be so much.

This is the start point. Time begins to spin like a wheel, accelerating. It begins to play out its thread, fast and faster. Sanguinius catches his breath. It's too fast, too fast for him to follow. Histories flicker past, like fire-cast shadows dancing on the wall of a cave, occasionally, almost subliminally, illuminating some mark or image painted there. A figure. An animal. A city. A handprint.

It's all too quick for him to comprehend, too fast, too much.

Except, he realises, he *does* follow. He *does* understand.

'I am…' he murmurs, 'I am–'

I am the end product of centuries of a Great Work, he comprehends, marvelling. *Me, my brothers, our sons, all of our kind, we are the culmination of a Great Work, and that work is nothing less than the salvation of human biology. I see the beautiful young world below has grown older and darker now, stained with damage and woe. The void around me has grown blacker, suffocating. The Ages of Strife and Long Night have come and gone, woefully damaging the human genome. It has fallen prey to grim genetic drift and degenerative mutation rates. The Great Work is not just to unify Terra and rebuild the infrastructure of empire, it is to rebuild the human vessel itself. To repair molecular codes, to arrest mutation and, where necessary, select for positive trait alterations.*

Pinprick specks of light flicker on the surface of the world, increasing in number, like the first shoots of spring from hard winter ground. They multiply. They flicker out among the stars too. They are minds. Psykers, proliferating unchecked, are a deeply destructive flaw, but the emergent Navigators are essential. Sanctioned genetic reconstitution is crucial for human growth, and in pursuing it, my father reaches a profound understanding of human biological structure and function.

Aeons subdivide. Centuries turn over, one by one, like tarot cards on a table. As they turn, rationality has to remain paramount, but emotions, though unruly and forever unpredictable, are still mankind's greatest assets. Long years of neuro research show my father. this beyond doubt. The human mind is an astoundingly powerful instrument. We are capable of almost anything. But without emotions, we would permanently operate at capacity, even when performing simple tasks. If our minds were machines, they would have to be filled to the brim with exhaustive, pre-programmed, pre-set instructions for every possible eventuality. This processing would demand a level of energy that no human, or even post-human, could ever maintain.

'That is the function of feeling?' Sanguinius asks, intrigued, his voice tiny in the vastness of the memories that shift around him. It is as though he is at last making sense of himself.

Now cells subdivide in place of aeons. The arch of heaven, the Milky Way, is a gene helix. Lives pass by, like the ticking of a clock, so very swift, each one filled with joy and sorrow, love and loss, success and failure.

Emotions are the very root of our supremacy as an organic species. Arising not from the cortex, but from root brainstem consciousness, they are reactive, and function as short-cuts to decision. They facilitate rapid thought and resolution, bypassing processed perception. We think and then act because we feel first. Emotions emancipate our minds, allowing for spontaneous and intuitive cognition, and they remove the need for densely pre-programmed brains. Emotions are symbols, instantly bypassing conscious decision and conveying more than words can ever manage.

'So they are fundamental, not vestigial traits?' Sanguinius wonders, fascinated.

The memory rapport fades. Sanguinius feels the loss of it. He has never felt so safe anywhere, or so intimately enfolded. He has never felt his father's mind so close.

They are still in the holding area. All heads around them are still bowed. Not even a second has passed, and no one has noticed the tiny interruption.

'Quite fundamental,' Caecaltus replies. 'They make us what we are. To create the primarchs and the Astartes without emotions would have doomed us to stagnation, indecision and failure.'

'The very things, those unique, individual qualities that made Horus Lupercal turn, are the same traits that will allow you to triumph,' says Systratus.

'My king, your father, would no more have made His sons without emotion than He would have removed them from Himself,' says Caecaltus. 'And He could have done both.'

'He considered that?' asks Sanguinius.

'Of course,' says Caecaltus. 'He rationally weighed every option. Anyway, there is your answer. That is why we suffer.'

+We suffer because it is the sad but necessary consequence of our ability to prevail.+

'Then I thank you,' Sanguinius says.

+For the explanation?+

Sanguinius shakes his head.

'For the curious gift of humanity. I have been called a god, father. I have been called an Angel, and looked upon as divine. I would rather the vulnerability of a warm and feeling heart than the cold mettle of a deathless god.'

The others approach: Rogal, adorned in shining golden plate inlaid with chrome and amber, and Constantin, caparisoned in lacquered auramite. Behind them, the assembled host stands ready, four companies of the most superlative warriors the galaxy has ever known.

And the most capable. Sanguinius understands that now.

'My Emperor, the platforms await,' Rogal says.

The hum of power rises. The lights flicker.

The Emperor of Mankind unsheathes his sword.

2:xxv

Fate proves cruel

In the Rotunda, the lights go out. There is a distant bang of mass discharge, a quake of overpressure that seems to shake the whole Palace, and a sudden stink of ozone. Consoles fail, and several hololith plates crack and craze spontaneously. After a moment, emergency power cuts in, and the chamber is lit by a ruddy glow for several seconds until main power returns.

Sandrine Icaro consults her data-slate, checks for confirmation, and then steps onto the central podium.

'Attention!' she shouts. 'Your attention!'

The voices around her drop to silence. Every face turns.

'Notification,' she announces. 'Teleport event confirmed as complete and optimal. Anabasis assault is underway and running.'

There is a burst of applause. Some present look upward involuntarily.

'Get to work!' she yells, climbing down.

At station nineteen, Tactician Jonas Gaston tries to get Icaro's attention, but she is surrounded by War Court seniors. The

Gilded Walk has just fallen and immediate responses must be decided. Sidozie, of the Chosen, sees Gaston's agitation, and crosses to him.

'Situation?' Sidozie asks. The young man is junior, inexperienced, drafted in at short notice to plug a gap left after Bhab. He is clearly close to panic.

'A signal, sir,' he begins, one hand pressed to his earpiece.

Sidozie checks the display. Gaston is manning overwatch and deep listening, monitoring traitor fleet operations in the hope of intercepting command transmissions.

'A signal?'

'Very broken… very faint…' Gaston says.

Sidozie plugs his augmetics into the station system and listens for himself. A reedy, scratchy whisper, like the scrape of twigs. He moves Gaston aside, and adjusts the filters with expert precision. He listens again.

Gaston sees the look on his face.

Sidozie increases gain to maximum, until the audio backwash is almost deafening. He strains to hear.

'*…Repeat, we are nine hours out. Nine hours out. Deploying now to wide formation assault positions, inbound. Terra Control, do you receive? Terra Control, can you respond? Repeat, we are nine hours out. Terra Control, respond. We need immediate tracking guidance. Light your beacons. We are extending to wide assault formation. Terra, hold your positions. Remain in secure defensive alignment. Hold your positions. That's all you need to do. Just hold. Repeat, we are nine hours out. Terra Control, respond. Acknowledge. Hold your positions and light guidance now. Terra Control, this is Guilliman…*'

'Oh, shit,' stammers Sidozie. 'Oh shit.'

He turns. He starts to bellow Icaro's name.

2:xxvi

_____

In ruins

As they charge towards the pitiful bulwarks and dug-outs before Radium Gate, the Imperial Fists hit their flank hard from the left. What was already havoc deteriorates into a savage, running melée in the smoke and the howling, cyclonic filth. Bodies crash into bodies, blades swing and smash, and armour buckles. The liquid mud is a foot deep, and splashes high as bodies topple into it. An Imperial Fist with twin axes, so doused in blood his yellow armour looks more like the plate worn by the IX, drives through the wheeling mayhem, removing heads and limbs. The Neverborn are screeching in the smoke-pall. Bolters bark and bang.

The Imperial Fist, roaring, takes down Itha Clathis of Second Company with a blow that sounds like a sledgehammer hitting tin, and sends blood and fragments of bone into the air in a stupendous, arcing fountain. He knocks Kaltos of Second aside with a glancing strike, then comes at Tyro Gamex of Third, gore stringing from his blades. Another figure blocks his path, intercepting him with an impact like two armoured transports colliding head-on.

Ezekyle Abaddon, First Captain of the Sons of Horus, wrenches out his blade. His foe is dead. Fafnir Rann is dead.

Abaddon crouches in the steaming mud, and tears off the corpse's helmet. No. Not Rann, after all. An Imperial Fist, one of the VII, but not Rann. In the confusion of the melée, he thought it was. And the man fought well, which seemed to confirm Abaddon's identification.

But it's not him. That trophy is yet to be taken.

Abaddon rises. Sons of Horus, giants in dirt-sullied plate, explode through the smoke past him, splashing forward, charging the line. Bolters open up, sustained fire. The smoke jumps with flashes and shadows. The weak, improvised defence of Radium Gate mounted by the Imperial Fists is about to collapse as fast as the Gilded Walk resistance. Dorn's master touch is gone. They are a shambles, rudderless, lacking cohesion, lacking strategy, reduced to impulsive and helplessly reactive efforts of repulse. Abaddon has lost count of the figures in yellow, red and white he has butchered today.

There is shame in this. It is not the victory he dreamed of, or the triumph he desired. Too much has been accomplished by infernal processes, by startling Neverborn atrocities that have exploded out of polluted darkness and thin air, or sprouted from the buckling ground. Not enough, not nearly enough, has been done the way he was taught. He may mock the Praetorians for their loss of military precision, but where is his? Abaddon is a warrior. He wanted to take the Palace with militant perfection and exemplary soldiering.

But this is no longer, in any way, a soldier's war.

He is sick at heart, sick to the gut. They have brought horror, and become horror. This was not the way his father ever practised, and it is not the victory his father promised.

Abaddon halts, lowering his blade. The Sons of Horus continue to stream past him on either side, bellowing in glee, giving themselves entirely to the weaponised insanity of the fall of Terra. Despoilers all.

Let them finish it. Let them take the Gate and dismember the defenders. He starts to trudge back up the broken slope, through the choking waft of ash, towards what passes for their forward command position. The vox clicks in his ear again. It's been doing that for half an hour, longer perhaps. Not the incoherent back-chatter of the mob, a signal: someone trying to contact him long-range. But the channels are washed out, or jammed, and each time he's tried to answer it, there's been nothing but garbled sounds and white noise.

At the line, where the Sons of Horus' spiked banners are pitched like the lank sails of funeral barges, the Mechanicum of the war-steads are arriving, leading columns of barbaric killing engines and rumbling saurian breacher-rams. Clain Pent, Fifth Disciple of Nul, stands aloft on the gibbet-balcony of a vast, tusked war engine, his limbs writhing like some manic conductor at a rostrum, orchestrating the advance and deployment via noospheric gesture. Eyet-One-Tag of Epta motions to Abaddon from her palanquin.

'First Captain,' she says, a human mouth framed and crowned by augmetic sensor-blisters. 'There is a repeated signal–'

'I am aware,' he growls.

'You do not respond?'

'My system is jammed–'

'Then avail yourself of my devices,' she invites.

Mastervox instruments are rolled forward in the acid rain. Adepts fuss and simper around them, cleaning dials. Abaddon takes a proffered plug and connects it to his suit sockets.

'Abaddon,' he says.

'Ezekyle, at last!'

It is Argonis. He sounds scared.

'Are you still orbital?' Abaddon asks, puzzled.

'Yes, yes. I've been trying to reach you. Trying for hours–'

'Just speak, equerry.'

'The voids, Abaddon. The voids–'

'What of them?'

'He's lowered them. He's lowered the voids.'

'What voids? Who has?' Abaddon asks.

'Lupercal, Abaddon. Lupercal has lowered the void shields on the Vengeful Spirit.'

Abaddon pauses. Toxic rain and liquid mud trickle off his visor.

'Are you still there? Ezekyle?'

'Say that again,' says Abaddon.

PART THREE

THE DAY WILL NOT
SAVE THEM

3:i

A warp-twisted hell

The abrupt silence is shocking.

It puzzles Caecaltus Dusk for a second, until he realises it just *feels* like silence because he is so accustomed to the distant, constant drone of war.

At my post in the Throne Room, day after day, the faraway rumble of warfare was so unremitting, I became inured to it, and inhabited it without regard. But here–

In a shiver, the background drone has gone, and only silence remains, a fossil imprint of missing sound.

The silence, the utter stillness, is tranquilising. Caecaltus feels numb. For a moment, the proconsul has to remember – actively, *consciously* force himself to remember – where they are and what they have come to do.

We have come to strike. We have come to undertake the solemn business of war against–

Around him, the golden demigods of the Hetaeron company are silent too, as though they, like Caecaltus, are unnerved by the sudden quiet. None of them has experienced the thunderclap of their arrival, for the savage boom of mass and pressure displacement was over by the time they were fully materialised. Vapour drifts from their armoured forms, teleport energy dissipates like forest mist, and sparks of recorporealisation backwash circle them like fireflies.

Proconsul Caecaltus takes a step forwards. Companions advance around him, spears aimed. As they begin to move, transmaterial dust residue sifts from their plate like flour. They move quickly. They move silently. They move in perfect coordination, spears raised. They encircle the almost luminous figure of their king and master, ready to protect Him from–

What was I expecting? Anything. Everything. But–

There is no attack, no ambush, no host of warriors waiting to repel their boarding action.

If this is a trap, and the Praetorian Seventh son was so sure it would be, then it is either an odd one or a poor one.

The assault site selected for the spearhead is Embarkation Deck Two, and that is where they are. It is a vast chamber, part hangar, part launch tunnel. The distant mouth of it, a kilometre away, shows the cold blackness of space, held at bay by integrity fields. Caecaltus turns slowly, surveying the long plasteel flight ramps, where guide lights blink on automatic, the raised galleries and skeletal gantries, the side holding bays, the munition silos. Above them, the immense manipulator gears and ship-clamps hang like ornithological limbs, grasps empty. Around them, on the launch rails and standing platforms, the Stormbirds are rigged for preflight. There are eight of them. They are painted white, and marked with the emblems of the XVI Legion Luna Wolves.

I would have thought they might be re-dressed by now in their new traitor liveries. I am surprised, indeed, that there are any here. Were they not all deployed, long since?

Caecaltus approaches the nearest launch stand, with Kliotan to his right and Andolen to his left.

Why is there no one here? The Stormbirds are rigged and ready, but ready for what?

He looks up at the sleek lines of the nearest craft.

The huge transatmospheric drop-craft were the backbone of all Imperial assaults during the crusade to remake the galaxy. Fine, trustworthy, graceful machines from an earlier time, their kind is now slowly being replaced by more functional delivery vehicles. Warmaster Lupercal has kept his in perfect condition.

And with them, from this deck and the other five like it on this mighty flagship, the Warmaster conquered half the stars in his father's name. From here, the ceramite deck plates beneath my feet, the Warmaster's sons set out, oaths of moment sworn, and accomplished deeds of valour and skill that aligned the peace of the Imperium. Sometimes, I was with them. I may even have gone to war in some of these very machines. I remember escorting my master on a war-drop in Stormbird Three during the Gorro Undertaking. Is that one of these?

Caecaltus begins to look for the tail-number insignia–

He stops himself short.

How am I allowing distraction into my mind? How am I sidelined by memory and nostalgia?

Where is my focus?

We have achieved primary site-to-site. I lead a company of one hundred Custodians in support of my master, who has drawn for war for the first time since the secret conflict in the webway.

Why can't I concentrate?

No one comes. Nothing moves. The deck is empty of figures, except the Lord of Terra and His Hetaeron. There is no sign of damage or decay, no dirt or spent casings from rapid turnaround and refit. The lights glow pearlescent. Atmospheric processors hum at the frontier of hearing. Fuel lines are still connected. On consoles and wall plates, screeds of luminous data flicker and shift silently.

If this was a ceremonial inspection, my master would pass the Warmaster's scrupulous presentation with approval, and commend his deck crews and servitor chiefs.

But it is not. It is not! This is the solemn business of war, not–

There are no servitors either. Not even dormant units in the charging racks of the side bays. Just the haunted, echo-less serenity of a shiftship holding orbit. It is almost hypnotic.

The proconsul's Custodes, golden phantoms, edge forwards and fan out wider, spears raised for instant reaction. In their midst, the Master of Mankind steps with them. Silence prevails. There is no ambient vox-chatter, nothing on the link, no noospherics, no psykanic activity. Everything is a soft, doughy emptiness.

How has our arrival not been detected? A bulk-teleport assault… the energy signature of that, and the contiguous heat-flare, that should have registered on the ship's sensoria like a missile strike–

No alarms sound. No warning detectors blink. There is no noise of activity, of armoured figures rushing in response.

Is this ship empty?

Caecaltus tightens his grip on his paragon spear. He feels something welling inside him. With frank astonishment, he realises it is fear.

I haven't known fear in centuries. Fear was an old friend, but we no longer speak, for I have no business with him any more.

Yet here he is.

The Stormbird on its launch rack to his right, its tail stencil is *eight*. Caecaltus thought it was *three* for a second, but no–

I thought we would be transporting into a warp-twisted hell, not this. I can't–

No noospherics. No vox. Not even a hint of immaterial activity. This chamber is as null-sterile as the vaults of the Sisterhood. How–

Where are we? I can't–

Caecaltus looks at his warriors, silent, auramite giants stalking forward against the bathing whiteness of the deck.

Don't they feel it too? Don't they–

The lights on the launching ramp wink on auto-cycle, blinking a pathway to blackness.

Where are Dorn and the captain-general and my lord's beloved Angel? Where are their companies? What–

Everything seems slow. Like a dream. Like a heavy dream. The silence glides into him, oppressive, like the shadow of the void, the deep, cosmic mono-note of the celestial deeps. *Can–*

Why can't I focus?

Caecaltus sees the main internal hatch, a bulwark of steel and adamantine. *Embarkation Deck VIII* is fusion-engraved across it.

My mouth is dry. I–

The *Vengeful Spirit* only has six embarkation decks.

Caecaltus should have noticed all of this. *All* of it. He was primed and alert, ready – perhaps readier than he has *ever* been – for the trial ahead of them. He should have noticed these discrepancies the second he arrived. But his mind is like sludge, like jelly–

I should have seen–

Caecaltus turns to look at Sentinel-Warden Kliotan at his right. He feels like he is moving in slow motion, suspended in thick fluid. None of them have spoken since their arrival. Whatever else might have broken the oppressive silence, their vox-link should be live.

There should have been immediate hortcode exchange and voice confirmation on arrival. My helm display is dead–

Only now, Caecaltus notices that too.

Kliotan turns to look at him. It is very slow. It takes a century for his crested golden helm to turn. Others turn too. The proconsul's Custodians all turn to look at him. They are as slow as sap, as slow as continental drift, as slow as the very slowest setting of a pict playback. They turn to look at him–

No, not at me. They are all turning to look at the Master of Mankind–

Blood wells from Sentinel-Warden Kliotan's eye slits and trickles down his faceplate like tears. It oozes and runs from the snarling mouth of his sculpted visor.

What is this–

It runs from the eyes of all the warriors around them. Caecaltus feels himself weeping blood too–

What's happening–

The slow silence ends.

Suddenly, there is nothing but screaming. Suddenly, the world is a blur of lightning-fast movement.

They come for Him. Weeping blood and shrieking, the Master of Mankind's own guardians come at Him from all sides.

3:ii

888

'Try it again,' says Sandrine Icaro. Her voice is brittle and sharp.

The Hegemon's Rotunda is hushed, but for the murmur of instrumentation and the occasional warble of an alert. No one speaks.

'Negative vox,' says the War Court officer at main communication at last. 'Negative noospheric link. Negative trace signal or transponder locator. Negative lock on teleport marker beacons.'

'Keep trying,' says Icaro. 'Ten-second cycle. They must be alerted to the situation change. They... *He* has to know of Ultramar's approach.'

And we have to know, thinks Ilya, watching from her station. *We have to know if they even got there.* The data reported by Lion's Gate port is deeply concerning. It suggests that all augury scans and sensoria reports are dubious at best, falsified or unreliably incomplete. Anabasis assault should have been called off. But who tells Him that He cannot do something?

There should be joy, the first real joy in months, a renewed hope of salvation. The Emperor has risen to lead the final fight, and the liberating fleets of the last, loyal sons, in all their fury, are but nine hours out.

But there is no way of confirming the signal from Guilliman, and no way of answering. The avenging sons come too late anyway, for their father has already committed and passed the point of no return. And, though nine hours close, the vengeance fleet is blind. It cannot find Terra in the warp storm wracking the Solar Realm, and Terra has no beacon to light to show it the way.

Ilya looks at the stations nearby, where senior tacticians have been analysing auspex returns and detection grid metadata since she first brought the issue regarding Target Principal to Icaro's attention. Sidozie also has two seniors running a forensic review of the teleport pattern log.

One of them suddenly signals to Sidozie. The Chosen reviews his data-slate, then hurries it across to Icaro. Ilya just gets out of her seat and follows him. She's at Sidozie's side when he presents the findings to Icaro. Icaro doesn't even bother sending Ilya back to her station. She is at the very edge now. Ilya can see it in her, the frantic, milling spiral of panic.

'What does this mean?' Icaro asks Sidozie.

'It's a transmission report coding,' says the Chosen. 'It is appended to all teleportation transfers. *One-one-one*, for example, signifies successful transfer, with complete materialisation integrity, at selected destination and–'

'I know that!' Icaro snaps. 'What is this? What is *eight-eight-eight*?'

'We… aren't sure, mistress,' says Sidozie. 'It appears to be an archaic error signature, usually expressing a teleport failure due to insufficient power. Either that, or it's some invasive scrap code.'

'What are you saying?' Icaro asks. 'Are they still here? Is He still here? Did they not transfer?'

'They are *not* here,' Sidozie replies. 'Throne Room confirms this. Power level discharge was also confirmed as optimal on all bulk teleport platforms. But we are also unable to hard-fix Target Principal.'

'But it's right *there*. Shields down. Wide open.'

'It appears to be, mistress. But, with repeated attempts, we cannot acquire solid target or location solutions on it.'

Icaro looks at him.

'What the hell does that mean?' she asks. 'What the hell does eight-eight-eight signify?'

'It means, mistress,' he replies, 'we have absolutely no idea where Anabasis assault went. We have no idea where He is.'

3:iii

Vigil

Despite the intense glare, it is possible to see the drops of blood trickling from the Sigillite's tear ducts.

Vulkan doesn't want to look. The light radiating from the Golden Throne and the figure upon it is too bright, and too sickly, and it chills him to see the old Regent in such extraordinary, silent pain.

But he must look. A last vigil. The most important of all.

The Throne Room has been emptied of all but key personnel. The Concillium adepts fuss at their tasks, nursing the wheezing stability engines. The Throne itself, radiating light like a miniature sun, sings. It is a high, constant note, a harmonic vibration, a fingertip running around the edge of a glass, but amplified to a level that could crack stone.

Vulkan wonders how long Malcador will be able to maintain control. How long can a man last like that? The energies pulsing through the Throne would cremate a mortal soul in seconds. Malcador is no ordinary mortal, but he is nothing

compared to Vulkan's father, and Vulkan knows how grievously his father suffered in that seat.

Malcador sits fixed, rigid, still as the stone effigy on the lid
of a tomb, but for the spasmodic twitch of his hands and the
tremble of his eyelids. His eyes have rolled back, showing
only white. His mouth is slack, as though palsied. His skin,
it seems to Vulkan, is beginning to crack, like the dry pages
of an ancient book.

The Sigillite has not spoken since he took the Throne. Vulkan
didn't expect him to. He knew the focus required for operation
was so onerous that there would be nothing spare to give. But
Vulkan found himself anticipating *something*. The Sigillite was
ever an ingenious man, with power to match his cunning.
Vulkan never liked him much, but he has always admired
him. The Regent had such a breadth of learning, and such a
hunger for knowledge. Vulkan suspects that one of the reasons,
beyond loyalty and necessity, that Malcador took the Throne
was that it would offer him a chance to see, to *truly* see, for one
lethal but spectacular instant, the greatest knowledge of all.
To operate the Golden Throne is to open one's mind entirely
to the etheric structures of the universe, and Malcador has an
exceptionally potent mind. The Regent's only task is to regulate the dangerously hypertensive webway, but in enhancing
the Sigillite's ability to do that, the Throne would also grant
him a unique perspective. Mindsight, foresight, farsight and
all other aspects of psykana would be amplified, providing a
metaphysical insight that, Vulkan imagines, borders on omnis-
cience. Thus would be unveiled the invisible underpinnings
of fragile realspace, the deep and eternal conjunction of mat-
erium and immaterium, the ephemeral patterns of the warp,
things that Vulkan, in all his journeys and all his years, has
never witnessed.

Vulkan had been secretly convinced that the Sigillite would

communicate something, or at least *try*. If not words, then a sign of some sort. Where Vulkan's father is infamous for withholding, and only ever alluded to things the Throne had allowed him to see, Malcador would want to share. Sitting there, in silent agony, he is surely learning things, more and more, with every passing second, things that could undoubtedly assist the war.

What could he be perceiving? The dispositions of the enemy? Radical techniques of defence? Esoteric methods of combating the Neverborn? Surely, all those things and more. Malcador, who, as Rogal Dorn's silent partner, had orchestrated the fundamental mechanics of the siege and every stage of their obsidional tactics, now has a superlative vantage. He can see all of the everything he could never see before.

Vulkan was certain that Malcador would be dying to communicate that, to use his insight to steer them, with utmost expertise, through the final battle.

Instead, he just seems to be dying. Forever.

Vulkan looks to the side. Abidemi has approached. The Salamanders Draaksward bows his head.

'Any word?' Vulkan asks.

'No, my Lord of Drakes,' replies Abidemi. 'The teleport chambers report transfer, and Hegemon Control confirms it. Anabasis assault is deployed.'

'But?'

'No contact, lord. My agents in Hegemon Control report some consternation.'

'Regarding?'

'Nothing official, my lord. But there are concerns that the situation was the trap our Praetorian suspected. Indeed, there is great doubt as to exactly where your brothers and our lord your father have gone.'

'Teleport signal capture? Redirection?'

'Perhaps. There is no data. They may be aboard the *Spirit* now, or the *Spirit* itself may have been a bluff.'

Vulkan looks back at the figure in the Throne.

'I think he knows,' he says.

'The Lord Sigillite?'

Vulkan nods. His jawline clenches. 'I think he knows and he wants to tell us. I think he's desperate to tell us.'

'Why, my lord?'

'Look at his mouth, Atok. See? The way it twitches, now and then? A shiver of the lips. I think he's trying to tell us something and he simply cannot.'

Abidemi hesitates.

'My lord,' he says, 'you should withdraw to a safer distance. It is too dangerous to be this close to the Throne for long.'

Vulkan nods, and sends the Draaksword back from the heat of the glare. He takes one last look before following.

'What are you seeing, Sigillite?' Vulkan murmurs. 'What are you seeing? Everything? Nothing? Or the broken fragments of our demise?'

3:iv

Fragments

It is the end, and not the end. The death, and not the death. The final fortress of Terra's Palace has less than a day of life left in it, but that day will never end. Linear time has gone, replaced by the warp's un-when. The vortical fury of the consuming flames will rage forever, and the very act of dying, even on the Golden Throne itself, has become immortal.

Demigod corpses litter the Gilded Walk, the Clanium Precinct, and the splintered ferrocrete wastes around the Palatine Ring. The corpses wear war plate, fabulously wrought, of yellow and red, white and gold. Inside each suit of war plate are bones and meat and rapidly cooling blood, and the end of dreams and duties and proud principles. Each corpse is an oath kept, a moment over. Each one is an ended history of prestigious deeds and courage that knew no fear. Each one contains a life story that no one will ever tell, for the remembrancers are all gone. There have been no last words, no final testaments, no mortal declarations. No one is left alive to harvest,

with narthecium and tender surgical reductor, their progenoid
seed, a thousand times as precious, by gram, than tritium.
Each demigod has died alone, unheard, unshriven, his dying
actions, by far the greatest of his already great life, unwitnessed.
There are so many of them.

Whatever else this endless day is, it is the end of the Astartes
as anything more than elite strike troops. They will never be
pre-eminent and numberless again.

Their banners are trampled underfoot, or soaked in gore, or
matted with mud. They drape over some corpses like winding
sheets. The symbols they marched under, and believed in with
their entire beings, shroud them in death.

The umbratic symbols of the foe are still raised. The great,
unblinking eye gazes from a thousand banners, staring with mad
glee at the devastation wrought by those who hold it aloft. The
red-and-ebon traitor banners flutter in the smoke-stained, firelit
twilight, flapped like batwings by the holocaust gales, shivered
like gooseflesh by the constant dysphonic roar of traitor voices.

More banners, and still more, are being manufactured to
join those already raised. In the spark-filled gloom, the smaller
and malformed Neverborn move in hissing gaggles behind the
main advance, flaying and peeling skin from the dead and the
almost dead, fashioning standards of human leather to hang
from bone frames. They huddle and squat in the glare and the
lagoons of blood, cackling and snuffling, using dagger-fingers
to score and prick out the shape of the great eye, symbol of a
pinchbeck god. They mark out eightfold stars. They whisper
names to themselves, and shudder with anticipation every
time that name is the Dark King.

Khagashu of the Night Lords walks through the slaughter-
fields beyond the Eirenicon Gate. Ahead of him, another of

the Palatine bastions is beginning to succumb to fire and shredding assault. Khagashu cannot see the ramparts falling. He is too far away yet, and the false night is too thick with cindersmoke. But he can hear the noise of it, carried fitfully on the bradycardic gusts of a heartsore wind. Rockcrete and adamantine, raised to withstand macro shells, is yielding to behemoth fangs and insatiable claws, and the sound of it is delicious.

Elated, proud, he struts with pavonine delight, and signals his scavenger gangs of feral humans, abhumans and cankered servitors to spread through the bloody spilth of the battlefield. Like children gathering shells and curious pebbles on a beach at low tide, they are collecting skulls.

Khagashu and his foragers have instructions that, though they were murmured to them by nothing more than shadows and damp air, they are quite determined to fulfil. They must construct carefully aligned mounds of skulls, according to strict ritual measurements, in preparation for the ascendant coronation.

Then there will be a throne to build. Khagashu isn't yet sure who it is for.

On the broad talus of the Irenic Barbican, one of the chief bastions of the Palatine line, an engine war escalates into sudden fury. Remnants of Legio Gryphonicus mount a ferocious repulse in an effort to keep the barbican intact for another thirty minutes.

All the rules are gone. Range factors are ridiculous. Churning out of water-choked culverts, support armour wrestles with the enemy treads, hull to hull, main weapons firing almost point-blank. Basilisk platforms are used like duelling pistols, head-to-head at zero metres.

New suns flare and fade in quick succession along the vast

earthwork edge as punctured reactors light off and go critical, wiping out everything around them. The radiating heat-wash is so intense, it instantly bakes the lakes of mud into dry seabeds cracked in star patterns.

Gharnak Omaphagia, disgraced Warlord of Legio Magna, is killed by engine-fire as it mounts the talus, disembowelled by shells that spin its torso aside in a cloud of oil. Leaking systems catch and *Omaphagia* immolates, a giant figure burning head to foot like some festival hecatomb on a heathen midsummer. *Khorness Gorewalker*, another daemon Warlord, pushes past it at main stride, mounts blazing. Three of the Warhounds mobbing its heels founder and fall on the massive rockcrete caltrops laid by the loyalist Mechanicus.

Gorewalker passes the prone carcass of *Indomat Celsior*, a Gryphonicus main engine that has been brought down on the slope. *Celsior* is on fire, its hulk swarming with a saprophytic mass of traitor ground troops. *Gorewalker*, kicking its way through tanks and maniples of House Hermitika Knight Armigers as though they are toys, is stopped at the mid-line of the embankment by sustained beam fire from the Warlords *Bellus Shockatrice* and *Argent Polemistes*. *Gorewalker* endures a great deal, far more than build-specifications ever dreamed of, before its hull bursts, rent by structural failure and the collapse of the immaterial energies empowering it. It staggers backwards, crushing its own ground support underfoot, but remains standing until *Polemistes* mass-launches rockets from its shoulder silo. The fizzling, vespine rockets hit *Gorewalker* in rapid succession, like a drumroll, draping its chest and shoulders with an intricate garland of small, overlapping detonations that blink-bloom around it, and then tip it off its feet. Its huge wreck slides two hundred metres down the slope, shovelling an entire assault squadron of tanks into the talus ditch.

The Warmonger *Castellan Corda* advances alongside *Shock-atrice* and *Polemistes*, adding its monumental support, its batteries harrowing the surging edge of enemy machines and men as they sweep up the earthwork.

But more giant figures are looming through the kilometres-deep smoke towards the barbican. They are not war engines of the Legio Magna, for though towering and humanoid like Warhounds and Warlords, they are not machines at all.

One takes to the air upon gigantic wings.

Zhintas Khan and eight other White Scars fight a running battle against a pack of the Lupercal's ferocious Astartes in and around the Botanicus Gardens. They have become *life-sellers*. Zhintas Khan is amused by the term. It was said to him, an hour earlier, by a Blood Angel called Khotus Meffiel, with whom he shared the brief but savage dismemberment of a Cthonian Dreadnought. Meffiel said that they, like all the loyal warriors left outside at the closing of the Gate, had just one responsibility to discharge: to sell their lives for the highest price they could get. What tally could they reach before death, now inevitable, overtook them? The concept added pride and zeal to an otherwise thankless duty.

What will my life sell for? Zhintas Khan wonders. His price stands at forty-four traitor lives. He parries with his tulwar, and decapitates a Sons of Horus legionary. Forty-five.

Not enough yet. Not nearly enough.

Propinquity Court is a single square kilometre of open park just off the Via Palatine, surrounded by the House of Atlases, the Albigen Belvedere, the Devotorium Mundus, and the cloisters of the College of Jurists. Across six timeless hours it becomes the site of five separate battles, each one depositing a new stratum of bodies and wreckage.

Here, Vigil Sister Vedia and squads of terrified militia drive back a force of traitor guards sworn to the observances of the Word Bearers. The fight is astonishingly brutal, and leaves the Devotorium on fire.

Here, Pyre Warden Ari'i, Sigil Master Ma'ula and Sergeant Hema of the Salamanders hold off three rallying assaults by the Death Guard, and only survive a fourth when House Cadmus Armigers arrive to support them.

Here, four units of the Hort Palatine are slaughtered by assault squads of the Sons of Horus led by Vorus Ikari in an action that levels the cloisters and descends into almost ritualised execution.

Here, Prefect-Captain Arzach of the Legio Custodes and his Companions fight and slay the Neverborn things found feeding on the dead.

Here, Captain Brastas of the Imperial Fists holds back a tide of World Eaters until, munitions spent and reduced to blades and shields alone, he and his men are finally overrun.

Propinquity Court is not alone in recording a catalogue of actions. Many streets, yards, gardens and courts in the Palatine approaches become the sites of multiple, contradictory battles, often overlapping, often without strategic sense as those loyal forces left outside the walls, those life-sellers, attempt to frustrate the enemy advance. Like the bodies of the loyal Astartes dead, the actions are not remembered, nor their significances noted. War has little or no memory. Feats of extraordinary prowess that would, in other times and other places, have been recorded and celebrated, are finished and forgotten even before the next wave of violence sweeps through, crunching obliviously over the bones of the valorous and the defeated alike. In the final ever-hours of the siege, such deeds and achievements take place that would fill a thousand books and swell the honoured archives of Terran military history, but all are lost and unremembered, as ghosts in the fog and smoke of their tumult.

Bödvar Bjarki gets back up again.

There's blood in his eyes, and most of it is his own. The last impact lacerated his head so deeply, his scalp is torn open.

At Nafus Crossing on the Delphic edge, loyalist units have been holding back the enemy advance for three straight hours, though time seems to have lost the definition it once had. Their numbers have dwindled with every transpontine thrust the Death Guard makes. Bjarki, Heaper-Of-Corpses, and one of the very few warriors of the VI Legion Space Wolves active on Terra, feels like he's one of the last defenders standing at Nafus.

Flexing his grip on his blade with blood-slick hands, he looks around. He's not one of the last at all. He *is* the last.

War-horns boom. He can hear the shrill warble of meltas, and smell the stink of cooking stone. Three times he has fought back the enemy bastards from the top of the mound of bodies piled at the north end of the bridge. Three times, he's been struck from the apex of that corpse-hill.

Each time he's clambered back up to hold the ridge of snapped bone and torn flesh, there have been fewer warriors with him. But Bjarki's thread is not yet cut, and though there are no *skjalds* to sing it, his saga is not done. Not yet.

He spits, and invokes the spirit of Fenris, the dark and silent slip of not-wolves running the black-and-white forests. He starts to climb the bodies again.

He'll make it four times. Five. As many times as it takes, or as many times as he has left. There are few wolves on Terra but, in the name of Russ, he will be a one man Rout.

Lantry Zhan, a forward observer for the PanCon Fifth and a shot-caller for the mortar squads, struggles to ascend a ridge

of rubble west of the Via Irenic. His brigade knows there are
Traitor Astartes close by, but they have no idea of numbers
or angle. It's taken Zhan fifteen minutes to find a decent vantage. Through his scope, from the ridgetop, he finally sights the
enemy. They are not Astartes. They are dire Neverborn things,
slope-shouldered ogres, that seem to be wallowing or playing
in the lagoon of a macro-shell crater. He adjusts focus. What
are those atrocities doing? What sport are they–

Zhan sees what they are doing. He snatches the scope away
from his eyes. He wishes he had never looked.

As they advance along the Metome Processional in the vague
hope of reaching the Delphic Line, Marshal Agathe finally
solves the riddle of the names, or the lack of them.

The ragged army group, some three thousand infantry men
hauling unlimbered, iron-wheeled field guns between them,
are hugging what's left of the Metome Wall as cover as they
advance. Enemy shells lob right over them, dropping into loyalist positions three kilometres to their north. They're like rats
in a gutter, three thousand half-named rats.

Agathe divided her army at Hermitage Gate during a lull
in fighting. She sent two thousand men, under Hort Captain
Martineaux, to hold the Tigris Arcades, and another six, along
with her Kratos tanks, under Sire-Militant Sklater towards the
Gilded Walk, a decision that she now realises was futile given
the firestorms blazing in that direction. Most of what she has
left are from the 403rd, plus a battalion of Vesperi.

She hears Phikes shouting angry orders as he urges the troops
along, heaving and grunting with the field guns. There have
been skirmishes: a close call with stegatank engines that were
trying to breach the wall, and a ferocious melée with necrotic
traitor zealots, stinking of the frenzon they were glanding as
they slaughter-charged the line.

Agathe tries not to dwell on the odd changes to the landscape. Not the widespread damage and upheaval, the uncanny alterations. Stone walls sheathed in damp skin. The ground, in places, like frozen meat, slowly thawing. Buildings rotting as though gangrenous. The foetor of corruption. She ignores the way certain parts of the processional seem to sigh with the echo of soft breathing, a suspirious tremble accompanied by a sticky breeze.

The Dark King is not a name she wants to consider. For it to appear on the damn wall like that suggests it has significance, and she doesn't want to understand why, because her imagination runs wild. It says a lot to be in this hell and still be afraid of something worse. The mind has an unparalleled capacity for destructive speculation.

But the 403rd's names are a less distressing subject for speculation. Most of the 403rd use forenames only, like Captain Mikhail, or nicknames, or just serial numbers. Perhaps–

One of the field guns gets mired. Men shout, and bring ropes to drag it clear of the sucking ooze.

'You don't use names,' she says to Mikhail, standing nearby. He glances at her, unsure what to say because it wasn't a question.

'Anonymity?' she asks. 'Or shame?'

He's reluctant to answer.

'You weren't ordered to service, were you?' she asks. 'Never mind. Don't answer. Don't admit anything. I don't care. But you and your men, you weren't ordered to service. There was no formal mobilisation at Gallowhill.'

'There wasn't time,' he replies, very quietly.

'No one came and rounded you up to serve,' she says. 'You just did it. Picked a name. Pulled weapons from the dead.'

'We had to do something,' he says.

Agathe understands that. 'Brave choice,' she says.

'Not brave,' he replies. 'There was nowhere to run. And once we fought clear, we figured the only way we could do any good was to act like we were authentic.'

'No, I think it's brave,' she says. 'And I don't care what you are if you stand on the right side. And your lack of names…'

'What about it?'

Agathe nods in the vague direction of the enemy, the stained horizon beyond the wall.

'They know our names,' she says. 'They seem to. Or they're learning them. The Neverborn. They call to us and leave whispers in the air. Like it gives them power over us. So I'm glad to have men with me who have taken care to hide theirs. Might make you live a little longer. The enemy's known my name for weeks.'

The man exhales.

'We'll be shot for this,' he says. 'When it's done, we'll be rounded up and shot as fugitives, won't we?'

'Probably,' she replies. 'But we don't know what awaits us after today, do we?'

They hear shouts and shooting. Marauders have burst into the gulley three hundred metres ahead. The fighting is already close and murderous. She can see bat-faced figures with needle teeth, lobed ears and clusters of spider-eyes. She can hear entrenching tools crunching as they are used as weapons.

They start to run. She hears the officer yelling serial numbers as he calls in his fire-teams.

No names. Just duty.

'Respond. This is Hegemon Control. Anabasis, respond and verify.'

The War Court junior at the mastervox station has been repeating the same words for long minutes now. Too many minutes. Sandrine Icaro has a rapidly growing list of other bulletins and priorities to deal with, but she cannot take her eyes off the junior and his patient but futile efforts. Nothing matters more than this. If Anabasis is lost, then the entire structure and purpose of the world as she understands it is gone.

Nothing seems real. She wonders if anything is. Everything has felt *unreal* to her since she fled Bhab Bastion. Icaro puts it down to partial amnesia triggered by the traumatic circumstances of that escape, but the sensation is not easing. Everything has acquired an odd, dreamlike quality.

She has no idea how she survived the assault on Bhab. She has no idea how she managed an evacuation, or made it back, unscathed, to the final fortress. She has brief memories of burning streets, of gunfire. More than anything, she has no idea how she got into the Sanctum. How did she do that before Eternity Gate closed? She doesn't even remember passing in through the Gate. She remembers Bhab, then the frenzy of the warzone, then being here, in the Rotunda, as though time, and distance, and direction, and relative position have all telescoped and twisted.

She fears it is all a dream. She suspects she's dead; that she died in Bhab Bastion, or in the streets outside, and everything since then has just been an illusion, the desperate imaginings of her mind as it died, the final flash-second of her life stretched out into a dream of all the things she wished and yearned and longed for.

She hopes it is. She hopes she's actually dead on the floor of the Grand Borealis, and that all of this is just the final firing of her cooling synapses. Icaro would rather that. She would rather be ensnared in the final millisecond of her life than for this to be real. She would rather be dead than for any of this to be true.

Let me be trapped in my own death, she thinks, rather than He be trapped in His.

3:v

Visions of heresy

It makes such perfect sense. Such perfect, rational sense.
Caecaltus isn't sure why it's taken him so long to appreciate it.
The Emperor must die. He *must*. It's the only logical conclusion
that anyone sane could reach. The Emperor must die–

No–!

The Emperor must die. He is mad, a mad monster, drunk
on power, and His tyrannical rule has lasted far too long. He
really must die–

Nooo–!

He must die *now*. It's the only way to stop the war. It's the
only way to protect the human race. The Emperor must die
immediately–

Please stop–!

He must be put down and destroyed as quickly as possible.
And who better to do that than the men built to guard His
life? Who else is strong enough? *Close* enough?

Please–

Who else has the peerless clarity of mind to understand the perfect, rational sense of it? The Emperor must die.

I can't–

Take that spear. Plunge it through Him. Free the species.

Shut up–!

It's all been arranged. The stage is set. Everything is ready. The Emperor won't see it coming, because He's a mad monster, and utterly deranged. All the hard work's been done. He's been brought out of hiding to His place of execution. He is defenceless. Now just take that spear–

Get out–!

The cunning of Horus Lupercal knows no limits. There is a reason his father named him Warmaster. He has arranged it, and made it all so easy. Look at the simple perfection of his stratagem. He set a trap so blatantly and painfully clumsy it can only *be* a trap, a trap so *brazenly* incompetent that the Emperor could not afford to resist it–

Stop! No!

He laid bait so staggeringly *unsubtle* that it spoke to delusion, to a loss of faculty, to hubris and arrogance, and beckoned with such graceless inelegance that even the infallible *Master of Mankind* was convinced His first-found had lost his wits–

You will stop–

And so the Emperor, proud and mad as He is, rushed into it, knowing full well it was a trap, yet arrogant enough to think He was ready for it. Ready for anything. More *powerful* than anything. More *mighty* than–

Noooo–!

No, indeed. The trap itself was the ruse. There was no way in creation for Horus to surprise his father, so he didn't even try. Instead, he let his father surprise Himself. His arrogance was His own trap. Now, take the spear–

* * *

Caecaltus Dusk resists. He falls to his hands and knees, weeping and spitting blood. The feral ingenuity of Horus Lupercal has undone him entirely. It has undone them all. Choking on his own gore, he goes into violent convulsions as he tries to break the insidious control that has been placed upon him. He wants to get up – *needs* to get up – and defend his king and master. Some of his brethren have collapsed, stricken like Caecaltus, but many of the other Companions have already turned on Him. Part of Caecaltus' brain, the part that he is resisting with every fibre of his being, is telling Caecaltus to get up and join them. It is screeching at him to become the utter contradiction of his nature.

There is a pain in his chest, an invisible knife through his heart, pinning him to the deck. All he can do is lie there, shaking and fitting, witnessing the horror as a blood-dimmed vision.

A vision of atrocity. Of heresy. Of natural law undone and duty desecrated. Of the most shameless infidelity. A king, turned on by his royal bodyguard. A monarch, surprised and betrayed by the ones he trusted most. A caesar, butchered by the captains he never thought to doubt.

We cannot be doing this, but we are. It is impossible for us to be doing it, but we are doing it anyway. Horus, you will pay for this. My King-of-Ages is alone. He cannot–

Blood jets.

The Master of Mankind decapitates Sentinel-Warden Kliotan before Kliotan can skewer Him with his lance. The Lord of Terra catches Sentinel-Warden Cazadris and Hetaeron Companion Kintara on the backswing of His burning blade as they rush Him. He deflects Shield-Captain Damorsar's halberd, and cuts him in two. Hykanatoi Krysmurthi weeps as his master beheads him, because he realises what he is being coerced to do.

You will pay. You will pay, you traitorous monster.

Shield-Captain Avendro cartwheels away, auramite splintering like golden glass, the long spray of his blood spattering the white hull of the Stormbird racked beside him.

The trap was in us, all along. There was nothing waiting for us at all. Your doors were wide open and your shields were down. There were no surprises waiting for our master except your profound mastery of the immaterium, which we have woefully underestimated. We knew your power was great, first-found. We had no conception of how great.

Host-Marshal Telemonis shreds through a guard rail, his headless form plummeting into the shadows of the under-deck sub-holds.

The Emperor came here ready for anything, first-found, so you prepared nothing. Misdirection. He was looking everywhere except at Himself. With His attention held, you reached in and, with formidable sleight of hand, took away His readiness. You took away His focus and determination, from the moment He arrived. You took it from all of us.

The Emperor's warblade, a brand of white fire, leaves burning magnesium after-streaks in the air.

You took away our keen edge by easing our minds into distraction and puzzlement, into reflection, into random thoughts. You did it with such precision we forgot ourselves. You did it with such concealed domination of will even our master couldn't sense your mind at work.

Companion Caercil sinks to the deck and slides apart in three pieces, like a perfect puzzle that will never be put back together.

And then you twisted the pristine souls of the Custodians. Each one of us was painstakingly restructured on a molecular level to withstand the corruption of Chaos, but you took the incorruptible and you broke our minds. You broke the unbreakable.

Sentinels Tyrask and Systratus thrust at their master with guardian spears, firing their integrated bolters.

We are shrieking because we understand what you have done to us. We are screaming because you have forced us to turn on the master we love above all things. We are howling because we are fighting it and we cannot resist.

The mass-reactive rounds explode against the rippling shield of His will, and He slices off the powerblades of their spears. Tyrask and Systratus get to take one step backwards before they are struck down.

You are forcing our master to kill us.

Sentinel Mendolis grazes the blade of his castellan axe against the Emperor's right pauldron, throwing sparks. Companion-Captain Vantix, wailing in lament, drives his warblade into the Emperor's ribs.

Blood jets.

You will pay, Horus! You will pay!

The Master of Mankind reels, then shreds Vantix into ribbons with His power claw. He sidesteps Mendolis' second lunge in a swirling billow of cloak, and runs His sword hilt-deep into Shield-Captain Amalfi's chest.

Each Companion He strikes down is a profound loss to humanity. Each one is a perfect creation of genetic and esoteric engineering, masterpieces hand-wrought with the most diligent and exacting labour. Each one is a boon companion and a friend, beloved as any son. And He is being obliged to destroy them one by one.

The peerless blade splits Mendolis open. It splinters Companion Heliad's visor and spins him off his feet.

Was that why, first-found? Was that why you made us your weapon of choice? The psychological effect? Did you think it would make Him hesitate? Did you think it would make Him vulnerable?

You clearly do not understand at all.

Vestarios Entaeron drops to his knees, clutching his ruined

torso. He crumples sideways. Sentinel Justinius misses with a two-handed swing, and does not live to try a second.

He is the Emperor of Mankind. He comes upon you in wrath, clad in His aspect of war. More than thirty thousand years of work will not be undone by your malice and spite. That He is required by you to kill His own, perfect warriors does not make Him falter or weaken His resolve.

It just makes Him all the more determined to vanquish you. He–

Beam energies rip across the flight deck. The Master of Mankind is knocked down.

Oh, Golden Throne. Oh my King-of-Ages–

The Emperor has fallen against the side of another Stormbird, denting the armoured flank and shaking it on its launch rack. The Tharanatoi squad closes in, encircling Him, the blood of their tears streaming down the ornate goldwork of their Terminator armour, their Adrathic weapons cycling for a second salvo.

He cannot let them hit Him full beam again–

The Emperor leans for a split second against the Stormbird, fighting down the lingering pain so He can refocus His will. A squad of Hykanatoi vault the guard rails to their master's right, racing up the launch ramp to flank Him.

The relic weapons of the Tharanatoi glow with power.

The Emperor raises His hand.

Imperial lightning ripples out, a brilliant neon blue. The searing forks scorch the deck and hurl the Tharanatoi into the air like sheaves of corn caught in a cyclone. One ricochets off a ceiling hoist, fragmenting. Two tumble over the platform edge and plunge down the shaft of the through-deck elevator. Two hit a racked Stormbird so hard their armoured bodies punch through the hull like breacher rounds. Four hit the deck with enough force to leave craters. One explodes, the power system of his Adrathic beamer jarred to critical instability. The catastrophic detonation throws others off their feet.

They sprawl on the deck around Caecaltus and the other handful of Companions convulsing in resistance seizures. Caecaltus rolls on to his side, shaking. He tries to rise, but he can't. He tries to reach for his spear, then pulls back his hand. He knows that if he touches it, the urge to use it against his master will become impossible to resist.

He sees the Hykanatoi bearing down the ramp on his master's right. He sees his master turn and look at the deck supervisor's console on the chamber wall a hundred metres away. He sees his master tense and spear the console with a telekine pulse, and then duck to His knees. The ramp's ion launch catapult fires the Stormbird He was thrown against. It slams over Him, past Him. Fuelling cables stretch and snap in clouds of sparks. Its engines and systems are dead, so it is merely dead weight, slung by the ion rail's accelerator. The Stormbird mows down and pulverises the Hykanatoi on the ramp. It keeps going, starting to tumble, down the entire kilometre length of the rampway, in an expanding, seething fireball, and finally obliterates as it impacts the invisible integrity fields at the deck mouth.

The Emperor rises to His feet. Loss, bitter pain and fury have broken the lulling spell of indecision woven by the warp. His will is now entirely clear and engaged. Before any more of the screaming Custodians can move or rise or act, He enforces it fully.

The deck lamps dim. Guide lights blow out. Consoles short and explode. Cables spit cinders and sag from the ceiling systems. All the Custodes still alive drop. Caecaltus collapses onto his face. They are all screaming and writhing. It is no longer in torment or grief.

It is simply in pain.

Pain will do it.

The Emperor applies more. Shrieking, Caecaltus can hear his master's booming wrath inside the buckling bones of his skull.

+I will burn your touch out of them, first-found.
+Do you see what I am now?
+Do you see what is coming for you?+

3:vi

Repulse

They have seen what's coming, and they prepare to meet it. War slides armies across the field and into conjunction, like playing pieces, to clash and compete, as though it is all some heartless, preordained game. Near Hasgard Gate, just short of the Delphic Battery's southern front, Fafnir Rann prepares to meet the enemy's next move.

Archamus has positioned Rann there, for Archamus is a grandmaster of war's merciless game. Rann takes his place under the broken arches of the Delphine Viaduct, its proud spans demolished by engine fire. Petrocarbonic smoke, luxuriant as velvet and as toxic as reactor dust, floods the street basin like a living thing, racing ahead of the advancing traitor line.

Archamus has just been named Lord Militant Terra. Signals are torn and patchy, and Rann is not sure of the significance of this. It suggests the chain of authority is somehow broken, or that Hegemon Control has devolved leadership to the field. It suggests great Sigismund is dead or occupied with other, vital work. It suggests the Praetorian Dorn is not able or available to lead the fight, which in turn suggests that the Lord Angel and mighty Valdor are also, somehow, gone.

Rann puts such doubts and fears from his mind. He assumes, for he is no fool, that some significant counter-strike is being planned or is already underway, a counter-strike that occupies the Emperor's three greatest champions.

He hopes desperately for its success. He feels no resentment that he cannot be part of it. The line must be held, and it is down to those remaining outside the sealed gate, men like him and Archamus, Aimery and Azkaellon, to do that work. They have been fighting relentlessly, without break or pause, for at least twelve hours, though Rann's chron system has become defective, and he is unable to track combat time precisely. It feels like months, longer than the rest of the siege combined.

Archamus has been calm and masterful since his authority was announced and authenticated. There is more than a hint of Dorn in him. His deep voice speaks to them over the crackling vox-cast, grim and exact, moving units like ivory markers on a regicide board. Archamus is in the thick of it too, somewhere close by the mayhem, fighting hand-to-hand as he runs the game in his head. Archamus chose to stay outside when Eternity slammed. Rann knows the old Huscarl well. He can't help but feel there is an incongruous note of delight in Archamus' commands. They are on the last stroke before midnight, in the belly of hell, but Archamus rejoices in the combat, freed from his desk-station at Bhab to join the fight.

Even if it is simply to die with dignity, blade in hand.

It is his right, and Rann won't deny him. Rann expects the same right himself. He cannot see a way they can prevail now, for too much has been lost, and the enemy is far too great, but they can serve as they were born to serve, holding fate back for as long as they can, and requiring the very highest price for their lives.

Archamus has sent Rann's units forward along the causeway below the viaduct, with a force of White Scars under Namahi, Master of the Keshig, to their left on the Via Atmosine. Rann can hear White Scars jetbikes and the chatter of their bolters through the billowing smog. Blood Angels, four squads at least, are reported as closing on his right, but there's no sign of them.

Relays report a surge of World Eaters pouring in from Hasgard along the viaduct approach. Rann spreads his formations wide, making up in coverage what he sacrifices in line density. His approach to warfare has always been more fluid than Archamus', less strict or formal. He knows this is why Archamus was elected to field command over him: Archamus has superior strategic experience, while Rann can do his best work at the cutting edge of the fight. Archamus expects this fluidity from him. He has directed the lord seneschal, but not specified any formal notions of deployment or fighting structure. He would not presume to do so, no more than Rann would presume to question Archamus' grasp of the battlespace dynamic.

When they come, the World Eaters are not alone. It is more a rabble, a disjointed, incoherent mass of Traitor Astartes and warriors of the Dark Mechanicum jostling together as they charge down the causeway towards the Via Atmosine. They are manic, unchecked and raving, drunk on the ecstasy of slaughter and the infernal forces that compel them. Many are indeed World Eaters, now rage-blind, their bolters long since discarded in favour of blades and tearing hands. Some still wear the *caedere remissum* crests of their kind, and bark blasphemies in the Nagrakali argot. Most are barely recognisable as Astartes: they are grotesquely swollen and distorted, reshaped by the warp into lumbering, ogre-like forms that bound and gallop down the rockcrete on all fours like giant apes. Their necks and shoulders are thick and hunched, like those of fighting bulls or boars. They squeal and bawl, their snouts and toad-mouths and other transmuted features bristling with tusks and horns and saw-edged fangs.

Among them, the soot-caked, skeletal figures of gun-servitors, some stilted and preposterously tall, some multi-limbed, some hunchbacked with heavy powercells or tanks for flamer weapons. Some ride artillery carriages mounted with swivel guns or pot-de-fer, or crew ornate, self-propelled zamburak fitted with autocannons and fusion sakers. Rann sees Death Guard too, ponderous and abdominous, leaking liquid pus from the seams of their distended plate, and Sons of Horus, fleeting, howling, crested shadows of wrath. But many are undefinable, Astartes so disfigured it is impossible to determine their origin Legion. They are caked in mud and gore, or transmuted into inhuman, Neverborn shapes, or have covered their plate with garish colours and obscene symbols that sear the mind if the eye lingers on them too long.

They are an onrushing wall of depravity.

Rann's sensoria render the tag-marker icons of most as degraded, pixelating smudges. A few markers remain legible, and Rann's skin crawls to see the names of old once-brothers and fine comrades appending such monstrosities.

'Line hold!' he roars on the company channel. Affirmation runes light up on the side-bar of his visor. In a day of the most ferocious warfare he has ever known, this is going to be an entirely new level of savagery. He marvels at the mettle and capacity of his brother Praetorian Imperial Fists, and the White Scars and Blood Angels too. They have all fought at exemplary levels in their lives, never found wanting, but on this last day of days, they have drawn on new reserves of speed and skill and fury. The level of violence required in this last stand makes every other war pale into insignificance and seem like a trifle. It is as though they have never really fought at all until this hour.

His fire-teams open up from behind planted shields. Leod Baldwin's heavy weapons group pumps cannon fire and bulk las at the approaching tide. The squads commanded by Tarchos, Devarlin and Halen rip off bolter shots. Rann's standing order was single shot to preserve ammunition stocks, but just as Archamus defers contact applications to Rann, so he defers to his warriors. They are men of experience. All have selected rapid fire because they know that in such a target-rich environment, no round will be wasted.

And they need to smash the momentum out of the enemy mass before it reaches them.

The raging blitz of fire lights up the smoke, and bathes the causeway in a flickering brilliance, and even underlights the broken arches of the viaduct above them. The front rank of the enemy bulk is chewed apart, then the rank behind, then the third, until those that follow are either shot apart or brought down by the corpses piling up in their path. Baldwin's cannon fire strikes a spidering zamburak, and it detonates in a wild globe of light that blows a smoking, burning hole in the enemy's ranks twenty metres in diameter. Everything caught within it is vaporised. Bolter fire from Halen's squad slays some bestial, Neverborn devil, four metres tall, and horned like a ram, that comes clambering and scything through the mob, maiming its own followers in a paroxysm of desperation to reach its prey. The diamantine-tipped mass-reactive shells stop it in a series of shuddering impacts, pummelling it, riddling it in showers of blood and meat, and finally disarticulating it entirely.

But the tide cannot be dammed. The enemy stampedes on,

clambering and scrambling across its own dead and dying,
like some conveyer system in a manufactory that blindly rolls
product into product even though the line is jammed.

Rann knew as much, even before his squads began their
barrage. He has already formed his melée squads between the
spaced-out, blazing fire-teams. The skirmishers, mostly Imperial Fists, but with some worthy White Scars among them,
are either men like Rann who specialise in the brute action
of hand-to-hand, or warriors who have lost their bolters or
expended their munitions in previous actions. Most have
been given storm shields. They draw up in hastate formations,
angled like ice-ploughs with their tips towards the enemy, the
flaring lines of each V dressed with overlapped shields. Chainblades rev. Powerblades ignite.

As the mass reaches them, the formations drive forward,
punching into the approaching line like broad spears. Rann,
an axe in each hand, is at the tip of one V. The impact is an
instant, jarring concussion of plasteel and ceramite.

As the melée squads drive in, raking like a serrated blade
into the enemy line, and breaking its integrity like a fork
turning soil, the fire-teams disengage, fluidly re-forming into
smaller Vs to plug the gaps between the teeth of Rann's formations. They dig in, bearing the pressure of the foe-weight
against them. Unity will not hold for long, but while it does,
the hastate formations broaden out, turning narrow spikes
into makeshift shield walls that open like wings.

From there, it becomes incoherent, a whirling maelstrom of
fury, a blur. Rann is in the very thick of it, orientated only by
the shield bearers at his left and right. His furious axe blows
overlap, hacking with mechanical repetition. The air fogs with
blood vapour, and fills with hammerscale and spinning chips
of ceramite. The din of armour striking armour, and weapons striking armour, and weapons striking shields becomes

one endless, grinding shriek, utterly deafening, a numbing metal torrent that reminds Rann of the ceaseless noise in the hammering rooms of the House of Weapons.

Rann has no idea what he is destroying. Every shape and movement in front of him is a target. His visor overloads with baffling data, unable to code and represent the mayhem fast enough. He knows his line will break at any moment. He can feel it buckling and stretching, losing cohesion as wave after wave of traitor bodies crashes into it. He is standing on bodies, climbing up the mound of dead that his men are making.

And too many of the dead are his own men.

3:vii

Out of madness and into insanity

Caecaltus feels his master ease His will. The pain ebbs. The shame will never go away.

Thirty-nine of the proconsul's company are dead. The rest sprawl, trembling. Some are too broken in mind or body to continue.

+If you can rise and stand with me, rise now.+

Caecaltus hauls himself to his feet. Twenty-seven others claw their way slowly upright. They cannot look at the Master of Mankind, such is their abject remorse. Caecaltus feels his lord reach out with mindsight and scan each one of them, blink-fast. Caecaltus feels it wash across him. The scan hunts for lies, for lingering deceit, for the smudges of remaining, implanted treachery.

There is none. The Custodes have regained their grip, though none will ever be the same again.

+Take up your arms.+

They obey.

Caecaltus looks at the rest of the Hetaeron company, those

who have not risen, who cannot get up. He feels another
tremble of psykanic power as his master extends a small
measure of grace to each, a final, soothing thought to ease their
suffering. Then the Master of Mankind ends them, quickly
and without pain, a needle of will to each that triggers a cata-
clysmic intracerebral haemorrhage, and instant death.

The lights flicker, stuttering the embarkation deck between
twilight and sickly glare in a fitful pulse.

+Proconsul?+

Caecaltus walks with his master between gilded corpses
towards the main hatch. The twenty-seven Companions follow
them. Caecaltus checks his sensoria and comms, but from
Dorn and Sanguinius and the captain-general, or any of the
warriors in the companies with them, there is no answer, only
the low and threatening crackle of the warp, like wood burning
in a grate. They should all be here, but they are not.

The Emperor and his depleted company face the hatch. The
Lord of Terra takes hold of its six-tonne adamantine mass with
His mind and crumples it like metal foil. He lifts it from its
frame and tosses it aside.

Through the shredded portal ahead of them, they see the
hallways of the *Vengeful Spirit*.

To his left, Caecaltus hears Companion Estrael shudder and
moan as his mind submits. The Emperor quickly administers
a needle of will to stroke Estrael out and end his torment.
The Companion falls to the deck. Caecaltus continues to gaze
at what lies ahead of them, trying to reconcile what he sees
without losing his grip on his own injured sanity.

Now *this* is the hell his master was expecting…

3:viii

The horror of names unchanged

Something breaks. Rann feels it go, feels the constant chest-to-chest, visor-to-visor compression slacken. He assumes his own formation is collapsing. But it is not. Managing, for the first time since combat-impact, to turn his head, he sees his line, though tangled and torn, is relatively whole. The slackening is coming from the enemy quarter, no matter that the enemy outnumbers them forty to one.

Somehow, the enemy has lost its focus and impetus.

'On!' he yells, though the order is not needed. His men drive on, shields held where shields still remain. Chainblades wail as they swing, and blurt as they connect. Rann buries *Hunter* in the skull of a Sons of Horus warrior, then finds the axe wedged, and uses *Headsman* to shear off the helmed head it is stuck in. For the next few moments, the blows he rains with *Hunter* use the wedged skull as a cudgel, breaking rather than chopping, until the helm, and the skull inside it, disintegrate and mash off his axehead.

They have space now. They are inside the reeling scrum

of the enemy, but there is space. The enemy isn't retreating, but it is separating. Rann cuts down a roaring World Eater, and smashes through a gun-servitor cart, and then sees, just ahead, the reason.

Through the whirl of bodies, he sees white jetbikes, riders striking from the saddle, cutting across the front of his line at an angle. Namahi's White Scars have punched in from the Via Atmosine, driving their machines and firepower into the right flank of the traitor host. The riders have no space for speed or manoeuvre. They are moving slowly, like horses wallowing in a river, deep in the enemy mass, ripping fire from their bike guns, point-blank, as they chop and hack with their swords and lances.

Rann is almost overcome by their bravery. The White Scars have willingly sacrificed their speed and mobility to penetrate the thick of the brawl and relieve the pressure on the left span of his line. They could have held back, spared themselves, or run harrying charges from a distance. But the White Scars' resolve, and their unflinching allegiance to the Imperial Fists, has never been more boldly affirmed. They have driven straight into the density, foregoing all of their trademark advantages, to support the Imperial Fists before they fell.

Rann hopes he lives to the end of this day, simply so he can take Namahi, Master of the Keshig, by the hand and embrace him as a brother. In an age when brother murders brother, this seems like a miracle of fraternity.

Rann leads his men in a slogging, shielded drive to link up with the White Scars. Artillery and mortar shells start to land along the line of the causeway as the enemy's support formations try to break the deadlock, heedless of their own troops within range.

Rann takes apart a Death Guard after a furious exchange of blows. The Death Guard's warhammer cracks Rann's pauldron in the exchange, and he feels tendons snap and bones bruise. Past the Death Guard, Rann strikes down a World Eater before it can bring its chainaxe to bear, then hacks apart two bulk weapon servitors. He reaches the nearest White Scars riders, Halen at his heels, and defends them from flank attack, driving back the warriors mobbing them. The fight becomes stagnant and dirty, just grinding to hold ground. He smacks aside World Eaters and bladed automata, then guts some skinless Neverborn thing that lunges at him. Some of the White Scars dismount, their bikes destroyed, and slash with their tulwars and long sabres double-handed.

Then Fisk Halen falls, toppled by a thundercrack blow that splinters his faceplate. Still alive, Halen tries to crawl free, using his tattered shield to fend off his furious attacker.

Rann slams in to protect him. His helm display makes identification. The marker: *Sor Talgron.*

Rann remembers Talgron, a fierce Word Bearer from the early days. It was said he died, following injuries received on Perception Primus, begging not to be interred in a Dreadnought chassis. Something has brought him back and granted him a second life. He is a giant, wrought from augmetics, bulging with synthetic power. His filthy armour is badged with parchment and pages of Lorgar's deranged litanies. His face, framed in crude bionics, is a raddled mass of burn scars. He wields a fizzling crozius that drips with dark, oily power. The mace head of the crozius is fitted with jagged side-blades.

Talgron is chanting something as he swings for Halen, like a form of blessing or benediction. He is almost crooning the words, the only ones of which Rann can make out are 'dark' and 'king'. Rann is convinced that the Word Bearer is making his utterances out of some twisted kindness, as if he is offering last rites to fortify the soul of the man he is trying to pulp into the rockcrete.

The most horrifying thing about him, Rann decides, is that he still has a name. Most have lost theirs in crackles of non-loading graphics, but Talgron still generates a marker. He is a monster, demented, a burned husk caged in bionics, his mind blown out by warp madness. But his name somehow clings to him. He is still Sor Talgron. This is the fate they will all face, Rann understands. Not to die, but to remain themselves, their identities preserved no matter how far the warp twists and mutates them.

Rann engages. It is like striking at a bastion wall. Talgron's machine form is so large, so powerful, it seems rooted to the ground. Rann's blades draw no more than sparks. Talgron scythes at him with the burning crozius, and Rann ducks back. Talgron chuckles.

He says Rann's name.

He says it fondly, as though he is greeting a long-lost friend. He offers his hand.

Repelled, Rann strikes again. Talgron grunts and swings at him. Rann tries to deflect the crozius, but the Word Bearer is too powerful, and the impact against *Headsman*'s haft almost spins Rann off his feet.

He backs away. A berserk World Eater lunges at him from his right, and he scythes, sending the brute flying with an understroke cut, keeping his eyes on Talgron. The giant is advancing, singing his litany to Rann. There is sadness in Talgron's blood-logged eyes, as though he is disappointed that his old comrade has rebuffed his heartfelt blessing.

Rann backs off further, avoiding each swing that comes at him. He does not know how he is going to overcome the Word Bearer, but at least he is drawing him away from Halen. He sees one of the White Scars dragging Halen clear. Talgron swings again, catching Rann well enough to chip his plate and rock him around.

Bedwyr and Cortamus rush to his aid. The three Imperial Fists, side by side, attempt to contain and stop the monstrous Word Bearer. Cortamus, too eager or too brave, dies almost at once, his head crushed into his body by a down-swing of the infernal crozius.

Bedwyr locks in, using his upraised storm shield to hold off Talgron's rain of blows. The sight of Talgron's name-marker reminds Rann that his display still has some function, despite the sensory overload and deluge of data. He locks a sensoria analysis of the Word Bearer's bionic form, pinpointing structural weaknesses using a scanning algorithm devised by Dorn himself for target integrity assessment.

It pings up a flurry of indicators, and Rann lunges in, with Bedwyr's shield warding him, striking with his axes. He swings not with the blind fury demanded by the fight thus far, but with a surgical accuracy, slicing the left knee at the outside of the joint, a block of servos above the left hip, and across the inside of the right elbow. Each impact severs motive systems, and causes lubricant and hydraulics to spurt. Talgron lurches back, hobbled, his augmetic body no longer obeying him as diligently as before. Rann puts another slice in across his neck, cutting a sheaf of cables.

Furious, wounded, Talgron tries to come at him, swinging his mace. Bedwyr's shield blocks the swing, but in that instant, Rann sees that the blade spikes of the crozius are in fact eagle wings, the aquila span of the Imperial icon.

It seems a bitter disgrace that Talgron is killing loyal sons with such a symbol. It fires Rann with incandescent anger and outrage. He puts *Headsman*'s blade across Talgron's breastplate, tearing off the pages of his gene-lord's book, and *Hunter*'s through the side of Talgron's cicatrised face.

Eyes wide, Talgron snorts blood from his nose, and dies for the second time. His immense bulk collapses with a crash.

When Rann turns from his kill, he sees that figures in red have joined the fight. The promised four squads of Blood Angels, delayed no doubt by other traitor warbands, have finally arrived, raking into the mass from the right with their gleaming longswords and stabbing lances. They are led by the noble Dominion, Zephon.

Their charging thrust, impressively as swift as any White Scars assault, catches the traitor mass across a new angle, squeezing the head of it between the Imperial Fists and White Scars formations until it bursts. The traitor host, harried by the loyalists, ebbs backwards into the smoke, its savage urgency lost to hurt and surprise.

An eerie, aching silence falls upon the causeway, now cleared of all enemy except their mangled dead. Rann lowers his axes. He knows it will not last.

Talgron's butchered corpse is carried off the field in the confusion by his brethren, and brought to Portis Bar. Later, in the terrible aftermath, he will be made to live again, against his abject wishes, for a third time, interred in the sarcophagus of a Dreadnought shell to endure the living death he had always rejected.

3:ix

_____

Unspoken

Even from a safer distance, Vulkan and Abidemi find it hard to tear their horrified fascination away from the sight of Malcador's eerie immolation. But they turn. Three of Malcador's Chosen are advancing along the nave, accompanied by a Sister of Silence and several other officials.

'Watch him,' Vulkan says to Abidemi, nodding towards the Throne. 'If he stirs at all–'

'I will, my lord.'

Vulkan leaves his son at vigil and walks down the nave to meet the approaching figures. He has no intention of straying far from the Throne. If Malcador perishes in his courageous efforts, or the hated enemy breaks in to take the Inner Sanctum, he has a duty to perform. The Talisman of Seven Hammers, a protocol retrofitted into the Golden Throne, can only be activated by Vulkan's command. Once initiated, it will destroy the Throne, and the Sanctum, and all the treasures of the Palace, entirely. Vulkan, the Maker, the Shaper, the demiurge-craftsman, will be the Un-Maker of all that the

Emperor has built, splitting the Palace and the world open before Horus can plunder it. If anyone claims the Throne back from Malcador, it will be Vulkan's father on His return. No one else. Horus will never get the chance.

The three Chosen are named Khalid Hassan, Moriana Mouhausen and Zaranchek Xanthus. They bear the sigil of the Regent on their cheeks. Vulkan doesn't know them well, but he trusts them because Malcador trusted them. They bow to him. All look pale with grief. With them are Kaeria Casryn of the Sisterhood, and Eirech Halferphess, Astrotelegraphica Exulta of the Higher Tower, along with several seniors of the Concillium.

'My lord primarch,' says Hassan. 'We bear confidential communication from Hegemon Control.'

He hands a data-slate to Vulkan. Vulkan reads it.

'When was this received?' he asks.

'Not long ago,' says Hassan. 'Mere moments, in fact, after Anabasis assault deployed.'

'So, another few minutes…?'

'Another few minutes and the operation might have been suspended,' says Hassan. 'Fate is cruel.'

'I think fate is very deliberate,' Vulkan replies. 'We receive this, just seconds after my father finally committed, and there was no going back? That's not an unkind coincidence, Chosen One.'

'You think… the timing is deliberate?' asks Mouhausen.

'I imagine the traitor fleet has been blocking all manner of signals,' Vulkan replies. 'They've jammed most of our comm-operations. For this to get through? At that moment of all moments? That's malicious gamesmanship. That's Lupercal deliberately letting hope come too late. His intent is to psychologically ruin us.'

'But you believe it to be genuine?'

Vulkan looks back at the slate, and rereads the transcript of Guilliman's transmission.

'I think it is. We'd easily identify a falsified signal. The codes are right. No, I think it's authentic because only an authentic message would be cruel enough.'

'Then the tragedy is, they can't find us,' says Xanthus. 'The saviour fleet, however close, is blind to us.'

Vulkan nods. 'And we can supply them with no beacon,' he remarks. He looks at Halferphess. 'The Astronomican is non-functional?' he asks, knowing the answer, but hoping to be surprised.

'My lord,' replies the Exulta, 'we don't even know if the mountain still stands. Bombardment has probably razed it. And, if it exists, we cannot perform a remote ignition. The infrastructure is too badly damaged, and the power conduits destroyed. Even if we had power to spare.'

'Then this hope is no hope,' says Vulkan, handing back the slate.

'My lord,' says Hassan. 'Exulta Halferphess has proposed that we might activate a temporary beacon here.'

'Here?'

'It would be makeshift,' says Halferphess. 'And there are inherent technical problems. But by channelling etheric power from the Throne–'

'No,' says Vulkan simply.

Psycho-able reinforcements are already being assembled, Casryn relays in thoughtmark. *The first are arriving now to supplement Sigil Protocol–*

'You mean to strengthen the Sigillite if his power ebbs?' asks Vulkan.

Yes. And more, if necessary. The Unspoken Sanction–

'Is a crime,' says Vulkan. 'We will support the Sigillite. We're not going to burn through–'

'It's been done once. It can be done again,' says Hassan. 'And we are all dying, my lord. The world is dying. Candidates would give their lives willingly to bring the Unspoken Sanction into effect, if it buys us more time.'

If the reinforcements are gathering already, in preparation, we could use their power to fire an emergency beacon, employing the Throne mechanisms and the choral systems of the Throne Room, Casryn signs. *The Adnector Concillium assures us it is feasible, and the Exulta can oversee–*

'Have you found enough of them, then?' asks Vulkan. 'Enough psyker volunteers?'

'Volunteers is a misleading term, my lord,' says Xanthus.

'Indeed it is,' says Vulkan. 'And it was my understanding that there was a dearth of alpha-rated psykers in the Palace. Prior to the siege, too many had been shipped out, on the instruction of your master the Sigillite, in order to engineer the concealment of Titan.'

'This… is true,' Hassan concedes. 'A significant portion of the Palace reserves were removed. They have not been replenished due to the situation. We are… limited.'

'And you'd expend those we have to light a fire that we hope someone will see, rather than keep them ready to support Malcador's efforts?'

No one responds.

'I won't entertain this,' says Vulkan. 'Not yet, at least–'

'My lord,' Hassan begins.

Vulkan looks at him sharply enough for the Chosen to flinch.

'There are other possibilities to explore first,' Vulkan says. 'Listen to me, all of you. I have longed for Roboute and the others to arrive, with all my heart. I can think of nothing more glorious than my brothers descending in fury to end this atrocity and grind Horus under their heels. I yearn for it, just as you do, and I feel the pain of that belated transmission.

But we are committed now, and more precariously balanced than ever. My father has taken the fight to Horus. He must prevail. Malcador, your master, has taken the Throne to maintain stability. *He* must prevail. Our duty, my friends, is to support them both, in every way we can, so they emerge victorious. An attempt to establish a rudimentary beacon here will jeopardise the function of the Throne, and the life of the Sigillite, and will expend our precious resources far too rapidly. And for what? The remote hope someone will see? It is a remote hope indeed. An empty promise. We will continue as we are. Casryn, have them bring in the first of the psycho-able to act as a choir of support. *Just* support. Burn them out, and you'll answer to me. We must help the Sigillite maintain his focus. As for my father, we will wait another hour, then re-evaluate if we have not heard from him.'

'The clocks are broken, my lord,' says Hassan.

'Then count on your fingers, Chosen One,' says Vulkan.

They nod.

'Go,' says Vulkan.

As they turn, he calls Hassan's name and draws him aside. The others stride away down the nave.

'Your master left you without warning,' Vulkan says.

'He did, sir.'

'And you were all bonded to him, I know. The loss must be very great. I can see it in you.'

Hassan nods. 'There was no time for farewell. And he will not return to us as he was, if at all.'

'Tell me, Hassan. Is it possible he is trying to communicate with us?'

'My master?'

'Yes.'

Hassan glances towards the distant Throne. 'I… What makes you ask?'

'A feeling, Hassan. I watch him, and I feel he's trying to speak.'

'To you?'

'To anyone who will hear. I thought perhaps, you, or…?'

Hassan shakes his head. The idea has upset him.

'My master knew that once he had consigned himself to the Throne, his focus would be absolute, my lord. Before he took his place, he dumped masses of sigilised information into each of us. It was a shattering experience. He conveyed, urgently and without his usual finesse, all of his thoughts and plans, and every last symbol of intention and unfinished deed, in the hope that we would enact them now that he could not. We are all still trying to make sense of his bequest.'

'Like a living will?'

Hassan nods. 'In a way, lord. My point is, he did that because he knew he would not get a chance to speak later. So, for that reason, I doubt your idea is any more than fancy.'

Vulkan takes him by the arm, a huge hand on a tiny mortal limb, and leads him closer to the Thone where Abidemi is standing watch. They feel at once the rising heat on their faces.

'His mouth still twitches, my lord,' Abidemi says.

'You see?' Vulkan says to Hassan. 'Hassan, he must have knowledge in him now beyond any wisdom he possessed before. Untold measures of it. I think he is desperate to communicate it to us or impart some sign. I believe he's trying to convey vital secrets that we should know. Things that could win this war for us.'

'I see his lips move,' says Hassan very quietly. 'I see he suffers a great deal. But I think it is involuntary. Just a tic. A nerve spasm.'

'I think he's trying to talk,' says Vulkan. 'I'm sure of it.'

'Well, not to my mind or my ears, lord,' says Hassan. 'If my master is talking, then it's not to me or to any of the Chosen.'

'If Malcador is talking, Hassan,' asks Vulkan, 'who is he talking to?'

3:x

_____

In torment

Daemons howling beneath me and at my back. Ice-bladed hyperborean winds carving at my mind. Moments of brain-freezing anomia, becoming ever more frequent. Pain beyond any limit I could have imagined. Pain in everything. I struggle even to exist. I fight, to temporise my mindsight and maintain plenary control. The Throne is a living thing, scalding with power and fury, a wild steed that no human was ever meant to master or break. It's trying to eat me alive. It's trying to consume me with hyperphagic lust. In the whirling darkness beyond the light, the Neverborn caw and press, dressed in dazzling raiments and cloaks sewn from the souls of saints. They tear at me, willing me to make a mistake, however small. Some tiny error they can exploit. They probe at the telaethesics to find a finger-hold, pecking holes as fast as I adjust. They try to spancel me to the Throne until my bones snap. They try to change my mind and make me one with their cause through bewildering acts of meticide that annihilate and blank whole portions of my mind. The pain is beyond unbearable. The assault beyond relentless.

But I can see. I can see it *all* now. I can see the full material distortion afflicting Terra, the infected and weeping halo of voidmist, the lethal saturation of the warp. I can see the delicate genius of the *Vengeful Spirit* trap, now that it is sprung. I can see how the Emperor has been tricked, not by brute force but by infinite subtlety. I can see the macabre and impossible intersection of *there* and *here*, *now* and *then*, conjoined in ways no one on Terra has yet realised. I can see how every one of our ploys is about to be undone, in ways we could not have predicted. I can see Roboute and the Lion, so close yet lost and blind. I can see my lord and friend the Emperor cut down, Sanguinius rotting in a grave-pit, Valdor driven insane, and Dorn lost, alone and cornered. I can see the shadow of the Dark King.

And I can see all this, because Horus is *letting* me see it.

What the Warmaster hid from the Emperor to lure him, Horus is showing me to torment me. The caustic images burn my brain.

I cannot speak. I simply cannot make my mouth move. I can barely make my mind work. There is no time to waste, for I have to concentrate through the agony and focus, just to keep the Throne functioning at a basic level. If I manage to speak at all, it must be precious words to the few who matter. Not poor Vulkan, at the foot of the Throne, waiting for an answer. Not even my Chosen, for they have been instructed already.

If I speak, every word must count. And it won't be words, because they are too difficult to form. It will be signs. It will be sigils. That's all I'm capable of now: signs, sigils, symbols, and every one of them – if I can manufacture any at all – must be sent, at the limit of my immolating will, to those that fate, luck and blind chance have left on the board in places where they might, just might, stand a chance of changing this outcome. Few will. Perhaps none will. In truth, all are likely to die. But if I can steer just one of them, nudge just *one* of them to take the right step…

A feeble whisper, I call to them. I know their names.

3:xi

_____

Zahariel in the mountain

Zahariel hears a whisper. It makes him pause in his work. He rises, and he listens. It is only the wind sawing through the mountain's deep amplifier vaults, but for a moment it sounded like someone saying his name.

Nothing. A distraction. The hollowness of the place soaks up sound and spits it back out at different angles. He looks around for Cartheus, Tanderion and Asradael, but they are in adjoining chambers, hard at work. Already, in mere hours, the four of them have reconstructed part of the sacred mountain's psionic lattice, reweaving the etheric filaments where they were burned out and torn by daemonic excess.

But it is hard toil, painstaking, and it quickly exhausts the mind. He knows why. The mountain has forever been a place of acute sensitivity, and now, as chaogenous power saturates the whole world, it is worn away raw. As he composes and configures the talismatic engrams, one misstep, one lapse in mental defence, could split his soul open. It makes him feel vulnerable and weak, and neither feeling suits him. It is like feeding a feral beast through the bars of a cage, knowing that the beast would rather feast upon him than the meat he proffers.

He has guarded himself. He has marked his armour with hexagrammatic wards, and taught his three brothers to do the same. The shamans of old did not come here to mark figures on the walls. Sympathetic magic was not about composing an image of some desired future. It was about making the future *present*. They knew the rock was just a membrane, not solid at all, but a veil on which the etheric world was projected. The images of hunters and hunted were just tracings of things on the *other* side. Zahariel has learned this from the ghosts of the shamans that drift around him in the darkness.

He tries to stay alert and focus. There is still too much to be done, and just days before the enemy arrives. At the very darkest recess of his mind is a thought he doesn't want to acknowledge, that he will not share with anyone, not Cartheus or Tanderion or Asradael, not even with himself. He is susceptible. A part of him wants to submit and allow the warp in. Not just the warp, but those who move through it, those who have themselves submitted and–

He catches his breath.

'Cunning,' he says, to nothing. 'Oh, that's cunning.'

It nearly had him. He nearly let down his guard. Something is trying to reach at him, to prise into his head. Something that can sense him. Something that is using the resonance of the mountain to show him some kind of sign. He has set his sword down while he works, but he goes to it, lifts it, and draws it. He thinks it's still here, watching him. He is sure he knows who it is.

The old enemy.

He studies the walls, with their flickering seams of chrysosite and quartz. He almost expects Typhus to loom from the shadows, hands extended to greet him. Typhus, so deeply drenched in the warp, has always known the secret, agnostic leanings of the Order hidden in the Dark Angels' heart. This is his guile at work, an effort to turn those he thinks might stand with him. This is his way of infecting minds and cracking them from within.

'Hell take you and your nightmares, Death Guard,' he says out loud. 'You cannot tempt us so. When you come, we will be ready, staunch and fresh upon the high cliffs while you crawl in the dirt at our feet.'

The lights in the rock throb, describing promises of truths and secret powers and deathless majesty. His blade shakes in his hand. He hears a buzzing in his ears. He yearns to know more. He–

He raises his hand, palm out, the warding gesture.

'I abjure you!' he cries.

The lights sparkling across the face of the wall go out. The membrane goes cold. The buzzing stops.

He is left alone in the cold depths of the mountain. The intruding presence has gone, and he has no idea what thought, what whisper, what mystic sign, fortified him against it. The lights slowly return, pulsing dimly in the crystal traceries. They show the truth now, no longer twisted by temptation and deceit, the future writ.

It is not the same future he read just hours before. What he sees is barely credible.

Zahariel turns and runs into the adjoining chamber. His footfalls echo and bounce in the stone gullet of the mountain. He finds Cartheus first.

Cartheus is kneeling in deep contemplation, repairing a psionic engram that fizzles in the air in front of him. Zahariel grabs him and hauls him to his feet, breaking his intense focus. The delicate engram shatters like glass. Cartheus, dazed, starts to protest. There isn't time for words.

There isn't time for anything.

Zahariel clamps his hand across the right side of Cartheus' head and communicates directly, by will. Cartheus gasps, staggers back a few steps, and then turns, without further word or question, and rushes away to carry the warning.

Zahariel sinks to his knees where his brother was kneeling. He breathes hard. Blood is singing in his neck, his throat, his temples. He reaches for the satchel under his robe. He pulls out the mask.

There isn't time.

There isn't time for anything.

Except this.

3:xii

Sindermann at Leng

'You shouldn't even be here,' the woman says. She's young and looks scared, but there's a defiance in her that is quite impressive.

Kyril Sindermann is about to reason with her: she's an archivist, and she's only doing her job. But Mauer just pushes past.

'Prefectus,' Mauer says, as though that explains everything.

'I'm sorry,' the archivist says. 'I can't allow it. Access to the Hall is forbidden. You need permission in writing, from the Sigillite, and only then to request a volume to be brought from the stacks. You can't–'

'Have you any idea what's going on out there?' Mauer snarls at her.

'Yes,' says the archivist. 'Yes, I do.'

'Will you display the same measure of defiance to the next person who comes to the door?' asks Mauer. 'Because it will probably be one of the Sons of Horus. They're inside. They're inside the Palatine.'

The archivist sags slightly. She's petite, and seems to Sindermann to have been made even smaller by the baggy, insulated coveralls she is required to wear. He's sure she's trying not to cry.

'I am Sindermann,' he says, as gently as he can. 'Authorised by the Praetorian to run the Order of Interrogators. This is Boetharch Mauer, chief officer of the Command Prefectus. Do you know what that is?'

The archivist shakes her head.

'The Interrogators and the Prefectus are both agencies created to safeguard what might be called the Imperial Truth,' he says. 'We work to protect the historical and factual essence of what makes us us. What makes the Imperium. We're trying to defend it against the forces invading us. I'm sorry, this is a longer conversation. Am I making any sense to you?'

The archivist doesn't answer for a moment. She looks past Sindermann, through the door she opened after their repeated knocking. The plaza beyond is empty, and awash with rain. It is a gloom of false twilight in which the groundcar they arrived in is barely visible. Every few seconds there is a flash, like the strobe of lightning, which makes everything outside starkly black and white.

But it isn't lightning.

The archivist murmurs something. Sindermann can't hear her over the hissing spatter of the downpour.

'What did you say?' he asks.

'I said... What do you want?'

'We've come, perhaps in vain, on a desperate mission of hope.'

'Hope?'

'I believe there is material here that might help us,' says Sindermann. 'Old material, perhaps restricted. Right now, I'm sorry to say, anything is worth trying.'

'I'm only junior,' the archivist says.

'Are you alone here?' Sindermann asks.

She nods. 'Everyone… everyone left,' she says. 'I think they've gone to fight. Or hide. And the Custodians assigned to guard the Hall were all withdrawn, without explanation, about an hour ago.' She looks at her wrist, and frowns. 'My chron has stopped. About an hour ago, I think.'

'But you remained at your post?'

'I didn't know what else to do,' she replies. 'I've worked here all my life.'

'Open this!' Mauer barks from the other side of the atrium. She's trying to drag open the huge wooden doors, eight metres tall, that lead into the main collection.

'Do you have keys?' Sindermann asks the archivist.

She does. She fishes a big ring of pass keys, both old mechanicals and advanced encrypted wafers, from the hip pocket of her coveralls. Sindermann follows her across the atrium. It's a huge space, four storeys high. The floor is checked with black and white tiles. The roof is a crystalflex dome across which night rain swirls. A single, immense electro-flambeau hangs from the apex of the dome, bathing the atrium in golden light. Sindermann, like Mauer, leaves tracks of muddy rainwater in his wake.

Mauer stands back. The woman selects a large brass key, and unlocks the paired doors.

They step into a vast, gloomy space. The air is soft, warm, climate controlled. The light is muted and diffuse. They are entering on the fifth floor. Over polished wooden rails, Sindermann can see the four galleried levels below. Above, fifteen more levels, each stacked and galleried, connected by spiral staircases and portable ladders. The central space is a wide oval.

He has never set foot in the Hall of Leng before. It is the

Palace's most significant library, a priceless collection of arte-
facts and data that exceeds even the Clanium, the Majestary
of Records, the Terran Collection, and the Augustian Library.
And it has always been the most restricted.

'Where do we start?' Mauer asks.

Sindermann shrugs.

'This was your idea,' she snaps, and strides away. She starts
picking along the nearest stack of shelves, examining spines.

Sindermann sighs. He's not sure it was. He starts to follow her.

'Perhaps I could help?' the archivist says.

He looks at her.

'If I knew what you were looking for?' she adds.

'This war has taken on a new and grim dimension,' he says.

'Daemons?' she asks. 'At least, that's what people are calling
them.'

'You've seen them?'

She shakes her head. 'I've heard things. I think that's why
most people fled.'

'Well, yes,' says Sindermann. 'The Neverborn. We can't fight
them as we fight other things... and Throne knows, we're barely
managing that. But the Hall of Leng is a special collection, is
it not?'

'Yes, sir.'

'What differentiates it from all the other libraries and archives,
even the most confidential, is that it contains forbidden and
outlawed material.'

She nods. 'It's said that this is the Lord Emperor's private
collection,' she replies. 'Not Imperial records, but the surviving treasures of Old Earth.'

'You say that as if you're not sure,' he says.

'Sir, I've worked here for sixteen years. It's an honour to
serve in such a special place. But I have never looked inside
a single book.'

'Never? But there are millions—'

'Nineteen point six million,' she replies. 'I care for them. That's the duty of the staff. We monitor the environmental controls, clean, maintain, repair and archive as necessary, and draw selected volumes from the stacks for examination. Which is usually for the Sigillite or one of his Chosen. We don't look at the books.'

'There seems something distressingly wrong about that,' he says.

'Not my place to say,' she answers. 'But I can access the catalogue. Perhaps direct you.'

'Well, good,' he says.

'So you're looking for... what?'

'The means to fight daemons,' says Sindermann. 'Perhaps grimoires. Incantations. Rites of banishment. Treatises of spells...'

He tails off. He can see the way she's staring at him.

'Such things exist here,' she says. 'Along with many sacred texts, the testaments and so-called holy books of all the banished and prohibited religions. But, sir, they are all superstitious nonsense. They were written in eras of ignorance and false faith. They are just old words on old pages, empty and meaningless, and they can no more fight daemons than I can.'

'Well, the daemons aren't daemons,' says Sindermann. 'Not in the sense of folklore and supernatural story. I have been aware of them for a long time, since a terrible encounter in a place called the Whisperheads. My knowledge is far from complete, but through careful examination of the ideas I have gathered over the years, I have come to believe that they are the forces of a companion dimension, a warped exoplanar space that conjoins our own material reality. We see them as daemons, for that is how our minds make sense of them, and they are certainly dreadful and destructive entities that operate beyond the laws of our reality. But they are not magick. They can be fought.'

The archivist tilts her head to one side, a moderately sarcastic look on her face.

'Good sir, if the daemons aren't daemons, why would you come here looking for spells to banish them?'

Sindermann smiles. 'Because the spells aren't spells either. My theory... and I confess it is a poor one, which seems to have come upon me as a flash of inspiration from some external source rather than a rationally composed concept... my theory is that this other space, this warped space, has interacted with our own throughout all of history. Down through the ages, even to the earliest times. The phenomena witnessed have had a deep cultural effect. They are the root of all ideas of the supernatural, of daemons and spirits, ghosts and devils. And, I venture, all religions too. Through history, man has encountered the unknown, and given it many names. And mankind has learned things about it. A body of lore, incomplete, I grant you, that has informed the operation of what we might call magicians.'

'Magicians, sir?'

'From the earliest shamans, painting on rock walls, to sorcerers and seers, witch-doctors and alchemists, prophets and wise-women, mediums and priests. They were the lucky ones – or unlucky, I suppose – the very few who glimpsed the otherness. And in their parchments and riddles, and their rituals and their scriptures, they recorded what they knew. Rules, untidy and makeshift rules, ideated for the divination and abjuration of the Other. I believe that some, perhaps many, were closer to the truth than they realised. Closer than our dismissal of them, at any rate. Some odd rite or incantation from fifteen or twenty thousand years ago might, by *accident*, if you will, retain some power that we can harness as a weapon.'

The archivist frowns.

'That seems unlikely,' she says.

'I quite agree,' says Sindermann. 'But I am too old and delicate to fight on the walls with a gun, and too mortal to face down an Astartes traitor. This is the only form of fighting I might be suited for. It is desperate. Very desperate, and probably futile. But I need to do something. And my dear friend the boetharch thinks the same way. So here we are, at your door, begging for help.'

'I don't know what you'll find,' she replies. 'I fear, sir, your desperation has led your imagination into riot.'

'Quite right,' he says. 'But I ask you this. What were you doing here?'

'I... I was maintaining my post, sir.'

'Knowing that the first thing to come to the door would probably kill you, effortlessly? And that you would not be able to resist in any way?'

'Yes.'

'But you keep your post in principle, because it's the thing you know how to do?' Sindermann smiles. 'I think we are rather alike. This foolish errand is, perhaps, all I know how to do. But consider... the Hall of Leng, unlike all the other libraries, is forbidden and guarded by Custodians. Well, usually. Doesn't that suggest to you there must be something in here of true power?'

She is about to answer, when Mauer's voice echoes to them.

'Having a nice chat down there, are you?'

They look up. Mauer is already on the gallery above. She leans over the rail and glares down at them.

'Listen,' she calls out. 'Listen to this... It says... "Of man's first disobedience, and the fruit of that forbidden tree, whose mortal taste brought death into the world, and all our woe, with loss of Eden, till one greater man restore us, and regain the blissful seat…" and then it says… "who first taught the chosen seed, in the beginning how the heaven and earth rose out of chaos…" Does that sound like a spell to you? Some kind of ritual?'

'It does,' says Sindermann. 'Hold on, I'm coming up.'

'She's touching it!' the archivist yelps, pointing at the old book, bent open in Mauer's hands across the wooden rail. 'She's reading it! That's not permitted!'

'Then you'd better come and keep an eye on us,' says Sindermann.

'Sir!' says the archivist. She regains her composure and starts running after him. 'Sir!'

He turns to look at her. 'What?' he asks.

'This idea you have, this notion… Where did it come from? Who instructed you to do this?'

For a moment, Sindermann remembers the Praetorian speaking to him on the roof garden in the rain. He'd said, 'Find some words.' He'd been instructing Sindermann to resume work as a historian, but the sentiment was the same. That, however, was long ago, before the Saturnine assault, and Dorn's words were not what had motivated him to come here.

'You know…' says Sindermann, with a shrug. 'I have no idea.'

3:xiii

_____

Keeler on her pilgrimage

On the Via Aquila, Keeler hears someone call her name, and it's not any of the millions with her.

'Are you sick? Euphrati?' Perevanna asks, but she greys out for a moment. She tries to steady herself. She knows what it is because it's happened before, just a few times. The nauseous, pre-ictal phase of vision. She had it at Lion's Gate. The world gets muffled, and her sight dims, and she can hear her own blood. She always assumes its Him, but He hasn't spoken to her very often, and she's never been truly sure its Him anyway.

'Euphrati?'

It passes. She straightens, and takes a breath. She can pass it off as tiredness. Perevanna knows everybody has long passed the point of exhaustion. It's never really a voice, and never really her name. Like this time, just a fleeting glimpse in her mind's eye of impossible light, a blinding brilliance above the world. In that light is her name somehow, not spoken but represented as a sign.

She feels sick. She suddenly thinks of all the times since the siege closed in and crushed their lives that she's thought she's heard her name called out. Most of the time she's dismissed it, just a voice in the ever-growing crowd. What if it's been Him every time and she's missed it? What if He's been trying to tell her something and she hasn't understood?

'I'll catch you up,' she says. 'Keep them moving.'

Perevanna looks at her for a moment, then nods.

She takes herself to the side of the road, and clambers up into the rubble to find a place to sit and catch her breath. In the Via Aquila below her, the exodus streams past. Eild reckons six million now, maybe more. There's no way of managing more than the roughest estimate. The conclave has been moving them north, away from the front line, though now it's a case of the masses moving the conclave. When they started out, trying to guide survivors, there was some sense of control. But the tide of refugees is now so vast it's moving of its own volition, like a great river or an elemental force, carrying the members of the conclave with it. She and the others have no more hope of guiding it or stopping it than they have of turning it around.

She doesn't know where they're going except north, and she's no longer sure why. The Via Aquila seems to have forgotten how to end. It's one of the main processionals of the central citadel, a vast highway, but even vast highways come to an end eventually.

This doesn't. They seem to have been trudging along it for hours.

She gets up and clears dust from her throat. A dry wind flutters the purity tag stapled to her coat. The river of souls below her, tight-packed and a hundred metres wide, stretches as far away as she can see to her right, where the bloom and fire-flash of war covers the sky, and also to her left, where there is just haze and drifting smog.

So does the Via Aquila. It's become impossibly, monstrously long, attenuated in ways that make her skin crawl, like the dimensions in a dream where the faster you run towards something, the further away it gets.

They are lost, on a straight road. They were lost, she thinks, before they even set out. She is glad of her brief vision and the sense of something calling to her, despite the nausea and discomfort it brought, because it gives her hope. Keeler had begun to think, for reasons she can't fully explain, that He had somehow suddenly gone from the world and left them all behind, that He had disappeared and was no longer in His place on the great Throne.

So long as there is a voice, there is a chance.

3:xiv

Constantin in his silence

He doesn't need to speak. From the moment the mass teleport unfolds them back into corporeality, they know that everything is wrong.

Everything, perhaps, except Dorn's prognostication of deceit.

Well, damn him. Damn him and his clinical, Astartesian projections of strategy. Of *course* it was going to be deception. Of *course* it was going to be a trap.

It's not even subtle. The waiting Neverborn pounce before they are even solid, biting and clawing at their molecular patterns while they are still resolving. Sentinel Geliden solidifies to find his subatomic integrity so disrupted he is missing his torso from the breastbone down. He topples in a cloud of scrambled cells. Companion Astricol materialises in several pieces, which fly apart in showers of immortal blood and bounce across the deck. He does not have time to know what greeting has met him. He is dead on arrival. Sentinel Valique appears, on fire from the inside.

The others in the company strike. Their reactions could

not be faster; reflexes that would shame mere Astartes. From pre-flare precipitation through materialisation through first daemon murders to their first kills, barely six nanoseconds pass. They are at pitched combat instantly, without prelude or warning, like pict-footage edited to play from the middle of battle. They are moving and killing before Geliden hits the deck, before the pieces of Astricol begin to separate, before Valique starts screaming.

Constantin Valdor truncates the daemon he appears face to face with. His power sword is in and through the thing before it can react. Its head – massive, horned, manged with disease – is still grinning in anticipation as it is sheared off its shoulders.

Valdor doesn't need to speak. His command over his Custodes is partly wordless neuro-synergy, and partly decades of relentless drill and rehearsal. The company moves as one thing, like a troupe of gymnasts, their performance at once both precise choreography and acutely nuanced reaction. Their conditioning and combat formats are cured into them, practised to the point of objective perfection, but the expression of them is ordained, demi-second by demi-second, by Valdor's neural cues. He doesn't need to speak because there is no need for verbal command, and because there is nothing to say anyway.

They are in a pit of daemons. Immediate lethal force must be applied.

And it is. Guardian spears lunge, stab and redress. Castellan axes hack and block. Integrated bolters and plasmics blurt and howl. Heavy Adrathics roar like afterburners. Greatswords slice. Misericordias bone and fillet. Where necessary, auramite fists and vambraces crush faces, block limbs or punch through chest walls.

Valdor is older than any primarch son, and his collated experience of war exceeds that of any of them. For the longest while, through the grinding lifetimes of the Unification Era and the early years of the Great Crusade, he had begun to believe, without complacency, that there was nothing in creation he hadn't met and killed. The civil war has shown him otherwise. It has revealed to him not just new, monstrous adversaries, but new *forms* of them. The galaxy seems to delight in presenting him with surprises.

He is never surprised. Surprise is a human handicap, and comes weighted with fear and hesitation. His response, always, is simply curiosity.

How may I learn to kill this?

He applies his curiosity now, with surgical focus.

He knows the primarch-children regard him as sullen and remote, like some malcontent uncle who begrudges their inheritance. They think him single-minded and stuck in his ways, unimaginative, and oddly unambitious. They assume he disapproves of them, of them and their Astartes, and believes they should never have been bred or birthed.

Valdor knows they think this of him, and he simply does not care. For the most part, they are entirely correct. He regards them as a profound mistake, the rare miscalculation of a brilliant mind. He considers them a disaster waiting to happen. He disapproves of them and resents them, for their boisterous and petulant emotions and the undeserved glory that flows towards them like iron filings to a magnet. He sees the civil war as an unequivocal vindication of those beliefs.

But those are political beliefs, and play no part in his duty, so he keeps them to himself. And the vindication gives him no pleasure, because pleasure is a human handicap, and comes weighted with extenuation and prideful satisfaction. He says little or nothing on the matter, except for occasional private rumination to those closest to him, of whom there are few. He keeps his counsel. It is not his place to express an opinion.

The primarchs are also correct in thinking him single-minded, but to see this as a failing reveals only that they have no understanding of his purpose. He, and those he commands, were built for one task: to guard the life of the Emperor. That is his duty, impressed into him at a genetic level. The primarchs speak of duty as though it is a solemn calling, and yet they flout it and shy from it at the slightest provocation. He is single-minded, because he has a single purpose. To see that as a fault shows they have no comprehension of duty whatsoever.

But they are wrong to believe him unimaginative. They would be surprised, profoundly, he thinks, at his curiosity. It is a baseline requirement of his purpose: to enquire, to examine, to learn, as constantly as his name implies, the nature of the galaxy so he may perform his duty with ever greater efficiency.

It makes him intellectually hungry, an appetite he sometimes feels on an acutely physical level. As the civil war unfolded, and the unknown exoplanar threat of the immaterium began to manifest, his mentor, He that Valdor guards, showed him a kindness, and gave him a gift: the Apollonian Spear.

What it pierces, what it bites, it knows. It learns, and transmits that learning to the hands that wield it. A weapon of revelation. A feast for a starving warrior.

What Constantin doesn't know, and perhaps can never know, is whether the Emperor gave him the spear as a simple practicality, to improve the performance of his duty, or if there was something more human, more unconditional, in the gift. Was it just to make Valdor a more effective warrior, or did his mentor feel pity and wish to placate his constant curiosity? Did He fear, perhaps, as his gene-sons rioted and turned traitor, because, allegedly, their needs were not met, that Valdor might break too? Did the Emperor think that Valdor would grow disloyal if his burning curiosity was left unsatisfied?

Was the spear a bribe? An inducement to maintain loyalty

and stave off resentment? An enticement to create the illusion that his needs were recognised?

He trusts it is not the case. The Emperor knows him better than that, surely? The Emperor *made* him better than that. To suspect that of Him is to think that the Emperor doubts him, and that cannot be, because doubt is a human handicap, and comes weighted with mistrust and anxiety.

The only way to know for sure would be to pierce the Emperor's flesh with the spear – if *it* could even do that – which would grant Valdor complete elucidation of all mysteries, but also entirely defeat the original purpose of his duty.

Better to regard the spear as merely an instrument vital to the accomplishment of his work.

Some rotting, dragonate depravity rears up at him, billowing from the shadows while being simultaneously half-made of those very shadows. Valdor ends it with his sword, a stroke that splits its body in a mesial slice and opens it like a book. But his sword, fresh-forged in the House of Weapons, has already chopped down two capering Neverborn with hirsine heads and lariat tongues, and a massive tarantulous form with a thousand compound eyes freckling its furred mass. The blade has begun to choke out, and some substance in the dragonate beast, some liquor or some energy, shorts out its power, entirely.

An emaciated giant, four metres tall and thos-headed, like the jackal-gods of the ancient Nilus, swings for him. Valdor ducks the sickle talons and the long, eight-jointed digits that bear them, and drives his sword in. But its energy is exhausted, its edge is chafed and dinted, and it is now only dead metal. Metal is not enough to tear this thing's hide.

Valdor back-steps, hurls the sword away – incidentally impaling some squealing lesser spawn that dared too close – and unlocks the spear from his backplate. Eight seconds

into the fight, eight seconds since materialisation, and a
master-crafted weapon is worn out.

The thos comes at him, hunched, head down, porpentine
quills rising like hackles on the base of its skull, its dog-teeth
bared, a ringent grin, not of delight but because, like a dog,
it is tasting him in the air.

Valdor makes no flourish. His technique is never ostentatious. With a twist of his hips, he drives the spear tip-first into
the thing's shrunken chest until the blade emerges through
the spine.

A moment. It's never pleasant. It never lasts longer than a
blink or a heartbeat. Valdor waits for it to be over, deadpan.
In the blink, in the heartbeat, a mystery is transmitted through
the haft of the spear, into his hands, into his soul, the mystery
of a grotesque and elaborate lifetime… Aeons of un-terrenitous
existence in the bloodwept eternity of the warp, various embod-
iments of flesh and bone, deep ravening appetites and desires,
a brief millennium worshipped as a deity by terrified priests in
a shadowed temple at Saqqara, nine more locked in a lightless
mastaba, a sojourn to a seething plutonium star on the hem of
the Milky Way, pseudo-names and apocryphal titles, symbols,
runes, glyphs, imprecations, prayers, rituals, allegiance to the
entity of Change, a name, a real name…

'M'han Thytt,' murmurs Valdor, uttering the dead thing's
name to take power over it, and so he will remember it the
next time. He jerks the spear out, and it comes free in a gout
of mud-brown ichor. The thos collapses.

He twists, using the base of the haft to trip an attacker,
before slicing with the blade. Another moment. Another blink,
another heartbeat.

'Qullqullech,' he whispers.

Twelve seconds into the fight. The Custodes have ignited
their arae-shrikes to broadcast blight-code that defeats and

confounds any cogitators or sensoria trained on them. Adrathic weapons are turned on the largest horrors looming from the darkness. Blades and lances flense smaller forms into bloody meat, or burst etheric instantiations into voidmist. As they fight, the automatic systems in the Custodians' wargear scan for vox, noospheric and psycho-active linkages, communication bands, positioning data and reference markers, and tactical connectives, hunting fast and wide with high-function cogitation capability.

Valdor knew it would be a trap. Unlike Dorn, he didn't regard it as a worry to be questioned and evaluated. He knew it as an operational certainty, simply to be expected. He knew it because the Emperor knew it too. The Emperor does not make mistakes, because mistakes are a human handicap, and come weighted with ignorance and poor judgement. The Emperor would not have commanded Anabasis without expecting deceit. The brat Lupercal had dared Him, and He had out-dared the dare by accepting.

This was always going to be a fight. A fight to the death, after all, was the desired outcome.

Nothing about this is surprising Valdor. Except, perhaps, for the fact that he has only lost fourteen men in the first seventeen seconds. He blocks and thrusts, dodges scything claws and biting maws, guts and skewers, endures moments, learns names and mysteries, maintains his singularity of purpose.

Then, in the thick of the melée, his suit link chimes. Search parameters exhausted. No data.

He keeps killing and learning as he ponders this. No data. No available vox or data linkage. No positioning. No contact with Hegemon Control or any of the other Anabasis companies.

No contact with Him.

He remains calm, killing a herpetine form as his mind whirs, ignoring, uncharacteristically, its name and secrets. Where are they? Where is He? Transition should have placed them all in Embarkation Deck Two. All four companies of the spearhead, no more than two hundred metres apart.

The darkness around them, the darkness that has entombed them for all of the twenty seconds since they arrived, is impenetrable and suffocating. The others should be close. *He* should be close. But Valdor somehow knows they are not. Even if he couldn't see them, or hear them, or scan them, or raise them on the link, he would know.

Intuitively, he would know that He was close by.

He is not.

And this is no embarkation deck. The walls, where visible, are taut sails of skin stretched like vocal cords. The floor is spoiled meat that extrudes fat white maggots when weight is placed upon it, like pus squeezed from a pimple. The air is a shivering etheric soup.

He is not here. Valdor has no data confirming His whereabouts or proximity. Valdor doesn't even know where he is himself.

He kills again, spit-speaks a name, then swallows hard. He has one duty, one duty, bred for it. He pursues it singlemindedly. It is his life. The preservation of the Emperor. And suddenly, he cannot.

Was *that* the trap? Was *that* the deceit? The torment that brat Lupercal chose for him?

To prevent him being the only thing he has ever been?

He does not panic. Others would. He does not. He doesn't even become anxious. Only those who know him best – and those would include the two Custodians fighting either side of him, Proconsul Ludovicus and Warden Symarcantis – would be able to detect the change in his mental state, the micro-increase in his pulse rate and breathing.

They both glance at him.

'Focus!' he snarls, the first verbal instruction he has issued.

The rate of attack is not diminishing. It is increasing. Entire menageries of atrocity are spilling out of the tangible darkness from every side, gibbering and laughing, whispering and mewling, like rushing waves of nightmare breaking on the margent shore of sanity. Breaking across his men, of whom, twenty-three seconds into the fight, only seventy-nine remain alive.

Are they even aboard the bastard child's ship? Did he divert their matter transmission? Change their destination using signal capture redirection? Did he send them into the webway? Did he send them into the warp itself?

Sparks flurry, embers in the air. Diocletian Coros is unloading bolt-round after bolt-round into a colossal tusked beast to bring it down. The concentration of shots has caught its straggled pelt alight. Tribune Diocletian has been obliged to act with such inefficient fury, because the tusked thing had been about to strike Valdor.

Who hadn't seen it coming. Distraction had broken his focus.

He nods his appreciation to Diocletian, turns, stabs a thing – half plump infant, half hornet – out of the air, mutters its name, then recomposes his formation via neuro-synergetics.

The daemon droves multiply, living darkness becoming solid things.

He is not scared. He isn't even angry, though rage is a weapon he always keeps close at hand. He hesitates to use it, because rage is a human handicap, and comes weighted with imprecision and unforced error. But he will reach for it if he must.

His curiosity lights him up. He needs to know. He *needs to know*. Not the names belonging to the participants in the misbegotten parade of murder around him, names that will simply edge him ever closer to the fringe of madness, but something true. Something real. Something he can fight with, or against.

He hefts the spear. It works against flesh, even immaterial corporeality, but not against inanimate materials.

The deck, though. The deck is maggot-puckered meat.

Valdor plunges the Apollonian Spear into the floor, or the ground, or the deck, or whatever it is or used to be.

A moment. A blink, a heartbeat. A mystery. A name.

Constantin Valdor shudders. It is twenty-five seconds into the fight.

'Vengeful Spirit,' he whispers.

3:xv

Azif

Adophel said three days. Adophel is seldom wrong. But he is wrong.

Corswain goes to the parapet below the Tertiary Portal. The Chapter Master is gazing into the drop, surveying the long channel of the pass.

'I can't explain it,' Adophel says before Corswain even speaks. 'I was sure we had time yet.'

He points. The scree slopes immediately below them are furred in deep ash and snow, but the lower realms of the pass are bare black rock, caught in the windshadow of the mountain. There is movement, undetected by any of the auto-sensoria they have set up. Corswain hears a buzzing. The *azif*, the night-scratch of insects, reckoned in the old deserts of Terra to be the call of daemons.

He sees, at a great distance, a stream coursing along the very bottom of the deep pass. It is just a trickle, like a fresh run of meltwater in spring. It winds beneath the rock-shadows, in and out of blackness, but where it catches the hyaline daylight, it glitters like tumbling jewels, blue and green. There's no way to easily judge scale, but Corswain can see that it's not men. A mass of tiny, gleaming shapes. A moving, advancing mat of–

Beetles. Flies.

A trickling stream of them, threading up the pass. How many must there be? How many billions must it take to make up a glinting black rill on the floor of the pass?

Far below, a gauze of mist drifts across the trackway. When it's gone, there is a figure standing there, gazing up at Corswain on the distant cliff. The stream of insects has halted, as though dammed, at the figure's heels.

It is Typhon. It is Calas Typhon, proud son of Barbarus, First Captain of the XIV Legion. He looks exactly as he did the day Corswain first met him, all those years ago before hell descended. His plate gleams in the cold light. He raises his hand in an almost fraternal salute.

'You are broken,' he says. Just a whisper, but Corswain hears it as clearly as he would if they were face to face. *'You are broken, Corswain, inside and out. Our long game of war comes down to this, and in respect of you, we offer a chance to submit. Submit to us. Do not attempt a final fight.'*

'You can offer me nothing but death,' Corswain yells back. He has to raise his voice so it will carry the thousand metres down into the pass. Typhon's soft reply comes effortlessly to his ear.

'Of course. Nothing but death. But it need not be by blade or violence. Submit, and it will be painless. A gentle decay into silence. We offer this in honour of your worth as a rival. No recrimination. Accept that you are broken, and take this gift from us. Spare yourself the pain of resisting the inevitable.'

The voice is commanding, honest, respectful. An offer of honour, warrior to warrior, mindful of dignity, courteous in manner. It is the integrity Corswain would show to a helpless foe. For a moment, he finds himself considering it. It would be so easy to let go, so sweet to relinquish the effort of–

'Sire. Your grace.'

Corswain looks at Adophel.

'Hell's blood,' says Adophel very quietly. 'The urge to agree is almost overwhelming.'

Corswain nods. 'You feel it too?'

'Like an ache in my heart. What's wrong with us? What is he doing to us?'

'He was always witch-blooded,' says Corswain. He looks around. A good portion of his forces are positioned to guard the pass, both above on the jagged lip of the cliffs, and on the skirt walls and fighting platforms below the portal. There should be more, but they thought they had longer. Many are still undeployed, or occupied in purifying the mountain's chambers. They thought they had three days. Adophel said three days.

How could Typhon have reached them so quickly? And why does he come alone, with only carrion flies and chirring beetles as an escort?

Corswain looks at his men. They are silent and motionless, as though they too have been transfixed by Typhon's offer. It feels as if their hearts have emptied.

Cartheus runs out onto the parapet. He drops to his knees and almost scrape-skids to rest at Corswain's feet.

'They are here!' he cries. 'Your grace, they are all here!'

'What?'

'He's beguiling you! Against all sanity, they are here already!'

Corswain blinks. It's not possible. Typhon has come alone. He should descend and finish him, for his gall, and set his head on a spike to greet the Death Guard army when it arrives.

Corswain turns and gazes down into the pass. 'Begone,' he yells. 'Or I'll cut you down where you stand.'

'*Pity…*' Typhon whispers. His figure is already dissolving into languid mountain mist. His last word echoes and repeats, slowly blurring with each repetition into the whirring scratch of azif. In the shadow-thwarted bed of the deep pass, the stream of blackness starts to move again, scuttling and scritching, inching between pebbles and stones towards the base of the portal.

But they are not pebbles, or stones. They are boulders and age-tumbled blocks. The gleaming shapes are not beetles and flies, they are men. Scale telescopes and shifts. Distance reduces, and the sheer cliffs of the pass seem to soar and tower. There is an army in the pass, a whole army at their door. It is plated in dirt, and where the thin light catches the moving plate, it glints and sparkles iridescent, like the wing cases of scarabs.

It swarms towards them.

'To arms…' Adophel croaks, then clears his throat and repeats the words with more force to clear the strangled break in his voice. On the walls and fighting platforms, the men shift, but it is slow and stunned with disbelief.

The air below is suddenly freckled with flies. The buzzing azif swells in volume.

'Raise the line!' Corswain snaps at his Chapter Master. 'Every man, every weapon we have!'

'Your grace–'

'Do it! You heard our brother Cartheus! He has no reason to lie, but by my soul, we are *blinded* by lies! Typhus infects us with his fever-dreams! Go! Go!'

Adophel turns and strides towards the portal, yelling commands. Arms and armour clatter as men respond.

'Are you sure of this?' Corswain asks Cartheus. 'What unfolds below… it's not just another warp-conjured trick to drive us mad?'

'Upon my life, *no*, your grace!' the warp-seer replies. Corswain sees the odd symbols and wards chalked on the man's plate. 'Zahariel has read it. He sent me with all urgency. They are here and upon us already.'

Corswain unsheathes his warblade, and glares down into the pass. The gulf below is full of churning black forms. Clouds of flies smoke the air like the vapour haze of a cataract. The Dark Angels had the advantage of height, and the natural choke point of the pass, but the enemy is already teeming up the rocks, like black water running uphill, against all laws of nature, impossibly ascending even sheer rock to the first of the fighting platforms, the grip and purchase of the warriors as sure and effortless as spiders on a wall.

He thought they had days to prepare, days to lay up their defence and edge their blades. They do not.

He raises his sword in the brumal light.

'Kill them,' is his only command.

3:xvi

Surfacing

The freight elevator, unused for months, takes almost twenty minutes to ascend from deep storage bunkers kilometres beneath the Sanctum. As it rises, it passes other storage levels, vast lonely halls, haunted by silence, that were once lined with rows of burnished war machines and stocks of munitions, enough to conquer a galaxy. But they have been picked clean, the cellars and reserves of the Palace stripped bare by the siege. War has emptied the vaults, leaving dim rockcrete compartments so vast, the entire human population of Terra could be contained there, sheltered from the surface onslaught.

If only anyone had thought to do it.

The elevator arrives, finally, with a shuddering clank, in a dispersal chamber adjoining the power plants that serve the House of Weapons. The chamber is also empty, apart from the abandoned freight haulers and exo-loaders that once handled the flow of armaments. They stand in the gloom like sculptures of orkoid beasts, their service to the war effort ended.

Amber warning lamps flash briefly. The elevator's tripartite hatch whirs open, and the Coronus grav-carrier rolls out across the chamber's floor, lifting a silent billow of dust. At other times, its arrival would have triggered security notices and brought Sentinels to investigate, even though this vehicle is one of theirs. But no one comes. John isn't sure if that's because the Alpha Legionnaire has run scrap code exploits to mask them from the automated security systems, or because there is no one watching any more. He isn't sure which of these ideas alarms him more.

The legionnaire brings the carrier to a halt and powers it down.

'Are we ditching this?' asks Dogent Krank, who has quickly come to like the well-armed and well-armoured reassurance of the Coronus.

'The mass-passageways of the lower Sanctum are more than large enough to accommodate a vehicle of this size,' says Actae.

John looks at her. 'I have a feeling,' he says, 'that He's not going to like us arriving unannounced and knocking on His door. I know for sure He won't like it if we roll up in a tank.'

John and Pech dismount first, John with his kitbag shouldered. They walk away from the carrier, looking for signs of life, feeling the infrasonic thrum of the nearby power plants in the air. The air is dead and stale, as though circ-processors have been shut down or set to conserve.

'The Sanctum,' murmurs John.

'Dispersal chamber six-nine-four,' Pech replies. 'About ninety minutes' walk to the Throne Room proper.'

John glances around at the emptiness and dust wistfully. His face and ribs still hurt, and his mouth and chin are bruised and scabbed.

'Not quite the Palace I imagined it would be,' he says.

'It's a service area, John. A utility vault. The formal areas of the Sanctum are quite grand. You won't be disappointed. In fact, you may want to brace yourself.'

'I was being sarcastic, Pech.'

'Ah.'

'You've seen them then?' John adds. 'The, uh… formal areas?'

'I've glimpsed them. Some of them.'

'You damn Hydra, you'll find your way into anything, won't you?'

'It's why we were made, John.'

'Well, my hat's off to you, Pech,' says John. He sets his kitbag down and rummages inside it to check he has everything. 'You did exactly what you said you'd do. You got us in. Into the Sanctum. Nigh on half the galaxy is trying and failing to do that, including several of the most gifted and powerful primarchs. You showed them, eh? Devil Lupercal should have put his money on the Alpha Legion. I guess that's why Erda sent you to us.'

'I suppose so.'

'Well, anyway,' says John, rising to his feet, with a slight wince as he braces his bruised ribs. 'My thanks. Sincerely. We literally couldn't have got this far without you.'

He casually pats the Alpha Legionnaire on the chestplate, an almost affectionate gesture of comradeship. When his hand comes away, it leaves something behind.

'Don't move, though, Ingo,' he says. 'Not a muscle. Please.'

'What have you done, John?'

John raises a hasty finger to his lips. 'I wouldn't even speak, if I were you. Seriously. Now it's set, it's acutely motion sensitive.'

Pech freezes, as much a statue as the derelict exo-loaders around them. His suit systems have already identified what John has done. The close-focus limpet mine anchored to his chestplate displays a small, red, blinking rune.

'Be resourceful, you said, so I'm being resourceful,' John tells the unmoving giant. 'I'm taking you out of the game, just like you told me to. Move, even slightly, and that thing goes off.

But don't move, because I don't want you to die. Just stay there. Really, *really* steady. I know your kind knows how to do that.'

He bends down, scoops up his kitbag, and reaches into it again. Behind them, the others are emerging from the carrier.

'I found a canister of them in that tank's storage locker,' John says. 'Same place as the voltvolver. One of your caches, I think. Now, you stay put. I'll sort out the rest of this mess.'

He walks towards the carrier. The others have all dismounted: Oll, the long companions, Leetu and Actae. The witch moves to meet him, her blind head cocked in curiosity.

'What's happening?' she asks. 'What's Alpharius doing? Why–'

John strides towards her. He lets the kitbag drop, revealing the psi-damper in his left hand, and flicks the pod's casing open with a snap of his wrist. He's ready for it, teeth gritted. She isn't, and it's going to hurt her more anyway.

Actae squeals, and falls to one knee, clawing at her head. John puts the damper down, just out of her reach, its soft, blue light glowing at maximum, and steps back. He pulls the voltvolver out of his belt with his right hand, and aims it directly at her head.

'Stay *down*,' he says.

3:xvii

Someone in authority

'Keeler!'

Again, the voice–

'Keeler! Mam!'

No, not some divine whisper. A real voice. Across the torrent of the flowing crowd, she sees Tang waving to her. Keeler jumps down and pushes through the press to reach her.

Tang has soldiers with her, members of the conclave, or willing civilian volunteers. They stink of promethium because most are carrying flamer units liberated from the munition wagons. Trial and error has shown that flames are the best defence. It's not much, because despite their vast numbers, they are not an armed force. But flamers can lay down screens of fire to drive off the raiding enemy units that harry the exodus, and fire is the best protection against the Neverborn, especially when they irrupt inside the refugee column. Fire has become the weapon of faith.

It's not much protection. If they are overtaken or surprised by an enemy main force, there will be absolute slaughter.

'What is it?' Keeler asks. Tang gestures to Katsuhiro, the trooper who has become part of their rabble. Caked in dust and masked like a bandit, he still clutches the child to his body. Keeler doubts he will ever let it go.

'Someone demanding to see someone in authority,' says Katsuhiro.

Keeler grins. 'Best of luck with that,' she says.

'He means you,' says Leeta Tang.

Keeler shrugs and follows them, walking up the ragged edge of the processional, in the stone-choked gutter, following the direction of flow. They move faster than the main body of the mass, which crawls, bandaged and blindfold, like a vagabond glacier. Katsuhiro and two flamer troops lead her and Tang off the main thoroughfare into an area of burned-out ruins. People from the exodus are resting there, propped on stone blocks and broken walls, easing torn feet and getting their strength back before rejoining the long march.

A little way in, Keeler sees a robed man indignantly arguing with Wereft and several more conclave soldiers. The robed man is injured, and his indignation has robbed him of what was once some stately dignity.

'What is this?' Keeler asks Katsuhiro.

'We saw a flyer come down,' he replies. 'A little Orgus 'thopter chopped by flak. Your man Wereft sent a team to check for survivors. Found this one.'

'Are you in charge?' the robed man asks as Keeler approaches.

'No one's in charge,' she replies. 'If you're here for any length of time, you'll realise that.'

'I require soldiers!' the man says. 'An escort detachment. You will provide them.'

'That's not possible,' she says.

'I told him it wasn't possible,' says Wereft.

'Then make it possible!' the man snaps.

'Sir, we can offer you support and somewhat limited medicae assistance,' she says, 'But beyond that…'

'Do you know who I am?' the man asks her. His anger is born out of fear, she can see that. She can also see that she *does* know who he is, to a certain extent. Up close, she can see the fine quality of his robes, the expensive silks, the mantle and crest of office disguised by dust and oil, the eyes that have been sutured shut for decades.

'This,' says Wereft, 'is Nemo Zhi-Meng.'

'Lord!' the man snaps. 'Lord! You will address me with respect!'

'With respect then, Lord Zhi-Meng,' says Keeler, 'you're shit out of luck. You can come with us, or you can make your own way. A dubious choice, I realise.'

He is stunned to silence. He sits down heavily on a slab of rockcrete, head bowed, and his shoulders start to shake.

'Step back, please,' Keeler says to the others. They back off and leave her alone with the man. She crouches in front of Zhi-Meng.

'I'm afraid authority has its limits now,' she says gently. 'Life too. Hell is here.'

'I know it,' he murmurs, nodding.

'I mean no unkindness, my lord, but all we can do is walk, in the hope of walking clear of this.'

He turns his face towards her. Though his eyes are long gone, the sacrifice of his art, his blindsight is sharp and knows exactly where she is.

'You're Keeler?' he asks.

She nods.

'I am–' he begins.

'Choirmaster of the Adeptus Astra Telepathica,' she answers. 'A lord of the High Council of Terra. One of the Senior Twelve. My lord, in other circumstances, it would have been a singular honour to meet you. Where were you going?'

'I was at Bhab Bastion,' he says. 'Trying to... to do my work. Reinforce the telaethesics...' He shrugs. 'Bhab is fallen,' he says.

'I guessed as much.'

'We tried to evacuate. My lifewards got me to a flyer, but–'

'This is not flying weather, my lord.'

Zhi-Meng laughs, a brittle laugh. 'It was a slaughter, Keeler. Great men and women, the Imperium's best, butchered in the halls, burned like kindling...'

'Men and women of all stations have been brought low by this, sir,' she replies. 'Come with me to the street outside and I will show you millions of them. War makes no distinctions when it comes to privilege, office or nobility, I'm afraid.'

'I was trying to reach the Sanctum,' he says. 'To rejoin the command structure and perform my duties–'

'I can't get you there,' she says. 'Eternity Gate is shut forever. Our duties are reassigned for us all. Ours, now – yours and mine – it's simply to survive, if we can.'

He nods. 'You're leading refugees out of the centre?'

'Yes, lord.'

'To where?'

'I have no idea,' she says. 'Nowhere in this world is safe, but I'm hoping some places are safer than others. Perhaps the northern districts, or even off the plateau itself, if we can get that far. To be honest, I think lack of food and water will kill most of us long before that, and if they don't, the enemy is at our backs and getting ever closer.'

'The world is broken,' he says. He rubs dirt off his cheek with the back of his hand. 'The last things I saw before I left my post... readings and data that made no sense. Time, dimensions... I mean the basic laws and fundamentals of the material world. They are corrupting. Terra is being dragged into the warp, Keeler. The natural laws of space and time can no longer be trusted to guide us. I know you know what the warp is.'

'Yes,' she replies.

'I have heard a great deal about you,' he says. 'One of the very first beyond the privileged few to glimpse the truth of our universe. That is correct, isn't it?'

'It is.'

'I confess, mam, I was one of those who voted to keep you incarcerated. To keep you locked away so you could divulge nothing. The truth was kept close for a long time, Keeler, for good reason.'

'I was taught the truth sets us free.'

'Sadly, no. And to say so makes you sound naive. Since the very first, I have known this. Since I was first elected to my role and inducted into the mysteries. To run the Telepathica, and support the Astronomican, I had to learn things that would curdle the mind. For all the Emperor's power, mankind exists on the very brink, under sufferance of the warp. Without it, we cannot maintain an empire, but it is our greatest foe. I have always petitioned, most strenuously, that the secrets of our universe must be kept from almost everybody. Then the likes of you come along, half-glimpsing something, and then speaking of faith and divinity–'

'I only speak of what I have seen, sir.'

'Without thought to the danger of it! The gods are false, Keeler. I have come to understand, through this horror, that there is a reason He prohibited religion and followed His instinct to shield mankind from understanding. The gods are false, but an awareness of the deep powers makes them real. The derangements of faith and belief stir up the empyric void.'

'I understand that,' she says. 'I understood it when it was first revealed to me. And for the longest time, that policy made sense. Ignorance was the best defence. The Emperor could shield us by our ignorance until His great plan was implemented and mankind could exist free of the warp. But Horus came.'

'Yes, Horus came.'

'And look at us, sir. Look where we are now. This can't be hidden or ignored. The warp is revealed to all and everyone. And the ignorance enforced upon us makes us more vulnerable for, lacking a better explanation, the masses see this as daemons and devilry which, of course, amplifies the effect. The ignorance that once protected us now magnifies the warp.'

'You are a more rational person than I expected, Keeler,' he says.

'Thank you. And I ask you this, because you may be one of the few who can answer... If superstitious dread amplifies the warp, might not faith fortify against it?'

'Faith in what?'

'In the Emperor. If fear agitates the warp into a frenzy, might not faith generate a stabilising calm?'

'You betray your lack of comprehension, Keeler. At the risk of gross simplification, such a mechanism would only work if the Emperor was a god, in the way that primordial entities of the empyrean may be called gods.'

'But what if He is?'

'Dear woman, I have stood in His presence. He is many things, but a god He is not.'

'I have met Him too,' she says.

'You have?'

'I have. He's here with me now. He is my hope. He is the hope of the millions in the street. He is the voice calling my name. He is the light. I think, sir, though I bow to your greater learning, that you have beheld it all but missed the point. You understand the detailed rubrics of your office, and the complex mechanisms of the Astropathica, yet fail to see...'

She stops, and sits down heavily. The nausea has overwhelmed her again, quite suddenly. There's a light in her eyes that makes the shape of her name, a shining voice that dazzles her.

'Are you all right?' asks Zhi-Meng. 'What happened?'

'I am… It's passing…'

'I felt that. Felt *something*. A wash of psykana, for a moment… Do you have the gift, Keeler? Does that explain your fanciful ideas?'

She clambers heavily to her feet.

'I don't know anything, sir,' she says. 'Really, I don't. I freely admit that my life has become cursed by mere flashes, all incomplete, of the greater truth. I have seen the lightning through a keyhole. I can only make what sense of it I can. But I know where we're going.'

'Who?' Zhi-Meng asks.

'All of us. I know where we're going, or where we're supposed to be going. I know where we need to be. I saw it, quite suddenly. A light. A guiding light. It is everything. It is the most important thing.'

'Do you mean a place where all these people will be safe?' he asks. 'Where *we* will be safe?'

'I don't know,' she replies. 'I don't think it's safe at all, but I know it's where we have to go.'

'How do you know? Who is telling you this?'

'I don't know that either,' says Keeler.

3:xviii

_____

Unless you fail

'What the hell are you doing, Grammaticus?' Oll yells.

'What I'm supposed to do, Oll,' John growls back, his teeth gritted, his weapon aimed at Actae's head. 'I'm looking after you. Watching your back. I've got them. Both of them.'

Actae groans, flopping over into a foetal position on the oil-spotted rockcrete.

'Stay *down*,' John tells her, the gun still aimed. He snatches a sidelong look at Oll. 'I had to wait until we were inside. Don't look at me like that. I know how dangerous she is. Alpharius told me all about it.'

'I know full well how dangerous she is,' says Oll, glaring at John in dismay. 'She pretty much told me herself.'

John sniffs and nods. 'Did she? Well, this is how it has to go.'

He glances at the others. They're all staring at him in shock, all except Katt, who has collapsed into Krank's arms. She's twitching and shivering.

'Sorry, Katt,' John calls out. 'Psi-damper. It was the only way, and there was no time to warn you.' He looks back at Oll. 'Just say the word,' he says.

'The word?'

'Come on, Oll! She's too dangerous to live. Just say the word!'

'For god's sake, John,' says Oll. 'I don't want you to shoot her.'

'Really? Knowing what you know?'

'I know she was sent to help us.'

'So she claims–'

'Erda co-opted her for a reason,' says Leetu quietly. 'Her, and Alpharius too. She brought us all together because we need each other.'

'Yeah?' says John. 'Well, I have the greatest respect for your lovely mistress, Astartes, but I don't think she knows everything. This Actae woman has an agenda of her own.'

'O-of course I do,' Actae gasps. 'And I h-haven't hidden it.'

'Turn that thing off, John,' says Oll.

'Oll...'

'Turn it off. You've got a gun on her. Let her speak.'

John hesitates. With a scowl, he crouches and deactivates the damper. He keeps the gun trained on Actae's skull the whole time.

'This is a mistake,' he says.

'My life's just one long series of those,' says Oll.

He looks at Actae. She's risen on all fours, panting as she tries to clear her head.

'I'm giving you a chance,' says Oll. 'The things you've said, I'm not going to lie. They scare me. I think you're crazy. But I also trust Erda's insight. She believes we need you, she steered you to us. So I'm not just going to kill you. Talk. Please.'

Actae raises her head. She rocks back and sits on her heels, trying to regain her breath.

'I'm the fail-safe,' she says.

'What does that even mean?' snaps John. Oll raises a hand to shut him up.

'Explain that,' says Oll.

'There are too many variables,' says Actae. 'Even you admit you're not sure what you're going to do when the time comes. Erda was providing options and opportunities. Alpharius was the way in. I'm the fail-safe.'

'If this goes wrong…' Oll begins.

'If this goes wrong.' She nods. 'If you fail to deliver. And, I swear, I have no idea why she has any faith whatsoever in you and your rabble. But I trust her insight too. Just like you. She is the future we might have had. She saw the dangers long in advance, but she was shut out and silenced. She sent me to help you, Oll Persson. I intend to fulfil that obligation. Help you in any way I can. I have demonstrated that intent already. Whatever I believe, I won't impose it on you.'

'Unless I fail,' says Oll.

'Unless you fail. If you can't achieve what you set out to achieve, then – and only then – I'll take my own measures. If Horus, as I believe, is too potent for any of us, even the Emperor himself… then I will try things *my* way.'

'Harness him?' John says. 'Harness the damn warp?'

'If I can,' she replies. 'Perhaps I can't. But I will certainly try, and I have an unrivalled insight. Whatever Horus was is long gone. He is an instrument now, a very powerful one, but an instrument, no more or less. Instruments exist to be used.'

'Oh, 'cause it's *that* simple,' John sneers.

She slowly rises to her feet. John's aim follows her up, and never wavers from her head.

'There are two sides in this, Oll Persson,' she says, turning her face towards Oll. 'That is the nature of war. Two sides must be defeated, or persuaded to alter course, in order for this conflict to end. That, or the galaxy and our species burn. You, Oll, are the weapon sent to stop the Emperor. If you succeed, you may be enough. But if you fail, I am the weapon sent to stop Horus.'

John starts to laugh. 'Shit, Oll,' he says. 'Are you swallowing any of this?'

Oll shakes his head wearily.

'Your words have a ring of truth,' he says to Actae, 'even if John can't hear it. But we've come a long way, and we're tired, and I can't see how we can trust you. You could be lying. You could be saying what you think we want to hear. You might even be telling the truth, but only because there's a gun to your head. The moment John puts away that preposterous handgun, you could turn on us.'

'So, you're saying I should shoot her?' John asks.

'Shut up, John,' Oll sighs.

'I'm sorry you don't trust me,' says Actae.

'So am I,' says Oll.

'But I understand. Our views of the cosmos are very different. Perhaps that's why Erda drew us together.'

'Perhaps. But I still see no way of trusting you from here on.'

'There is a way,' says Leetu quietly.

Oll glances at him.

'There is a way,' Leetu repeats. 'A safeguard. A way of keeping watch on her thoughts in case she tries to deceive us.'

'Go on.'

'It would be demanding. An unpleasant hardship.' The Astartes looks over at Katt, who is beginning to stand unaided, her hands shaking. 'A psykanic link. The witch lets the girl watch her thoughts. One mind open to the other. The girl would act as a leash. If the witch even thinks of behaving contrary to your wishes, we'll know. Likewise, if the witch tries to hide her thoughts, the girl will know that too. She can warn us.'

Leetu stares at Katt.

'It's a big ask, I realise,' he says.

'I'll do it,' Katt says without hesitation.

'Katt-' says Oll.

'I will do it. I'll watch her like a hawk.' She steps forward and glares pugnaciously at Actae. 'Well? You call it,' she says.

'Let you into my mind?' Actae replies, a look of mild disgust on her face. 'Let you in, to see everything-'

'It's that,' says Katt, 'or Grammaticus pops you in the forehead.'

Actae lifts her hand sharply.

'If you let me *finish*, girl,' she hisses. 'The idea is repulsive. My mind is my own, and I shudder at the thought of some grubby urchin ransacking my secrets and my memories. But my comfort is not the issue. There is far too much at stake. If that's what it will take for you to trust me, Oll Persson, so we may continue... So be it.'

'Wait,' says John. 'She's talking about trust. There's no trust in this! She could falsify her thoughts, wall off parts of her mind-'

'I could do all those things,' says Actae. 'But I won't, Grammaticus. That's the point. I need your trust. I have nothing to hide.'

She turns her face towards Oll.

'Well?' she asks. 'Do you trust me? Do you want to trust me?'

Oll thinks for a moment. He walks over to Katt and hugs her tight.

'Don't do this if you don't want to,' he whispers. 'It will be a lot. It will be unpleasant.'

'It's all right,' she whispers back, resting her head on his chest. 'I think I've finally worked out why I'm here.'

Katt pulls away from him and faces Actae.

'Go on,' she says.

Actae smiles. It is not a comforting smile. 'As you wish, child,' she replies.

She dips her head slightly. Katt blinks, and she lets out a little gasp. Oll can tell that the contact is immediately distressing, but Katt breathes hard and clenches her fists, determined not to show on her face the horror flooding her mind.

'There,' she says, with some effort. 'Not so hard. Not so bad.' She tries to flash a smile at Oll, but it's more of a grimace.

'What happens now?' asks Zybes.

Oll crosses to John, places his hand on the top of John's gun and gently pushes his aim down. John scowls at him, then submits and tucks the weapon away.

'This is a mistake, Oll,' he says quietly.

'Like I said…'

'I had them both. I won't get that chance again. You understand this is why I'm here, don't you?'

'To make amends, for things you did or should have done in other lives.'

'Yeah, that,' says John. 'Whatever. Oll, I threw my lot in with you to protect you. To get you where you need to be, that's all. You have to let me do that.'

Oll nods.

'I mean it,' says John. 'Let me look after you. Let me get you there. Stop overruling me. I don't have your scruples, Oll. Your moral compass. Let me do the dirty work so your hands stay clean. Damn it, I should have just shot her.'

'Well, don't ask my opinion, then.'

'I won't,' says John. 'Next time, I *won't*. Stay out of my way. I'll just do what needs to be done to save your sorry arse. No consultation. I won't give you the chance to talk me out of it.'

'Fine.'

'Fine. Because you can talk your way out of anything.'

'That,' says Oll, 'is basically what I'm counting on.'

John snorts in disdain. He picks up the damper, drops it back in the kitbag, and looks over at the motionless Alpharius.

'Right,' he says to Actae. 'Free him.'

'I'm sorry?' Actae replies.

'I know about the code word. The pre-conditioning. The path you've set him on against his will. Change Orphaeus. Abort it. Switch it to something else.'

'I can't,' she says.

'Don't give me that. Switch it to Xenophon. Let him be his own man.'

'I repeat, John Grammaticus, I can't.'

'She can't,' says Katt. 'She's not lying. Once Twentieth Legion plan conditioning is triggered, it can't be undone…'

'It can only be revoked by Alpha Legion auto-hypnotix, a deep neural process that is quite outside my expertise,' says Actae. 'I'm sorry. There's nothing I can do about it.'

'You can activate the poor bastard but you can't shut him down again?'

Actae doesn't reply. Katt, wide-eyed with worry, nods on her behalf.

'Shit!' says John. 'You utter… *Shit*!' He claps his hand to his head and stares at the floor.

'John?' Oll asks.

'Get them moving, Oll. Get them all moving. Leetu, take point. I'll be right behind you.'

They all look at him, then start to move away across the chamber towards the distant hatch.

John blows out a breath to settle himself, and then walks over to the unmoving Pech. He stands facing the frozen giant, so Pech can see him.

'I'm sorry,' he says. 'Truly. Don't try to answer. Just listen. You know I can't take that thing off you. Not with you coded the way you are. You know I can't risk it. I'm sorry it's played out like this. I know you'll get out of it. You'll find a way. I dunno, maybe micromovement over a period of weeks or months, you'll finally deactivate it and take it off. You people are good at that sort of thing. But I can't take it off you now. I know you understand why.'

Pech makes no response.

'So,' says John, with a shrug. 'Sorry. If I get a chance, you know, afterwards… if there is an afterwards… I'll come back. I swear. I'll come back and unlock it. Just don't move in the meantime. And if I don't get the chance, well… like I said. Sorry. Not the way I wanted it to go.'

The Astartes remains utterly silent.

'Right,' says John. 'Well… Goodbye, Pech.'

He turns and walks away after the others.

The Alpharius is still standing there, motionless, long, long after they have gone and the hatch has closed behind them.

3:xix

Rogal in the desert

Rogal Dorn spends a century in the yellow desert until he finally concedes that there is no way out of it.

After a century, he also believes there is no way into it either, although he is in it, which suggests that this is untrue. A small fact to cling to. He came here. He was brought here. There must have been a way in, once.

Unless he has always been here. After a century, that starts to feel like the truth.

He meticulously orders the facts he can be certain of. Every day, he collates the available facts. Every day, for a century, there are fewer and fewer of them. The sun rusts them away. He is here. Fact. The desert is endless and the sunlight unrelenting. Fact. Something, technological or metaphysical, intercepted his teleport pattern and diverted him to this wasteland. Fact. None of those who departed with him are here. Fact. This is not the Target Principal, the *Vengeful Spirit*. Fact.

But it is a trap. Fact.

He is alone. Fact. He knows exactly who he is. Fact.

'I am Rogal Dorn, Praetorian of Terra, primarch of the Seventh Legion Imperial Fists, seventh-found son, defiant and unyielding,' says Rogal Dorn to the hot and empty desert air.

The desert is boundless, a soft sea of yellow sand, the colour of his Legion's plate. The sky is a hot white haze, the colour of his hair. There is no sun, except that everything is sunlit. There is a breeze, parched and dry, that comes intermittently, and lifts the soft sand from the crests of the dunes in horsetail plumes to make new dunes nearby, grain by grain.

There are walls. Ancient stone walls, faded pink, and bleached by light. They are too high to climb and they serve no purpose he can identify, for they keep nothing in and nothing out, and merely stand, crossing the dunes in forking, geometric lines. There are walls either side of him, suggesting but never admitting that he is caught in some gargantuan labyrinth.

He tries and fails to climb them. He listens at them, hoping to detect sounds from the other side, but he does not. Some days, he ascends to the top of the highest dunes, and from there, as the breeze lifts the sand around his feet, he can almost see over them. Almost. Enough to see the odd, angled lines of their arrangement and the fact that, beyond them, lie more dunes, and other walls, and more dunes.

Fact.

Every day, for a century, he orders the facts he can be certain of.

He is here, and no one else is. Fact. He is alone. Fact. His pattern was diverted. Fact. This is not the Target Principal, the *Vengeful Spirit*. Fact. It is a trap. Fact. The desert is endless and there is no way out. Fact.

There is no way in. Perhaps.

He knows exactly who he is. Fact.

'I am Rogal Dorn, Praetorian of Terra, primarch of the

Seventh Legion Imperial Fists, seventh-found son, defiant and unyielding,' says Rogal Dorn.

The bodies are here. They are all long dead and they are all his sons. They are scattered across the dunes and piled up against the bases of the walls, for kilometres. They wear the yellow plate of the VII Legion Astartes Imperial Fists, but they have been here so long that only dry white bones reside inside them, and the plate is abraded by breeze and sand, so all numerals and identifier markings are worn away. He doesn't know who they were, except that they were once Imperial Fists. They may or may not be the men who formed the company he left with. He can't be sure. Those men, hand-picked, may be here, but if they are, why were they long dead when he arrived? And who are all the others? There are far, far more than a company-strength of men scattered across the dunes. There are thousands. Tens of thousands. Yellow plate is piled like metal shingle along the foot of the walls. Many times he attempts to count them, to reach an accurate number which he can add to his list of facts. But he always loses count, some days after ten thousand, some days after twenty, for there are so many, and it is impossible to know where he started counting and where he has finished. He tries to mark them with his sword as he counts, cutting a notch in each pauldron. That scrupulous method gives him a figure of thirty-seven thousand four hundred and nine, before he loses count and forgets if he has notched a pauldron or not. Besides, his sword-edge is beginning to blunt, and he is weary, and there are still so many more, more than those he has already counted.

Unsure, he starts again.

He orders the available facts.

There are very many dead, and the desert is endless. Fact. The walls are very slightly too high. Fact. There is no sun, but the light neither rises nor sets. Fact. It is slightly cooler in the shadow of the walls. Fact. There is no way out. Fact.

There is no way in. Is that a fact?

'I am Rogal Dorn, Praetorian, primarch of the Imperial Fists, seventh-found son, defiant and unyielding,' says Rogal Dorn.

The desert is yellow. The light is white. The walls are very slightly too high. He sits in the cool of the shadows, day after day, amid the litter of yellow armour, and recites the available facts to himself. His sword is notched. He is alone. The breeze lifts feathers of sand from the ridges of the dunes like spindrift from the sea. There is no way out.

This is a trap. Fact.

'I am Rogal Dorn. I am. I am *Rogal Dorn*. Primarch of the Imperial Fists, seventh-found son, defiant and unyielding,' says Rogal Dorn.

The desert is yellow at first. In the course of a century, it darkens. He doesn't notice it at first until, years later, seated in the cool shadow of the wall, he realises that the yellow of the dunes has become darker. It has become pinker, like the faded pink of the ancient stone walls. The sky is darker too. It is blue-white, hot blue-white, the colour of his eyes.

The yellow plate of the uncountable dead is beginning to rust. It is turning brown. It is rusting and, fleck by fleck, is slowly blowing away. Is that why the dunes are growing darker? Is it rust mixing with the sand?

He orders the available facts. Facts are his arsenal, knowledge his strength. Every battle he ever won, he won through application of knowledge. He is starved of facts. It is hard to know how to fight without facts to guide his actions. There are few here, fewer every day. There were more before, but many of them have rusted away.

In the siege, there were facts. Too many facts. More facts than there are grains of sand in this endless desert. Only he could order them all, and count them, and use them. That's why he was Praetorian. He never told anyone at the time, but it was a crippling burden. He longed to be out from under the constant weight of facts, the accumulating piles of data. In the months of the siege, he longed to be free of that weight. He longed just to fight as a man, as a warrior, with a sword. He longed for the simplicity of that. To fight, face to face, hand-to-hand, the freedom of physical war. By the end, it was all he wanted. To be free of the infinite data, the relentless pressure, the constant mental war, and just take up his sword and fight. To join the others on the walls and release himself into the joyous liberty of physical combat, where only instinct and reaction mattered, and his mind could rest. To stand, to fight, to kill, and not to think. Just for a while. Please. He never told anyone that.

That was all a long time ago. He barely remembers it. But he is sure there was a siege.

'I am Rogal Dorn, primarch of the Imperial Fists, defiant and unyielding,' says Rogal Dorn.

His sword is notched and blunt. He is very tired. These walls, bleached pink, are not the walls he longed to stand on. Things become simpler, here in the shadow of the walls where he sits. Facts rust away. There are fewer and fewer of them every day. There are no days because there are no nights.

Years pass, and it grows darker still. Where yellow became pink, pink becomes brown. Everything has rusted. There is nothing yellow left, except some tiny shards of yellow cera-mite and plasteel around his feet. Everything is worn out. He believes the entire desert is just grains of rust, that there were once far more bodies, and that other centuries, which must have passed before he arrived, had worn many of them away to form the endless desert where he found himself. The dunes were the rust particles of other suits of plate and other sets of bones, reduced by light and breeze.

He orders the available facts. He counts the bodies that remain. He gives up and starts again. The blade of his sword is beginning to wear away. He begins to like the fact that there are fewer facts to order and arrange, fewer things to take into account, less data to process and triage. He remembers longing for that simplicity. When was that? Long ago. Perhaps during a siege. He remembers yearning for it, anyway, and oddly, now he has it. There is simplicity here, in the cool shadow below the walls. There is very little to put in order. He is alone. There is no way out. The walls are very high. His sword is a shank of worn metal. He was going somewhere, but he never arrived. There were people with him, but they are not here now, or they are rusted to flakes in the cool shadow of the walls.

They are probably long dead. Whatever he was a part of – a siege, was it? Whatever it was, it must be over by now. Long over. Losers defeated, victors decided. It's out of his hands now. It's no longer his responsibility.

It's a relief. He thinks he longed for it, once. He forgets. His memory is rusting. It's a great relief, just to sit in the cool and be. Not to think. Not to decide.

'I am Rogal Dorn, of the Imperial Fists, defiant,' says Rogal Dorn.

3:xx

Measureless

They walk through empty golden halls, and across floors of gleaming marble that soak up the sounds of their footsteps.

'Is this what you expected?' John asks.

Oll shrugs. The scale of the Palace is breathtaking, designed, he supposes, to inspire awe if not outright fear.

'He always had lofty ideas about Himself,' he replies.

John smirks. 'That's an understatement,' he says.

'It's not pride, though,' says Oll. 'Not really. Not the way you or I would think of it. The man I knew...' – he sniffs slightly as he says the word 'man' – 'the man I once knew, He didn't really care for majesty or material riches. It was all just a means to an end. Everything was. The palaces, the titles, even the face He wore, they meant nothing to Him. All that mattered was what they meant to other people. They were just aspects, John. Signifying devices. To carry authority, He had to look the part. To rule a galaxy, He needed a palace like this. I assure you, He would have as soon lived as a monk in some stone cell, or in a hut on barren moors... He needed nothing. But no one would have taken Him seriously. This monstrous, taste-less edifice is simply the natural conclusion of His progress.'

'What, just theatre?'

'Dangerous theatre,' Oll replies with a nod.

Another hallway yawns before them, cased in gold and lined with statues, and filled with taut silence, the painted ceiling so high it seems just a bar of pale sky.

'It's everything I expected,' says Oll. 'Except the emptiness.'

'Yes,' says Zybes. 'I thought we would have been found by now. Long since. Found and challenged.'

'There's no one here,' says Krank.

'I think everyone is at the walls,' says Leetu quietly. They are all talking quietly, even though no one is around, afraid of raising their voices in such a hallowed place. 'Every soldier, every warrior, those that would ordinarily guard this place day and night.'

The Legion-less Astartes gestures to alcoves that line the aureate walls between the towering statues. They look like shrines, but Oll knows they can't be. He realises what Leetu is suggesting. The alcoves are made for sentries to stand in eternal vigilance. Oll has to adjust for scale, for the alcoves are so large. Giants stood here, golden giants, he is sure. But they are gone now. Even the elite lifewards are at the Delphic walls, fighting the last fight, and no one is left to patrol the emptied hallways of the final fortress. He and his long companions have only got this far because the place has been abandoned. No one has expected intruders at the very heart of things, for nothing is supposed to have got this far.

'We should find someone,' says Krank.

'What for?' asks Zybes.

'Well, we can't just wander around aimlessly,' says Krank. He's clearly scared. 'We're here on official business, aren't we? We should find someone, and tell them we want to see Him right away–'

'How do you suppose that will work out for us?' Katt asks, though Oll knows it's Actae asking the question, using the girl as a mouthpiece. 'We're intruders in the sacred heart of all things, and our intentions are ambiguous at best. It would be quite a feat, and quite incriminating, merely to explain how we got here.'

Katt looks at them, her eyes not quite her own.

'They will find us soon enough, and I, for one, am in no hurry to greet the golden warriors again.'

'So… we just find this Throne Room place?' asks Zybes.

'Yes,' says Oll. 'We find this Throne Room place.'

'Will we, though?' Krank asks. 'We've been walking for hours. What seems like hours. This palace is endless, and every hall looks like the last one…'

Oll feels it too. He tells himself it's just his imagination, but it truly feels as though they are walking some implausible, stately labyrinth. He has a poor history with labyrinths. He still has bad dreams about Knossos. He wants to ask Leetu if he can borrow the skein of thread the Astartes carries in his bag, so he can tie knots to finials and mouldings and the fingers of gilded statues and mark their way, for fear they are simply doubling back on themselves.

Perhaps they are. Perhaps He already knows they are here, and is playing games to deceive and confuse them. Perhaps He has no interest in the distraction of an uninvited audience, and is keeping them at bay with His psychic wiles. That would be just like Him. Delaying the inevitable.

'I will find you,' Oll mutters.

'What?' says John.

'Thinking aloud,' says Oll. 'Leetu? I saw you carry twine in your bag. Can I use it?'

The Astartes pauses, and then produces the ball of red thread, wound around its fid. He hesitates before handing it over. It is the property of his mistress, and he's loath to give it up.

Oll takes it with a nod, cuts off a short piece, and ties it around the ankle of a golden statue. He tosses the twine to Zybes.

'Every chamber we come to, Hebet, every room,' he says, 'do the same.'

Zybes nods, baffled at the purpose of his new task.

'Becoming paranoid, Ollanius?' Katt asks.

'Speak for yourself,' says Oll.

'I'm not paranoid. Just suitably apprehensive.'

Oll looks at Actae. 'I meant literally, speak for yourself. Stop using the girl. She's not there for your use, she's just keeping an eye on you.'

'Very well,' says Actae. Katt sighs slightly, as if some weight has eased from her.

They start walking again.

'You think He's toying with us?' John asks Oll quietly.

'I wouldn't put it past Him. He doesn't want to have the conversation I want to have.'

They pass into the next hall, then the next, treading softly. Each chamber is as glorious and intimidating as the last, the statuary as solemn, the alcoves as empty. But except for some details – the colour of the inlaid marble floor, the pose of statues, the designs of zodiacs and monads engraved on the auramite walls – they seem like the same halls, repeating.

They also seem so clean. So clinically clean, sterile, more like a laboratory than a regal dwelling. There is no smell, no grime. After the long companions' unmeasurable years of travel, through dark places and mummified cities, the caves crushed by time, the saponified landscapes of xenos realms, the squelching morass of forgotten battlefields, the raddled husks of hive arcologies in torment, the death-rattled tumult of exoplanar corpse-continents, they have become too accustomed to constant filth and dirt and foulness. This place, this

Palace, is too perfect, untouched and pure. Even the service hall where they first arrived, the dispersal chamber, a utility space, even that was unnaturally immaculate, but for a layer of dust that was, itself, unpolluted. These rooms, in their spotless clarity, seem acutely wrong to them.

And they seem purposeless. Halls that lead to further towering halls, anterooms opening to other cavernous anterooms, the constant soft hush of a gallery or mausoleum, the glitter of the giant pendulum lights. Approach rooms and colonnades lead to more approach rooms and colonnades, and arrive nowhere. Is the scale and proportion of the Palace so inhuman that it defies expectation, or is the scale playing with their minds?

In each chamber, Oll makes sure Zybes ties off a loop of thread.

The auramite doors at the far end of the next hall stand ajar, as though someone passed through in a hurry without caring to close them. The hall beyond is yet another arcade of heroic statues and empty alcoves, glowing soft amber in the light of the electro-flambeaux.

They move along it. Zybes fusses with his thread, then hurries to catch them up.

'Quite a journey we've had,' muses John.

Oll nods.

'Through caverns measureless to man, eh?'

'I didn't take you for a student of poetry, Grammaticus.'

'I'm not. I wasn't. The words just drifted into my head. All sorts of verse I was made to read when I was young. Never had much time for it. Funny how memories come back.'

'After lives as long as ours,' says Oll.

'*Caverns measureless to man…* I certainly remember that one. Keats.'

'Not Keats. Coleridge.'

'Be quiet!' Katt yelps suddenly. They turn and look at her. Actae is twisting her head from side to side, as if searching with her blind eyes.

'What is it, witch?' John asks.

'*Hide,*' hisses Actae.

3:xxi

Fragments

The Lady Lucia Galika Tamerocca hides, though it is a poor form of hiding. The heavy drapes of the grand chamber have been closed, the last chore of her household staff before they fled. The room is gloomy, but for the lamp at her side.

The Lady Lucia Galika Tamerocca has put on her finest gown, with its vast train and skirts of lace and silk. She has put on her best powdered wig, and she has rouged her cheeks. This is how she would dress whenever she, along with the high-born scions of other noble houses, was summoned from her palatine mansion to a formal event in the Sanctum. The room trembles. She hears the windows shiver in their casements.

The Lady Lucia Galika Tamerocca watches her beloved song-birds flutter and chirp in the huge and ornate birdcage on the table in front of her. How unafraid they seem. The cage is too heavy for her to carry, for she is an old woman, and she would never have left them behind. She considered letting them go, setting them free, but like her, where would they fly to?

The Lady Lucia Galika Tamerocca has decided to stay, to hide in the curtained darkness until whatever finds her, finds her. She is too dignified to run. She is of noble blood, and this mansion is her family home. She will not be driven out of it by mindless curs, no matter how brutal they are. The room trembles. Dust drifts down from the ceiling.

The Lady Lucia Galika Tamerocca keeps her seat, despite the sounds that rise like a storm around her house. This is her home. She absolutely will not run. She is nobility, and nobility does not flee, and besides, who would feed her birds? She hears something scratching at the chamber door. They are here now. Very well. So be it.

The Lady Lucia Galika Tamerocca has a laslock pistol in her lap.

Face down, Sergeant Hetin Gultan of the Royal Zanzibari Hort hides among the dead by pretending to be one of them. The dead are his men, and mud clasps them all. The enemy approaches, stalking from the smoke. He hopes he will pass unnoticed, but he will not.

The World Eaters smell fear, and the dead are no longer afraid.

Barthusa Narek of the Word Bearers stays hidden. Concealed in the rubble of a smashed fortification, he watches the cities of the human home world burn.

The Word Bearers who accompanied him to Terra and the final fight are dead. Most were killed when their drop-ship was hit by battery fire on the assault run. The rest he killed himself. Once on the burning fields of the Throneworld, one mote swept up on a war of global scale, he had no need to keep pretending he was one of them, or that he shared their manic ambitions. There's only one death, one end, that interests him. He's tracking his prey.

Hidden, invisible, he scopes from the rubble with his sniper rifle. He has standard ammunition left, and he'll use that as he pleases. He has one fulgurite bullet remaining too, and he's saving it.

When he finally locates his father, Lorgar, he will load it and use it.

There is nowhere to hide. Something down the street, a traitor engine by the sound of it, is raking Kucher's position with some kind of cutting beam, some hideous area-denial weapon. The beam, scarcely thicker than a whisker, is only visible when it passes through smoke. It cuts through everything it touches like a hot wire. It cuts through brick, stone, metal and armour. It cuts through Kucher's men. He sees it slice the corners off buildings, cleanly sectioning stonework like soft cheese. He sees it prune light poles and drop them like logs. He sees it pass, like a flawless surgical blade, through the tops of helmets, through torsos, through limbs. The corpses of nine men are already piled on the pavement, cut into astonishingly geometric cross-sections. There is so much blood.

Kucher yells at his squad to move and find cover, but there is absolutely nowhere to hide. Sergeant Geera falls, precisely severed at the waist. Trooper Vaskol loses both legs at the knees and collapses like a bolster. Trooper Herch leans against a wall, and then half of him slides away vertically in a sudden out-welling of blood that leaves the rest of him propped up like a dissection plate in a medicae treatise.

Kucher hurls himself into cover behind the command Aurox. He feels the vehicle shudder slightly, and sees a meticulous hairline crack suddenly running along the hull, end to end, at chest height. Kucher smells burned meat and the coppery stink of blood.

He looks down at himself as he falls apart.

The skitarii, vassals of the Dark Mechanicum, think they are well hidden. They have clambered up the flying buttresses of the shell-struck manufactory, and gained access to the lowest tier of the flat roofing. They move in fire-teams, lugging the disassembled parts of three heavy fusion mortars between them. Torrential rain pelts down across the roofscape, and vapour swirls up from the galvanised panels of the flat roof. The skitarii flash encrypted binharic data-bursts to and fro. On the next level up, they will unpack their cargo, and assemble the mortars for firing, dropping a string of fusion bombs on the unsuspecting loyalist forces dug-in behind the manufactory's eastern wall.

The skitarii are from the Kal-Tag Delt sub-branch, a purpose-specific clade designed for line infiltration, and group-unified by stealth-adaptive coding. Their power sources are baffled to mask heat profile, and their motivators frictionless and damped. Despite the weapons and munition canisters they carry, they move in virtual silence; their body armour – layers of long, ceramite leaf panels that encase them like feathers – is matt-grey and non-reflective. They are virtually invisible to auspex and modar. Their optics and sensoria are particularly large and sensitive.

Nevertheless, there is someone waiting for them on the flat roof. He is crouched in the rain, a sword flat across his knees.

The skitarii register surprise-code. They were hiding/concealed. How did the Astartes legionary hide/conceal himself from their hiding/concealment? How did he get there without detection, to be hiding/waiting for them?

Their binharic queries go unanswered. Loken rises to his

feet, chainsword purring as he extends it out to his right. He draws Rubio's blade in his left hand. The Kal-Tag Delt register no fear. Fear is not a coded option for them. They set down the mortar components and rush him. They have calculated the variables. They are many and he is–

–into them, without hesitation. Blades loop and hiss in the rain, shredding armour leaves and plastek, spraying debris and severed limbs into the air. They stab at him, they shoot, but he is moving too fast, and he is in among them, impaling and carving, smashing one skitarius into another with crushing force. Rubio's blade smokes with angry power as it slices through tubing, through wiring plaits, through mechadendrites, through torso-plate, through helmets surgically fused to skulls.

A skitarius folds under the fury of Loken's chainsword like torn foil. Broken leaves spin up from the impact. Loken turns and rakes Rubio's blade through the thorax of a particularly large Mechanicum warrior. Its chest explodes in sparks and fragments of circuitry. As it teeters, systems ruined, he delivers a hard kick to its belly that smashes it off the edge of the flat roof, and knocks three others of its kind off the lip with it.

The remainder scuttle back from him, fast-processing the conclusion that he is an unexpectedly dangerous impediment. One flash-burns out a noospheric signal, calling in immediate fire support with no heed for the integrity of itself or the surviving members of its unit. Such is the pragmatic war-logic of the skitarii. This impediment is too dangerous and must be obliterated as a priority.

One and a half seconds later, an auto-slaved launcher unit three streets away fires a hunter-seeker missile vertically with a sucking roar of fire-wash. The missile climbs on a tail of blue flame, arcs and plunges. Loken sees the twinkle of it, and leaps. The entire flat roof annihilates as it

impacts, and two of the great stone buttresses collapse, folding like weary limbs.

In the courtyard below, Loken rises to his feet. The flagstones
under his boots are cracked from his sure-footed landing.
Cinders flutter down around him in the rain. He glances up
at the burning rooftop he just vacated. The flames swirling off
it are almost incandescent. He sheathes Rubio's blade, then
uses the tip of his chainsword to probe the broken bodies of
the four skitarii he kicked off the roof. They are smashed and
crumpled on the yard's flagstones around him. One stirs, and
starts to gurgle out some kind of reboot code. Loken applies a
little pressure and lets the chainsword saw its head off.

He takes stock. He was sure he just heard someone call
his name again. The yard, mysteriously, seems familiar. Rain
sheets down. An abandoned groundcar stands off to one side.
The flagstones are littered with broken glass and lumps of
burning debris from the destroyed roof above. Ahead of him
are the doors of a large building. But everywhere looks the
same now. Everywhere is a repeating desolation of darkness
and rain and rubble.

His sensoria detect movement. He slides into hiding and
awaits the next encounter.

They scramble to find cover. There was an alarming note of
fear in Actae's warning. The only possible hiding places are
the vacant alcoves, the ornate recesses where giant sentinels
once stood. They crowd into the shadows of three of them,
pressing in behind the elaborate frames.

A procession passes down the hall. Soldiers of the Hort
Palatine in ceremonial regalia march in, streaming – as it
seems to Oll – from nowhere. They are escorting what looks
like a column of prisoners: men and women in simple cream
robes. These prisoners appear scared, or at least apprehensive,

and the stink of psykanic power wafts from them. There are over two hundred of them. Behind them come two cowled figures in green robes, conversing in low voices; behind them, two terrifying Custodians in gold bearing castellan axes of immense size.

In one of the alcoves with Actae and Katt, Oll tries to squeeze himself against the wall and remain hidden. Through the fretwork of the alcove's frame, he sees the agitated psykers herded onwards. For a second, it seems as though ghosts flutter around them, half-seen shades, but he's sure it's just a trick of the light. Then the Custodians pass by, and he shrinks in even more tightly, for they are beautiful and dreadful both at once.

It takes a long time for the procession to disappear into the next chamber. They hear doors close. Oll peeks out. The hall is empty again.

'Psykers,' he murmurs.

'Submitting to sacrifice,' Actae says.

'What do you mean?'

'It wasn't clear. Their minds were clouded by something. But the figures in green, they were two of the Sigillite's Chosen. I could hear some of their thoughts. This is the fifth recruitment today. They are gathering the psycho-active, tithing them… as a safeguard of some kind. Something called "sigil", an unspoken sanction. Taking them to the Throne Room to…'

'What?' asks Oll.

'I saw their thoughts, Ollanius,' says Actae. She turns her blindfold face towards him. 'The Chosen were just as scared as the reinforcements they had conscripted. They're not sure what's going on, but the Emperor has risen from the Throne and has engaged upon some sudden new plan.'

'What do you mean, "plan"?'

'I don't know,' says Actae.

'She doesn't,' says Katt. 'And they didn't know either.'

3:xxii

The place and manner of my execution

Of course, they granted him a gaoler too. A guardian to watch over him, to take him to the laboratorium and back, and to stand in vigil outside his door, day and night. The guardian is a golden giant named Amon Tauromachian. Early on, Fo couldn't really distinguish the brute from others of his kind, but he's come to know him, as much as anyone can come to know these kinds of facsimile gods. Amon seems thoughtful and almost kind (well, compared to that vicious killer the captain-general), if the word can be applied to a three-metre-tall genetic monster in laughably ostentatious gilded war plate.

Amon is his gaoler, his guardian, and now, it seems, his executioner.

'It's time then, is it?' asks Fo, looking up from his books.

Amon reaches up and disengages his neck seal. He lifts the helm from his head. The poor monster seems to want to look Fo in the face, unmasked, as though this conveys some sort of respect or dignity.

'Directives have been issued,' Amon says, his voice the soft rumble of a storm on a neighbouring continent.

Fo scowls to himself. He sets aside his book. He hasn't been allowed a pen or any means of making a record, and the walls of his quarters (unlike the noctilithic walls of my squalid cell in the Blackstone, from which I also learned so very much) are impervious to marking. But he has modified the nail of his right index finger so that it can impress individual letters and numerals in the books he's been given, and he has perfected a kind of inverted braille by which he can record, secretly, his private thoughts and ruminations. Once he's dead, the books will probably be discarded, or returned to some library without anybody noticing the slight dimples and stipples embossing the pages. They'll never know what he wrote, or the secrets he hid.

'Issued, eh? May I ask who by?' Fo says.

'I have not been told,' says Amon. 'I have simply been instructed to discharge my watch of you, and hand you over. I am–'

Fo raises a hand quickly to silence him.

'Oh! Please, Amon. Don't make your next words "only following orders". Do me *that* decency, at least.'

Amon opens his mouth and closes it again. An almost imperceptible expression of distress crosses his broad features. It *was* what he was going to say, of course. The idea that Fo knew that reinforces his concerns that Fo is somehow learning to manipulate and read him. Amon has been told all the stories about Fo's legendary and almost superhuman genius. Almost all of them are lies, or at least wild exaggerations. Fo is just a clever but frail old man in a paper suit. There is no way he can control a being like Amon, not by hypnosis or auto-suggestion or subliminal micro-direct, or any means biomechanical, or chemical, or *anything*.

But Fo is clever. Fo knows that the one thing he has left is his reputation. It's not what he can do, it's what they *think* he can do.

Fo gets up. He brushes down the paper of his smock.

'Those orders, Amon. What were they?'

'To guard you. You know that.'

Fo nods. One of the most powerful beings on Terra has been charged to guard him. Such creatures do not waver or relent in any way. They cannot be influenced. Indeed, the Custodes (each one brilliant in his own way) indulge in ingenious games to test themselves, to predict, imagine and out-think any possible ploy that might be used against them to disrupt their function. They cannot be out-thought. They are always projecting every possible variation.

But this, Fo reasons, creates an unusual loop of bio-feedback. It is a pleasingly simple sequence: the Custodes cannot be out-guessed. The Custodes are utterly diligent in their duty. One has been appointed to guard him. Fo has a (undeserved, really) reputation for being superhumanly ingenious. Thus his Sentinel scrutinises him with greater and ever-greater degrees of analysis, trying to identify what ingenuity Fo is about to use. Of course, there is none. Fo is just an old man in a paper suit, with no means whatsoever to influence or manipulate a Custodian (can anything do that? Can anything turn them? I doubt it), but Amon *suspects* he can (or will try) and so is constantly alert, constantly watching for tiny tricks and minute tells.

The mere expectation that Fo is about to try something is breeding a kind of paranoia in Amon that is slowly impairing his performance.

So, in fact, Fo has *two* things left. His reputation, and the way that reputation interferes with Amon's vigilance. Fo need do nothing at all (and I can do nothing *anyway*) and the

Custodian will slowly lose himself in ever-decreasing loops trying to predict what the trick (which is genuinely nothing) is.

'Follow me,' says Amon.

'Can I bring my books?' Fo asks. Amon nods.

Fo gathers them up. He offers the bundle to the Sentinel.

'Do you want to check them, or take custody of them?'

Amon looks at the bundle. He is evidently wary that they are part of the non-existent trick.

'You can carry them,' says Amon.

'So, where are we off to?' Fo asks as they start to walk.

Amon doesn't reply.

'Oh, Amon,' says Fo, 'show a condemned man the respect of conversation. How's the war going? Have we lost yet?'

3:xxiii

The honour of Angels

And, at the last, they cannot hold them. The long martial feud that has existed between their Legions, between Angels of Darkness and Guardians of Death, between the great war-captains Corswain and Typhus, seems pitiful and meaningless, merely the blunted games of the lists or the dainty sport of the tourney ground. It feels preposterous, a cheap and empty jest, that Corswain and his men have ever counted themselves the victors, or ever believed themselves the superior army.

For there is no stopping this.

The Death Guard comes, in a form and manner so changed, in mien so unlike before, it is as though their paths have never crossed, and the Angels of Caliban are no more than children, dressed for play with paper armour and wooden swords, surprised by real bandits or set upon by winter-hungry wolves. Lines break, shields shatter, defences topple in candent clouds of sparks, fighting platforms burn and collapse.

This is not the Death Guard they have known, and met, and matched on other fields. This is some fevered derangement, some altered version, plucked from the secret nightmares of Caliban: the old foe, but not the foe, some new thing wearing an old name.

Some horror.

Corswain believed he had begun to understand the chaogenic touch of the warp, and steel himself against the diseased state of the Death Guard.

But the narrow mountain pass has become a black pit, the stink a scalding gag of carious meat and liquid fever, the air a blizzard of blowflies, white ash and black snow. The Death Guard host bursts across their battlements and fortified slopes like a pestilential wave, drowning everything beneath its surge.

Swarms of man-things in swollen, bloated armour ascend the gloomy cliff-faces with insectile determination. They clamber and grimp up sheer rock that no human or demi-human should be able to scale, and pour out across the upper platforms, slaughtering and hacking. Dark Angels who have withstood the most ferocious xenos forces are cut down and torn apart in moments. Bodies pile and begin to rot from the very instant of death. Flies are everywhere, everywhere, billowing from visors and screaming mouths, spewing like smoke from the fluted horns and finials of Death Guard plate, sawing the air with their deafening roar of azif. Comms fail, stripped of all meaning beyond the static skritch of wing cases.

The light has failed too, filtered to an achromatic nothing by the fly-clouds and the airborne chitin dust. Blood is almost white where it splashes rock and armour, and black where it spatters snow.

Corswain fights. With him, on the ravine ledge, Tragan of the Ninth Order, Vorlois, Bruktas... and others close enough to touch at arm's length yet masked anonymous by the fly-blown murk. The mechanisms of their bolters have jammed, clogged with insect filth and crushed fly-bodies, so they fight with blades, damascened longswords and heirloom hand-and-a-halfs smeared with a gurry of black, caustic pus. Corswain rends dark armour and spills diseased entrails. He kicks the slain and dying foes from the rampart, casting them back into the faces of those clawing up behind them. He splits helms and breaks blades. Each blow sprays blood that adds to the slench dammed by the rampart lip. Men slip in blood, wade in it to their shins. It drizzles the air, a prisk of aerosolised gore that films their wargear and drips from their elbows and pauldrons.

And in it all, he knows one thing.

They are going to lose.

Corswain knows this, in his heart, as sure and certain as any pledge he has ever made. It is not the enemy's fury, nor his uncounted numbers, nor the plague of his contagion. These are things they might have withstood, for they are ten thousand sons of Caliban. No, it is not that the Death Guard is going to triumph; it is that the Dark Angels are going to lose.

For their courage has gone. Their resolve. Somehow, somehow the very heart of them, that has always faced down enemies, no matter the odds, seems to have dissolved like ice in the sun. Their will has failed.

He tells himself that it is the corrosive magick of the warp, that Typhus has infected them, through the gifts of Chaos, with a distemper that has robbed them of their determination, and sapped their vigour. He can see it in those around him, like Tragan. He can feel it in his own bones, an ache, a wasting despair, a futility. He tells himself that this is Chaos at work, weakening the mettle of the Dark Angels.

But it is gnawing in his mind too. The buzzing azif tells him this is *his* fault. *His* alone. This loss will be *his*. He has led them to this end. His ten thousand followed him, for years, from war to war, never doubting his leadership even as they faced the suicidal run to Terra and the horrors of the Hollow

Mountain. They followed him, without hesitation, even though they knew it would be to their deaths, for they believed in him, and believed their seneschal would make their life-price count, achieving some victory on Terra that would matter.

But it will not. They have come, like fools, it seems, to waste themselves on the shores of hell. They will accomplish nothing but death, squandered by a leader who thought he knew better. This is Corswain's folly. This is Corswain's defeat. They have loyally followed him because he was the voice of the Lion, but his roar was an empty promise. He was too bold, too confident. He has not led them to glory, just to a humiliating and pointless doom at the hands of their arch-enemy. Corswain has failed their trust and, their belief gone, they are failing him, spirit broken, fighting with lacklustre anguish simply to prolong the bitter ending.

It's not true. It's not true, Corswain tells himself, fighting bodies with his steel, and the buzzing with his mind. *I have not wasted this effort and I have not wasted these men. In the face of the fall of Terra, in the face of the triumph of Ruin, any attempt, however long the odds, was worth making. The Lion himself would have done the same, and I would do it again. We had to try. This falter of faith, this withering of self-belief, it is just the miasma of the warp, weakening us from within. If we can but find ourselves, if we can remember our spirit but for a moment–*

He cannot even convince himself. His limbs are leaden. He will die on this cold mountainside, his body fattened with maggots, with ten thousand sons of Caliban dead around him. Whatever vainglorious notion of heroism brought him to the birthworld, it is revealed as utter falsehood by the swarming, tenebrous majesty of the plague-bearing foe.

But still he holds, by some thread. Still he holds at the rim of the pass, bodies piling around and under him, his sword's edge chipped and notched, swinging at the clumsy, taliped beasts that claw over the lip of the cliff and shamble towards him through the fog of flies and cinders.

He sees Tragan fall, carried over in the soup of blood by multiple attackers. He splashes to him, cleaving assailants off his brother, hauling bodies away and despatching them with frenzied blows. Tragan is on his back, struggling to tear free and regain his feet.

A mace clubs Corswain from behind. He reels, and then, like Tragan, is mobbed in a scrum of Death Guard. Hands seize him, pin him, threatening to rip his limbs from his body. He tries to fight. A Death Guard brute, larvae pouring from its mouth-slot like rice, raises the mace to mash his head.

The brute combusts.

His bulk, wreathed in plasmic fire, collapses, molten metal fused to blistered meat. The mace drops into the mire.

More beams sear out of the blizzarding insect clouds, engulfing others. Heads un-form like hot wax. Corswain stumbles forward, released, his armour spattered with droplets of molten Death Guard plate.

A figure steadies him.

'Stand firm, your grace,' it says.

Plastered in mud, blood and a crust of crushed insects, Corswain looks up and sees hope in the most unexpected form. A sign. A silver mask.

'Stand firm, great seneschal,' says Lord Cypher.

3:xxiv

Discovered in their doubt

'We should follow them,' says Oll, shouldering his kitbag.

His companions look at him uneasily. 'The psykers?' asks Krank.

'Yes,' says Oll. 'At a careful distance, of course.'

'Why?' asks John warily.

'Because they were being taken to the Throne Room,' says Oll. 'What have we found, John? Just one anonymous damn hallway after another. Do you want to keep wandering in circles, or follow someone who knows where they're going?'

He walks towards the doors at the far end of the hall. Graft starts to trundle after him obediently, and a second later, Zybes and Leetu follow. The others hesitate. John glances at Actae.

'Risen, you said?' he asks her.

'That was the word framed in their minds,' replies Actae. 'It was emotionally dense. The idea that he is risen carried immense significance for those people.'

'I'll bet,' mutters John. He hurries after Oll, and catches up with him at the doors. Oll's got his ear to them, cautiously preparing to open them.

'Wait,' says John.

'Why?' asks Oll.

'I think…' John begins. It's like he can't bear to say it. 'I think we might need to reconsider our options.'

'No,' says Oll. He looks at John and sees that, for the first time, John Grammaticus looks properly scared. Oll can almost see the confidence leaking out of him.

'If He's risen,' John says, 'if He's left the Throne… then He's committed to some new plan. A new tactic. An endgame.'

Oll nods.

'So He'll be even harder to reach.'

Oll nods again. 'And even harder to stop,' he agrees.

'So we should reconsider,' says John, 'before it's too late.'

The others have gathered around them. John's sudden fear is contagious, and they all look rattled. Oll realises their morale is finally caving in. It's not as though they ever had much of a chance anyway, and every step of their journey has been skin-of-their-teeth luck. But all along John's been the dynamo, a source of eager determination, sometimes irritating, always intense, that's kept them all afloat. That daredevil, almost manic fire has gone out, quite abruptly, and without it, everything seems very cold and uncomfortably real. They can no longer ignore the immeasurable folly of their mission.

'No,' says Oll. 'We're not going to reconsider anything. We push on.'

He reaches for the door handle. John grabs his wrist.

'We could still get out,' John insists. 'Use the knife. Get these people to safety–'

'I said no,' says Oll, pulling his hand free of John's grip. 'You don't get to recruit me and then back out at the last minute. I never wanted to do this. You talked me into it. So here we are. And it's already too late. The knife won't carry us out of here. It couldn't get us in here, remember?'

He opens the doors. Another long, silent hallway confronts them, entirely empty but for the demigod statues lining its walls. The light is the gold-leaf glow of early summer.

'Hebet? Tie another thread, please,' says Oll as he starts to advance along the hall.

Zybes nods, and trots over to the nearest statue, unwinding the twine. As he waits, Oll looks back at the others. John is loitering in the doorway, reluctant to enter the hall.

'What are you afraid of?' Oll says to him.

'Failing,' John answers. 'Dying. Getting everyone killed. Him.'

'Me too, John.'

'You don't show it.'

'I have my faith, John,' says Oll.

John laughs sarcastically. 'Oh. That,' he says.

'Trooper Persson believes in god,' says Graft, rotating its upper body segment to face John. 'He is pious. He is a man of faith. He will be guided by that faith to do what is called "good works". This I have recorded about him on a number of occasions.'

'Faith is meaningless,' says Actae. 'It is an outmoded concept. A crutch for the puerile and the ignorant.' She turns her blindfolded eyes towards Oll. Her poise is arch and superior. 'Or is faith,' she asks, 'against all rational sense, your guiding principle in this whole endeavour, Ollanius? If it is, I regret ever getting involved.'

'Ignore her,' says Katt. She looks at Oll. 'Just lead us and we'll follow.'

'Yeah,' says John. 'What "good works" should we do now, whatever the hell that means?'

'Good works means to endeavour to help others who require

help,' says Graft, 'without expectation of reward or profit. It is not conditional on self-benefit. This I have rec–'

'Oh, shut up!' says John. He glares at Oll. 'Do you know what? That pious streak of yours was a charming little quirk for about a century. It's beginning to wear thin.' He points at the tiny Catheric charm around Oll's neck. 'That's bullshit,' he says. 'Your "god" is–'

'What I have faith in is my business,' says Oll. 'You have faith too. You had faith in me. That's why you came to me and begged for help. You had faith that I could do this. Where's that gone?'

John looks aside sullenly.

'The things we've been through to get here, John,' says Oll. 'You've never flinched. I'm sure you've been afraid many times. Terrified. I know I have. But you've never lost that faith in me until now. Why is that?'

'Oh, I'm sure you're going to tell me,' says John.

'I think it's because we're actually here,' says Oll. 'I warned you, the Palace is a weapon. It's messing with your mind. It's purposefully designed to be intimidating, to make you feel small and powerless and lost–'

'This... dangerous theatre?'

'Right,' says Oll. 'It's all for show. The architecture is intended to swallow us and make us feel like nobodies–'

'Oh, we're nobodies, all right,' says John.

'We're nobodies who made it all the way to Terra,' says Oll quietly. 'We're nobodies who got inside His damn Sanctum. These last-minute fears are just a subliminal reaction to the weaponised environment. It's crushing you psychologically, exactly the way He wanted it to.'

'No,' says John. 'The witch said He's risen. Risen from the Throne. What does that tell you, Oll?'

'It could mean anything,' says Oll.

'It means,' says John, 'that He's not here any more. All this bloody effort getting here has been for nothing.'

'Don't talk that way,' says Zybes. 'It sounds like you're giving up.'

'No one's giving up, Hebet,' says Oll. 'John's faith may be wavering, and I understand why, even if he refuses to admit it. But mine isn't.'

'Faith!' John snorts. 'Is that really all you've got?'

'It's all I need,' says Oll.

'How about a plan?' John growls. 'Or is that god of yours going to show you some kind of sign?'

'Maybe he will. Or maybe we work this out for ourselves.'

'What are you saying?' asks John. 'We just have to tweak our plan a little?'

'Plans are hard to revise when they don't exist in the first place,' says Actae.

'Just… don't talk!' Katt snaps at her.

'As you command, my leash,' Actae replies sardonically.

'Of course Trooper Persson has a plan,' says Graft.

'Does he?' asks Actae. 'This would be the plan he refuses to share with any of us?'

Oll doesn't answer. He's suddenly frowning. He's looking intently at John.

'Well, there's our sign,' he says.

'What?' Katt asks.

'What's wrong with your face?' Oll asks John.

'Nothing!' John says.

'That's my point,' says Oll.

John touches a finger to his mouth and chin tentatively. Then he gropes at his ribcage and shoulders.

'That rogue Alpha Legionnaire did a serious number on him,' Oll says to the others. 'But there's not a mark on him any more.'

'I don't understand,' says John, bewildered. 'Nothing hurts. No bruising. My lip isn't split, and my tongue—'

'What's happening?' asks Zybes in alarm.

'It's the aegis,' says Oll.

'The what?' asks Krank.

'The Sanctum's psychic shield,' says Leetu.

Oll nods. 'Correct,' he says. 'It's His aura. A projection of His will…'

'It holds the warp at bay,' says Actae, 'and protects from empyric assault.'

'Indeed,' says Oll. 'But it can have a healing effect too. Like a side effect. Back in the day, it was considered a miraculous property of His palaces and fortresses. Wherever He was, He would extend His will as part of the site defences. But people who were granted an audience, or came inside His protection, they were often cured of disease or restored to health. It was just a by-product of His intense psychic presence.'

'Which means He's still here,' breathes John.

Oll nods. 'Which means He's still here,' he agrees. 'We're inside the aegis. Your injuries have vanished. We have to be really close to Him. It's not as though He can have someone else maintain the Sanctum's aegis in His place.'

Slowly, John begins to grin at Oll. 'Damn you, Oll,' he murmurs.

'See? Sometimes you just need a little faith,' says Oll, smiling back at him.

'Faith is your department,' says John. 'I don't touch the stuff myself.'

John hoists his kitbag and they stride together towards the next set of golden doors. The others exchange glances and then hurry to catch them up.

'So we've still got a chance?' asks Krank.

'I think we have,' says Katt.

'I think Erda was a fool to believe in either of these men,' says Actae.

Oll approaches the imposing doors, preparing to open them, but John stops him.

'Let me,' he says. 'My business is watching your back while you get things done, remember? What did you call them, eh, Graft? "Good works"? Let's do some of those.'

He nods to Leetu, who raises his weapon to cover the doorway. John listens at the doors, then takes hold of the handle.

'Ready, Argonauts?' he asks, grinning back at them. His confidence has returned, as quickly as it fled. Contagious as his fear, the return of his familiar, cocky grin draws a smile from Katt, Zybes and Krank.

He swings the huge doors open. The tip of the levelled sentinel blade is aimed directly at his face, even though it is rested at the hip.

'Submit instantly,' says the Custodian giant, 'or be destroyed.'

3:xxv

The Angel in flight

The Blood Angels of Anabasis take Embarkation Deck Two. They sweep the sub-deck prep chambers, the adjoining service crypts, and both the principal and secondary access routes. Terminators led by Khoradal Furio snap left as soon as the arrival site is claimed, and burn through the aft control blocks and duralium stores, securing tertiary engineering and port power relay four within eight minutes. Sarodon Sacre's assault formation make even better progress, clearing ventral eighteen and nineteen, cutting the primary power relays to the ninth quadrant (port) autoloader assemblies, and then establishing control of the interdeck connectives at five points. The squads of Maheldaron, Krystaph Krystapheros and First Captain Raldoron elegantly leapfrog Sacre's blocking action, mine and disable the entire port-side auspex array, then break through cleanly into the deck twelve interlace and punch a route directly to the main spinal. By then, their primarch and the Sanguinary Guard have reached them.

The spear-tip bites deep into the flank of the *Vengeful Spirit*.

The fighting is brutal and intense. Rogal's projections were entirely accurate. The Sons of Horus, plumed and ferocious, resist with magnificent resolve, even though they have been taken by surprise. Within seconds of the initial teleport flare, the ship is screaming with alert klaxons, and the vox is wild with directives deploying squads down-ship to supplement and reinforce the units that have confronted the initial boarding. It was everything Sanguinius expected: no one, not even the elite of the Immortal Ninth, storm-boards an Astartes flagship without meeting the most savage resistance.

And these are not just Astartes. These are the warriors of the legendary XVI. These are the peerless Luna Wolves, against whom every other Legion, no matter how much they deny it, measure themselves. Sanguinius has broken into their home, their ship-fortress, the heart of their Legion. No one commits such an outrage without suffering the most lethal reflexive reaction.

Sanguinius doesn't waste time analysing the defiance he faces. Even if there was a way of knowing what percentage of the XVI had been deployed to surface action, there is still no means of calculating the odds or determining how many Astartes are present on the *Vengeful Spirit*, for nobody has any reliable data on the Legion's current size. What confronts him is merely a blistering and exemplary resistance, and he matches it with a blistering and exemplary attack.

Nor does he distract himself with consternation at the fact, obvious from the very first moment, that *only* his company, just one-quarter of the Anabasis assault, has transitioned successfully. There is no sign of the other formations, of Rogal, Constantin or his beloved father, and all links to Terra are jammed. Was it teleport malfunction, or worse? Will the others arrive on their heels, belatedly, any second? Are they already here, elsewhere on the vast ship-fortress, misdirected somehow and out of contact?

Such speculations are pointless. He is here. He is committed. There is no going back. There is a compliance to deliver, and an illumination to achieve. If he has to accomplish that with just a quarter of the intended force, then he will.

At least it's not a trap. The flagship was entirely unprepared for their shock assault. He has seen the disbelief and indignation on the faces of those he has killed. To their credit, the Sons of Horus do not break. Of course they don't. They rally and adapt with unhesitating dedication, just as his Blood Angels would if the situation was reversed.

Some Legions, like Rogal's, Roboute's and Ferrus', are famed for their immaculate presentation and discipline. Others, like Leman's and Konrad's, are notorious for their savage, feral aspect. His Legion and Lupercal's, the IX and the XVI, always had one thing in common: they combined both. Each presented as formidably noble and disciplined, with the drilled precision and gleaming perfection of an Ultramarines high cadre, yet each could, in the blink of an eye, unleash unrestrained hell as monstrous and wild as any Fenrisian Rout. That is what made them special. That is what made them the best, the most feared, and the most celebrated of all the Legiones Astartes. Majestic ferocity. Feral discipline.

And now the Astartesian exemplars meet each other, face to face, in a death match to discover which is truly the finest Legion.

It is positively childish to think of it in those terms, as a competitive test between rival champions, but to think of it in any other way is to dwell on what's really at stake, and Sanguinius has no need of such mental shackles. He and his men fight as they have always fought, for the peerless glory of the moment, for unqualified victory, to prove their superiority, brazen in their pride and audacity. He told them to affect this mindset. In the final moments before departure, as

they assembled their cohort on the platforms of the bulk teleport, those were his last instructions to them. Fight for victory
alone. For the simplicity of absolute achievement. Think not
of the significance, nor the odds, nor the consequences. Think
not of vendettas or grudges or perceived slights. Put from your
thoughts all notions that you are avengers or redeemers or
saviours. Just fight and win for the honour of demonstrating
your unmatched superiority. Fight as Angels.

And so they do. And so they have. He has seen their arrogant glory before. He has never seen them match this. Each
Blood Angel is a bright devil, a radiant monster, glorious in
crimson and gold, leaping and vaulting, fast as thunderbolts,
furious as the shining wrath of heaven, blades and spears
raised aloft, teeth bared, voices loud and wild with courage.
They are almost too fast to follow, too bright to behold, too
beautiful to contemplate.

The Sons of Horus, for all their courage and ability, seem
like crude ogres of the primordial midnight. Each of the Sons
of Horus is a fallen angel, an abyssal hero, dark as shadows,
bracing and recoiling, sulphurous as the searing rage of hell,
shields and chainblades held to block, eyes blazing, voices
roaring with denial. They are strong as bedrock, too dark to
perceive, too terrible to pity.

But he almost pities them.

Their dead litter the hallways. Their broken plate fumes and
burns. Their traitor blood, once so *noble*, washes the decks.

These are decks he knows. Knows well. In this ship, with
these men, with this great lord, Sanguinius first rode the stars
as a son of man. The Cthonian warlord mentored him, and
taught him the ways of man's war long before Sanguinius ever
joined with his own sons. He was part of them, a brother,
an honorary son of Horus, taken in and welcomed as one
of their own.

He knows this ship well. He learned it by heart. He knows these warriors too, and every nuance of their astonishing technique.

He exploits that knowledge unashamedly.

It is because he knows the unique fingerprint of the *Vengeful Spirit* that the Blood Angels knew to sweep the sub-deck prep chambers and the adjoining service crypts as soon as Embarkation Deck Two was taken. It was because he knew the layout of both the principal and secondary access routes that Khoradal Furio's Terminators snapped left instead of right as soon as the arrival site was claimed. It was thanks to him they understood the urgency to burn through the aft control blocks and duralium stores, and secure tertiary engineering and port power relay four before turning through-ship at the more obvious target points. Only his insight allowed Sarodon Sacre to clear ventrals eighteen and nineteen, and cut the primary power relays to the ninth quadrant (port) autoloader assemblies, for on other vessels of the class, the primary power relays are seated beneath ventral twenty-two. Minutes would have been lost locating the correct relays, and there would have been no time to advance and control the interdeck connectives. Only he knew that the port-side auspex array was sheathed in unusually heavy diamantine plating, which would require mines to breach and destroy. The squads of Maheldaron, Krystaph Krystapheros and First Captain Raldoron would never have reached the deck twelve interlace before the Sons of Horus sealed it, and besides, they would not have had Sacre's blocking action to cover their flank, because they would still have been searching ventral twenty-two.

It is because of him, and his intimate memories of the flagship, that they have already breached the main spinal, the primary artery of the ship.

It is because of him. And it is because of Horus. It is because of the friendship they shared, the time they spent, the love that bonded brother to brother, the secrets they revealed to each other without hesitation. Sanguinius knows this ship like any in his own fleet, because Horus taught him the lay of it.

The love is gone now, cold and dead. Bitter fury fills its place. Sanguinius is taking the ship with devastating precision, deck by deck, because he once loved his brother, and that love was reciprocated. He exploits his privileged understanding of the *Spirit* with simultaneous regret and delight. His father told him emotions had been preserved for a reason, so he rejoices in both. He mourns the great Lupercal of old, the peerless, charismatic friend, who taught him the ship level by level, and had no idea that one day his generosity would orchestrate his defeat. He hates the foul Warmaster of the present, who has betrayed everything and everyone, including his old self, by creating a weapon to spear his own flank and unerringly find his very heart.

Sanguinius even delights in the applied formation of his men: a spear-tip. The trademark of the Luna Wolves, the bravura method of so many of their victories, a tactic Horus taught his brother so he could similarly excel.

Sanguinius turns the spear-tip on the warrior who devised it.

He fights. He kills. He advances. He savours the delight of advantage, and the ironic reversal of betrayal. He embraces the satisfaction that Horus all but briefed him on the specifics required to take the XVI flagship all those years ago, as though, subliminally, he knew that one day it would have to be done. He feels no remorse, and he ignores the pain.

But the pain does not ignore him.

The main spinal is the greatest of the ship's titanic longitudinal hallways, as great in scale as some of the fine processionals of the Inner Palatine. It is a space three decks deep, and runs as a grey steel canyon, arch-roofed and buttressed with grand scissor arches, for five kilometres through the heart of the ship, like the long naves of antique cathedrals laid end to end.

It was impressive: the major vaults of Gloriana-class void-ships always are, the ostentatious extravagance of the ship-wright's art, an architectural statement of power and majesty. I will build a ship to traverse the stars, and in it I will place such vast and humbling chambers it will seem as though I have lifted a great palace into the sky. Such is my ambition, my magnifi-cence, my confidence in the colossal over-power of the immense drive systems that they will propel such a vanity of excess mass across light years with ease. There will be no economy of volume. Those who come to these vessels as visitors will weep in awe that we are so mighty we bring our fortresses to them.

Main spinals are meant to be awe-inspiring. Sanguinius recalls his own sensations of intimidation when he, a winged giant, first walked its length at Lupercal's side, struck dumb by the spanning archways, the suspended rows of martial banners that marched to infinity, the Luna Wolves and crowds of ship's crew, Navis Nobilite and common serfs that thronged the illu-minated upper galleries, and cheered him from the overlooking decks and raised terraces. He remembers being confounded that all of this could be contained within a single ship.

But it seems mere function to him, now. A wide and inde-fensible route of advance down which to charge, an expressway to the enemy's heart, and an invitation. It seems squalid, too. The gilding is flaked and worn, the illustrious banners long gone, the gleaming deck stained with oil and coolant. The XVI always favoured utility over flourish, and this long approach seems to have been stripped back and made barren, like some low-deck service corridor, or the coldly spartan cloister of some grimly ascetic monastery. The air is cold, the light glaucous, and the Sons of Horus who crowd at the marble rails of the upper galleries are no longer cheering.

His advancing parade is garlanded by ticker-tape streams of bolter fire and raining petals of las. The punished deck cracks and pockmarks with such intensity it soon resembles the pores and crinkles of old skin. Plumes of dust and grit spring up around him and his men like sudden fields of wheat.

His Cataphractii advance into the hail of gunfire, sparks dancing off their sculpted plate. His tactical squads dart to the side of the spinal, using the pillars of the lower archways as cover, blazing return fire up and across the cyclopean space, and raking the upper galleries. Balustrades explode, showering dust and lumps of mangled stone and metal. Torn figures fall, striking the deck far below.

Sanguinius and his elite guard take wing.

3:xxvi

Seeking meaning where none may exist

They move through the stacks in the velvet gloom, with no
particular process or plan, just picking and tasting at random,
like children loose in an orchard, drawn at whim to the next
promising fruit. Already, the rows behind them are piled
with books pulled from shelves, or left open and abandoned
on lecterns and side tables. The young archivist would be
dismayed, but Sindermann has sent her off to consult the catalogue listings. Mauer shows a fascination Sindermann would
not have expected from so terse and pragmatic an officer. She
seems almost enraptured by what she is finding, and keeps
calling out lines and verses for Sindermann to scribble down
in his old, dog-eared notebook.

He hears her rattling out the latest thing that's taken her
eye. He only catches the last few words.

'"...awake, arise, or be forever fallen!"'

'Wait. Slower. Say it again.'

He can't keep up with her urgent dictation so, by the end of
the first hour, she is transcribing annotations on her data-slate,

and they content themselves with calling out lines to each other through the stacks, sometimes a distance apart, so that the words of Old Earth echo in the stilted space of the Great Hall, uttered aloud for the first time in perhaps ten or twenty thousand years.

Mauer reads out something else, her voice coming to him from beyond the stacks where he is rummaging.

'"It little profits that an idle king, by this still hearth, among these barren crags–"'

'I don't think so,' he tuts.

'Wait, Sindermann. It goes on... wait... "Some work of noble note may yet be done, not unbecoming men that strove with gods... one equal temper of heroic hearts, made weak by time and fate, but strong in will, to strive, to seek, to find and not to yield."'

'Is that a poem?' he calls back, lifting down a heavy, leatherbound volume of what appears to be late 37th century political speeches. 'Mauer? Is that a poem?'

'I think so,' she replies. A pause. She appears suddenly, in the shadows at the end of the shelves, studying a small book. 'A Lord Alfred? It's hard to tell. The pages are so faded. Lord Alfred. Was he a High Lord?'

'I don't know,' he replies.

She tuts, and discards the book onto a nearby pile.

'What is a poem anyway?' she asks.

Sindermann sighs. Her approach is so random, he's finding it hard to concentrate. 'Mauer,' he says, 'I don't really have the time to explain the cultural function of lyric verse. I think you know what a poem is.'

'Of course I know what a poem is,' she snaps. 'I didn't mean that. I meant... what's the point of a poem? And when does a poem stop being just words and become something else? When do words gain power? Under what circumstances?'

'Power?'

'You know what I mean. The reason we're here.'

He does know what she means, and yet he still can't answer. If any abreactive magick lurks in the Hall of Leng, he has no idea how they will find it, or recognise it if they do find it. Where does verse, or prose, or memoir stop, and ritual begin? Can things be both at once? Are there incantations of control stashed here in this great collection, under lock and key, or merely the indulgent scribblings of the ages, the fancy of idle men in easier eras, who set out to do no more than praise a lover, or articulate some feeling, or describe a flower or, perhaps, merely rhyme for the sake of rhyme? The arts, whatever they might be, have come to play an increasingly insignificant role in Imperial life, eroded by Strife and Old Night, until they are vestigial memories, non-functioning organs dwarfed by rational science and secular industry. He recognises, belatedly, his own lack of knowledge. Did the arts ever have a purpose, at any time in history, or have they always been decorative? Does some art have true function and capacity and other art not? How does he, with a mind raised in the schools of the modern Imperium, even tell?

'I have found a *Metaphysics of Old Albia*,' Mauer calls out from beyond the shelves, 'and something called the *Codified Ministrations of Narthan Dume*.'

'Add them to the pile, Mauer,' he calls.

'I have.'

'Listen,' he says, propping a book open in his hand. '"I met murder on the way…"'

'Why is that significant?' she calls back, unseen.

'Horus went to Murder. Urisarach, which he called Murder…' he trails off.

'What's it from? A grimoire?'

'*The Mask of Anarchy*,' he replies, reading the title. 'It says, "Rise like Lions after slumber, in unvanquishable number…"'

'Does that mean the First Legion?'

'I don't know,' he says. 'I doubt it.'

They are both idiots, he decides. Idiots for embarking on this. He sees them both for an instant, as if from a distance through other eyes, himself and Mauer, an old man and a stern woman, lost and alone in the shelf-maze of an abandoned library, seeking meaning where none may exist. An effort of monumental desperation, without plan or forethought, driven by apocalyptic fear. This, he thinks, this is why people believe in gods. This is how they come to believe. In fear for their existence, they seek meaning in the dark, any meaning they can cling to, building false gods from nothing, assembling false significance from random scraps that were never connected or meant to be connected. It is exactly, precisely the kind of manic, superstitious pseudo-faith that the Emperor erased from human culture so that mankind could be free to build and make and know.

'How about the *Principia Belicosa*?'

'Skip it,' he replies. 'That's merely a record of conventional warfare.'

He doesn't even know why they came here. Not any more. The desperation of the hour notwithstanding, two sensible, sane people came here to... *what*? Two people, millions of books, trillions of words. What were they even thinking? He can't remember whose idea this was, his or Mauer's, and if it was Mauer's, then the folly of it seems so unlike her. Yet she went along with it, and seems more caught up in it than him.

'"At the still point of the turning world, neither flesh nor fleshless. Neither from nor towards, the still point, there the dance is... Where past and future are gathered..."'

He ignores her voice. It is as though something told them to come here. As though, without words, someone sent them here.

If there was something here, something of true worth and value, surely the Emperor or the Sigillite would have come to fetch it long since? The Hall of Leng, so piled with books and words, perhaps that's all it is. An emptiness, a trove of junk and memories left over from the distant past, a museum of antique and useless ideas.

A museum of trifles. Yet He kept it. He preserved it all, in one of the most secure locations in the Sanctum. That, to Sindermann, is the true marvel, and the true tragedy. An unexplored, unexploited wealth of past ideas. Of high art. Does it make Him more a god that He sequestered it, or more human that He, perhaps out of sentiment, could not bring Himself to discard it?

'"To see a world in a grain of sand, and a heaven in a wild flower,"' Mauer reads out, walking into view, '"hold infinity in the palm, and eternity in an hour." I like this one. I don't know what it means. Do you think it means the wall or the gate?'

'Mauer.'

'The wall or the gate? What do you think? I think–'

'What is the Hall of Leng?' Sindermann interrupts. 'After all?'

'What?' she asks, leaning around a shelf-end to look at him.

'What is it? A treasure house of the riches of Old Earth? In which case, why is no one ever given access to it, or scholars granted admission? Or is it just His–'

'His what? Sindermann?'

'His scrapbook? His attic? His private casket of mementos and bric-a-brac?'

'You think it's *that*?'

Sindermann shrugs. 'I think it has a ridiculously vast building devoted to it, if it is. But then, everything about Him is on a scale beyond our understanding.'

'Are we wasting our time?' she asks, lowering the book in her hands.

He looks at her, and shakes his head in doubt.

'Do you remember what prompted us to come here, Mauer?' he asks.

She starts to answer, then stops. She has no answer, and he can see that it troubles her.

'It's in our minds, isn't it?' she whispers. 'The warp. It's made us mad, and we don't even see it. It's in everything. It planted some insane notion in our heads and off we ran like...'

'Idiots?' he suggests.

Mauer scowls. 'No,' she says. 'No, Kyril. No. There's something here. I'm sure of it. Think how this place was locked and guarded. How secure. The Emperor is pure rationality, and it is not rational to build a place like this unless it guards something of actual value. Keep looking.'

She glances back at the book in her hands. '"...the sacred river ran, through caverns measureless to man, down to a sunless sea,"' she reads. She tosses the book aside. 'Not that, obviously. Keep looking.'

The young archivist reappears suddenly. She gazes in dismay at the books scattered on the chequerboard floor, but decides not to say anything. She has a data-slate in her hand.

'I have consulted the catalogue,' she says nervously. 'I think I may have located some items in special storage.'

'Where?' asks Mauer.

'Collection eight-eight-eight,' she says.

'Which is where?'

'Down here,' she says, gesturing.

They freeze. A heavy thump has just rung through the echoic space of the vast library.

'That was the main doors,' the librarian whispers.

'Someone's here with us,' says Mauer. She draws her sidearm. 'Someone, or something.'

3:xxvii

Arise

Below the Hollow Mountain, the wind shifts.

Corswain gazes at the silver mask.

'Do not ask,' says Cypher. 'Do not question it, your grace. I have been with you all along. I stand with you now. That is all you need to know.'

His words echo in the ether, carried and amplified by profound psionic force. The choking clouds of flies billow back.

'Sons of the First, your duty to your seneschal, please,' Cypher declares, his voice piercing every mind on the hill-slope and cliffs. 'He gave you an order. Kill them.'

Immediately, he is at the edge of the black rock, over which the pullulating droves of the Death Guard are still spilling. He begins to mete out death to all unwise enough to come across the lip at him. His sword splits open black armour like blisters. His plasma gun torches men whole, and sends their molten bodies hurtling down the cliff in pyretic streaks.

Dark Angels rush to his side, like lions out of slumber. The spirit that was lacking surges back. Faith finds its steel.

It is the work of the Librarius. A supreme effort of will and one, no doubt, they have been striving to achieve since the Death Guard magicks settled upon them all and the battle first began. Corswain knows it is their doing, though it marvels him to the core all the same. The revelation of Cypher is miraculous, but it alone could not have overturned his vanguard's despondency so quickly. Cartheus and his brothers are working in concert somewhere, magnifying the effect, echoing the image of Cypher into every mind. It is bravado, the theatre of war, but it has a dazzling effect.

As he runs to Cypher's side, sword raised, Corswain knows he will not question it. Not now. Not ever. The symbolic office of Lord Cypher is a curious and ancient part of the Legion's hierarchy: a warrior assigned by the Lion, masked and always anonymous, charged with the custody of the secrets and traditions. In such wise, he is a tradition of secrets himself. Where he chooses to reveal himself, and which battles to fight, are always subject to his own decision, except that he always stands true in the darkest hours, for there is no greater tradition or discipline within the Legion order than the pursuit of perilous victory.

And this fly-blown hell is a dark hour indeed. Corswain had no notion that Lord Cypher was hidden in his ranks. He thought him far away, perhaps abiding within the echelons of his father. He thought the power of Cypher's presence a blessing he could never wish for.

But here he stands, like some divine sign from the Emperor.

It seems impossible, but Corswain will not question it. That itself is contrary to tradition. His descent to the furnaces of Terra have shown him the impossible too many times. This day alone, endless in scope, has been filled with daemons and phantasms, with vile impossibilities made flesh. It seems just and right that one impossibility should manifest in their favour.

A sign perhaps. A portent that the Lion yet lives, or that the Emperor has noticed their minor efforts in the general tumult of the stricken world.

Do not question it. Rejoice. Rejoice and fight. To have Cypher make his stand with you is the greatest accolade of the Legion. It lauds you, and marks you and your battle out as the most vital and deserving. It is a living symbol that means the spirit of the First Legion is focused upon you.

And the spirit is here without doubt. As the swarms of flies flurry back, so too the clouds of doubt and hopelessness. The malediction of Typhus, the warp-conjured ailment cast upon them all to wither and kill them as surely as any Death Guard steel, burns off them like morning fog in hard sunlight. Their minds are clear, their hearts, their souls.

It does not mean victory. The fight is still insurmountable, the miserable odds beyond calculation, but if they fail, if they fall upon the black cliffs of this mountain, they will die as Dark Angels, not as broken men, and in their dying they will give bloody account of themselves.

If victory belongs to the polluted filth of Typhus' host, then it will be bought only by the most hellish price.

Corswain, Hound of Caliban, lays in beside Lord Cypher, beside Tragan, beside Vorlois, beside Bruktas, who is missing an arm but warring anyway, beside Harlock and Blamires and Vanital, beside Erlorial and Carloi and the gun-shields of the Third Order, beside men who had utterly lost their way mere minutes before. Now they fight again, butchering to clear the cliff. Splinters fly and blood gouts with such force it rains back upon them. Corswain is plastered in gore and mire and frass, flies stuck to him like black gems. He splits corcoid beak-visors and opens armour with such force, the ceramite is pleached around the gaping wounds as the bodies tumble away. He hears the shrieking zinzulation of chainblades from every side.

Then that too is muffled by a wail of tempest air. Flashes bloom along the run of the black pass, explosion followed by explosion, wracking the foe far below, and hurling bodies into the air like dolls. The fire blossoms are vast, bleached white in the mockshade monochrome of the blighted air. Craft shriek low overhead, sweeping from the mountain and down the length of the pass, Stormbirds and Thunderhawks, raining munitions on the Death Guard mass. They are Dark Angels ships, the very craft that brought them to Terra, charged with the last of the fuel and warheads, and sent aloft by Adophel.

Corswain watches them turn and bank along the narrow ravine. He watches the rolling, fiery wake of their lethiferous bombardment, sending clonic shockwaves through the tight-packed foe below.

He lifts his sword in the half-light with a fury he thought had left him forever. Words come to him from somewhere.

'Awake, arise or be forever fallen!' he yells, and the Librarius carries his command to every soul on the field, as both a threat and an unwavering promise.

3:xxviii

'On, I said, Ikasati!'

He ignores the pain.

Aloft, his wings powering, he races like a missile, the Sanguinary Guard at his heels. Their speed and sweeping agility make them hard targets to track. They bank under and between the spans of the scissor arches, using the screen of these great structures to shield themselves from chasing gunfire. Now the ceiling and the arches stipple and pock, a mirror of the ruined tracts of floor.

Beyond the third great arch, with some broken feathers eddying from his wings, Sanguinius turns hard and swoops in upon a gallery on the second level. The Sons of Horus there baulk as they see him stoop at them like a plunging eagle. He falls upon them.

Two Sons of Horus are smashed over the gallery rail by the backstroke of the blade *Encarmine*. Two more are impaled on the spear in his left hand. Another is broken under his feet as he lands. He swings the spear, throwing off the skewered dead, sending their burning corpses flying to tumble other Sons of Horus like skittle pins. *Encarmine* rips, a bar of red light, and two more fall, cut asunder through the torso, blood dappling his feathers like rain. Another crashes his warhammer into the primarch's thigh, and loses his head for his temerity. A bolt-round detonates against Sanguinius' breastplate, causing him to wince and stumble. The officer, a company captain, fires his boltgun again, but Sanguinius has already hurled the *Spear of Telesto*, and the shots fly wild as the officer is staked against the back wall of the gallery, his feet dangling.

Sanguinius ploughs into the mass, slicing *Encarmine* two-handed. The blade passes through ceramite and plasteel, through chainswords trying to strike, through boltguns rising to fire, through storm shields held in frantic defence, through chestplates, pauldrons and helms. Clouds of blood vapour, smoke and splinters billow around him like a halo.

Encarmine splits a massive Terminator, one of the vaunted Justaerin, but wedges fast in the thickness of the plate. Sanguinius releases the blade, pushing the dead Terminator away, while wrenching the huge warhammer from its dead fingers.

With that trophy, lavishly wrought and weighted with a uranium core, he continues his merciless advance, cracking armour, splintering visors, and pulping the organics within with transmitted hyper-concussions. Hammerscale sprays from crumpled plate. Blow by inhuman blow, he clears the gallery, leaving bodies buckled in his wake, and breaks his way beyond the arch into the next gallery, another proud span of colonnade where once the Luna Wolves stood, cheering his name. Their inheritors die miserably in the same spots.

He slaughters, and ignores the pain.

Proud Taerwelt Ikasati meets him, coming the other way. The Sanguinary Guard's golden wargear is running with gore. With sword and fusion maul, Ikasati has purged the next gallery along. Below them, Furio's squads make rapid advance down the main floor, the hail of suppressing fire much reduced.

'My lord…' Ikasati says.

Sanguinius tosses the hammer aside. The head of it is deformed from furious employment. It strikes and cracks the gallery wall, and falls to the deck.

'On,' Sanguinius grunts. He turns to recover his spear and sword from the corpse piles.

'My lord–'

'On, Taerwelt! On, and again! No pause! We clear these galleries one by one! Purge them, and cut our way to the traitor's heart!'

Ikasati switches from battle-cant to informal Aenokhian, and his voice drops. 'My lord, you are hurt–'

Sanguinius frees *Encarmine* from the dead Justaerin and glances down. The bruise of soot on his chestplate where the bolt-round hit him still smoulders. The pain is hard to ignore now.

'You were hit…'

'On, I said, Ikasati!' Sanguinius growls. The Sanguinary Guard stares at him, then nods, and leaps from the fractured balustrade, wings wide.

Blood is leaking from the seams of Sanguinius' abdominal armour. The blood is dirty, and he can smell the sickly rot of it. He barely felt the bolt impact, and it did not cause this wound. It simply angered the older injury he carries, the one he has been most carefully concealing. Angron's blade bit him deep, deeper than any wound he has ever sustained, and he is certain that the blade was toxic with infection. He can feel the poison in his blood, the clammy numbness of his organs, the tear and grind of the unhealing wound every time he moves. The dressings he packed across his torso have ruptured.

He grits his teeth. He can ignore it. He did not foresee

Angron as his killer, so this wound is not fatal. This will pass. It will heal. Besides, he only has to keep going for a while. They are almost there. The day will reach an end. He will reach Horus very soon.

He jerks the *Spear of Telesto* from the wall where it pins its smouldering kill.

He will not halt until he gets to the end. The end, or whatever else might be waiting for him there.

3:xxix

Another authority

The place is empty and cold; grey rockcrete walls lined with arterial pipework. They walk together, side by side, a demigod giant and a tiny old man in a rustling paper suit. Fo can hear the distant, muffled thump of explosions. It really *is* getting close.

'Who do you guard me from, Amon?' he asks.

'You are… a prisoner, and therefore must be guarded.'

'Yes, obviously, but…' Fo pauses. 'Sometimes I wonder, are you guarding me from things that might harm me, or are you guarding everything else from me?'

'Can't it be both?' asks Amon.

'I don't know. Can it?'

'I think a basic definition of the role of a guard is both. It certainly can be both. Is this some kind of game?'

A tone of wariness again (aha!).

'I hear you like games, Amon.'

'I do not. But I am good at them.'

Fo nods. He can feel that loop of paranoia tightening. 'I can presume, then, that at least part of your duty is to guard me, which is to say, protect me from others?' Fo asks.

'It is.'

'Protect my life?'

'It is.'

'Protect me from harm?'

'It is. Rather, it was. Directives have been issued. My duty function is completed. You are to be passed to another authority.'

'That,' says Fo, 'sounds alarming. Tell me, if you don't mind, for it seems we are about to part company forever... You say your duty function is completed. How do you know?'

'I have been informed so.'

'But, really... when does duty end? "Only in death..."? Isn't that the mantra you fellows like to bark, given half a chance?'

'No,' says Amon. 'The phrase you refer to, I believe, origi-nates with the Imperial Army. They are mortal, and therefore death is a more practical increment by which to measure things.'

Fo smiles. 'Was that a joke, Amon?'

'No.'

'Are you sure? Not even a tiny bit of one? I distinctly caught a hint of dry wit at work there.'

'It was not a joke.'

'Oh,' says Fo. 'How very disappointing.'

They reach the small laboratorium. The hatchway stands open, and the lights inside are on. They do not stop, but as they pass, Fo sees a team of high-grade servitors inside, their body cowling painted black. They are hard at work, dismantling and tagging his apparatus, and packing it away in insulated cargo crates.

'He's confiscating it, then? Your lord and master, Valdor? Confiscating my work?'

'It is complete,' replies Amon. 'You completed it. It is being secured.'

'And so I become a disposable asset,' says Fo. 'I probably shouldn't have said it was complete, should I? Might have lived a little longer that way, eh, Amon?'

'Haven't you lived long enough?' asks Amon.

Fo doesn't answer him, not even with a quip.

He has just seen what is waiting for him at the far end of the long, dank corridor.

3:xxx

Wolf at the door

Head down, weapon raised, Mauer fans her hand. *Keep low! Keep hidden!*

Sindermann doesn't need to be told. He cowers, heart thudding, below a reading table, with piles of books as a useless bulwark. He realises the little archivist is tucked in behind him, her arms wrapped tight around her upraised knees, trying to make her small form smaller still.

He sees the abject terror in her eyes. He reaches out and clasps her hand.

The boetharch prowls forward, sidearm braced, steering between the laden shelves. The smell of aged paper and book-must seems unbearably strong suddenly. The smell of dead history.

Another soft thump. Movement. Something moving on the floor below.

Then silence.

Mauer presses in against a bookshelf, her back to it. She

undoes the red buttons of her coat so her upper body can move more freely. She listens.

Nothing.

Then another stirring, brief. Heavy feet, but moving softly, across black and white tiles. Or is it stairs? She moves around, glimpses a shadow, and ducks back. The shadow was big. Imposing. Though seen only for a second, it was not human.

Where is it? She waits. She listens. She smells the faint odour of wet metal. Of fyceline.

Of blood.

Where *is* it?

She flops onto her knees and crawls along the stack row, then peers out to get a better look. But the shadow's gone. There's only the sepia light, the sombre shadows of the racked shelves, the gleam of the burnished handrails, the sound of rain on the roof.

Mauer swallows hard. If she fixes it with a clear shot, can she bring it down? Something that big? Is she fast enough? Has her service weapon got enough power?

No, she isn't, and no, it hasn't.

But they're dead anyway, if she doesn't try.

She hears a noise, from an entirely different direction. A rustle of parchments. She wriggles around. Another sound, from the opposite direction. A book, flipped through, then cast aside.

Where the hell *is* it?

'"The day will not save them, and we own the night."'

She has no idea where the voice is coming from. It is deep and powerful, a minatory tone. Pages rustle. Another book examined.

'Not his words, then, after all,' the voice muses. 'Stolen. He claimed them for his own, but this attributes it to an "Amiri Baraka", back in the early millennia.'

Where the hell is the voice coming from? Above her? Below? To her right?

She leans to her right, gun raised.

From her left, a sword blade rests gently against her neck. A shadow falls across her.

'I could hear you,' says the voice. 'I knew you were there, from the moment I entered.'

Mauer turns slowly, the blade at her throat. The Sons of Horus legionary is an immense silhouette standing over her.

'Did you think you could kill me?' it asks.

'No,' she says, her voice shaking but honest. 'But I was going to try.'

The shadow nods.

'Leave her alone!' Sindermann yells. He bursts into view at the end of the stack, glaring at the shadow.

'Leave her alone, I said. What the hell are you doing here?'

'Exactly my question,' says Loken.

3:xxxi

Say it

Later that century, the rusting brown cast of the desert and the walls and the sky have grown darker still. It is red. Everything and everywhere is red, like blood, the colour of blood, scarlet out in the sunlight, across the endless dunes, and crimson, madder and orchil hues in the darker shadows of the wall.

He remembers, sometimes, longing for blood. The fire of blood, the gush of blood, the physicality of blood. He wanted that simplicity. He wanted to fight, in a blood fight, spilling blood close up, not fight with his mind from a distance. He wanted to put the mental fight aside, give up the crippling, endless puzzle of war, the never-ending facts and data, and just be a man with a sword. Just give up. Stop thinking and give in. Just fight. Just fight, mindlessly. Just be free. Just fight and kill, for blood. For blood, the colour of this desert. Just blood for the sake of blood, simple, released, unthinking. Just blood. Blood for–

How long ago was that? Who was there?

Does it matter? Which side was he on?

He tries to order the available facts. He was a warrior who just wanted to kill. They wouldn't let him. They wanted him to think. They wanted him to decide everything. They wanted him to order the available facts because they said he was good at it. He didn't want to decide. He didn't want to have to make those decisions. It was killing him. He never told anyone that. He wanted to stop and make somebody else decide, make somebody else order the available facts. All he wanted to do was to go to the walls and forget it all and fight, a man with a sword.

Just fight. No thought. No decisions. Just fight, mindlessly, free, the way the others did. Just fight. Spill blood. That's all. Just blood. Blood for the–

Just give up.

'I am Rogal Dorn, defiant,' says Rogal Dorn.

Just give in.

'I am Rogal Dorn,' says Rogal Dorn, sitting in the crimson shadow under the red wall.

Are you even that? Were you ever? Just give up.

'I am Rogal,' says Rogal.

Not even that. Don't think. That's all you really wanted, isn't it? Not to have to think any more? You can do that here, in the shadow of the wall. Just give up. Give in.

He orders the available facts.

'I...' he says. Is there anything he's certain of any longer? All the facts have rusted, and all the thoughts have gone. There is only blood. That's all he really wanted. Give in to that.

'I...' he says.

Just blood. Say it.

'I...'

Say it. Say blood. The thing you wanted.

'Blood,' he says softly. Soft as the flecks of rust the dry breeze lifts in horsetail plumes from the ridges of the dunes.

Say it again.
'Blood.'
Who is the blood for?
'For–'
Say it. Who is the blood for?
'Blood for the–'
For? For whom?
He's waiting for you. You just have to say it.

3:xxxii

Our father in hell

Proud ship, proud *Spirit*, I see what you have become. Even from this great distance, my embattled mindsight can see what his excess has made of you. I can perceive the truth of it, whole and entire and terrible, for my mind is not shuttered by deceit like the brave sentinel souls who travel with my lord and master.

I want to help him. I want to stand alongside my beloved friend, the Master of Mankind, and aid him in his fight. But I can't. All I can do is watch, from my excruciating perch on the Golden Throne far away. Horus Lupercal is allowing me to witness this. I can smell his cruelty. He hopes the sight of it will break my concentration so I lose control of the Throne.

I will not. *I will not*. But I cannot help but look, and what I see is a whole agony in itself.

I see a hell-pit, a realm of horror that my lord's first-found has wrought, mistaking it for heaven. Perhaps the great Lupercal is now so far gone this seems like a heaven to him. His gods – gods that are not gods – have lied to him.

The lies are so very convincing. Fleetingly, they fool even my master. I see him forced to blink and look away as he advances, to shake off the visions of gold and lustrous pearl, the pure white light that bathes everything in a glow like sunlight on fresh snow. It reminds him of the great Himalazian peaks, silent and unspoiled, when first he climbed them, lifetimes ago, and stood, and breathed the empty cold, and looked upon the white dazzle of the top of the world, and decided that this would be where he would raise my city. It was a place that knew eternity.

This place knows it too. This poor, proud ship is a ship no longer. The four, the False Four, have made it a bridge to infinity, matter fused with unmatter, a pathway from sane reality to insane ether. The entire Solar Realm is subsiding into the warp, and the *Vengeful Spirit* is the focus, the primary pathway between realms.

I see that my master, for all his great power, is finding it hard to concentrate and hold on to the truth. The compounding lies of heaven and hell are so very convincing. It is all too easy to become lost in private fantasies born of doubt, or secret fear, or burning need. The warp tempts us all. I fear for all who embarked on this assault with him: Constantin, Sanguinius, Rogal… wherever they are, they may already be lost to delusions manufactured to exploit their smallest flaws.

My master's Companions, the pitiful remains of the Hetaeron company, for all their preternatural gifts, are entirely beguiled by the lies. They see heavens of their own, madly beautiful or beautifully mad. Warden Xadophus sees an Elysian temple of glass and gold leaf, sunlight beaming from a pale dome. Custodes Frastus beholds a serene field of glory, surrounded by alabaster pillars under a bright noon sky. Prefect Andolen perceives the halls and galleries of a golden palace, lined with auramite effigies of heroes, paved with silk-sheen marble.

The others too: it's hard to track. Their thoughts, usually so steeled and focused, are slippery with amazement and wonder. They see around them the glory of the Inner Sanctum, the Palace they have guarded their whole lives, replicated in every detail, but magnified in scale and richness a thousand times, more lavish than any citadel their master ever built. To Proconsul Caecaltus, he that I marked with my sigil, the company advances along the Gilded Walk, yet it is ten times broader and a hundred longer, and gleams beneath a sky more pure than any Terra has ever known. To Karedo, it is the Hall of Worthies, flanked by statues and roofed in crystal, which marks the final, western approach to the Silver Door. To Ravengast, this is the cryselephantine Yulongxi Passageway, which leads to the cloisters of the Imperial adytum.

Lies. All lies. They are all so amazed at the radiant kingdom, they see not the menace suffusing every inch of the place, at every hand. Frastus, pausing to marvel, sinks slowly into the golden floor, unaware of his descent as he vanishes from view. Braxius, lost in rapture, disappears quite suddenly. I think the golden statues took him, yet they are quite still, their frozen gazes turned away innocently. Andolen stops, and leans back against an engraved auramite wall in contemplation. The wall begins to pull him in, without a ripple, as though he is being gently lowered into molten gold.

I see this happening. My mouth moves, silently screaming. I want to call out, but they cannot hear me. They do not see what I see: the nightmare black, the rot, the filth, the *truth* that briefly replaces the palatial glory every time I blink.

I see my master turn and yell Andolen's name. Andolen stirs, and smiles to see his lord. He is half-sunk in the wall. There is no seam or line where the gold of his plate ends and the wall begins. My master grabs his hand and tries to pull him free.

He sinks further.

+Andolen, awake!+ I hear my master cry. Andolen blinks, confused, then alarmed, slowly realising his plight. My master cannot pull him free. He won't let go. He stakes his sword in the deck and, with his free hand, grips the limb of a vast aureate statue nearby to anchor himself. He hauls, yet still Andolen won't come loose. The statue feels cold to my master's touch, even through his gauntlet. The statue is one from the Hall of Worthies. It depicts one of the primarch sons. I don't know which one. My master grips the leg so hard the gold deforms, ruining the sculptor's perfect line of thigh and knee. I see the crafted shape of harness and plate, the laurels on the head, the sceptre held high in the left hand, the loop of frayed red twine tied around the fingers of the right hand.

+Awake!+ my master roars. He will not let the lies consume them. Straining to pull Andolen clear, he unleashes his will to drive the radiant cloud of falsehood from their brains.

+Awake! Please. Know yourselves. Wake from this stupor or be forever fallen.+

They wake. Some of them, at least. Others are too far gone. They wake, by his will alone, and see the ship as I see it. They see the darkness and the decay, the cancerous steel of the deck, the diseased bulkheads. They see their master gripping a half-broken stanchion as he tries to haul Andolen from an oozing wall of meat that is sucking him in like quicksand.

Andolen is screaming. The most terrible sound in creation, to hear a Custodian cry out in fear. Others start forward to help their lord: Xadophus, Karedo, Caecaltus. But all they drag free is Andolen's arm, torn off and blurting blood.

Frustrated that their lies have been exposed, the spirits of the ship become vengeful. They sweep in from all sides, wide-mawed and roaring, from the darkness, snatching men off their feet even as they turn in confusion.

I see what the cursed first-found is trying to do. Or rather, I see what the four that *rule* him are trying to do. This is them at work, the predators in the long grass. All four have deployed their gifts here, to stop my lord, because they fear him. They are targeting the Hetaeron Custodians because they dread the killing power each one represents. They are trying to pick them off, one by one, through violence or madness, until my master is forced to stand alone. Further, they are trying to weaken my lord and dilute his power. The Custodes were built to protect him, but the four have turned them into a burden, forcing *him* to protect *them*, for only if he shares his will and mind-sight with them, diminishing his own power, can he keep them alive and alert.

Once more, the insidious cruelty of the warp is demonstrated to me. It fights not fairly if it can fight with cunning. It wants no match with my lord and his warriors on an equal footing, for it has no doubt as to who would win that. It turned my lord's men against him when he first arrived, now it turns them into an encumbrance. It knows, and mocks, his love for each of them, and it knows he will not see them wasted and destroyed. It obliges him to mete out his strength to them, so they can at least see the truth, and fight it. It seeks to weaken my great lord and wear him down until he is at last alone and vulnerable.

These are the treacherous blood games it wishes to play. Well, my lord and Master of Mankind has some skill in such games.

The *Spirit*, once-proud ship, is but a ruin, no more than a derelict, decayed tomb, like the benighted space hulks we have sometimes found, drifting and lost between stars. The warp has eaten it away, and where it has not rotted and disfigured, it has transmuted and diseased. The decks are scarred and dislocated, the walls rusted and soiled. In places, it has split open so that the hull gapes wide into the void. But it is not the hard vacuum of near-Terran space that glares back in, nor are they familiar constellations that I see glinting through the torn and collapsed hull-skin. The *Vengeful Spirit*, just like the rest of the immense traitor fleet, just like Terra itself, and the entire Solar Realm, is half-sunk in the immaterium, much as poor Andolen was half-sunk in the wall. What surrounds my lord now, what permeates his first-found's flagship, is the leaching, cankered voidmist of the empyrean, flooding into realspace to claim it as its own. This increasing flux is what pollutes Terra, and deforms it, and reduces it, and mangles spatial dimensions, and revokes time, and allows the Neverborn and dead to walk. Horus' ship has not been spared the dissolving touch of Chaos it has carried to the Throneworld and unleashed.

You have brought the Emperor face to face with Chaos, first-found, closer than when he sat upon the Throne or walked the shrieking halls of the webway, perhaps closer even than when he last faced the four, and took their fire from them on Molech. You have brought Chaos to his very door, and forced him to look it in the eye.

Do not, then, expect him not to *use* it.

I see him look down at his hands. They are sheathed in auramite, because it is almost quantum-inert, and thus most efficacious in the manipulation of immaterial forces. Bare skin is better. This much he knows. He tears his right gauntlet off, hangs it from his harness, and seizes the immaterium with bare hand and a bared mind. It is scalding and alive with anger, but my lord is no longer constrained by the constant duties of the Throne. That is my burden now.

There is no time. There are no clocks. There is no pain. My master hears only the crackle of the warp. I watch as he harnesses that sound and uses it as a focus, a drishti, to regulate his work.

The immaterial presses at him. It seeks to overwhelm and

drain him, but he understands its fire. It is the same fire he stole from the four annihilators, and used to keep them at bay, the same fire he has wielded, for centuries, to drive them back whenever they have come too close. They flinched then, from their own fire. They flinch now.

You have forced this confrontation, first-found. You have brought my lord into a realm of Chaos to face you. Did you think that would weaken him and grind him down? How can he grow weak when there is limitless power around him to draw upon? You do not put out a fire by throwing fuel upon it.

He draws upon your flames. Over the millennia, he has worn many masks, each suitable to the task at hand. His mind, his greatest gift, allows him flexibility in such things. Now you see him at his truest aspect: as terrible as he can be when terror is the only recourse. He is *ordo ab chao*. He is *lux in tenebris*.

The Emperor lights up your pitiful, wretched ruin of a ship. He burns back your perfidious darkness. He empowers his ailing Companions, and rekindles their courage. He shares his searing mindsight with them, banishing the false heavens and murderous paradises you conjured to drown them. He sharpens their senses and the edges of their blades. He fires the cryptochromes in their eyes, the retinal proteins he wove into their construction that lets them read magnetic fields, and allows them to see the actual, physical structure of this place behind the congealing lies and illusions. He boosts their data-depleted senses and banishes the cognitive dissonance created by the isotopic space around them.

Despite the inhuman pain that wracks every atom of my body, I rejoice at the sight of it.

Refreshed, renewed, the Custodians form up around my lord. Xadophus, Karedo, Caecaltus, Taurid, Ravengast, Nmembo, Zagrus… the last of the few. They see through your nacrous dreams, first-found, to the spoil-heap desolation they veil, the botched pipes and curdled waste, the fibrous decks seethed with a filigree of worm tracks, the dripping ceilings and sloughed wall panels, the dangling cables and broken fittings, the litter of bones and the oozing stacks of skulls.

Your darkness billows back like squid ink. The gathering Neverborn, some quite the most enormous of their ilk I have ever glimpsed, scream mirthlessly at my lord's baleful fire, which scorches their minds. They surge forward.

Golden blades meet them. The stench of their blood and bursting organs infects the air, the nidor-reek of their meat and fat burning as powerblades cut through it, but it cannot overwhelm the osmogenesia, that pure odour of sanctity, that surrounds my lord and his Companions.

They drive forward, smashing through the daemons' energumenical mass, possessed by will and power and abreactive fire. The decks shudder as infamous beasts collapse and die, or stagger, howling, back into the shadows, trailing blood or mauled limbs. Horned things, tusked things, insectile horrors come apart under raining blows and roaring shells, deliquescing into slicks of aithochrous sludge, or spattering the walls and floors with sizzling ianthine blood.

My master begins his vastation, advancing blow by blow and death by death, into the dark heart of your lair, searing away the evils that you throw at him, edging ever closer to your abditory, *your* inner sanctum. Your attempts to stop your father have forced his hand, obliging him to become stronger, to reject notions of mercy, to adopt the aspect I hoped he would never have to wear. I am reluctant to admit it, but this pleases me. I am almost delighted to have lived just long enough to see his ultimate fury unleashed.

The things he slays, dead, undead, or Neverborn, incinerate in outrage at the power he is wielding. They see him for what he is, first-found. They see him in the aspect you have forced him to assume: Emperor, Master of Mankind, thanetiser of daemons, annihilator of the annihilators, bearer of stolen fire, death-bringer to the false and pitiful four.

He is here, first-found. In rage, in extremity, in theandric fury, he is here and he is coming for you, with all of the vengeance and malice you are owed.

No more restraint. His reluctance is gone. He will take great pleasure in obliterating you. For I hear his mind ringing through the warp.

+I am here, Horus Lupercal, and for you, I am the end and the death.+

3:xxxiii

Somewhere

Somewhere, in the outer darkness, four voices start to laugh. It is cruel laughter. They laugh, and begin to whisper the name of the one who is now here.

They lisp and hiss the name.

Over and over.

The name.

The name of the Dark King.

PART FOUR

IN THE MIDST OF CHAOS

4:i

Terminus

He takes a breath. He swallows his grief. He raises his green cowl to shadow his face, so that no one can see the pain in his eyes.

Xanthus, Chosen of Malcador, slips down the shadowed cloisters that flank the Imperial Sanctum. Like all of the Chosen, wounded by sudden loss, he dearly wanted to maintain his vigil in the Throne Room, but there is too much to be done. *Far* too much. The Chosen have been working tirelessly since long before the war began, their toil all but invisible. History will not record their efforts, or even their names. The Sigillite called them, fondly, the 'hidden seamsters of the Imperium'.

How he will miss him.

Though they will go uncelebrated, the achievements of the Chosen are as great as any performed by the Astartes or the Excertus Imperialis. Under the Sigillite's covert direction, they have woven and maintained the fabric of the Imperium, balancing all the vying offices and institutions of governance,

as a cunning and entirely discrete arm of political adminis-
tration. They act as a lubricant to allow the great gears and
cogs of authority to turn without jamming. 'Few decisions of
significance have been made in the Palace,' the Sigillite once
boasted, 'without one of my Chosen in the room.'

Great Terra, he will miss him.

Xanthus believed that, when the final hours came upon
them, the workload would ease. So much is rendered trivial
by the approach of an apocalypse. Instead, though it seems
there is nothing anyone can do except wait for some kind of
conclusion, the Palace seems busier than ever. The heart of
the Sanctum beats frantically. War Court seniors and aides
of High Council lords and ceremonial officials rush past,
each on his or her hasty task. Petitioning nobility pack the
mass-passageways around the Throne Room, craving admission. Sentinel guards clear pathways through the crowds,
crowds of Terran aristocracy gathered like pleading common-
ers, to allow Oblivion Knights to lead through processions
of psycho-able conscripts. Some of the Chosen help super-
vise these scared, tithed herds. Sigil Protocol is now being
implemented in full force. Concillium work-crews bring in
additional areopeaic devices in wagons hauled by abhuman
gangs. The devices, each one huge and strange, like sound
mirrors wreathed in filament wires or the tarnished anvils of
blacksmith giants, will be conjoined with the Throne mechanisms to improve stability. To prolong the Sigillite's... well,
not his life, but the progression of his death.

He will miss him so badly.

All the halls and processionals are packed: the Hall of
Worthies, the Hall of Swords, the Mencavite Hall, the Martian
Approach, the Hall of Celebrants, the Calisto Galleries. They
swarm with ushers and lords, household serfs and dominion
governors, Navis Nobilite and high-status servitors.

Xanthus knows that, in truth, most of them have very little urgent business. They are finding things to do, inventing tasks and hectic purposes, simply so they can congregate in the Throne Room approaches where they feel they will be safest. Even here, deep below ground, tremors can be felt. The Delphic is beginning to submit to the enemy's assault. Very soon, the traitors will be inside the final fortress.

He pushes through the crowds of purposeless activity, following worthies through to Mencavite, and then heading along the echoing Yulongxi Passageway towards Martian. The Chosen still have genuine errands to run.

Such was the Sigillite's parting gift. A monsoon download of unfinished business. In addition to his stinging bereavement, Xanthus' mind aches from the raw psionic deposition. All the Chosen are still mentally struggling to prioritise the tasks the Sigillite left to them, muddled and unfiltered, in his living will. Xanthus has, as far as he can tell, sixty-seven to perform, though there may be others tumbled into the recesses of his mind. Each one, in another age, would have been the most essential thing that had to happen in the Palace on a given day. But they will have to wait, because his priority now is the performance of a duty that was left to Hassan, the most senior of their kind, because Hassan, in his seniority, has been called away to the Antirooms by a sudden security crisis. Hassan has mentally passed the duty to Xanthus. It is a thought-file marked *Terminus*.

'Get it done,' Hassan said. As soon as Xanthus studied the engram, he understood the relevance and the urgency. The sodality had already been instructed.

'Without delay,' Xanthus had replied.

So he runs, without delay, down the Yulongxi Passageway to Martian. It is a matter of Imperial Security, of interdisciplinary politics. The autonomous authority of the captain-general must be checked. If, as the Sigillite believed, the Imperium survives this day, it cannot emerge with the Legio Custodes, already frighteningly powerful, holding quite so many cards.

Moriana Mouhausen, of the Chosen, is waiting for him in the Martian Approach. Like Xanthus, she had tasks of her own to perform and, like Xanthus she has been co-opted to Hassan's purpose. Like Xanthus, she is poorly hiding her grief.

'Have you found her?' Xanthus asks.

'I have,' she replies. 'Is she really the most appropriate proxy for this?'

'According to Khalid, yes,' he says. 'She has talents that can be exploited to achieve leverage, and Khalid reminded me that she has previous experience with the subject.'

'I have reservations, Zaranchek,' Mouhausen replies. 'If we fail in this, the implications–'

'I know.'

'I'm saying, she is unaligned, potentially divisive, and bears no authority in the Palatine–'

'The same could be said for us, Moriana. Couldn't it?'

'Even so, she–'

'She can hear you, you know.'

They both look aside. 'She' is waiting nearby, leaning diffidently against the engraved gold panels of the Martian Approach. Either side of her stand the officers of the Hort Palatine who have escorted her here as requested. Nearby, the polished ouslite floor is scattered with red petals. There are sprays of flowers in glass vases on every demi-lune table along the length of the approach, and none have been attended by the household staff in days. They are silently shedding petals as though they wish to lose excess weight and be better able to flee.

'You are Andromeda?' Xanthus asks.

'Seventeenth of that archetype,' she replies. She straightens up. Her grey robes have a soft, feline flow. Her chrome hair glints in the light of the vast electro-flambeaux overhead. 'You are both of the Chosen?'

Xanthus nods.

'And this concerns Fo?'

He nods again.

'Am I to understand this is an unofficial errand?' asks Andromeda-17. Xanthus reads her grin of curiosity as amused relish. He dares not imagine how the Selenar gene-witch reads him.

'It comes from the highest authority–' he says.

'Well, not the highest, eh? Not *the* highest. From your master, which is significant, but not the same thing.'

'It comes from the highest authority present on Terra,' says Moriana.

'Oh,' says Andromeda. 'That's interesting. And I'm sure you won't elaborate on what that means.'

'This is a delicate matter,' says Xanthus, 'of high priority. A smoothing of interaction between two different agencies.'

'Back-room politics? Underhand?'

'If you like.'

'Between Malcador's lapdogs and…?'

'The Legio Custodes.'

Andromeda-17 raises an eyebrow.

'How very Machiavellian,' she says. 'Do you know who that was? Never mind. I would say that this kind of political intrigue seems pathetically inappropriate under the circumstances. We're all going to die. What machinations could possibly be so important that they have to get done now? But you mention Fo, and the Custodes. I presume they wish to assume control of the little monster and his weapon, and the office of the Sigillite would rather they did not?'

'They already have the weapon,' says Xanthus. 'We may or may not be able to secure it through official channels.'

'The Sigillite is allowing them to keep it?' Andromeda asks. 'You know what it *does*, right?'

'The weapon is a last resort,' says Moriana. 'The Sentinels understand this. It is classified Tier XX as a Terminus Sanction. Once the crisis has passed–'

Andromeda laughs. '*Once the crisis has passed…?*' she echoes.

'Once the crisis has passed,' Moriana reaffirms, 'the weapon will be removed from Custodes supervision and placed in more appropriate hands.'

'Meaning yours?' Andromeda smiles again. 'Don't worry. I know you won't answer that. I get it. The weapon isn't important. The mind that made it is. Because the mind that made it can *replicate* it.'

'Correct,' says Xanthus.

'So the Custodes want the maker securely in their jurisdiction. *Once the crisis has passed*, they want to be left holding all the cards. Ready for the *next* crisis. Or just to clean house after this one.'

'The Custodes intend to execute him,' says Xanthus.

'Ah, I see,' says Andromeda. 'A miserable death for a miserable creature, and entirely deserved. But I appreciate that the office of the Sigillite doesn't want to lose so vital an asset. The last lord of Old Night represents a weapon that would make the Chosen a more powerful institution than the primarchs or the Legiones Astartes. The power of life and death over the god-king's creations. In the present circumstances, many would see that as a good thing. The brave Custodes certainly seem to.'

'Do you?' asks Moriana.

'Not my place to say,' she replies.

'We have a window of opportunity,' says Xanthus. 'A temporary power vacuum, if you will. We procure Fo now, or the opportunity will be lost.'

'You're thinking about the future still? How brave.'

'The present is out of our hands,' says Xanthus. 'The future is our only viable concern. You engineered his release once. Will you assist again?'

Andromeda nods.

'I'll take it from here,' Xanthus says to Mouhausen. 'Get back to your duties.'

She nods, and hurries away, beckoning the officers of the Hort Palatine to follow her.

'We don't have much time,' Xanthus says to the Selenar gene-witch. 'Directives have been issued, and the Custodes are already en route.'

'You realise I hate his living guts, don't you?' she asks.

'That,' replies Xanthus, 'hardly matters.'

4:ii

Close work

They take back a little ground. Just a little, and it's meaningless in the grand scheme of things, but it matters. To Fafnir Rann, it feels like a proactive achievement after hours of mindless resistance.

When the enemy thrust chokes at the Delphine Viaduct, Archamus, Second Of That Name, orders in sustained bombardment from the high batteries. The firestorm, delivered by principal wall guns built to kill engines and void-ships, cuts a molten canyon-scar across the southern limits, and catches the mass of the enemy fall-back between Fratary Bastion and the ruins of the Hasgard Gate. The bombardment lasts six minutes, and Rann has no idea how many traitors die in it, but the number would be in the high thousands. A signal victory on another day: today, high thousands are just a drop in the traitor ocean.

The senior Huscarls call for entrenchment to take full advantage of the Delphine win: dig in along the viaduct line, and fortify that link in the stretched chain. Immense formations of

Sons of Horus and World Eaters are driving in at the loyalist line to the east and the west. In under an hour, the mauled traitor prong driven back behind Hasgard will be ready for a second bulk assault.

But Rann has other ideas. If they can extend their line as far as Hasgard, they can form a salient from which to strike at the eastern and western traitor masses flank-wise rather than simply head-on. Archamus concurs. The salient won't hold for long, but every minute bought back is another minute of the Emperor's life.

The terrain beyond the viaduct is a smoking mire where nothing is identifiable any more. Heat radiates from the mud banks, the pulverised rockcrete and the lagoons of slime steam. In minutes, Rann's advance is specked and pied with liquid mud. Namahi's riders, scouting ahead through the vapour with their servo-raptors, return with auspex surveys. Nothing lives between their position and Hasgard, but sensoria read life-traces in the surviving bunkers and blockhouses below Hasgard. The enemy has taken shelter there, and dug-in, hoping to hold a beachhead in preparation for their reinforcements.

'Close work,' says Zephon. Rann nods. That's exactly what it will be.

Every hand in the advance rises. Rann won't ask anyone to undertake a fight he wouldn't tackle himself. Fisk Halen volunteers, of course, but Halen is now bareheaded, his nose and mouth hidden by a rebreather, his ruined helm ditched. Rann gives him acting command of the advance instead, and asks for his bolt pistol. Halen hands it over without hesitation. Rann chooses Leod Baldwin and Val Tarchos. Zephon chooses Rinas Dol and Kystos Gaellon. Namahi dismounts and calls two of his riders to follow him.

Is this posturing? Rann wonders. The two field leaders, Blood Angels and White Scars, electing to go because Rann did? With

Namahi, it's a possibility, but not for the usual reasons of pride or rivalry. Rann knows the White Scars have always felt the outsiders in the loyalist formation, deployed, contrary to their usual role, by necessity in the siege defence. From the start, they have been viewed as the junior partners, second to the Blood Angels and the Imperial Fists, a mobile force unsuited to defensive war-work. The Keshig-Master is simply seeking to underline that his brothers are willing and able to do whatever is required. As far as Rann is concerned, the White Scars have been proving that every day since the siege began. Their honour is beyond doubt, and their status alongside the Imperial Fists and the Blood Angels irrefutable.

In Dominion Zephon, there seems no swagger either, though the Imperial Fists and Blood Angels have long enjoyed a contest of honour. Zephon, almost wordless, seems clinically matter-of-fact. He's going because why wouldn't he? In that, Rann thinks, he simply conducts his leadership as I do. No fuss, no devolution of responsibility: face it yourself, or dare not expect it of others.

The nine advance, through the mud-lakes and swelter. The liquidised ground is already baking and cracking in the post-bombardment calefaction-shock radiated by the area. The air swims with heat distortion. The complex of bunkers is half-buried in the caking ooze.

It will be close work, as Zephon said. Close confines, close quarters, clearing chamber by chamber. Baldwin and Tarchos have clamped their main weapons, and drawn pistols and combat knives. The Blood Angels and White Scars have done likewise, drawing bolt pistols, and where the Blood Angels have poignards, the White Scars have edlel or gutting blades. Large weapons or long blades will be cumbersome inside.

Rann locks his twin axes across his backplate, and takes out his own pistol and Halen's. Zephon, similarly, keeps his keen sword, *Spiritum Sanguis*, in its scabbard across his back. He has left his brace of precious volkite pistols – powerful, but impractical for the kind of combat ahead – in the care of one of his lieutenants in the advance, and borrowed a blunt-pattern bolt pistol. To Rann, the Exarch of the High Host, like all Blood Angels, seems a creature of splendour and rich panoply, so it reassures him to see Zephon favour plain functionality over ornate wargear.

They turn off their active icon marker transmitters, and fan out along the northern limit of the bunkers. Rann moves with Zephon, scaling a huge, frozen wave of mud onto the top of a blockhouse. A shell has punched a hole in the roof, a circular wound through three feet of rockcrete, surrounded by snapped and twisted rebar.

Since the fight at Clanium Square, Rann has noted a difference in Zephon. He doesn't know the Blood Angel well, by reputation mainly, but he knows him well enough. The Dominion was once known as a warrior of fury and passion, but now carries himself differently, moves differently. Even his voice, when he does speak, seems affect-less. Rann hasn't marked it much until now, because there has been no room to think, but here, in the steaming silence, he is obliged to watch his kill-partner closely for signals and gestures. The beauty and grace, so typical of the IX Legion, is still there, but Zephon now reminds him, he realises, of some exacting natural predator, driven by a hardwired impulse to kill and feed, but entirely and scrupulously in control of that urge. The wild bravado has gone, and in its place is just the dense, lightless silence of menace. Rann wonders what might have effected such a change in the once noble warrior, but he need only look around. This war has done it to all of them, and to everything they know and value. It has hollowed them out, left their eyes empty and their expressions blank, and scraped the gilt of glory off all their deeds. Mere purpose remains, blackened and scorched, the duty to kill until killed. Valour, glory, pride, triumph… such Astartesian qualities are gone and bankrupt.

It pains Rann to see Zephon so; to see a glorious angel clipped and dulled, all spirit vacated. Rann has always thought of the Blood Angels as the exemplars of martial prowess, not just great practitioners like the Imperial Fists, but paragons of inspiring prestige. It pains Rann, for in Zephon's grim emptiness, he sees his own, and sees the hollow soul of every loyal son left on Terra.

He checks his melancholy thinking, for the work is upon them and intense focus is required.

Rann listens for sounds in the bunker below, and tracks for heat spots. He gestures to Zephon, then takes the lead, dropping feet first through the hole.

Inside, it's a lightless oven of mangled debris. He advances, slowly, silently, with both pistols raised. His visor penetrates the darkness for him, resolving a green ghost-fog where the contours are shattered blocks and twisted metal, collapsed internal walls and the mashed pulp of those who were in the bunker when it was split and blown out from the inside.

Zephon drops in behind him, and they spread out in parallel. Rann's visor passive-tags Zephon with an icon so Rann can track him and not target his movement in error. He reaches a hatchway into a connecting corridor. Torn struts and pipework jut from the ruptured rockcrete. Rann raises his pistols either side of his head, then swings through the doorway, a gun aimed in either direction.

Empty. More layers of wreckage strewn underfoot. Dust clogging the air like mist. Zephon glides past him, pistol up, dagger low. He pulls in against a bulkhead, and covers the angle as Rann moves up past him. Room to the right. Vacant. Room to the left. Two corpses: World Eaters demolished by overpressure where they cowered.

Rann covers Zephon. The Blood Angel moves left. Another chamber. He aims through the door as Rann switches past him. Tight angle. Nothing visible within. Rann nods, and Zephon rotates in. Three more bodies, destroyed by monumental shockwaves, compressed against the rear of the chamber like flotsam. Next, an adjoining chamber, a sub-communication duct. The cables of main-system vox-casters drape like vines from the torn ceiling. A 'caster bank has fallen sideways, three tonnes of metal tilted against the wall with its broken mechanical guts spilled out.

Rann enters first, pistols aimed. Zephon covers, then crosses behind him, so they loop the slumped bulk 'caster. The World Eater, his left leg trapped, is hidden by it, but they know he's there. Their sensoria picked up his corrupted icon marker, his pulse, and the cycle of his plate systems from outside. He's been trying to gnaw his leg off to get free.

When Rann swings around at him, he grunts and grabs for his bolter. Zephon's poignard has run through the back of his skull by then, the tip projecting between his teeth like a tongue. Black blood spatters the caking white dust.

A half-open blast hatch, misshapen by air pressure. Rann goes first. The approach hall of a billet area. The hall was tiled, and half of the white tiles still cling to the walls. The rest are strewn and shattered on the deck. There is a little more light. Low-level auxiliary power feeds the caged overheads. They flicker, and the swirling dust makes the shadows undulate. Rann prowls in, covering a doorway with his left pistol and the hall ahead with his right. Zephon slips past him as he stands watch, then rolls around the doorway into a second chamber. Clear. Rann moves on. More tiled walls, some shedding tiles like fish scales. The doorway into a large barrack area. The insignia of the Hort Palatine has fallen off the wall. Most of the long line of metal lockers are still upright. In the bay-end, dirty water pisses and fizzles from broken shower pipes. Rann gets a faint contact, but he can't lock it. Just motion. Not all of the enemy have functioning marker systems any more, or they have shut them down. He signs to Zephon, who follows him in. Rann hugs the wall to the left of the locker bank. Zephon slips down towards the bay-end to flank him. His sensoria paints a large alcove or archway beyond the lockers.

They both freeze as they hear the rapid, muffled discharge of bolt pistols. The sounds echo through the ruined bunker complex. One of the other clearance teams has engaged. Rann longs to know who, and to know status, but he won't go vox-active in case the enemy pinpoints him.

He takes another silent step.

Something behind the locker bank opens fire with an autocannon.

4:iii

High risk

There are two of them, standing like statues beside the hatch of the main elevator bank. Fo lives in a state of constant transhuman dread, appalled at the monstrosity of His creations. He had just about got the measure of Amon Tauromachian, but these...

'What is taking so long?' one of them asks.

'Nothing,' replies Amon. 'Just final supervision checks. The subject is registered high risk. He is a genius, according to the Mondavardi Scale, and of high cunning. Thorough supervision checks were required.'

'You flatter me, Amon,' says Fo, trying to hide his gnawing terror, trying to ignore the ice in his guts. These things, these monsters, they are the beasts assigned to kill him.

The Eastern Approach elevator bank has been locked down by a Custodes override. Xanthus and Andromeda take the service stairs, rattling up the dingy ferrocast steps. She is younger than him, fitter, but she has to race to keep up such is his dedicated urgency.

'Do we have a plan?' she asks.

'I was leaving that to you,' he replies.

'Then I'll improvise.'

They exit on the secure floor. Almost at once, he checks her, and pushes her into the shadows. She frowns at him, but he points. Ahead, the service passageway runs for fifteen metres and then opens into a vestibule where main corridors converge on the elevator bank. She sees two immense figures in black armour: Custodians, but of some sub-order she doesn't recognise. As they watch, two more figures arrive at the head of the corridor to face the pair in black. One is a golden Sentinel, and she's quite certain it's the one named Amon. The other, a tiny child beside the other three, is Fo.

'What are they?' she whispers.

'Wardens of the Sodality of the Key,' Xanthus whispers back. 'We're too late.'

4:iv

Eight individuals

Khalid Hassan, Chosen of Malcador, enters the Antirooms. He has, he believes, no time for this, but the orskode alert indicated *security/intruder*, and that obliges him to attend. He's had to trust Xanthus with his primary duty, and that feels wrong. He *does* trust Xanthus, completely, but the Sigillite legacied the thought-file marked *Terminus* to him, and he feels as though he is dishonouring his master's wishes by delegating.

The Antirooms are an annex of gold and glass thirty minutes brisk walk from the Throne Room. They fall under the jurisdiction of the Custodes, though they are officially maintained by the Sisterhood. There are forty-six such facilities in the Sanctum precinct, and another nine in the Hegemon. The moment he enters, Hassan feels the bite of the artificially generated null space, the pinch across the bridge of his nose and the pressure below his ears.

Sister Vigilator Mozi Dodoma awaits him, her wrists resting across the long quillons of the biedhander planted tip-down in front of her like a staff. The sword is almost as tall as she is. At her side towers a Sentinel, Hetaeron Companion Ios Raja.

'An intruder?' Hassan asks.

'Several,' replies Raja, though Dodoma is thoughtmarking the same word.

'Some panicked nobility penetrating a secure area?'

'Outsiders,' says Raja, again interrupting Dodoma's deft signing.

She looks at him.

'My apologies, Vigilator,' he says.

The outsiders were apprehended near the Hall of Worthies, she signs, her greatsword resting against her collarbone. *The Custodes have secured them but–*

'Wait,' says Hassan. 'Outsiders?'

Yes, Chosen One.

'Forgive me, but in the circumstances, isn't that supposed to be absolutely impossible?'

The very reason we summoned you, she signs. *The breach requires the most senior authority.*

And that's me, thinks Hassan. In the Palace, outside of the Throne Room, that role falls to me.

'Show me,' he says.

He follows them. Armourglass airgates hiss open. The gleaming gold of the walls reflects from the crystal diamantine floor. In the inner suite, the air is cold and the bite of the null fields stronger.

Eight individuals, Dodoma signs as they walk. *Four human, as far as we can assess. Two psykers. One servitor mechanical. One Astartes.*

'Of dubious provenance,' Raja remarks. 'A hybrid, in my judgement, or some malformation. Perhaps immaterially altered.'

'Which Legion?' Hassan asks.

No Legion.

'That's absolutely not possible,' says Hassan.

'Hence my estimation,' says Raja.

'Are these... traitors?' Hassan asks. 'Is this the first wave, the first penetration? An advance scout–'

Dodoma's hand moves, switching from elegant thought-mark to the curt simplicity of battlemark. The gestural meaning is simply: *?*

The core of the inner suite is a ring of cells made of non-resonant crystal set in ornate psycurium frames. Hassan can see shapes inside, figures in eight of the glass boxes, but the crystal has been opaqued so they remain silhouettes. He notes that the anti-systems of the suite have been raised close to maximum. Items have been laid out for examination on a long glass table. Psyber-skulls hover over them, probing them with whisker-thin beams of light, bobbing and darting like hoverflies as they process information.

Hassan sees weapons, most of them regular army-issue, with the magazines or powercells removed and placed beside them. He sees a voltvolver of arcane design, then a bolt pistol. It's old, with a gold-wire grip and a side-mounted sight.

'Phobos pattern,' says Hassan.

'No,' says Raja. 'Actually an M-six-seven-six Union Model autobolter. It predates Imperial pattern designation.'

Old, agrees Dodoma.

'An antique,' says Raja.

Hassan picks it up. It is extremely heavy and he has to use both hands. There is no Legion marking on it at all, not even a designation stamp or code number.

'Which Legions used these?' he asks, putting it back down carefully.

Dodoma makes the *?* again.

'And this... Astartes... has no insignia?'

'None,' says Raja. 'His armour pattern is also antique. The chestplate was stamped LE two.'

He also carried these, signs Dodoma.

Beside the gun there are several grubby satchels. Psyber-skulls are carefully unpacking them, an item at a time, using miniature mechadendrites and extensor probes. Hassan sees a deck of cards. They're old too, handmade, slightly worn. He starts to turn the top cards over, one by one, laying them out in a line. Tarot cards, simply rendered, made of plascard. He recognises a few of the designs... *The Harlequin* of discordia, *The Eye, The Great Hoste, The Shatter'd World, The Labyrinthine Path, The Throne* reversed, *The Hulk, The Moon, The Martyr, The Monster, The Lightning Tower* and *The Emperor*, all major arcanoi. He turns another. *The Dark King.*

'A poor reading,' remarks Raja.

'One might expect no less,' replies Hassan. He knows the tarot, in various arcana variations, is in common use, though officially frowned upon as superstitious vulgarity. He also knows that the Sigillite often privately consulted a deck, and placed great credence by it, and that the deck he used had allegedly been designed by Him, though under what circumstances the Emperor would lower Himself to such esoteric practices, Hassan can't imagine. What strikes him about these crude cards is the similarity to the designs on Malcador's liquid-crystal wafers. Tarot is ubiquitous enough, but massively variable in style. These might have been copied from the Sigillite's personal deck.

The last card he turned unsettles him. Hassan has been made aware of current concerns regarding that symbol. He looks at the next item laid out on the glass. It is a primitive stone knife.

'What the hell is that?' he asks.

'I don't know,' replies Raja, 'but it troubles me.'

'Did these people resist?' Hassan asks, looking at Dodoma and the Companion.

'No,' says Raja, 'though they were furtive, and moving to avoid discovery when detected. They did not resist.'

'Did they offer explanation? Excuse? Justification for their presence?' asks Hassan. 'Did they make... I don't know, demands?'

One, signs Dodoma. *And it's all they've said. They request audience with someone in authority.*

'Really?'

Their leader repeated this. Strenuously, though he remained calm and non-confrontational.

'Their leader? They have a leader?' Hassan asks.

Dodoma takes him over to one of the crystal cells.

This one, she signs.

Hassan adjusts the gold dials on the fascia and the crystal gently de-tints. A man stares out at him. He is old. No, not old. Worn, Hassan decides. His grubby clothing is faded, ex-military and commonplace. His skin is dirty and weathered by sun and the open outdoors, which Hassan has not visited in a long while. He looks like nothing special at all, just another army dog-soldier, a 'script, one of the billions dragged in to bulk out the Excertus and man the walls. But there is a curious strength in him, an intent, a dreadful solemnity in his eyes.

His mouth moves. Hassan adjusts another dial to bring up volume.

'Repeat,' he says.

'I am Ollanius Persson,' the man says, his voice relayed by the vox-speakers built into the cell.

'I understand you request audience with someone in authority?' says Hassan.

'That's not what I said at all,' the man replies.

'Oh. I was told–'

'I said take me to your leader,' the man says. 'Take me to see *Him*.'

4:v

Closer still

Rann leaps backwards as the wall shreds.

Broken tile sprays in clouds of dust. The shots stitch around and start to hit the locker bank, punching through the thin metal of the back-to-back uprights. Some of the locker doors on Rann's side deform or are blown off completely. Several rounds slice clean through and strike the facing wall. The end section of the lockers is rapidly mutilated and fractured.

As the shooting starts, Zephon darts around the opposite end of the lockers, and is body-slammed by a Sons of Horus legionary. The two of them crash backwards into the shower bay, Zephon underneath. The legionary, his huge form sheened in white dust, has a power fist, and tries to punch down into Zephon's face. Zephon twists sideways, and the fist shatters the tiled floor of the wide stall. Zephon's gun-hand is pinned. As the power fist rises again, he stabs up into the armpit with his poignard. The Sons of Horus warrior howls, writhing. Zephon tears his other hand free, and fires two bolts up into the body on top of him, blowing the torso apart, and coating the white tiles and white dust of the shower bay with blood.

Rann is forced back to the barrack room doorway by the rate of fire. He ducks outside, using the thick wall as cover, feeling it quake as heavy-calibre rounds smack into it. A few rounds spit through the open doorway and explode against the opposite wall of the corridor.

Pistols raised, Rann holds position, weathering the storm. His visor shows him a heat source moving around the locker bank, but most of that is muzzle flash and superheated smoke. The gunfire is now so intense it is dislodging tiles on his side of the wall, sloughing them off the rockcrete so they shatter around his feet like crockery.

Then the shooting stops. Rann doesn't hesitate. He swings back into the doorway, already firing both pistols. The Sons of Horus warrior with the cannon, now emerged from behind the ruined locker bank, takes one shot in the chest and another in the face, and is hurled back into the lockers, which further buckle under his impact until they have become a crumpled hammock of twisted metal supporting his corpse.

Rann keeps moving. He sees a third Sons of Horus legionary beyond the bank, and drops him with a headshot. He reaches the archway. Zephon is back on his feet and moving to join him. A bolt-round sings out of the archway, missing them both. Zephon, with a better angle, fires four suppressing shots through the arch, and Rann pivots in.

The air is thick with dust. He kills a Sons of Horus legionary with a single shot as he comes through, and the traitor's toppling body actually wipes a brief man-shaped gap in the airborne dust as it collapses. Rann switches right, right hand, single shot, and puts another traitor into the tiled wall, a plume of gore rising above his head more magnificent than any topknot. Simultaneously, left hand, ninety-degree angle to the right, single shot down the length of the chamber to drop a Sons of Horus warrior attempting to run for the rear hatch. Zephon's behind him, firing two shots to the left into the haze.

Rann keeps moving. Bay to the left, single shot, left hand. Hall to the right, single shot, right hand. His multitasking ability is not confined to an ambidextrous use of war-axes. Ahead, a service hall. Two figures. Both pistols, side by side, square-on and blasting. Both figures jerk and then sprawl.

'Replenishing!' he snaps. Zephon has already jammed a fresh magazine home, and puts timed shots down the service hall as Rann reloads his pistols.

More gunfire spits through the dust to their left. Zephon rotates, cool and methodical, and snap-shots a Sons of Horus legionary off his feet.

Rann *keeps* moving.

4:vi

Directives have been issued

'He will offer no challenge to us,' one of the Wardens says with a hint of scorn. They are twins of Amon Tauromachian, armoured giants. But where Amon's plate is gold, theirs is blackened and ash-dark. (Is this the garb their kind wear for executions?) It is peculiarly terrifying. The gold armour of the Custodes seems to celebrate their majesty and (albeit ineffectively) minimise their threat. To cake them in black seems blatant, and designed to emphasise their menace.

'Aren't you going to introduce me to your friends, Amon?' Fo asks, barely keeping the wobble out of his voice.

'No,' says Amon.

'Well, I don't trust them.'

'That has no significance,' says one of the monsters.

'I assure you, it does to me,' says Fo.

'Your trust in us, or lack thereof, has no bearing on the performance of our function,' says the other monster. 'It is immaterial.'

'Oh, now there's a loaded word I wish you hadn't used,' says Fo.

'Your considerations of vocabulary do not concern us,' the monster says.

'Irrelevant is an appropriate synonym,' says the other.

'It is,' agrees Fo, 'but even so. Tact? At a time like this... You gentlemen are so very precise in all things, so very, *very* precise, and there you go using a word with quite alarming connotations. At a time like this.'

'This dialogue is irrelevant,' says one of the Wardens.

'To you, perhaps,' says Fo. 'Not to me. And not, actually, to Amon.'

'It is,' says Amon. 'It is irrelevant.'

'Well, no. Agree to disagree, Amon. I would like to know who these people are before you let them walk off with me. I don't trust them.'

'That has no bearing on anything,' says Amon.

'It has a great bearing on your duty, Amon. Who are these men? I don't trust them. When does duty end?'

Amon pauses. He glances at the giant figures in black.

'This is Aedile-Marshal Harahel. This is Companion Shukra. They are Wardens of the Sodality of the Key.'

'Ah,' says Fo. 'The ones that shut things away. The ones who keep safe all the dangerous things. Am I a dangerous thing, tribune? Have you come to shut *me* away?'

'Directives have been issued,' says Harahel.

'Or have you come to kill me?' asks Fo.

'Directives have been issued,' says Shukra.

'So I gather. By whom? Who has issued these directives?'

'That is–'

'Don't say irrelevant,' says Fo. 'And *absolutely* don't say immaterial. Because it's very relevant.'

'Your opinion has no bearing,' says Harahel.

'I'm sure it doesn't,' says Fo. 'But Amon's does. It's his duty to guard me. His duty was instructed by Captain-General Valdor, and it has not yet concluded.'

'Our directives were issued by the captain-general,' says Shukra.

'Oh, now we're getting somewhere. Amon's directive was authenticated. Wasn't it, Amon?'

'Yes.'

'Are your directives authenticated?' Fo asks.

'Of course,' says Harahel.

'Follow us now,' says Shukra.

'Have you seen their authentication?' Fo asks Amon.

'No.'

'Then how do you know they are genuine? Please, Amon. Think. Your kind do not make mistakes. To make a mistake is to fail in your duty. Your duty is my life. Your duty has not yet ended. Do not make a mistake now and end your duty in error.'

'Be silent,' says Harahel.

'There, you see?' says Fo, glancing at Amon, and wagging a finger at the giant in black. 'A demand. Almost a threat. Not the rational presentation of accurate fact that your kind follows to the letter. Please, think. You've seen the hell outside. You've seen the doom falling upon Terra. The warp is in everything, Amon. Nothing can be trusted. It's turning brother against brother. Primarch against primarch, oppositions that should not be possible, such is the will of the Emperor, and yet–'

'Be silent,' says Shukra.

'We have to do something,' Xanthus whispers.

'Wait,' says Andromeda, watching the exchange by the elevator bank carefully.

'Some improvisation, as you promised–'

'Just wait, Chosen One,' she hisses. 'I think the old flesh-crafter is about to demonstrate why he is so dangerous.'

'Be silent,' repeats Shukra, cutting Fo off again.

'Another demand!' cries Fo. 'You see? I do not trust them, Amon, because nothing can be trusted any more. Nothing! Except I *do* trust you. So, do you trust *them*?'

'Be silent,' says Harahel.

'Follow us,' says Shukra.

'Show me authentication,' says Amon.

The Wardens stop and look at him. There is no way to read their expressions behind their soot-black visors, but Fo is certain it is indignant fury.

'Step aside, Custodian,' says Harahel. 'Your duty is discharged.'

'Not yet. Confirm and authenticate your directives.'

'Directives have been issued,' says Harahel. 'Confirmation of those directives may be obtained from the captain-general.'

'Obtain them,' says Amon.

'This is not currently possible. Captain-General Valdor is unavailable.'

'Obtain them via neuro-synergetics.'

'This is not currently possible,' says Aedile-Marshal Harahel. 'Captain-General Valdor is not present on Terra, and neuro-synergetic link is unviable.'

'Then I cannot release the subject to you,' says Amon.

'You will not block us,' says Harahel.

'Step aside,' says Shukra.

'No,' says Amon.

They stare at each other. Amon's face is expressionless.

'Step,' says Harahel. 'Aside.'

'No,' says Amon.

'Tauromachian…' Harahel growls.

'If my lord the captain-general is unavailable, obtain authentic confirmation from another source,' says Amon. 'Authentication hierarchy states that suitable alternatives for a Tier XX directive are the Throne, the Lord Praetorian, or the Sigillite. No other sources are appropriate.'

'No,' says Shukra.

'Do so, or we have an impasse,' says Amon. 'There is no alternative.'

'There is,' says Harahel, taking a step towards Amon.

'I believe it would be an ironically fitting end to this cataclysm for Custodes to enter into conflict with Custodes, Harahel,' says Amon quietly. 'The bitterest betrayal of all that our beloved Emperor could face. Treason is the sport of bastard primarchs and their crude Astartes sons. It is their flaw, not ours. We were made better than that, weren't we?'

4:vii

An invincible calm

'"A commitment to war must be absolute, for once killing has been done, it cannot be undone. Thus the true justification of war must be determined before commitment is made,"' Loken reads out, '"but when war is made against daemons, there need be no other justification than it is a war made against daemons." This, from a manifesto on combat written in the two hundred and seventy-seventh century.'

Loken lowers Sindermann's notebook, and turns back a page or two.

'That's a long time ago, Kyril. The depths of Long Night,' he remarks. 'Arresting, I'm sure, but I'm not sure of the purpose of any of this.'

'Neither are we, Garviel,' says Sindermann. He has explained his efforts once, and he's tired of repeating himself. Rain beats on the high roof of the Great Hall, and thunder-that-isn't-thunder rolls outside. They have gathered around a reading table in one small corner of the gloomy library. Sindermann sits, weary. Mauer leans against bookshelves, her arms folded. The young archivist hugs the shadows behind them, timid. All three are watching the grey Astartes as he stands, examining the books and notes.

'"There is shadow under this red rock, come in under the shadow of this red rock, and I will show you something different from either, your shadow at morning striding behind you, or your shadow at evening rising to meet you. I will show you fear in a handful of dust."' Loken looks up from the notebook. 'Why that one?' he asks. 'Why note that one?'

Sindermann shrugs. 'I don't know. It seemed to resonate at the time. That was one you called out, boetharch. I just scribbled it down.'

He looks across at Mauer.

'Do you remember?' he asks.

She shakes her head. She's still staring at Loken. 'You still haven't accounted for your presence here,' she says.

To his left, Sindermann feels the young archivist shrink further into the shadows of the stacks. The Astartes, his plate pitted and flecked with blood and dirt, simply terrifies her. She can do nothing except stare at him and cower.

Loken looks over at Mauer. He has removed his helm and set it on the table. It doesn't make him any less intimidating.

'I have no account to make,' he says.

'Shouldn't you be,' asks Mauer, 'I'm just guessing now, *fighting* somewhere?'

'I was,' says Loken. 'I thought I was. I was at Praestor Gate. The heart of it. I was moving with a formation of Dorn's men to engage at the Processional of the Eternals.'

'And?'

'I heard gunfire, close by. I went to the assistance of your colleague, Ahlborn, is it? Ahlborn. I went to his aid.' He pauses, and turns another page. 'Ninety-fifth century allegorical verse? Really?' he asks. He looks at Sindermann quizzically, and shrugs.

'And then?' asks Mauer. 'You were with Ahlborn?'

'I've known you a long time, Garviel,' says Sindermann. 'You often hesitate to speak when you can't make sense of facts.'

Loken glances at him. 'There are no facts, Kyril,' he says. 'Everything is broken.'

'I don't quite know what that means,' says Sindermann.

'The part I left out,' says Loken. 'I was at Praestor Gate. I heard gunfire close by. I went to help Ahlborn. But then, I was at Scholaster Hall on the Via Aquila. That's where Ahlborn was.'

'Praestor's twenty-four kilometres from there,' says Mauer.

'Twenty, but yes. However, to me, it was a street away.'

'You must have lost track of time,' says Mauer. 'In the heat of battle–'

'No,' says Loken.

'A blackout–'

'No,' Loken repeats. 'I considered all of those things. Fatigue. Confusion. Acoustic shock. But it keeps happening.'

'What do you mean?'

'I lost Ahlborn on the Via Aquila. We were looking for Keeler. I thought I was heading for the Lotus Gate, but I found myself on the Via Terranic. So I tried again. Two streets across from Terranic, I was at the Metome Wall. Places, leagues apart, folding into other places. No matter what route I took. Multiple times, it's happened. In the last hour, I've been from Lion's Gate to the Palatine to the Sanctum. Locations hundreds of kilometres apart.'

'But Eternity Gate is sealed–' Mauer begins.

'In the last hour?' Sindermann asks.

'What time is it?' Loken asks, though it seems more like a challenge than a query.

'The clocks are all stopped, sir,' says the archivist from the shadows, daring a whisper. Loken looks at her, and she flinches.

'She's right,' he says. 'That's the first true statement anyone's made. The clocks have stopped. Time has unwound. Time and dimension. I suspected as much, and I said so to Ahlborn. I'll say the same to you. The warp is in us so profoundly, everything is changing, compacting, contorting. Places are touching that shouldn't touch, melting and fusing with each other. The Palace… and I suspect all of this world… is blurring and realigning as a deranged labyrinth. Time has stopped, and distance is meaningless.'

'Is this… a weapon turned on us?' Mauer asks. For the first time, Sindermann hears a hint of fear in her voice. 'The sorcerous powers of the foe, collapsing our–'

'It could be,' says Loken. 'It could be the work of the Crimson King. It could be any of them. One final twist of the knife to tumble us into madness and ensure their triumph. But, if you want my personal opinion, I don't think it is. I think it's a symptom. A by-product of the war. My cursed father has brought the entire power of Chaos with him, and unleashed it upon Terra. The whole world is drowning in the immaterium, and the physical laws around us are changing. First it was dreams and nightmares, possessions, then the birth of Neverborn things. Now it is the fabric of reality itself, unravelling. Chaos has infected Terra, reshaped it according to its own rules as it draws us into the bosom of its realm.'

The archivist suddenly starts to cry. Sindermann gets up to comfort her.

'This is how you came here?' he asks.

'When I found myself in the Sanctum,' says Loken, 'I tried to get to the Delphic, to serve there. Each time I did, I found myself in a rainswept courtyard. The times I tried again, each time, the same courtyard. The one outside this hall. It is as though something wants me to be here. This place. So, the fourth time, I went along with it and came inside. And found you.'

'Are you saying you think you've been directed here?' asked Mauer. 'By who? By what?'

'By something,' says Loken. 'At first, it was all random. But since I reached the Sanctum, it has seemed deliberate, as if I was being shown a sign. Something wants me at the Hall of Leng. I suspect the Sigillite.'

'Why?'

'I am chosen by him, and he has often been in my head these last weeks. But he has always spoken to me, and made his presence known. I don't know why he doesn't speak now. I want him to tell me what he needs me to do here. When I came in, I thought it would be obvious.'

'And it's not?' asks Mauer.

'It may have something to do with your work,' says Loken, 'but the rationale for that isn't even obvious to you.'

'What was the last thing he said to you?' asks Sindermann.

Loken shrugs. 'Combat directives, and that was days ago. Nothing pertinent. He simply plants instructions into the minds of the Chosen to keep them tasked. He is, as you can imagine, busy.'

He pauses.

'But I'll say this,' he adds, 'when I was at Praestor Gate, just before I went to help Ahlborn, a phrase popped into my head. Just very suddenly. I think it was something you quoted to me years ago, Kyril, aboard the *Spirit*, when you were an iterator and I sat in your audiences. I don't know why it came back to me.'

'You were a rewarding student in those days, Garviel,' says Sindermann with a sad smile. He pats the young archivist on the shoulder, and finds his kerchief so she can dry her eyes. 'What was the phrase?'

'"In the midst of chaos, I found there was, within me, an invincible calm,"' says Loken.

Sindermann frowns. 'I don't recall quoting that,' he says. 'I'm not even certain who it is. Is it Poul Kertus Varik?'

The archivist, blowing her nose, says something.

'Camus,' she repeats, a little louder. 'It's Camus.'

'Whom I have not read,' says Sindermann.

'There's a copy here,' she says.

'So you *have* read books?' says Sindermann.

She flushes. 'Some, I confess.'

'There is definitely a copy here,' says Mauer.

They look at her. She is holding up her data-slate, the screen towards them.

'I wrote this down,' she says. 'I'd given up calling things out by then. It was the last thing I wrote down before Loken arrived.'

On the screen are the words, *In the midst of chaos, I found there was, within me, an invincible calm.*

4:viii

A problem of jurisdiction

Unbearably calm, Harahel pauses.

'We will obtain authentication,' he says. He gestures, and the elevator hatch behind him hisses open. He steps in with Shukra. In the doorway, he turns and looks back.

'When I return, Tauromachian,' he says, 'your duty will be over. All of your duties. Valdor will see to it himself.'

The hatch closes.

Amon looks down at Fo. 'I will conduct you back to your quarters, and we will await their return,' he says. They turn to retrace their steps, Fo shuffling along in Amon's shadow.

'Thank you, Amon,' says Fo.

'I did not do it for you, Fo.'

'I know. It was simply attention to the logic of duty. But thank you anyway.'

'Look at you two, bonding,' calls Andromeda as she steps out of the service passage shadows behind them.

Amon turns to study her. His spear is already raised and gleaming.

'Didn't take you by surprise there, did I, Custodian?' she asks.

'I have been aware of you both since you entered this level seven minutes ago,' replies Amon. 'It is not my place to interfere with the business of one of the Sigillite's Chosen or one of his companions. Unless it interferes with mine.'

Xanthus walks up behind Andromeda, who is standing, arms folded, smiling at Fo.

'The security of this subject and his device are a priority concern of the Sigillite too,' Xanthus says. 'We have come to assist, Custodian.'

'I was not notified,' replies Amon.

'There's a lot of that today,' says Andromeda. 'Things are a little busy.'

'What are you doing here, gene-witch?' Fo asks, his brow furrowed.

'Do not communicate with them,' Amon tells him.

'The Sigillite has instructed that the subject be placed in our recognisance,' says Xanthus. 'The Chosen will take charge of him.'

'I was not notified,' says Amon, 'and it appears to conflict with the captain-general's directives. And this female has a history of unauthorised behaviour and subversion, especially with regard to the subject. So, no.'

'Those directives cannot be authenticated,' says Xanthus.

'Yes, we heard that much,' says Andromeda.

'Incorrect,' says Amon. 'Custodial directives *have not yet been* authenticated. They will be. Until then, my duty function, which is authentic, remains in place. Tell me, Chosen One, can your directives be authenticated?'

Xanthus pauses.

'No,' he admits.

Andromeda shoots him a sharp look. 'Nice going,' she mutters. 'Leave it to me, I said.'

She turns back to Amon and smiles.

'No one's directives are being authenticated today,' she says. 'Frankly, it's a mess. You can imagine why. We're going to have to use our own best discretion.'

'Why is nothing being authenticated?' Amon asks.

She shrugs. 'As I said. A mess. It's as if there's no one actually in charge any more.' She looks at Xanthus. 'Who *is* in charge, right now?'

Xanthus clears his throat.

'In the field, Lord Militant Terra Archamus,' he answers in a reluctant mumble. 'At Hegemon Control, Mistress Tactician Sandrine Icaro. In the Throne Room, the Primarch Vulkan.'

'Really?' says Andromeda, genuinely surprised. 'When I said mess, I…'

'What of the Emperor?' asks Amon. His spear lowers a little.

'Oh, you poor boy,' says Fo. 'They really have kept you in the dark, haven't they? Left you to your duty. Abandoned you at your post–'

'Be silent,' growls Amon.

'So where is the high and mighty Emperor?' Fo asks Xanthus. 'Run for the hills? I don't blame him. I'm surprised that oaf the Praetorian and the blowhard Valdor haven't evacuated him by now. Picked him up, kicking and screaming, and carted him off to the last express out of town. Have they quit too? Run away? Are the lifeboats full of rats, looking back at the sinking ships? What about the one with the wings? And the Khan fellow, you know, big moustache–'

'The Warhawk is dead,' says Xanthus. 'The Praetorian Dorn, Sanguinius, Captain-General Valdor and the Emperor have committed to the war.'

'Great merciful gods,' breathes Fo. 'It really is the end of the world. And your Sigillite?'

'The Regent occupies the Throne,' says Xanthus.

'Well, then he's dead too,' says Fo.

'Not yet,' whispers Xanthus. Andromeda hushes him with a gesture.

'Custodian Amon,' she says. 'It seems to me we are dealing with a problem of jurisdiction. The Custodians and the Chosen both want control of this maggot. Your orders are clear – to guard him, yes? I understand, absolutely, that those orders cannot be relinquished until you are relieved of duty. Might I also be correct in thinking your duty includes making sure he finishes his work?'

'His work is completed,' says Amon.

'No, it isn't,' she says.

Fo stares at her, eyes wide. He has no idea what she's doing.

'The subject confirmed it,' says Amon.

'Him?' she asks. 'He lies, Amon. He'd never hand over a finished commission if it meant he was of no further use. He has neglected to include a vital component. The weapon won't work.'

'If that was true,' says Amon, 'Fo would have played that trick already. If he'd left a loophole as insurance, he would have used it. Just now, to evade the Aedile-Marshal. Instead, he was obliged to appeal desperately to my function imperatives. You are the liar.'

Andromeda laughs and claps her hands. Her laughter, echoing down the dank corridor, seems brittle and out of place.

'Very good,' she says. 'I forget how perceptive you creatures are. So easy to mistake you for a dumb, unthinking statue. Fair enough, Amon. You got me. So I'll level with you. He's not lying. Fo's clever. But he's not *that* clever. His weapon is based on biomechanical principles, which is his field of genius. Flesh-eating phages, I presume, sir? Tailored to the biomatter code of Astartes and primarchs?'

Fo nods. His eyes are bright. This new lie is unexpected (and I am enjoying it very much).

'Fo has little or no knowledge of the warp, however,' says Andromeda. 'His weapon will kill Astartesian flesh. I'm talking a galactic slaughter. The crowning glory of his horrible career. But the Astartes aren't merely flesh, are they? Nothing is. Each body is connected to a soul, and each soul is inextricably linked to the warp. That is the nature of reality, and not something Fo has studied. So, if activated, his weapon will not entirely purge the Astartes. It will leave a significant portion of their essence in the warp. I say that again, for emphasis... *in the warp*. And what's out there, what threatens us, is barely physical any more. Horus Lupercal certainly isn't. The traitors, Amon, are immersed in the immaterial, soaked in it. So even if the weapon works, it will not destroy the right targets. It is hardly the last resort Valdor hoped for.'

'I admit,' says Fo, grudgingly (for I am perfectly happy to play along with this ruse), 'that *is* the Emperor's genius. To meld the immaterium with the physical in the creation of his sons. I ignored that component. I really didn't think it through. But then I have never studied these factors.'

'You see?' Andromeda says. 'Amon, your duty is not fulfilled, because Fo's work is not complete. The Chosen and I are here to make sure it is completed. *Properly*. And time, my friend, is against us.'

'What are you proposing?' asks Amon.

'You heard him,' says Andromeda. 'He said it himself. He hasn't studied these factors. We must allow him to, immediately.'

'That would certainly help...' says Fo.

'The data repositories are too far away,' says Amon. 'The Clanium has fallen. The Hall of Leng is too distant and probably inaccessible–'

'The Sigillite keeps a small private archive in his retreat, Custodian,' says Xanthus.

'Very well,' says Amon. He turns immediately and starts to

lead Fo away. Fo looks back at them, mouth wide in mock amazement.

Andromeda glances at Xanthus. He shrugs a 'what the hell?' at her.

Im-pro-vi-sing, she mouths to him.

4:ix

My life for Lupercal

No one is listening any more. No one. He has lost control.

'I am First Captain,' says Abaddon, almost to remind himself. No one else is listening.

He thought it would be glorious, when it finally came. He thought the end would be glorious, a victory beyond victories, an illumination beyond illuminations. The crowning triumph. The greatest achievement of any warrior.

But it is not.

It is more horrific than he ever imagined. It is an unfathomable atrocity.

He was steeled for it, of course. A man, even a warrior as infamously ruthless as Ezekyle Abaddon, does not go into such an undertaking blind. He resolves himself, he centres his mind, he inures himself from the carnage that will follow. He makes himself ready, not just for the pain and the blood and the loss and the effort, but for the mental carnage. This is Terra, the Throneworld. Any other action pales by comparison, and not merely in scale. This is the biggest war he has ever been part of, but he's indifferent to that. To invade *Terra*, to conquer it and bring it to compliance, that is an act of desecration. It is the ultimate iconoclasm, a breaking of oaths and a shattering of rules. It requires an inhuman strength of will. To turn against your species and your cradle-world, to turn against your creator, to turn against everything you were, and renounce it all.

That takes singular resolve.

But he was prepared for that. Abaddon has made his choice, long since, and he is strong. He was ready to witness the horror, ready to mete out the havoc, ready to withstand the conceptual shock of what he was doing. He was even prepared to stand alongside the daemon-things that disgusted him in order to get the deed done.

For, after the end, there would be glory. A triumph. A peerless victory. A tyrant would be dead, a toxic regime overthrown. His kind would be free, his beloved father vindicated and crowned, and a new and better world born from the flames.

Abaddon had oathed that he would do anything that had to be done, without flinch or hesitation. For, beyond anything, it would prove his worth. His loyalty. His courage. His ability. The victory would be his, for he was the lord commander on the field, his father's chosen proxy, the tip of the spear, a new master of war and mankind, who would deliver the *coup de grâce* and claim the greatest feat of all.

It would all be worth it.

But it is not. And he is not. No one is listening any more. He has lost control. And this is not something to which the word 'victory' could ever be applied.

It is obscenity.

From the burning slopes of Coriolis Park, fast by the blood-washed bastion of Auguston, which cooks like a dirty rag, he sees the swarming host engulfing the fortresses of Lycia and Naxos, the palisades at Crucis Hill, the broken line of the Via

Aquila and the ramparts of Marquis Bar. He sees the sundering towers toppling one by one, in fire and debris, their flanks disintegrating, falling away like calving glaciers. He sees buildings scalped and eviscerated. He sees the sudden uprush of titanic dust clouds as spires are levelled, filling streets for kilometres at a time. He sees the burning spans and collapsing bridges, the furnace line of the horizon, the uncounted dead and the unnumbered deathless.

Sixteen kilometres ahead, Antiphrates Fortress, perhaps the last of the Palatine bastions, enters its death throes. Explosions shudder beneath its skin, and the entire fortress, a colossal island of stone and steel rising above the Palatine Zone, begins to slope, capsizing like a yacht at sea, wallowing into the stagnant mire that the landscape has become. Everything – stone, ground, rock, metal – has begun to ooze, seeping clotted filth and tar like fat rendered from meat. A cheer goes up as Antiphrates succumbs, a throaty roar of a million voices that shakes the sky. Ekron Fal has accomplished this cataclysm. Ekron Fal and his Justaerin and his screaming hosts. Ekron Fal, veteran of Isstvan, a true monster of destruction whose Cataphractii plate shifts and seethes and changes like a living thing.

Ekron Fal, who has ignored all of Abaddon's summonses.

To the west, fifty kilometres, a line of pestilential smoke marks the advance of the Catulan Reavers and their Word Bearers retinues. At their head, their master Malabreux, reckless Tarchese Malabreux, joyful in his killing, the superlative terror-soldier, carrying the profaned banners of Bhab Bastion aloft to boast of his deeds.

Tarchese Malabreux, who has refused to acknowledge Abaddon's repeated commands.

No one is listening.

From where he stands, on the burning slopes, Abaddon feels

as if he can see all the way to the very Delphic Battlements, though they must be sixty kilometres distant. The Delphic, the proud Delphic. With Antiphrates and the Palatine principals gone, the Delphic is all that remains, a final rampart girdling a final fortress. It is already assaulted at almost every side. Serob Kargul, Lord Contemptor, and the Death Guard have reached it. Lord of Silence Vorx and his Death Guard echelons too. The wild hosts of World Eaters are gouging at its southern hem. Vorus Ikari, captain of the Fourth, that unbridled sadist, is there. So too Taras Balt and Third, singing their Davinite doxologies. So too Kalintus and Ninth, Dorgaddon and Tenth, Zistrion and Thirteenth.

So too all the daemons of hell, and the gnawing, restless dead who will not lie down and be damned.

Vorus Ikari, Taras Balt, Kalintus, Dorgaddon, Zistrion, them and the rest besides, who have disregarded his signals, and declined his instructs, and spurned his demands for vox-contact.

'The command link is down,' his adjutant tells him, 'there is too much interference to establish contact,' and 'Captain Ikari's seniors report he is in the thick of combat and a link is impossible,' and 'No response from Captain Dorgaddon's units,' and 'Third command repeats that Captain Balt cannot disengage to speak with you at this time.'

No one is listening. No one wants to listen. They are lost in their lusts and consumed by that which consumes them. More, and more damning, they think it is Abaddon's cupidity that issues these demands: that he wants this victory for himself, that he wants this glory, and that he resents their gains and seeks to restrain them as they race ahead.

If only they understood. How can he make them listen?

'I am First Captain,' he murmurs.

'My lord?' His adjutant, Ulnok, approaches up the slope.

'Speak.'

'Captain Beruddin commends himself to you. He reports Fifth Company is now closing on the Delphic, and has engaged with White Scars forces. He urges you to join him without delay so you may cherish this triumph as brothers, and break the wall together. He regrets he cannot link with you directly while engagement is ongoing.'

Abaddon spits on the ground.

'Logistics?' he asks.

'The flight cadre stands ready for your word, sir. They have fuelled and prepped as you instructed.'

'Then I give it.'

'They…' Ulnok hesitates. 'Lord captain, the pilots direct me to say there is no suitable landing zone in this vicinity.'

'Then I direct *you* to ask them to select one. Have them tell me where they can set down, if they would *be so very kind*. Have them select a damn site, *any* site, and I will draw my companies there.'

'Yes, lord. To… uhm, *embark*, lord?'

'You heard me.'

Ulnok hurries away.

'Airborne assault, my captain?'

Abaddon turns, and sees Baraxa descending the slope to join him. At the heels of the Second Company captain come Sycar of the Justaerin and Fyton of Seventh.

Baraxa, his helm removed, reaches him and bows his head.

'Airborne?' he repeats, with a wary smile. 'A rash gamble, Ezekyle. The Delphic and its voids are as strong as shit. They'll burn 'birds out of the air. I admire the flourish, but we'll take the final fortress better on foot.'

'No flourish, Azelas,' says Abaddon. 'No airborne assault.'

'But I just heard you say–' Baraxa begins.

'You came, then?' Abaddon says, cutting him off. Sycar and Fyton have joined them.

'Well, you summoned me, so why would I not?' Sycar replies.

'You were most insistent, First Captain,' says Lycas Fyton. A curious pattern has begun to appear on his face in the last few weeks that looks like some kind of dermal infection, but which seems to be scarification. There is a fresh gash across his brow that appears to be welling yellow ichor.

'No one is listening,' says Abaddon.

'My lord?' Baraxa says, frowning.

'I was insistent because no one is listening,' says Abaddon. He gestures at the burning world. 'No one. Not any more. I am First Captain but that, it seems, means nothing. Everything is broken. Everything is madness.'

'We came,' says Sycar.

Abaddon looks at them, and nods, mastering his rage and remembering himself.

'I need you to understand,' he tells them, his voice low. 'This isn't pride. This isn't some fit of indignation on my part. I am not trying to hobble the other companies so that First can claim the laurels.'

'We… didn't think it was,' says Baraxa.

'And it's not remorse,' says Abaddon. 'Not at all. No last-minute qualm or compunction, even though…'

He pauses, and looks back at the atrocity behind him.

'Even though, brothers, look at what we've done.'

'Then why summon us?' asks Fyton, his tone curt. 'Seventh was locked in at Polemos Bar, alongside Sixteenth. We had Dorn's puppets falling before us. Thane himself, his back to the wall–'

'Everything is broken,' says Abaddon.

'Ezekyle–' Baraxa begins.

'Listen to me! Everything is broken! Everything we stood for, the structure and discipline of the Sons of Horus. The things that made us the very best of all, ruined and gone.'

'Because a few damn orders have gone astray?' asks Fyton. 'This day is like no other, Ezekyle. This victory unparalleled. I think even *you* might forgive the heedless energy and zeal of our captains as they race to conclude this business. Let them have their moment and revel in it.'

Hé pauses.

'Let me have mine,' he adds.

'Think for a minute,' says Abaddon. 'One damn minute. What we do today shapes us for tomorrow. What we are now, we will be afterwards. The Sons of Horus, like the Luna Wolves we were, are the finest of all Legions, the personification of controlled precision in war. And here, in this cataclysm, on this day of days, we forget ourselves and fall apart. Our values and authorities are lost, discarded, ruined–'

'All this because the seniors have disregarded a few of your signals?' asks Fyton.

'Enough, Lycas,' whispers Baraxa.

'No, not enough,' says Fyton. He looks at Abaddon. 'You are a great man, Ezekyle. Finest warrior I ever saw, and I am proud to call you brother and commander. But this pique is unbecoming.'

'Fyton,' Baraxa growls.

'Shut up, Azelas,' says Fyton. 'It ill-suits you, Ezekyle. To stand at the edge of the rear line and pitch a fit of indignation when your orders, barked from a great distance, are overlooked? Where are you, man? It should be *you* at those walls, leading from the front. The captains should be begging *you* for the chance to follow at your heels. They should be pleading with you for an order that lets them stand with you in honour.'

'I was there,' says Abaddon quietly.

'You were there?'

'I was there the day this began,' says Abaddon. 'I was there at the front, all the way from Lion's Gate when it fell, all the way along the Gilded Walk and the Grand Processional, right there at the front, Lycas, carried by the energy and the glory, rejoicing in this triumph.'

'Then why are you here?' asks Fyton. 'Why the hell are you here, skulking in the rear lines, squawking orders like a–'

'Enough!' Baraxa snaps.

'Because,' says Abaddon, looking directly at Lycas Fyton, 'everything is broken.'

'Brother, captain,' says Fyton, his tone more moderate. There is concern in his eyes. 'I know you have misgivings. You always have, and I understand. I know you lack trust in the etheric powers we employ, and think we should not invest ourselves so much. I understand. The warp calls who it calls. It is a friend to us, and without it, we would not have taken this seat of power.'

'Wrong,' says Sycar. 'This is a soldier's war. Always has been. We don't need Neverborn filth to fight it for us. This is about us. The stand we make. The rights we seek to avenge. I understand Ezekyle's position. We have surrendered too much control to the immaterial–'

'No,' says Fyton. 'Not *wrong*, Hellas. How can you think that? All we do, we do for the Lupercal. He is the one who has ordained this. He is the one who has invested us so. He chose the immaterial as our weapon, and it has served us well. He has perfected its use, and thus made this triumph possible. He has shown us how to control it–'

'Has he?' asks Abaddon.

'Of course,' says Fyton.

Ulnok has returned.

'Well?' asks Abaddon.

'My lord, flight cadre has selected Sacristy Field, to the south of Hasgard Gate. They report the terrain there will support a landing operation.'

'Tell them two hours,' says Abaddon. 'Tell them I want Stormbirds for six companies.'

'Yes, my lord.'

'We are embarking?' asks Fyton, puzzled.

'Yes,' says Abaddon. 'Those that have deigned to respond to my orders are embarking. That includes you and Seventh, Lycas.'

'Embarking for what purpose?' asks Fyton. 'An airborne run at the Delphic would be insan–'

'We are returning to the *Spirit*,' says Abaddon.

The three captains stare at him.

'Are you joking?' Sycar asks.

'Are you mad?' asks Fyton.

'Everything is mad, and everything is broken,' says Abaddon. 'We should all be returning, every last one of the Sons of Horus, but you're the only bastards who would listen.'

'We are this close to the finish!' Fyton cries, holding up a thumb and index finger almost touching. 'You've lost your way, Ezekyle. Lost your way and your mind. No one is pulling out. We're at the *walls*, brother! The fortress is ours! You'd have us withdraw at the very last gasp, and give up all we have achieved?'

'Malabreux can finish it,' says Abaddon. 'Ikari can finish it. Fal can raze the place to the ground and carry the tyrant's head out on a stick, for all I care. They're at the walls, as you say, so they can finish this murder. Our place is at our father's side.'

Fyton starts to protest again. Baraxa silences him with a raised hand. He stares at Abaddon.

'Why?' he asks. 'Why, Ezekyle? What do you know that we don't?'

'Our lord Lupercal, who I love more than all things, needs us,' says Abaddon. 'He has taken leave of all sense. I believe now, more than ever, he has become too enthralled by the powers he has unleashed. You asked where I was, Lycas. Ask instead where is *he*? Where is Lupercal? He should have led this from the front. He has not set foot on this world. He has not raised a hand in this fight. I have longed for him to be the Lupercal I know, and he has not.'

'So… this is, what… churlishness?' Fyton asks. 'Vexation that he has left the tiresome hard work to you? He's Lupercal, you child. You're the First Captain. This is your damn job!'

'My job, Lycas, is to protect the person of my beloved father, whatever ails his mind,' murmurs Abaddon. 'First and foremost, my life for the Lupercal. No oath matters more, not even the illumination of this pretend god and his gaudy palace. No one is listening to me. Everything is broken, and we must make haste to mend it before it is lost forever. Lupercal, our Legion, everything we are.'

'What do you know, Ezekyle?' Sycar asks. The Master of the Justaerin's voice is very small, just a hoarse whisper coming from his immense plated form. There is a hint of fear in it.

'I have spoken with Argonis,' says Abaddon. He sighs. 'Damn, it feels like an age ago. The hours are broken too. I've been trying to rally you all ever since. Kinor says the voids have been lowered. The *Spirit* is wide open.'

They gaze at him.

'If it's a ruse,' says Abaddon, 'then it's a private one known only to our father. Horus himself ordered it done. I think he is taunting our enemy. I think he is, in all madness, inviting direct contest. Our foe may be close to death, brothers, but he has fury left in him yet, fury that will double and redouble given such reckless opportunity. I believe our Lupercal has underestimated the danger of this gambit. I do not even think it was his choice. All I know for certain is that our main force is here, wading in the mire and ignoring commands, and he is on the *Spirit*, essentially unprotected. I have called in the

Stormbirds for immediate return. We move now. The fight is not here, brothers. The real fight is not here at all.'

4:x

Closest

The blockhouse galley and food stores are deep inside the bunker, and the walls there are brick-built partitions, for there is no need to replicate the shell-proofed ferrocrete skin of the outer shell.

It is a suboptimal place to fight.

Las-shot chops through two and even three thicknesses of bricks, filling the air with rust-red dust and a pungent stink of burned oxides. Bolt-rounds blow out holes a metre wide. Everything is close range. There is no long range. Even the shots coming from the adjoining mess hall are travelling far less distance than in the open field.

Rann's visor detects the density of the rockcrete spars of the bunker's frame. They stand like pillars every five metres, infilled with brickwork. He uses one as cover, as gunfire tears out the brick courses either side of him. He reloads. Auspex return reads four: two in the galley behind the wall, two more in the communal space beyond. Zephon, behind a bulkhead at the other end of the corridor, is trying to line shots into

the mouth of the mess hall doorway, where a fifth and possibly sixth shooter lurks.

Between them, they have killed twenty-seven traitors since
entering the complex.

The traitors in the galley space unleash fury at the wall
behind him. Lumps of brick, mortar chips and clouds of red
powder spray out around him. Rann waits for the beat, the
brief moment when the boltgun reloads, then he spins out,
firing both pistols through one of the holes his enemies have
conveniently made for him in the wall. He kills the Sons of
Horus legionary with the boltgun outright, slamming his huge
bulk backwards into a stove unit, and clips the traitor with
the heavy las.

The latter barks in anger, and lurches for cover behind a
stack of drums for dry goods storage. Rann races to a second,
lower hole in the brickwork, and puts two bolt-rounds into
him, bursting him and one of the drums. The Sons of Horus
legionary sinks, slack, into a seated position, spoiled protein
meal pouring out over him like sand.

Zephon is still clipping off shots at the other end of the
corridor, and the shots are being answered. The air is filmed
orange with brick particulates. Rann moves again, kneeling to
use one of the lowest blast holes. The low angle gives him a
clear line along the length of the galley, past the prep counters
and the row of stewing kettles to the doorway of the chamber
beyond. He fires rapidly, both guns, driving the two traitors
there into frantic cover.

Rann reloads. He's about to hose again when his visor
flashes a marker to his extreme right. A corrupted wolfshead
icon.

The Sons of Horus warrior, a massive, distorted brute, is
charging him down the narrow access corridor. He is carrying
a heavy, rectangular storm shield in front of him, and firing

a bolt pistol over its top corner loop. Rann scrambles backwards. Two bolt-rounds hit the wall beside him, covering him in red dust, a third clips his right greave. Only half-upright, Rann scrabbles in retreat, returning fire, but the shield soaks everything up, the explosive impacts searing harmlessly across its surface.

Rann ducks into the galley doorway to evade the shooting charge, knowing it will expose him to the Sons of Horus in the chamber beyond. As he swings through the galley door, he empties the pistol in his right hand at the rear-galley arch to keep the shooters in cover, then clamps the empty pistol to his plate and draws one of his stowed axes.

Quarters are still too close for this kind of weapon, but he is acting on pure instinct. He lets *Headsman*'s haft slip down through his hand so he is holding it at a mid-point, as a hatchet. As the charging traitor draws level with the doorway, Rann, so coated in brick powder it looks as though his yellow plate has rusted, swings out to greet him, and buries the head of his axe squarely in the shield boss. Now he has a split second, and leverage. He hauls on the axe haft, prising the shield away from the Sons of Horus legionary's body, and puts three rounds into the opening with the pistol in his left hand.

The traitor drops, unguarded torso blown out point-blank. The shield drops with him, clamped to his arm. Rann drops too. The killers in the communal space beyond the arch have resumed fire, further mangling the galley doorway.

Hunched down, Rann puts one foot on the edge of the fallen shield and frees *Headsman*. He stows it, then drags the shield off the traitor's arm. Incoming shots chew the wall behind him and the doorway beside him.

Still crouching, he reloads both pistols. There won't be time once he's in it again. He clamps one pistol, takes the other in his right hand, and hoists the shield onto his left. He glances at Zephon. The Blood Angel, at the far end of the corridor, is still trading shots with the enemy in the mess hall. Rann knows, from his brother's stance, that Zephon is about to break cover and charge.

'Hold!' he shouts, but Zephon is already racing for the mess hall doorway, head down, pistol barking.

If Rann moves to support, it'll open them both to the traitors in the communal space. A simple, tactical choice.

Rann raises the shield and charges the length of the ruined galley. Shots hammer off the shield, bucking it in his grip. He reaches the archway, and kills one of the defenders immediately, firing over the loop: a shot to the throat, then another to the belly as the Sons of Horus warrior folds away. The other is to his left, just inside the room. Rann turns on him, shield raised, now taking fire at zero distance, the impacts threatening to wrench the shield off his arm. He just keeps moving, slamming the shield into the Sons of Horus legionary, driving him back against the chamber wall. The traitor is pinned for a second. Rann slots his pistol over the loop, rams his entire weight and power into the shield, and puts a single bolt-round through his face.

He steps back. The immense dead weight of the Sons of Horus warrior slithers to the floor, leaving a sticky track of gore down the wall. Rann can hear shots exchanged in the mess hall. Still, he takes a second to check the chamber, to make sure there's no one else in hiding, and no one about to storm in from the access beyond.

Then he goes back, fast, shield up.

Zephon is just inside the mess hall doorway. Two traitors are sprawled dead at his feet, and he is grappling hand-to-hand with a third. At some point since Rann last saw him, Zephon's helm has been torn off or discarded. He's been hit at least once in the shoulder, his pauldron scorched and buckled. Rann's instinct is to help him, but fierce gunfire is coming at them both from deeper in the room.

Rann ploughs past Zephon into the hall, shield up, drawing fire. Two more traitors: another of the Sons of Horus and a World Eater, both marker-tagged with corrupted gibberish. The Sons of Horus traitor is to the right, firing a boltgun. The World Eater is to the left, closer, but not shooting. Rann guesses the brute's heavy cannon has cooked out and jammed. He prioritises, advancing on the Sons of Horus warrior, emptying his magazine. His target, in partial cover, holds his ground, doing the same. Bolts hammer the shield. The Sons of Horus legionary's last shot finally cracks the shield diagonally. Rann's last shot explodes the traitor's head in a splash of blood, bone and ceramite flakes.

Rann leaves the ground. The World Eater, a huge beast, has abandoned his jammed cannon and slammed into him from behind. Rann is caught in a vicing bear hug, his feet milling. The World Eater is yowling in his ear, coating Rann's right pauldron and the side of his helm in viscous spittle. Rann drops his empty pistol and tries to break free, but he has no purchase, and he's clamped to the beast's chest by his captured shield. His left arm is almost crushed. He can feel his plate creaking as though it is about to fracture and split. His torso is compressed. The World Eater is terrifyingly strong, far stronger than any Astartes, for it is not truly Astartes any more. It is beyond transhuman. Right in front of his wedged face, Rann sees its ugly, white talons cutting into the edge of his shield, its huge hand, flesh swollen and almost translucent, folding the shield like the cloth of a cloak.

He realises his war is about to be over.

4:xi

A personal connection

'You see,' says Hassan, 'that's simply not possible. And even if it was possible, I wouldn't allow it. You don't seem to me to be a stupid man. Did you think I *would* allow it?'

'I think if you thought about it, you might,' says Oll.

They sit, facing each other, in one of the Antirooms' interrogation chambers. Like the cells, like everything, it is wrought from crystal and gold, and entirely inert. Hassan's simple chair is auramite. Oll's is a more complex affair of crystal and psycurium, fitted around him as though ready to restrain him, recline him, and present him for cranial surgery. Either side of him are field generators fashioned to resemble seated Bhutanese dragons, their long, swan necks curling upwards to present their open mouths either side of Oll's head, as though they are roaring in his ears. A single command, and they will be: the mouths are the speakers of null-field emitters and pain goads. The dragons are, of course, wrought from gold.

'The only reason we're having this conversation,' says Hassan, 'is that you and your companions have somehow got inside the Sanctum. That requires close investigation. Otherwise, your claims, your demands–'

'I understand,' says Oll. 'We are interlopers. Trespassers. At any other point in history, we would have been arrested and thrown into some oubliette. I imagine, time was, you got idiots trying to get in all the time. Petitioners, madmen, pilgrims… people who just wanted to get close and touch greatness. I doubt any of them ever got further than the outer limits of the Dominions. But these are not those times, and I am not one of those idiots.'

He sounds reasonable. He sounds sane. Hassan is trying to be reasonable too, more reasonable than he feels he should be. There's something about this man, his calmness. It struck Hassan the moment the cell glass de-tinted. This 'Persson' is intensely steady and assured. That would be unusual enough under normal circumstances: the strays and lunatics who attempt access to the Sanctum are usually so overcome by the scale and awe of the place they are manic and raving by the time – a very short time – they are apprehended. But this man is alarmingly serene. The Palace doesn't scare him, or even seem to impress him, and neither does his proximity to the heart of everything. And neither does the insanity raging outside. Hassan has better things to be doing, but this distraction is compelling.

'I advise, again, we execute him and the others,' says Companion Ios Raja.

Oll turns his head gently, and regards the Custodian standing at Hassan's shoulder with a relaxed, almost wry glance.

Throne of Terra, even a damn Custodian doesn't bother him.

'So noted, *again*, Companion,' says Hassan. He looks at Oll. 'He doesn't scare you?'

'Of course he does,' replies Oll. 'But I'm tired. I've come a long way, and I've seen some shit. You'll forgive me, but it honestly feels like too much effort to get worked up.'

Oll leans forward a little. The motion sensors in his chair chime.

'There isn't much time... Hassan, is it?' he says. 'I have a duty to perform that is so important, it... it's way beyond any of your rules and edicts and commandments. It's outside of official structures, even the grandiose structures of your almighty Imperium. It is, I suppose, personal. Yes, personal, though it affects everyone and everything. Please, Hassan. You seem like a decent man. I need to see Him, face to face.'

'How could it be personal?' asks Raja. 'No one has a personal connection to the Emperor.'

Oll pauses.

'I'm sure they don't. But He's known to me. We knew each other once.'

'No one could vouch for this unlikely tale,' says Raja.

'*He* could,' says Oll. He looks at Hassan. 'You're one of the Sigillite's people, aren't you? A chosen man? Then you know what it's like. To be one of the very few people in existence to have a personal connection to a being like that.'

Hassan nods. The reminder is sudden and painful. It reminds him of his grief, of the urgent work he has to do, of the scale and multitude of things slipping away, undone, every second. This is a waste of time. It might even be a trick of the warp, a soft and reasonable invasion where violence has failed, though none of the Antiroom systems detect a trace of that.

'Explain it to me,' says Hassan. 'Once more, simply. I will make a judgement. That will be the end of it. Explain who you are and what you want. Unfold to me the matter you wish to discuss, or the message you wish to convey. Account for the two unsanctioned psykers in your company, and the warrior who seems to be an Astartes but most assuredly is not. Begin.'

Oll sighs. His chair chimes again as he sits forward, rests his elbows on his knees and steeples his fingers. He leans his mouth and chin against his thumbs for a second, thinking.

'My name is Ollanius Persson,' he says. 'I have travelled a long way to meet with a man I once knew. A long, long way, further than you can possibly comprehend. The people with me are companions who have joined me on that journey to help me. They are innocent of any crimes that I know of. You should let them go. Let them leave the Palace. I suppose that's not possible. I need to speak with Him. I beg you to let me do that. I am here to help.'

'Help... what?' asks Hassan.

'Help end this nightmare. I hope. Actually, I don't know if I can do that. But at least, help stop it becoming something infinitely worse.'

'Your story is both flimsy and ridiculous,' says Raja. 'There is nothing you can say that–'

'Actually, there are two things,' says Oll reluctantly. 'Do you know what a Perpetual is? Do you understand what is meant by the term "Perpetual"?'

'Mythologically, yes,' says Hassan.

'You're looking at one,' says Oll. 'Bit of a let-down, I'm sure, but there we go. I was born something over forty thousand years ago, here on Terra. I am a Perpetual. So is the Emperor. So is, I believe, your Sigillite master. We are kin. I demand the right to speak to my kin. They would both be aggrieved to know you have blocked my effort to meet with them.'

There is a long pause.

'What,' says Hassan quietly. 'What is the second thing?'

'This Palace,' replies Oll, 'this Sanctum. Right now, it is the most secure place in the known galaxy, protected by things like that.'

He gestures at Raja.

'You might want to ask yourself,' he continues, 'how the hell I got in here, and what else I might be capable of doing.'

4:xii

Control, not controlled

The captains stare at Abaddon for a moment, then Sycar and Baraxas turn aside and open vox-links to instruct their companies waiting nearby.

Fyton glares at Abaddon.

'These were not your orders,' he says. 'You chide the others for disobedience, but you are disobeying the direct commands of the Lupercal. For shame, Ezekyle.'

'Did you not hear me?' Abaddon asks.

'I heard a brat complain about hard work,' Fyton replies. 'I heard a soldier repudiate his oaths of moment. I heard a Son of Horus doubt the reasoning of Horus Lupercal, Warmaster, believing he knows better.'

'Fyton–'

'If Lupercal has set a trap, Abaddon,' says Fyton, 'then it is his trap. He knows what he's doing. He always does. If he hasn't informed you of his plans, then it is because you, First Captain, are not part of them.'

'Our lord father has lost control,' says Abaddon.

'If you say so,' says Fyton. 'I will not be returning. Neither will Seventh. I am staying to fulfil my orders, orders he gave me, not you. I suggest you do the same, or prepare yourself for a future in which you are no longer First Captain of anything.'

'I gave you an order, Fyton,' says Abaddon.

'I do not acknowledge your authority, Abaddon,' says Fyton. He turns, and begins to walk back up the smouldering slope.

'Do *not*, Ezekyle,' Baraxa whispers to him.

'Do not what, Azelas?' Abaddon asks.

'Strike him. Kill him. The man's a wretch. And barely a man any more. But you are Ezekyle Abaddon, First Captain, First Company, Sons of Horus. Everything may be broken, everything may be lost, but while you are still *you*, our Legion retains discipline and control.'

Abaddon nods.

'I mean, it,' says Baraxa. 'Don't descend to their level. They are contaminated. They are consumed. They have no control, just as you fear our father has no control, for the warp controls them. But you, Ezekyle, *do*.'

'I know.'

'Then, you keep it.'

'I will,' says Abaddon. He nods again. 'I will. Control, not controlled.'

'Good,' says Baraxa. 'Then there is still a Legion.'

'Yes, still. Now, can we make ready?'

'We can make ready, Ezekyle. We can embark, your hands unsullied. Besides,' Baraxa adds, 'that's why you keep the Master of the Justaerin close and loyal.'

At the top of the burning slope, Captain Fyton turns as Hellas Sycar calls to him, and topples as the black-clad Terminator destroys him with a single blow.

4:xiii

What others call the Throne Room

'What's happening now?' John whispers, as soon as he is close enough to Oll.

'We are making headway, I think,' Oll replies.

'Do not converse,' snaps Ios Raja. He is in front of them, leading the way.

'Or being taken for execution,' Oll whispers. 'It could go either way.'

John had been removed from his crystal cell and placed with the others under guard in the armourglass atrium of the Antirooms. They had waited, watching, as on the other side of the crystal wall, Sisters of Silence had packed some of their possessions into a small, duralloy negation crate. John had seen the athame go in, the ball of twine, Leetu's cards, and his shears and torquetum. The rest – their weapons, carry bags and personal effects – had been left on the examination table.

Once the crate was packed, it was handed to Companion Raja. Then other Custodes, along with several of the Sisters, had closed around Oll and his long companions and escorted them out.

A last, long walk begins.

They have joined a main processional, moving at a brisk pace, with the green-robed Chosen at the head, alongside Raja, who carries the crate in front of his chest like an offering. Custodians and Sisters flank them, and follow on behind. In the cell, John had formulated a dozen escape plans. None of them fitted this scenario.

The Custodes are everything the Custodes should be: indomitable golden monsters. John can see no way to out-smart, out-run, or escape them, and he certainly can't fight them. The Sisters are worse. They are so hard to track, even when you know they are there, shifting like smudges in the air. And they are blanking what gifts he still possesses.

'Did you strike a bargain?' whispers John.

'I said all of us, or nothing,' Oll replies.

'All of us what?'

'Do not converse!' Raja snaps again, without looking around.

'Your leader has requested an audience with the supreme lord of Terra,' says the Chosen to John over his shoulder.

'Sharp ears,' John replies. 'You're our leader now?' he whispers to Oll.

'Shhh!' Oll replies.

'Due to certain factors,' the Chosen continues, 'I have granted this. The audience will be brief. My lord cannot leave his location, so we are going to him. You will all answer any questions put to you in full, without deception. Lies will be detected and punished.'

'Great,' murmurs John.

'This is what we wanted,' Oll whispers.

'I don't think it is,' says Actae.

John glances back at her. The witch's skin is pale and clammy.

Like him, and like Katt too, Actae is suffering the suppressive presence of the Sisterhood. She is clearly struggling the most, which suggests to John her psykanic powers are significantly more than anything he or the girl can muster.

She is also rigid with apprehension. John can see it. It's the Custodians. From what he's been told, it was their kind that killed her the first time she died. Is it fear she's registering? Hatred? Or just recollection?

Behind Actae and Katt come Krank and Zybes, both anxious and wide-eyed, then Leetu, who carries his helm under his arm and zero expression on his face. Last of all, Graft trundles at their heels, oblivious.

They turn off the processional into another, equally grand, equally gilded, equally empty. Their footsteps ring out across the marble: all except, John notices, the footsteps of the Sisterhood. They pass statues, the effigies of the great and good, the noble and the dead. John sees Oll glance at something.

'What is it?' he whispers.

There's no way to pause, or go back and look. Oll shakes his head.

'What?' asks John.

'I thought I–' Oll starts to say. He shakes his head again. 'It doesn't matter.'

'Cease conversation,' Raja barks.

The processional reaches a huge mass-passageway, fusion-cut through the bedrock. The delicate glow of the electro-flambeaux becomes the sickly glare of sodium lamps. As they turn into the vast tunnel, they feel a cold breeze, and catch in it the smell of oil, rock, fyceline and smoke. John has no idea why any tunnel needed to be built on such a scale. What the hell ever needed to move along it? The air is climate-controlled, but it still feels damp, as if they're in a cavern at the bottom of the world.

There's something ahead. It seems large, but they take minutes to reach it. Slowly, step by step, its sheer size begins to become evident. It's a portal of cyclopean proportions. A door.

A silver door.

'Oh god,' he says.

'Do not speak,' orders Raja.

Even when it's impossibly big, it still seems to take hours to reach it. John realises he's breathing fast, too fast. This is why they came. Here. This place. This terrible place. But now they're actually here, he wants to be anywhere else instead.

They approach the Silver Door, the last door of eternity. They halt.

'Hassan, Chosen of Malcador,' the Chosen calls out to the burnished Custodes Pylorus. Lances at their sides, heads raised, they seem like yet more decorative statues, but for the slight flutter of their huge red plumes in the tunnel breeze.

'By His will be done,' calls Hassan.

The Silver Door opens.

What lies beyond, slowly revealed as the door swings wide, numbs John's mind. His thoughts drain away. Nothing he has seen in his life, not even the scale and dimension of the Palace they have navigated so far, can cushion the impact. The space, the soaring arches, the light. He has no words. Even he, the logokine, has no words. It is indescribable. It defies his ability to accommodate it. It is endless, beyond scale, defiant of dimension, both glorious and paralysing, magnificent and awful. There is singing, and it's inside his head. The air itself is lustrous and alive.

Hassan leads them in.

A figure awaits them, dwarfed by distance, but amplified by grandeur. It is a god. John hates himself, but there is no other word for the being they are approaching. A god. Supreme. Transcendent. Cloaked and gigantic, god stands with his back to them and waits as they walk the last kilometres of heaven to his feet.

When they get there, John realises there are tears streaming down his cheeks. He wants to fall down and beg forgiveness. He wants to scream into the awful light and the terrible beauty and the living air.

'Kneel,' Raja barks.

They kneel. John, Zybes, Krank and Katt, all at once. Zybes is weeping, hands clasped. Graft's pistons hiss as the servitor lowers its chassis. Actae, reluctant for a second, stoops to her knees, and bows her head. Leetu drops to one knee, his face still raised, proud and in martial respect, his helm clamped under his arm.

Finally, Oll kneels too.

'You know me,' he calls out.

'You will not speak!' Raja cries.

'He does,' says Oll. 'He knows me. This isn't necessary.'

'Oll–' John hisses through his tears.

'This... abasement... it is undignified,' Oll calls out. 'It is the tawdry protocol of one too used to power. It is beneath you. And it is no way to treat an old friend. You know me.'

The god turns to look at them. Raja, and the Custodes escort, and Hassan, and the wraith-sisters, all bow.

Oll's face falls in sudden surprise. 'You do *not* know me,' he whispers.

'I do not,' says Vulkan. He stares down at them. He points to John Grammaticus.

'But I know you,' he says.

4:xiv

Magical sympathy

'There must be something here,' says Loken. 'For him to steer me here, however obliquely, there must be something.'

'Must there?' asks Mauer. 'If you're right, and all has become delusion, then there is no logic. No purpose. No connection. No scheme. The recurrence of that phrase was just a coincidence, the echo of insanity in a madhouse.'

'Or minds joining together,' says Sindermann. 'Minds, thoughts, ideas… warping into each other, binding together, creating synchronicities and connection. What Garviel described, what's happening to the city… it's probably happening to our minds too. An interconnecting labyrinth. An abstraction of ideas–'

'Bullshit,' says Mauer.

'The distribution of warped space effect is clearly uneven, as yet,' says Sindermann. 'Some places more than others, some locations more connected to the immaterium, or interconnected by the immaterium, than others–'

'If Terra is sliding into the empyrean, then it will be true of everywhere soon enough!' Mauer retorts.

'Yes, but why certain places first?' asks Sindermann.

'There is no logic! It's madness!'

'No, no,' Sindermann says, shaking his head, starting to pace. 'Some places… some places are more susceptible than others. More sympathetic. Like people! Some people are affected more rapidly than others. It could be a resonance, a… a… quality of materia… perhaps a legacy of pain, or thought or… or… psychic activity. This place, the Hall of Leng, it's always been considered special…'

'Because of the things in it?' asks Mauer.

'Yes, but the site itself. Leng. Mauer, the entire Palace was built here because of the mystical significance of certain locations within its bounds.'

'Alleged,' says Mauer.

'That's true, isn't it?' he asks the frightened young archivist.

She nods. 'The Palace, it is said, was built here because this has been a sacred place since the rise of man,' she says. 'The Emperor chose it. The Himalazian Zone contains many sites of ancient, ritual significance. The Palace was raised to contain all of them within its precincts.'

'And Leng was one of them,' says Sindermann. 'A sacred site. We can't explain what brought us here, Mauer, beyond some deluded notion. But something brought Garviel here too. Perhaps it was the Sigillite. To me, that proves that we were right to come here. That there is something here worth finding.'

'You are inspiring as ever, Kyril,' says Loken. 'But what have you actually discovered?'

Sindermann sags. He glances at the scattered books around them.

'Well…' he says. He sighs.

Loken picks up Sindermann's notebook again. 'Have you tried saying any of these things aloud?' he asks. 'Reciting them?'

'Yes,' says Mauer.

'And?'

'Nothing happened. Nothing at all.'

'Nothing happened *here*, you mean,' says Loken, 'nothing you were aware of or witnessed. Perhaps they are having some more distant or general effect? I heard your echo, Mauer, from far away. Or vice versa.'

Sindermann looks at the archivist suddenly.

'Hang on,' he says. 'What were you saying? You were telling me something, just as Loken arrived. Something about a special collection–'

'Collection eight-eight-eight,' she replies.

'Take us there,' he says.

4:xv

_____

Kill or fall

There is a jarring impact. Without warning, Rann is released. He falls to the floor, rolls aside, and turns to see the howling World Eater slowly sinking to its knees. Namahi, Master of the Keshig, is right behind it, gripping its hair with one hand. With the other, in an almost frenzied blitz of hammering blows, he is stabbing it repeatedly in the neck and shoulders with his edlel.

He doesn't stop. He just keeps stabbing, hand banging up and down like a steampress, two blows a second.

Finally, he lets go and steps back. The White Scar's white chestplate and visor are drenched in backspatter. The brute, dead on its knees, topples forward. Namahi looks at Rann. He jerks a thumb over his shoulder, indicating the chambers beyond the mess hall.

'Everything is clear, lord,' he says.

Rann gets up. He gestures towards the route that he and Zephon came.

'And that way too, Keshig-Master,' he replies.

Then he goes to Zephon. The Sons of Horus traitor he was grappling with is dead, and Zephon is hunched over the corpse, battered and wounded.

'Still alive?' Rann asks.

'As much as any of us,' Zephon replies.

Rann clasps Zephon's hand and pulls him to his feet. The Blood Angel's hair is matted with gore, and his beautiful face is a mask of blood, but his Astartesian metabolism is already closing burst vessels and clotting. Rann sprays him with the last of the counterseptic from his belt-pack to wash the blood out of his eyes. The damage is ugly but superficial. There's not much more he can do.

'I told you to hold,' he says.

'I chose not to,' Zephon replies. 'We got it done. There's no time to "hold" any more, Rann. It's kill or fall.'

Rann nods. He glances at Zephon's last three kills, crumpled on the mess hall's floor in a swill of blood.

Their throats have been torn out, as though ripped open by the bite of a wild beast.

4:xvi

A collection of secrets

She leads them down spiral stairs to a lower level. There is a heavy door, but her ring of keys opens it.

'We are seldom allowed in here,' she says, as they enter.

It is another wing of the library. Sindermann is sure there are others besides. They follow the archivist down a wide, dark staircase. There are framed pictures on the walls, held in humming suspensor fields, but it's too dark to really tell what they depict. Sindermann glimpses pale shapes, and abstract forms, ghost faces looking back at him, darkened by time and thick varnish as much as by the fustian gloom.

The chamber below is wide and low, with a barrel-vaulted ceiling. It is cast in a blue, twilight glow of auxiliary lighting. The archivist pauses at the foot of the staircase, and uses a wafer from her keychain to activate a wall panel. She throws a series of switches. One by one, the main lights come on: dull glow-globes hung at intervals like pendants on long cables. They rouse slowly, like embryonic suns rising to main sequence brightness. Their light is yellow, the colour of old paper or worn bone, and barely banishes the chamber's shadows. Gloom lurks, reluctant to be evicted, between the many rows of high shelves, and lingers below the desks and reading tables.

The air smells of electrostatic and paper dust, of cotton and vellum, of dry age delicately suspended in subtly moderated stasis fields. It smells, to Sindermann, of ancient learning, of forgotten thought, of ideas so old they have not been held alive or kept warm in human thoughts for centuries, and have grown cold and inert. Old learning, but new to him and his modernistic principles of scholarship and examination.

The shelves of books run, not as straight rows, but as a geometric maze, interrupted in places by islands of reading tables. Stretches of the walls are hung with more paintings, and still more are stacked, side-on, like tall, slim books, in racks beside plan chests, humidified cabinets and stasis displays.

'Where do we even begin?' asks Mauer.

Sindermann starts to walk along the nearest row of pictures. Automatic sensors light each one as he comes close in a downward fan of pale radiance. Extraordinary things. The light reflects white from the old varnish and lacquer of oil paintings, and gleams off gilded frames. It glows ivory from the handmade papers of blockprints and engravings, and from the pale primed canvases of abstract works. He stares, then moves to the next, one light field dimming in his wake as the next comes on. He reads the marker tags below the works, the names of artists and mystics… engravers, painters, designers and visionaries from across four hundred centuries of human civilisation.

He feels almost breathless with awe.

'Kyril?'

'We do what we did before,' he says, gazing at an etching of a descending god or an ascending devil. He can't tell which.

'We try at random. Let synchronicity and coincidence guide us. All the angels of the library. The warp is making its connections. We'll let its providence work for us.'

He turns to them. There is a smile on his face. He raises his hands, a conductor bringing his orchestra to attention.

'What else can we do?' he asks.

They spread out. He crosses to the nearest shelf, trying to clear his mind and let chance, or some dowsing, subconscious force direct him. His fingertips drift along ancient spines, some frayed, some repaired and rebound, some too worn to read. There are names and titles unknown to him. *Rapturous Beasts, The Book of Glass Hands, Autoclone Illumin of Luna Habitat, Liber Bidoph vel CX, Revelati Draconis...*

He takes one down.

'We need gloves,' the archivist announces.

Loken, nearby, raises his huge, plated hands and shows them to her. She shudders, and quickly hurries to inspect a different stack.

Loken picks a book at random. '"Bright star, would I were stedfast as thou art,"' he reads out. '"Not in lone splendour hung aloft the night..."' He shrugs and closes the volume. 'I don't think this will work,' he says.

'No, no, Garviel, we just need to be patient,' Sindermann replies. 'We just need to allow ourselves to be receptive. Learn how to hear the... the... What did they used to call it? The muse. That piece you just read–'

'This?' asks Loken, holding up the book.

'Yes,' Sindermann nods. 'As you read it, I was just reading this. Listen... "one bright star, to burn and heap the ashes of the moon".'

He looks at Loken expectantly.

'And?' asks Loken after a pause.

'Stars, Garviel! Stars!' Sindermann says eagerly. 'Two books, chosen by chance, read simultaneously, both speaking of lone, bright stars! You see?'

'No, Kyril.'

'The connection, my boy! The subtle synchronicity! As though things are aligning. We just have to see those connections... Oh, don't look at me like that. "Bright star, alone..." What are the chances of that concept occurring, just like that, at random, the moment we walk in here?'

'I would think... quite high,' says Loken. 'I would think that it's not much of a coincidence, and that the word "star" is not unusual, and is probably used a lot by poets. Poets being poets.'

Sindermann hesitates, then nods and puts the book down.

'The Clavicula Incubi,' Mauer calls out from nearby, reading along a shelf. 'The Five Books of Novopangaea, The Combinatorial Art of Merzhin Ambrosianus...'

'Slow down, Mauer,' Sindermann murmurs, not looking up. His initial rush of enthusiasm has dampened. He turns the pages of another book he has pulled arbitrarily. The Sortes Astronom. They're going to need translator systems, he realises.

'Enochian Chants,' Mauer continues, urgent, 'A Catalogue of Alexandria Biblios Compleat, uhm, something called Al Azif–'

'Let chance guide you!' Sindermann calls back, trying not to sound encouraging and not as annoyed as he feels. 'Don't overthink. Imagination, Mauer. Synchronicity.'

'What is the Dark King?' Loken asks, appearing at his side again.

'The Dark King?' Sindermann asks. 'I don't know. A reference to the old cartomantic arcanoi, I think. Why, have you found something?'

'Just this,' says Loken, holding another frail volume open. 'This says it's a "concordance of fraudulent and false gods". You see here, where it fell open? Rex Tenebris. It says it means "the Dark King".'

'I believe that's Proto-Gothic,' Sindermann says, frowning. He takes the book from Loken. 'Yes, I recognise some of these names... all the forgotten and banished gods here, look. *Dyeus*, known as Iuppter... Anpu-Anubis... Enlil... Baal... ah, yes. Rex Tenebris. Why does it interest you?'

'I heard the name spoken outside, several times,' says Loken, 'another chant of the damned and the Neverborn. I heard it at the front line, and in the streets, and from the mouths of daemons. It feels significant.'

'Perhaps.'

'Maybe it's just a new name for the Lupercal,' says Loken. 'Their chants and cries are hardly sophisticated. "The Emperor Must Die" lacks nuance.'

'Indeed, Garviel. But let me see what I can find.' Sindermann glances encouragingly at Loken, but Loken has already vanished along another row. Sindermann takes down another book, and flips it open indiscriminately.

Then crowned in his stead, the Dark King.

Startled, he feels a shiver. He puts the book back quickly and selects another.

One that is once born immortal is born again as a king of All Darkness.

He's starting to panic. The random incidence of the phrase is uncanny. It's what he hoped might happen, but now it's actually happening, it scares him. He pulls another book, bound in shagreen, opens it on an unpremeditated page, and reads:

The black shell cracks, thus he ascends, in the timeless time, and is elevated to the gods, to reign as a dark-crowned king.

4:xvii

Horus, rising

He is approaching now, fast, angry. You can feel His rage, and it amuses you. Finally, after all these years you have prompted an emotional reaction from Him.

Your father is just a man, after all.

He is brimming with fury, and burning with power. *Such* power. He is shining in your mindsight like a star. You had Him encased in a stifling, muffling, sense-depriving shell of pure, black immaterial force, but He has cracked that open, and now He burns a path towards you.

The *Vengeful Spirit* creaks and shakes at the fury of His approach. He is so strong, so powerful, any being in the galaxy would shriek in eternal dread and hide in the depths of hell rather than face Him.

But there is nothing in the galaxy like you any more.

You no longer have to hide. You no longer have to conceal your power behind veils of secrecy and deceit. If He'd had an inkling of how strong you'd become, He would never have dared come to challenge you. So you wrapped all of yourself in un-when, in skeins of timelessness… your presence, your thoughts, your soul, your power. You muted your mind, took shelter in the past, in memories, in hesternal seclusion, behind artificial masks of dementia and madness. You allowed nothing to give you away, for just a glimpse of your true self would have stopped Him in His tracks and made Him flee.

There's no going back now. He's approaching, and you no longer have to hide. You rise up. You cast off your masks and disguises, and stand revealed. It's liberating. Intoxicating. Those around you – your warriors and officers, your sons, the other things that lurk and whisper – they cry out in dismay at the sight of you. The revelation of your new aspect is too magnificent for them. Their eyes burn. They fall to the deck, weeping and screaming and soiling themselves.

You are a star, too. You are a tower of lightning. You are a king above kings. You do not underestimate the nature of the fight that is about to take place, the last battle. It will be testing. It will be hard. Your once-father is strong. But you are infinitely stronger. You are Horus Lupercal ascendant, chosen of the gods.

And He, when all is said and done, is just a man. So, if necessary, He will die like one.

He has taken your bait. He has run headlong into your trap. He has entered your kingdom. You control everything here. You control the board and every move that is made. There is not an atom of the *Vengeful Spirit* that does not obey your merest thought. It is no longer a ship. It is a place of execution and apotheosis.

Your once-father, the tyrant, the liar, the false Emperor, thinks He has come to confront you on a warship in orbit. He has not. He has come to the inevitable centre of all things.

He thinks He can fight the future. He can't.

This is where it will be decided.

This is your realm now.

4:xviii

A Realm of Chaos

'What about this?' the archivist says. Her voice makes Sindermann start so much, he drops the book.

'Are you all right?' she asks.

'Yes,' he replies, trying to slow his breathing. It's just words, just a random recurrence of words. A fluke. A psychological trick. He was looking for synchronous magic. Of course it would shake him when it seemed to appear. 'Yes. Of course,' he says, steadying himself. 'What were you saying?'

'My hand just landed on this one, sir,' she says. She is holding up a book to show him, a small volume, of evident age. The binding is so worn, he can barely read the spine. He leans in and squints.

'A *Primer of Enuncia*,' he reads. 'I don't know what that is.'

'Look at this!' Mauer calls. She hurries past them lugging a large and heavy folio, and sets it down on the nearest reading table. Sindermann and the archivist go to join her.

Mauer is turning the pages. The folio is large, and contains, loose-leafed, old sheets of parchment and what look like maps.

'The name caught my eye,' she says, untying the ribbon closure. '*Regno Kao.*'

'A Realm of Chaos,' says the archivist.

'Which reminds me,' Sindermann says to her. 'I was going to ask if you have a translation device.'

'I do,' she says, summoning a psyber-skull from its niche. 'But the name is written there, on that label beneath the original title.'

She points. Sindermann feels stupid. His anxiety is undermining his usual diligence and precision.

'Keep up, old man,' Mauer snorts. She opens the folio, and starts to rifle through the sheets inside.

'Look at that,' says Sindermann, stopping her from turning another page. 'Is that a map? A city?'

'No, a labyrinth,' says Mauer.

'Or both,' says Loken, suddenly behind them, looking over their shoulders. 'What does that say, the legend?'

'*Urbs Ineleuctabilis,*' says Mauer, sounding it out. The archivist has beckoned in the psyber-skull, a device formed, it seems, from a canine skull fused to a simian one, then bound in gold and brass. It hovers, buzzing, over the table and passes a quick bar of red light across the chart.

<The Inevitable City,> it declares, speaking in a monotone smear of noise that is simply sampled sounds edited to simulate words.

The four of them stare down at the chart for a moment.

'It's nothing,' Mauer decides. Her urgent, impatient mind has already dismissed it. 'Some old myth. Let's get back to work.'

'It looks like the Palace,' says Sindermann.

'It doesn't,' says Mauer. 'It's just some old fantasy. Some nonsense.'

'Something led you to it, Mauer,' Sindermann says.

She scowls. 'Well, I don't entirely subscribe to your search methodology anyway, Sindermann. "Let chance guide you"? Honestly, I'll humour you, but it's a suspect and frankly bull-shit approach. We should be more rigorous, maybe consult the data-catalogue–'

'It does look like the Palace,' says Loken in a quiet voice. 'I mean, it doesn't and it does. Some aspects are entirely wrong–'

'Please,' says Mauer. 'Not you as well. I think we've become too suggestible. We're seeing patterns and connections where none exist. There's a word for that–'

<Apophenia,> the psyber-skull whirs, <Pareidolia.>

'Whatever,' she snaps. 'Let's get to a more systematic–'

'Look again, boetharch,' says Loken. 'This map shows a location of convoluted madness. Agreed. But the double-helical shape? Like the notation for infinity? And see, where the gates are marked? And the principal structures? They echo the layout of the Zone Imperialis.'

'No–' says Mauer.

'I have spent hours in these last few months studying dia-grammatics of the Palace Dominions,' says Loken. 'Tactical schematics, combat assessments... I tell you, the comparison is uncanny. This could be a plan of the Palace, made by a child... or an unsettled mind...'

'All cities look alike,' says Mauer. 'In their basic components–'

'All cats look alike in the dark,' says Sindermann, trying to ease the tension between the two.

'Not helpful,' says Mauer, shooting him a look. She points to the map. 'I'm familiar with maps of the Dominions too, Astartes. Yes, there are a few points of correspondence. But there are far more discrepancies. If that's the Sanctum, what's that? Or that? What's that structure? If that's the Lion's Gate, what is that? Please, can we move on?'

'It looks as though maps have been interlocked or overlaid,' says Sindermann. 'The diagrams of two cities, superimposed. Perhaps more than two–'

'Where are you getting this from, Kyril?' Mauer asks. 'There's no scale, no measurement, no definition. There's no evidence this was even drawn as a proportional representation–'

'What if this is…' Sindermann pauses. 'What if this somehow depicts what the Palace is becoming? The intrusions of the warp? The superimposition of other places or times? The realignment and distortion Garviel was describing?'

'How would any of that feature on an old map?' Mauer snaps.

'When was this composed?' Loken asks the archivist.

'There is no date or origin for the work, sir,' she replies. 'Except some alleged provenance that it was part of "The Book of Chaos Foreseen". Nothing can be verified.'

'What of the text here, along the edge?' Loken asks.

The archivist touches the psyber-skull gently, and it bobs over the section Loken is indicating. The bar of red light slides slowly across the faded brown ink of the old cursive penmanship.

<Yette knowe this is the true and everlasting place of made-ness and lyes that concealeth all truth within its manifold streetes and fyne gates, which hath stoode since before time was and will stand throughe time and unto beyonde all time, eternal, and is withoute anye time, for it was builded in the Darke, and in the everlasting Darke remaines. It standeth forev-err beyonde all mortal sight, as beyonde a mirror upon the other side, seen only in visions and the most fytfulle dreams, subjecte to constant motion of currents and ethereal tides, and is the House of Ruin and insanity both, for within it dwelleth the four who haunt the dark, and besides them, many other vacant thrones and diverse spirits of revenge and ruination. It lyeth but a mere lifetime's journey from Calastar, yet therein

its walls and turrets join, by masons' craft, to the walls and turrets of that impossible city, and so too but a moment's eternity from the City of Duste, and also close by Uigebealach, whiche it is and is not, and thereby it is and is not alle things and places thereafter and before, freed from alle reason–>

'Enough,' says Loken.

<–and upon the Daye of Dayes it will become so all thinges, and its gates will devour all the Works of Man, and also Man, and all the angels and stars betimes, and the mighty works of Man will be as nothinge and despaire, and all peoples forgot and all empires unremembered, and all who look upon it, as throughe one great Eye, shalle say I weep now at the inevitable triumph of its Ruin, for ruin it is and ruin it brings–>

'Enough.'

The psyber-skull falls silent. The bar of red light winks out.

4:xix

Supplicants

'Stand up,' says Vulkan.

Grammaticus stands. 'You remember me, my lord?' he asks.

Vulkan's eyes are superheated red, the blazing glow of the world's core.

'I remember you,' he says. 'Barely, as a dream. When we met, my mind was not my own. But it is hard to forget the face of the man who killed me.'

Ios Raja sweeps around, a golden blur. The blade of his spear stops a hair's breadth from John's throat.

'Killed me, and in so doing contrived my salvation, I should say,' says Vulkan. 'Lower your blade, Companion. This man gave his life so that I could live again. But for his sacrifice, I would not be here to stand with Terra.'

'That was years ago,' says John, as the gleaming blade moves away from his neck. 'And a considerable simplification.'

'Perhaps,' says Vulkan. 'There were other elements in play, on Macragge and afterwards. But you played the key role. And you surrendered your life for me.'

He pauses.

'Yet you stand before me now.'

'As you stand before me,' says John.

'You speak as though you know the curious logic of a Perpetual existence,' says Vulkan.

'In part,' says John. 'But I am not of that rare kind. A rough facsimile, for a while. Not even that now. When I gave you my life, sir, I was not brought back as a multitude. I am mortal, with but one life. You, I trust, have many left within you.'

John puts his hand on the shoulder of Oll, kneeling beside him.

'This is the man you should be talking to,' he says. 'He certainly knows that curious logic.'

'What is your name?' Vulkan asks.

'John Grammaticus, sir,' says John. 'And this is Ollanius Persson.'

Oll rises slowly to his feet.

'I would relish a conversation with you both,' says Vulkan. 'However now, clearly, is not the time. I can barely justify this interruption to the work. But Hassan reported your remarkable intrusion, and your unusual demands. Both required the consideration of the most senior authority. I cannot leave my post here, so you were brought to me. I want an account. You will make it brief.'

'I came to see your father,' says Oll.

'From where?' asks Vulkan.

'Calth, but that's irrelevant. In truth, the past. I knew Him once, a long time back. I would speak with Him again.'

'He never mentioned you,' says Vulkan.

'I'm sure He hasn't. But then, has He ever mentioned much?'

Vulkan raises an eyebrow slightly.

'You came as a group?' he asks.

'Travelling companions, fellow survivors of Calth,' says Oll.

'The journey has not been easy. We've needed each other. I humbly ask that you have the Vigilant Sisters step back, for they are causing suffering to some of my friends.'

'Security must be maintained!' Raja snaps at once.

'Have the kind Sisters back away,' Vulkan says to him. 'Or would you like to insult my fortitude further?'

Raja bows his head and, at his thoughtmark, the Sisters and the Custodian escort step back from the group, forming a much wider perimeter. Oll hears Actae sigh in relief. Raja remains at their side, with Hassan, the negation crate he was carrying set on the lustrous floor at his feet.

'Thank you,' says Oll to the primarch. Vulkan nods.

'What was your business with my father?' Vulkan asks.

'To discuss with Him the course, purpose and meaning of this conflict.'

'Do you bear new intelligence?' Vulkan asks. 'Information about the foe that could prove decisive?'

'Probably not,' says Oll.

'Then I wonder why he would discuss it with you.'

'Because we have discussed wars many times,' says Oll. 'We have planned them together, and we have fought them together. He has, in the past, valued my perspective.'

'You are a soldier?'

'Once upon a time.'

'Your martial wisdom must be significant if he took counsel from you.'

'I'm just an ordinary soldier,' says Oll. '*Was* an ordinary soldier.'

'Yet one who evidently values his military skills enough to risk misadventure,' says Raja, 'to come a great distance, by his own admission, and seek to speak them aloud.'

'The Companion makes a good point,' says Vulkan.

'This is the end war, sir,' says Oll, looking squarely into

Vulkan's eyes. 'Perhaps the end and the death of everything. A soldier would be failing in his duty if he did not do whatever he could.'

'I sense you are being sparing with the truth,' says Vulkan.

'Some things, great lord, are for His ears alone,' replies Oll. 'Can I speak with Him?'

'No,' says Vulkan.

'May I ask why?' asks Oll. 'This is your decision?'

'It is a matter of practicality,' says Vulkan. 'My father is not here. You cannot speak to him. I am the most senior authority on Terra, which is why you are speaking to me.'

'Where is He?' asks John.

'At war,' says Vulkan.

'Then what of the Sigillite?' asks Oll.

Vulkan turns slightly, and with one gesture of his mighty hand, indicates the pulsing light that fills the Throne Room far behind him. It is a terrible radiance, the living light that began to gnaw at them all when they first entered. It smells of compressed pain and torn hopes, of burning gold and whispering agony. Against the glare, Vulkan is backlit like a cliff at sunset.

'Malcador,' he says, 'occupies the Throne in my father's stead.'

Oll peers into the light until his eyes begin to ache and a migraine blossoms in his skull. He can just see, in the distance, tiny specks of figures toiling in the glare, the shape of curious machines. He can almost pick out the shape of a colossal throne, raised up in majesty. He cannot make out a figure on it.

He opens his mouth to speak, then closes it again. The Emperor has gone, and all the senior commanders save Vulkan with him, and the Sigillite is lost in the technological inferno of what mortals laughably refer to as 'the Throne'.

They have arrived too late, and it's all been for nothing.

4:xx

Fragments

Titan engines grapple, hand-to-hand and claw-to-claw, on the precipice lip of ragged cliffs that were once Dorn's insurmountable walls.

Corpses drift in rank grey water where gas bubbles rise off sewage. High above, on grilled decking and walkways, men brawl by firelight with blades and hooks and clubs. It is frenzied. Blood drizzles down through the walkway grilles towards the grey water below. The living can no longer remember why they are fighting. The dead no longer care.

Sojuk of the White Scars sheaths his blade in the torso of a Word Bearer. Jetbikes roar past him, cannons firing as they rush the enemy charge. Sojuk longs for their speed and freedom. Time, cold and dead, has wrapped its weight around him like loops of heavy chain.

* * *

Men run through the smoke, from nowhere, to nowhere, lugging their weapons and their lives, muttering prayers and bewitched by battle-madness. From somewhere close, the industrial thunder of mega-bolters.

Ruin roars. The Palace screams. Maximus Thane yells to be heard, and tries to rally the last of his men, but there, on the tattered edge of the Gilded Walk, they are too busy selling their lives for the highest price to hear him.

Agathe wrenches her bayonet out of her enemy's gut. The fight rages around her along the length of the razor-wire line. They are not going to reach Primus Gate. The gate and its fortifications are probably gone anyway. The stone walls of the culvert have become mottled flesh, and are covered with names.

Closing in, Neverborn spectres call her by hers.

Corswain, the Hound of Caliban, lifts his bloodstained sword. The blade gleams in the half-light, but that half-light is merely the cold, phosphor glow streaming from the eyes and mouths of the ink-black Death Guard driving up the pass and splintering his lines. There is nothing but shadow beneath the Hollow Mountain. Corswain has raised whole mounds and hills of corpses, and set them aflame, but the mountain itself remains dark.

Zephon edges his blade with a whetstone, preparing for what will surely be the last battle of Hasgard, and his last battle too. Fafnir Rann watches him, loading shells into his bolter.

On the burning plains, a giant throne of skulls sits empty, awaiting the imminent coronation.

* * *

Mangler claws gouge open the Shadowsword's flank, and something inside it detonates. The blast wrenches the Shadowsword's huge bulk into the air, like a rider bucked from a horse. Jera Talmada, in the turret of her Banestorm, sees it land, burning from within. She orders 'Load!' but the Banestorm's main weapon has seized. She orders full reverse, knowing there is nothing behind her that is any different from the carnage ahead.

Armies tear into armies in ranks a thousand men deep and ten thousand wide. Spears jab, lifting bodies. Guns boom, shredding others. Broadswords and tactical spathas cleave helmets, crush skulls and tear pseudoflesh. Skin rips. Blood sprays. Bionics short out and fail. Plasteel cracks. Psykanic energy roils and lashes. Aggression is channelled by hypno-indoctrinated commands, or coded machine pulses, or obsessive training, or merely by a tenuous sense of self. The quaking air reeks of glanded combat stimms and piss and blood and fear. Every warrior carries another's death in his fist. The turmoil is unending and unbearable. Horns boom. Fire vomits from the punished ground. Adrathic wrath scorches the air. Bodies buckle and melt in waves of xenophasic heat. Tracked behemoths clatter over mud and wire and bones. Voltaic lances gouge and shatter against shield walls, and plated phalanxes punch through infantry lines like chainfists. There is rout and overrun, panic and disarray. Loyal corpses, breathing yet, but doomed, rush forwards under standards of foliated skulls and splayed eagles, caked in ash and gore, to meet the screaming host of treason, which smashes into their dented shields under banners made of entrails and flags of unblinking eyes. They bear their Neverborn lords with them on biers, swollen-bellied, horned beasts that whisper unutterable names through blood-flecked lips, or play flutes fresh-fashioned from human femurs. Carious bodies pile up and slither, twenty, thirty, forty deep. There is a hircine stink, a reek of nidor, the dry burn of weapon-generated ozone. They kill for the living and kill for the dead, and kill because killing is all that remains. The bony touch of mortality is upon them all, and their deaths will last forever.

It is the final triumph of Ruin, hymned by the spit and crackle of the warp.

Thus is the malison of Chaos. The world hangs badly, at an angle. Above, in the supernal realm, the lochetic nimbus of the opening warp burns against the blind, unconstellated void, turning in the thestral glow like the wheel of all fortunes, licking spears of lightning down to strike and tumble the last steeples and towers of Terra. It is a great eye, like the eyes on the drenched banners far below, its pupil blazing, its sclera bloodshot. It observes the shrieking psychomachia of the species, and devours each and every soul that flies up, a furnace spark. It gazes down upon the rock that they call the world as it is dismantled wholesale by a relentless concentration of absolute fury. It witnesses the end of the world, the end of Terra, the end of the rock that they kill on and for.

The four watch too, the False Four, through the eyes of their avatars in the dreaming shadows of the Lupercal Court: the dripping, red-plashed Father of Massacres, the trembling, feverish Grandchild of Decay, the languid Drinker of Delights, shaking with algedonic glee, the squirming, unstable Beast of Change. They see the plan ended, ruined and unfinished, and signify their approval of that repudiation with the bloody prints of their gnarled and sutured hands. Their laughter becomes the avalanche roar of a falling world.

* * *

'Respond. This is Hegemon Control. Anabasis, respond and verify.'

The War Court junior at the mastervox station keeps repeating the same words. She is the third junior to occupy the seat, taking over the task in rotation, repeating the same signal every twenty seconds. Sandrine Icaro and the other seniors in the Rotunda are now sure, beyond any doubt, there will never be a reply.

Bloody teardrops trickle down Malcador's desiccating cheek. The heat radiating out of him is now so intense, they evaporate before they've barely formed.

4:xxi

_____

The Dark King

Oll feels himself sag, the hope and determination that has fuelled him, thus far, now draining away. The exhaustion he has kept at bay for so long sweeps in like a tide. The air around him shimmers, dazzling with motes and filaments of light thrown, like cinders, from the immolating Throne. He hears the creak and shiver of the vast chamber's huge arches tensing in the outflow of raw power. He hears the pure song of the astrotelepaths running through the tumult like a single thread.

'It is me or no one,' Vulkan says to him. 'Is there anything you wish to say?'

Oll shakes his head.

'Then I cannot vouch for your purpose or presence,' says Vulkan, 'and I believe you are nothing more than a distraction. Besides, I am sorry to say, I suspect your motives.'

Raja has brought him the crate, and is holding it open. Vulkan inspects the objects within. Arcane aeldari instruments, a ball of twine, a handmade tarot…

'Can you explain this?' Vulkan asks. He is holding up the athame.

'Just a stone knife, my lord,' says Oll quietly.

'I know stone and I know rock,' says Vulkan, 'I know all the elements of the mineral realm. It is that, yes, but it is more besides. An ugly thing with a deep shadow.'

'It struck me, my lord,' says Hassan, 'as an artefact of particular evil.'

Vulkan drops the athame back into the negation crate, as though unwilling to hold it for long. He takes out Leetu's old deck, and starts turning the cards, one by one.

'My lord,' says Hassan. 'I noted that a particular card features in this set.'

'Indeed?' muses Vulkan. He stops. He's found it.

'Indeed so,' Hassan replies. 'I discovered it at the random turn of a card–'

Vulkan holds the card up.

'Is it a symbol you know?' he asks them. 'A concept? Do you understand some greater meaning? The name of it shivers on the lips of the enemy and echoes down the colonnades of the webway.'

'The name, sir?' Oll asks.

'The Dark King,' says Vulkan.

'Wait–' says Leetu, suddenly confused.

'This name is spoken?' asks Actae abruptly, interrupting him.

'It is said repeatedly, almost as a refrain,' says Vulkan. 'Do you know it?'

'Trust her not, lord,' says Raja.

'She will answer,' says Vulkan. He looks at Actae, and bids her stand. Actae rises, and Katt gets to her feet at her side. 'Do you know the name?' Vulkan asks. 'A true meaning?'

Actae tilts her blindfold head, as if struggling, either with pain or some mental battle.

'Not as our word, in our language,' she says. 'But perhaps in the un-tongued languages of the immaterium. Do you mean to say "the Dark King"?'

To Oll, the words are exactly the same, its sound and phonetic value identical. But when the witch says it, the name suddenly has a sharp edge. Katt shivers at it, and Oll feels John wince.

'It is the same phrase,' says Hassan.

'No,' says Actae. 'Names have power, and they are mutable. Meanings may shift and change. One thing becomes another. That phrase has a simple enough meaning for us. But in other places its meaning is quite different and specific.'

'What places?' Vulkan asks.

'In the warp, sir. In the unresolved realms of possibility that only prophesy can see. In the day of days when time runs out. Oh, by the lights of the stars… it has been spoken?'

'It has,' says Vulkan. 'The Sigillite and my father both, they said it represented an ending, and a death.'

'And more,' replies Actae. 'The Dark King is more.'

Again, as she says it, Oll feels it cut the air, like a razor against soft skin.

'Pity's sake,' murmurs John, 'every time she says it…'

'What?' asks Oll.

'I mean, I can hear what she's saying, and I can see her damn lips move, but there is another meaning hidden inside the phrase. I hear echoes of aeldari, and other xenos lexicons. Like they all have the same words, or that many meanings have all converged on one sound.'

'What are you talking about?' Hassan snaps.

'Listen to him,' says Oll. 'He is a logokine, and words to him are living things.'

'Explain the meaning,' says Hassan.

John shrugs helplessly. 'I can't… just with a sense of inevitability and… and extinction.'

Leetu has risen to his feet. 'My lord primarch,' he says softly, 'that card was not part of my deck. I have owned those cards for years. They were a gift from my mistress. I know every one of them, front and back. I have never seen that card before. It was not in my deck when I came to this palace.'

Vulkan frowns at the card. 'Yet it is clearly made by the same hand, to the same stylistic design, and of identical materials,' he says. 'Chosen? Have it examined by cartomancers and scryers. And you... Tell me what you know of it at once.'

'Lord,' says Actae, with some reluctance, 'the Dark King is... it is the name first written in the time before man, and repeated ever since, unbidden, by the prophets of all species. It is a name symbolising the rising god to come.'

'There are no gods!' scoffs Raja.

'You're a fool,' Actae tells him. 'Before the fall of the aeldari, there was no fourth power of Chaos. The gods of Chaos breed and multiply, propagating like storms through the empyrean. They are born in turn, though they have all existed forever. Time has no meaning for them. The fall of the aeldari did not cause the birth of She Who Thirsts, merely her occurrence. So too with all other gods, be they foul entities of Chaos, or divine forces of sentient power.'

'She Who Thirsts was born out of the death of an entire sentient culture,' says John.

'Such is the inevitable fate of all advanced, psychic species,' says Actae. 'And the Dark King is our fate. This war, my lord, is not one of loyalists against traitors. It is not about the conquest of Terra and mankind by Chaos. It is certainly not about a son at war with his father. This is the Triumph of Ruin. Horus and the Emperor have taken their conflict to such a pitch, that we are about to suffer the same fate as the cursed aeldari. The human race will die in birth-fire, consumed by blood-rage, pestilence, violent transmutation and blind desire. And from the grave-pyre of our civilisation, the broken galaxy will see Horus rising, absolute and complete, as a new, true and terrible god.'

She bows her head, shivering. At her side, Katt looks across at Oll with an expression of hopeless shock.

'She's telling the truth,' she says.

4:xxii

Handprint

He has lost sight of the others. Collection 888 didn't seem as extensive as the Hall's upper galleries, but its twilit, mazy layout has enveloped him. He can hear Mauer's voice, now and then, and occasionally a word or two in answer from Loken, somewhere beyond the shelves that surround him like walls.

Sindermann walks the length of another row of stasis-held pictures, the lights blinking on as he gets close to each one. He sees a faded, extraordinary painting entitled *The Tower of Babel*. He stares at it for a long time. Was it a particularly favourite piece of His? Cherished for its technique, or simply its immense age? Does it have a meaning? A pertinent meaning he can decipher?

Next to it, an arresting expressionist piece called *The Five Thrones* by an unknown artist working in the last years of the 66th century. It shows the distant, chair-like structures at a distance, so they appear huge, the size of buildings or pyramids. They are set within a city of strange design, viewed as through some curtain of flames. Is it a view of hell from outside, or heaven seen from hell?

Sindermann looks at it until it no longer makes sense, or perhaps makes too much sense. He has begun to suspect that no meaning may be extracted from anything in the library, for he and the others have no frame of reference. There is no way to understand the nature of the curation. If they knew why each piece was kept, they could begin to identify the significances.

He opens one of the sliding cabinets, and a light comes on inside illuminating a large, preparatory sketch. The delicate pencil work has somehow survived millennia. It is evidently a technical copy, made by hand, of an original work now long lost. There is no label. It shows a hunt or chase. There are antelope and bison, side-on, mid-leap, and startled deer breaking and running. There are men, with bows and spears. All the figures are crude and stylised to the point of simplicity. Sindermann imagines the original was a piece of parietal art, displayed on the wall of a cave or chamber, rendered in oxides and charcoal. Only this traced copy remains. Despite the simplicity, he can see the motion and energy, the urgency of the hunt, and even the arcing path, between hand and fleeing antelope, that the cast spear will follow. He can see the flank where the spear will strike. At the edges of the image there are additional marks that seem to indicate vegetation or undergrowth, and shapes seem to lurk within those marks. It's not clear what they are. Perhaps they are supposed to be other animals, or concealed predators lying in wait. Beside them, in the corner, is the outline of a human handprint.

It's not so much a picture, Sindermann decides, more a diagram, a visual plan. It's so old, Sindermann doubts anyone has an idea of its full significance any more, or could explain the maker's intent. He sighs. He closes the display cabinet, and wanders through the winding stacks to find the others.

Mauer is sitting, perched, on the top of a rolling ladder.

'According to the' – she pauses, and checks the cover of the book in her hand – 'Last Chronicles of the Lemurian Kingdoms, "All kingdoms on the Earth fall and perish when those that rule become absolute in power."' She looks down at him. 'So there's that,' she says.

'Where is the archivist?'

They both look around. Loken has reappeared.

'Where is she?' he asks.

'Here, sir,' says the archivist. Sindermann realises she had been in the shadows nearby the whole time.

'A question,' says Loken. 'Follow me.'

He turns and starts to walk. Warily, the archivist follows him. Sindermann glances at Mauer. She jumps down off the rolling ladder and they fall in step behind.

Three rows of shelves over, Loken comes to a halt in front of the wall.

'Where does that lead?' he asks.

'Sir, I… I don't know.'

He looks at her. 'You work here. You must know.'

Deeply scared of him, she shakes her head.

'I really don't,' she answers in a fragile whisper.

There's a hatch in the wall. A large hatch. It's not a door like the one they entered by. It reminds Sindermann of a security hatch, or even an airgate. It is robust and heavy duty. He can see the marks of wear and use around the sill and the seal rim. It's old. It's been in service for years. The grey steel looks like dirty ice in the gloom.

'It must go somewhere,' Loken says. 'Is it an exterior hatch? Or does it secure another collection? If the latter, then it must be something significant.'

The archivist shakes her head.

'It has to go somewhere,' echoes Mauer. 'Do you have a key?'

Again, the archivist, struck dumb with nerves, shakes her head.

'I don't remember seeing it when we came in,' says Sindermann.

'Neither do I,' says Loken. He turns to the archivist. 'Please,' he says, 'I understand you're scared. But where does the hatch go? Is it a secure area you are not allowed to enter?'

'Sir,' she says. She swallows hard, her voice tremulous. 'I'm trying to tell you… I don't know where it goes because I didn't know there was a door there.'

'You didn't know?'

'Sir, I have been in here several times over the years. I have never seen that door before in my life.'

Mauer draws her sidearm.

'Everybody step back,' says Loken.

They do so, but not far. They stand and watch as Loken approaches the hatch. He traces his fingers across its surface, and studies it closely. He presses his hand, palm flat, against the wall to try the lock mechanism.

To his surprise, there is a thump, and the hatch slides open. A gust of stale air blows out. Sindermann smells smoke, the cold hint of a fire gone out.

Beyond the hatch is a metal corridor with grilled decking. It is quite unlike the design and fabric of the Hall.

Loken glances back at them.

'Stay here,' he tells them. 'I mean it.'

He steps through the hatch. The corridor is dim. Pipework threads the walls. There are lamps set in the ceiling, but they are deactivated or broken. Small, emergency lights in the wall emit a soft, amber glow.

He takes a few steps. He has a rising, disconcerting sense of familiarity. He dismisses it. Foolish. All Imperial architecture looks alike. The same templates are used everywhere. This could be a bulk hallway anywhere in the Palace, a corridor in any–

Loken stops. There is a designator mark stencilled on the wall panel. He reads it, then reads it again to make sure he isn't going mad.

He retraces his steps and walks back into the library.

'Well?' asks Sindermann.

'I'm going to explore further,' Loken says. He wants to tell Mauer to summon support, but he knows that no one will answer her calls. He wants to tell them to run, to lock all the doors behind them and get the hell out of the Hall of Leng, get the hell out and hide.

But he knows there is nowhere left to hide.

Nowhere is safe. The Sanctum is no longer a sanctuary. He doesn't want to panic them. Panic will help no one. Their last minutes or hours shouldn't be spent in terror, because terror and death will find them soon enough.

'Stay here,' he says instead. 'Don't follow me.'

They stare at him.

'Do you understand?' Loken asks.

'Yes, yes,' says Mauer.

'What is it, Garvi?' asks Sindermann.

'Nothing, I hope,' Loken replies. 'A service corridor. A sub-access. Let me just check.'

He looks Sindermann in the eyes for a second. The old man nods.

Loken turns, and steps back into the corridor. Inside, he presses his hand against the interior plate and the hatch slides shut behind him. It knows his touch. His biometric print. Of course it does. He would still be in the record. At least Mauer and Kyril and the archivist can't open the hatch and come after him. It won't respond to their touch. It has never granted any of them full clearance.

4:xxiii

My father's house

Once the hatch is shut, he unclamps his helm from his waist, and puts it on. He locks the neck seals and wakes the visor. Over his back, he draws *Mourn-It-All* and Rubio's blade.

Loken begins to walk forward. He pauses at the stencil marker and reads it again, just to make sure he hasn't made a mistake.

He hasn't.

He is standing in *Sub-Access (Port Ventral) 423762*.

He is aboard the *Vengeful Spirit*.

TO BE CONTINUED IN
THE END AND THE DEATH: VOLUME II

ACKNOWLEDGEMENTS

The author would like to thank the Siege of Terra team – Aaron Dembski-Bowden, Chris Wraight, John French, Gav Thorpe, Guy Haley, Nick Kyme and Jacob Youngs – for their answers, feedback, reference citation and general support during moments of extreme 'siege-face'. Big thanks also to the 'without whom' department of Rachel Harrison, Karen Miksza, Jess Woo and Nik Abnett for their scrupulous attention, and to proofreaders Jake Stow and Kirsten Knight and the translation teams for several full-stretch catches. A standing ovation, please, for the artists: Francesca Baerald (the ravishing map), Valera Lutfullina (busts), Mikhail Savier (black and white internals), Mauro Belfiore (the primarch portrait internals) and, of course, Neil Roberts (that gorgeous cover).

The author would also like to express his appreciation to Tom McDowell at Black Library, Andy Hoare and Tony Cottrell at Forge World, and to Max Bottrill and everyone else at Games Workshop for their advice, guidance, support and confidence.

ABOUT THE AUTHOR

Dan Abnett has written over fifty novels, including the acclaimed Gaunt's Ghosts series and the Ravenor, Eisenhorn and Bequin books. His work for the Horus Heresy includes the first book in the series, *Horus Rising*, and the three-volume-long conclusion, *The End and the Death*. He also wrote several novels in between: *Legion*, *The Unremembered Empire*, *Know No Fear*, *Prospero Burns* and *Saturnine*. He scripted *Macragge's Honour*, the first Horus Heresy graphic novel, as well as numerous Black Library audio dramas. Many of his short stories have been collected into the volume *Lord of the Dark Millennium*. He lives and works in Maidstone, Kent.